"Pam Hillman has done it again—stolen both my sleep and my heart with a breathless novel unlike any I've read. From a Natchez auction block to a time-worn Mississippi plantation, this is a journey richly written and historically alive, a unique and gentle love story that is truly a promise kept."

JULIE LESSMAN, award-winning author of the Daughters of Boston, Winds of Change, and Heart of San Francisco series

"Hillman crafts a tale with fascinating, down-to-earth characters. If you are a fan of Westerns, you will enjoy this. Livy is a character who will steal your heart."

ROMANTIC TIMES, 4-star review for *Stealing Jake*

"In this romantic historical, Hillman's characters wrestle with grudges, vengeance, and wanting what they feel they deserve. But they learn that the sins of their fathers must be forgiven along with their own trespasses if they are to live in freedom and experience the joy of love."

CBA RETAILERS AND RESOURCES on *Claiming Mariah*

"[Hillman is] gifted with a true talent for vivid imagery, heart-tugging romance, and a feel for the old West that will jangle your spurs."

JULIE LESSMAN, on *Claiming Mariah*

"Pam Hillman's debut novel, *Stealing Jake*, is a little gem of a story and a credit to Pam's talent as a writer."

RELZ REVIEWS

"A fantastic read for fans of Western romance."

RADIANT LIT on *Stealing Jake*

The Promise of Breeze Hill

THE PROMISE OF
BREEZE HILL
A Natchez Trace Novel

PAM HILLMAN

Tyndale House Publishers, Inc.
Carol Stream, Illinois

Visit Tyndale online at www.tyndale.com.

Visit Pam Hillman's website at www.pamhillman.com.

TYNDALE and Tyndale's quill logo are registered trademarks of Tyndale House Publishers, Inc.

The Promise of Breeze Hill

Designed by Jennifer Phelps

Edited by Erin E. Smith

Published in association with the literary agency of The Steve Laube Agency.

Scripture quotations are taken from the *Holy Bible*, King James Version.

Scripture quotations in the discussion questions are taken from the *Holy Bible*, New Living Translation, copyright © 1996, 2004, 2015 by Tyndale House Foundation. Used by permission of Tyndale House Publishers, Inc., Carol Stream, Illinois 60188. All rights reserved.

For information about special discounts for bulk purchases, please contact Tyndale House Publishers at csresponse@tyndale.com or call 800-323-9400.

Library of Congress Cataloging-in-Publication Data

Names: Hillman, Pam, author.
Title: The promise of Breeze Hill / Pam Hillman.
Description: Carol Stream, Illinois : Tyndale House Publishers, Inc., [2017] | Series: A Natchez Trace novel
Identifiers: LCCN 2017001889 | ISBN 9781496415929 (sc)
Subjects: | GSAFD: Christian fiction.
Classification: LCC PS3608.I448 P76 2017 | DDC 813/.6—dc23 LC record available at https://lccn.loc.gov/2017001889

Printed in the United States of America

23	22	21	20	19	18	17
7	6	5	4	3	2	1

The Promise of Breeze Hill *is dedicated to my oldest son, Sean.*

In some ways, Sean reminds me of Connor O'Shea. From an early age, Sean was always bringing home stray kittens and puppies and protecting and defending the weak from aggression. Once someone left a litter of puppies in the parking lot at school. Sean and his buddies put the puppies in the back of his truck, fed and watered them, and at the end of the day, they made sure all the puppies had a loving home to go to. At least one puppy—if not more—came to live with us.

Sean has grown into a fine young man who would do anything to provide for and protect his wife and baby girl.

That's just what a hero does.

Chapter 1

Natchez Under-the-Hill on the Mississippi River
MAY 1791

Connor O'Shea braced his boots against the auction block and glared at the crowd gathered on the landing.

Vultures. Ever' last one o' them.

The stench of the muddy Mississippi River filled his nostrils, and the rude shacks along the riverfront reminded him of the roiling mass of humanity in the seaports back home in Ireland. Hot, cloying air sucked the breath from his lungs, and the storm clouds in the sky brought no relief from the steam pot of Natchez in May.

Dockworkers shouted insults at each other. Haggard-faced

women in rags scuttled past as grimy children darted among the wheels of rickety carts. One besotted fool lay passed out in the street, no one to help him or care whether he lived or died. As far as Connor knew, the man could be dead already, knifed in the dead of night when no one would be the wiser.

A commotion broke out at the back of the crowd and all eyes turned as a gentleman farmer shouted that he'd been robbed. The man chased after a ragged boy, but the moment they were out of sight, his compatriots turned back to the auction, the incident so common, it was already forgotten.

Connor ignored the chaos and focused on the high bluff overlooking the wharf.

Ah, to be up there where the wind blew the foul odor of rotting fish away and the scent of spring grass filled a lad's nostrils instead. And be there he would.

As soon as someone bought his papers.

"Gentlemen, you've heard the terms of Connor O'Shea's indenture," James Bloomfield, Esquire, boomed out. "Mr. O'Shea is offering to indenture himself against passage for his four brothers from Ireland, an agreement he had with his previous master."

A tightness squeezed Connor's chest. After serving out his seven-year indenture with Master Benson, they'd come to a mutual agreement that Connor would work without wages if the influential carpenter would send for his brothers. Benson's untimely death had squashed his hopes until Bloomfield suggested the same arrangement with his new master. One year for each brother. Four years.

No, three and a half. Assuming Bloomfield made it clear in the papers that Connor had already worked six months toward passage for the first of his brothers.

But who first? Quinn? Rory? Caleb? Patrick?

Not Patrick, as much as he wanted to lay eyes on the lad.

Having fled Ireland eight years ago, he'd never even seen his youngest brother. He'd start with Quinn, the next eldest. The two of them could work hard enough to bring Caleb over in half the time. He'd leave Rory to travel with Patrick.

Pleased with his plan, he panned the faces of the merchants and plantation owners spread out before him. Surely someone needed a skilled carpenter. Dear saints above, the mansions being built on the bluff and the flourishing plantations spread throughout the lush countryside promised enough work to keep Irish craftsmen rolling in clover for years.

He spotted an open carriage parked at the edge of the crowd. A barefoot boy held the horses, and a lone woman perched on the seat. Eyes as dark as seasoned pecan met and held his before the lass turned away, her attention settling on a half-dozen men unloading a flatboat along the river's edge.

She looked as out of place as an Irish preacher in a pub, and just as condemning.

He stiffened his spine and ignored her. It didn't matter what she thought of him. He needed a benefactor, a wealthy landowner with ready access to ships and to Ireland. And he planned to stay far away from women with the means to destroy him.

The memory of one little rich gal who'd savored him,

then spit him out like a sugarcane chew would last him a lifetime.

"I say, Bloomfield, what's O'Shea's trade?"

"Joinery. Carpentry. He apprenticed with the late John W. Benson, the renowned master craftsman from the Carolinas."

A murmur of appreciation rippled through the crowd of gentlemen farmers. Connor wasn't surprised. Master Benson's work was revered among the landed gentry far and wide. Unfortunately, Master Benson's skill with a hammer and a lathe hadn't saved him from the fever that struck no less than six months after their arrival in the Natchez District. With the man barely cold in his grave, Connor now found his papers in the hands of the lawyer, being offered to the highest bidder.

But regardless, no one offered a bid. Connor squared his shoulders, chin held high, feet braced wide.

The minutes ticked by as Bloomfield cajoled the crowd.

Oh, God, please let someone make an offer.

What if no one needed a cabinetmaker or a carpenter? What if Bloomfield motioned for him to leave the platform, his own man, belonging to himself, with no way to better himself or save his brothers from a life of misery back home in Ireland, a life he'd left them to suffer through because of his own selfishness?

All his worldly goods stood off to the side. The tools of his trade. Hammers. Saws. Lathes. He'd scrimped and saved for each precious piece during his years as a bonded journeyman to Master Benson. He could sell them, but what good would that do? He needed those tools and he needed a benefactor if he would be any good to his brothers.

Finally someone made an offer, the figure abysmally low. Connor gritted his teeth as the implication of his worth slapped him full in the face. But the terms. He had to remember the terms. Every day of his labor would mark one more coin toward passage for his brothers.

A movement through the crowd caught his eye. The barefoot boy made his way toward Bloomfield and whispered something in his ear. Connor glanced toward the edge of the crowd. The carriage stood empty, and he caught a glimpse of a dark traveling cloak as the woman entered the lawyer's small office tucked away at the base of the bluff.

"Sold." Bloomfield's gavel beat a death knell against the table in front of him. "To Miss Isabella Bartholomew on behalf of Breeze Hill Plantation."

Cold dread swooshed up from Connor's stomach and exploded in his chest.

A woman.

He'd been indentured to a woman.

He closed his eyes.

God help him.

Isabella Bartholomew pulled back the faded curtain in the attorney's office and glimpsed the Irishman's eyes close briefly as the gavel fell. Relief, maybe?

Or despair?

Unsure if Mr. O'Shea might be the man for the job, she'd hesitated to buy his papers, but hearing that he wanted to secure passage for his brothers swayed her in his favor. Surely Papa would be pleased with her choice.

Thoughts of her father swirled in her head. His strength was returning as slowly as cotton growing in the field, inch by painful inch. She couldn't see his progress, but he'd surprise her with a halting step or his gnarled fingers grasping a spoon. Small victories, but so much more than they'd dreamed of eight months ago.

Connor O'Shea jumped down from the platform. Butternut-hued breeches, roughly mended, hugged long legs. A handwoven cotton shirt, worn thin, stretched across broad shoulders. Leather lacing up the front hung loose, revealing the strong column of the man's throat.

Long strides brought him closer to Bloomfield's office. Isabella whirled from the window, unwilling to be caught staring. She hurried across the small room, skirts swishing, to stand beside a crude table strewn with papers.

The Irishman stepped through the door and removed his hat in one fluid motion. Stormy, moss-green eyes clashed with hers before he bowed stiffly in submission.

Isabella fought the urge to apologize. This arrangement wasn't about master and servant. She would have offered the job to a freemason if one could've been found. Her chin inched up a notch. She would *not* feel guilty. It wasn't her fault the man's master had expired and his papers were for sale.

"You do understand the terms, don't you, lass?" His Irish lilt rumbled throughout the close quarters.

"Of course I do, Mr. O'Shea."

"I'm no' a slave." His square jaw jutted.

Isabella stiffened her spine. "Breeze Hill does not deal in slaves."

Having clawed his way up from the bottom, her father preferred freemen and bonded servants—men and women with a vested interest in seeing that the plantation flourished. Neighboring plantation owners had tried to convince him otherwise, but he refused to listen. When pressed, a faraway look came into his eyes, and he'd say that no man had the right to own another.

He would say no more on the matter.

"Forgive me, Miss Bartholomew. I stand corrected." The Irishman gave a slight bow, his wind-whipped dark hair falling forward over his forehead.

He didn't look the least bit repentant. As a matter of fact, his clenched jaw and wide-legged stance made her wonder if he regretted putting forth such terms in the first place.

No time like the present to find out. She didn't have the time, the money, or the patience to transport him all the way to Breeze Hill if he'd already changed his mind.

"Mr. O'Shea, a fire destroyed an entire wing of my family home last fall, and I need a skilled carpenter to rebuild it." Memories of the flames that destroyed their crops, a third of their home, and almost took her father's life flashed across her mind, but she pushed the horrific images back into the recesses where they belonged. "From Mr. Bloomfield's glowing recommendation, you are that man. If you're unwilling or unable to fulfill the terms of your indenture, now is the time to say so."

"No, ma'am. I'm willin'." The words grated, like a hammer pulling a nail free from a board.

She eyed him. His words and his tone were at odds with one another. But what choice did she have? Her father was obsessed with repairing the damage to Breeze Hill, and Connor O'Shea had been the first carpenter she'd found in Natchez.

No, that wasn't entirely true. Mr. O'Shea was the first carpenter she could afford. She squished down the thought that Breeze Hill couldn't exactly afford him now. But there would be plenty of coin after the fall harvest to send for the first of his brothers. And by then, her father would be recovered, Leah would have her child, and all would be right in their world.

As much as it could ever be without Jonathan.

"Very well. We'll lodge here in Natchez and be on our way on the morrow."

Bloomfield stepped in, and before she could change her mind, she signed the papers indenturing Connor O'Shea to Breeze Hill. When Bloomfield slid the papers across the table, her indentured servant took the quill in his large, work-roughened hand and scratched his name on the paper in barely legible script. With papers in hand, she led the way to the carriage, where Toby waited. She smiled and waved a hand at the lad. "This is Toby. He's one of our best stable hands."

"Thank ya, Miss Isabella." The youngster grinned.

"Toby, help Mr. O'Shea load his belongings; then we'd best head on over to the Wainwrights'." She glanced at the moisture-laden clouds. "Looks like we're in for a rain."

The woman gathered her skirts in one gloved hand. Connor stood by, not knowing whether to offer his hand to the haughty miss or not. He knew his place and knew from experience how easily the wealthy took offense. Before he could make up his mind, the stable boy stepped forward and assisted Miss Bartholomew into the carriage.

He noticed a discreetly stitched tear along the hem of her outer skirt as she settled on the worn leather seat. He frowned, his gaze raking the rest of the carriage, the old but carefully repaired tack, the mismatched horses. From the looks of the conveyance and Miss Bartholomew's mended clothes, would the plantation coffers be able to fulfill the obligation of sending for his brothers?

"Miss Bartholomew . . ."

The question died on his lips as two riders careened down the bluff, heading straight toward the outdoor auction. The color drained from Miss Bartholomew's face, and she gripped the edge of the seat.

The riders, both lads on the verge of manhood, reined up beside them, hair tousled, clothes dusty and sweat-stained.

"What's wrong, Jim? Is it Papa?"

"No, ma'am. It's Miss Leah."

"The babe?" If possible, she paled even more, and Connor braced himself in case she might faint.

"I don't know, ma'am. She just said to hurry."

Miss Bartholomew took a deep breath and scooted to the edge of the seat.

"Jim, I'll ride on ahead. The rest of you follow on the morrow with Mr. Wainwright's party."

Jim twisted the brim of his hat in his hands. "Miss Isabella, you can't travel the trace alone."

"Thank you for worrying, Jim, but I don't have a choice. It's much too soon, and Leah needs me."

Connor realized her intention and reached for her hand, assisting her from the carriage. Grateful eyes, laced with fear, pierced his before she turned away, intent on her mission.

Would the boys stop her? When the lads didn't protest, Connor grabbed the horse's reins just below the bit. Decent stock, the lathered animal still needed rest before making the return journey.

"Mistress, it's too dangerous."

"I'm going." She faced him, a stubborn jut to her chin.

"I may be new to Natchez, but I've been here long enough to know the dangers of traveling that road alone."

"Mr. O'Shea, I won't argue that fact." She stood tall, the top of her head barely reaching his chin. "But my sister-in-law needs me, and nothing you can say will prevent me from going to her. Stand aside."

Her chin thrust forward, dark-brown eyes flashing, she somehow made him feel as if she looked down at him instead of up. He took a deep breath, struggling to remember his place. She owned the horses, the carriage, and for all practical purposes, she owned him and the three youngsters gawking at the two of them. Well, if she meant to dance along the devil's backbone, then let the little spitfire flirt with death. No skin off his nose. But at least he could give her a fighting chance.

He addressed the stable lad. "Those carriage horses broke to ride?"

"Yes, sir."

He faced Miss Bartholomew, having a hard time showing deference to a woman as daft as this one. "Mistress, if it's all the same to you, let the lads switch the saddle to one o' the fresh horses. This one could do with a bit o' rest, if ye don't mind me saying so."

She looked away, the first sign of uncertainty he'd seen. "Thank you, Mr. O'Shea. In my haste, I didn't think of the horse. Jim, do as he says, and be quick."

Two boys scurried to unhitch the horses from the carriage while Jim stripped the saddle from one of the lathered animals. In moments, they had the mare ready, and Connor assisted Miss Bartholomew into the saddle, taken aback that she didn't have any qualms about riding astride. He glimpsed a fringe of lacy ruffles just above a pair of worn leather boots before her skirts fell into voluminous folds around her ankles.

"Jim, make haste to Mr. Wainwright's. He'll see you all safely home on the morrow." She spoke to Jim, but she looked at Connor as if she left responsibility for the boys on his shoulders.

"Yes, ma'am. Will you be all right? Shouldn't I—?"

She reined away, the animal's hooves kicking up dirt as it raced to the top of the bluff and disappeared northward. Connor shook his head. Crazy woman. To take off in a dither just because of the birth of a babe. The whole lot of them would probably arrive before the child made an appearance.

"I'm such an idiot." Jim threw his hat in the dust and let out a string of curses. "Why didn't I go with her?"

"She didn't give you much choice, lad, rushing off like she did." Connor led the extra horse toward the carriage.

"It's a day's ride to Breeze Hill."

Connor whipped around. "A day's ride?"

"Yes, sir. And the Natchez Trace ain't safe for nobody, especially a lady. Mr. Bartholomew will have my head, he will."

Connor raked a hand through his hair. Daft woman.

"Saddle up the other horse, lads. I'm goin' after her."

Chapter 2

OH, GOD, not Leah too. Not the babe. Please, God.

Fear clogged Isabella's throat as she left the outskirts of Natchez, her horse's hooves pounding out a staccato rhythm that rivaled the rapid beat of her heart.

Was God listening to her prayers born out of desperation? She wanted to believe He was. Surely He wouldn't take Leah and the babe, too. A hard knot of resentment lodged in her throat. But that hadn't stopped Him from taking her mother and Jonathan.

Was she casting blame where it wasn't due? Her heart hardened. God might not have taken them from her, but He'd allowed their deaths. So wasn't it the same thing?

Shame followed on the heels of her resentment, and she was torn between asking God to save Leah and the babe and asking Him to forgive her unbelief.

When her mount stumbled on the rutted lane, she was almost glad for the distraction. She grabbed for the saddle horn and eased back on the reins. She'd do well to set a slower pace. No need in breaking her horse's neck or her own. She squirmed in the saddle, unused to riding astride. But riding astride was the least of her worries right now.

The last year had brought many changes into her life. She'd gone from being the pampered daughter to becoming the caretaker, not only of her father and her widowed sister-in-law, but of the plantation itself.

Bulging clouds rolled in, and a fine mist began to fall, rain no longer a threatening possibility, but a reality. A twinge of fear at the journey ahead snaked through her as she eyed the tall pines closing in on each side of the trail. Should she turn back? But what if Leah lost the baby? What if her sister-in-law died? Even as she battled her indecision, Isabella continued toward home, reasoning that the rain would be in her favor. No one, not even the thieves who plied the trace, would suspect anyone of traveling on such a dreary afternoon and into the night.

She heard a shout and glanced back. Connor O'Shea sat astride the other carriage horse, his boots dangling below the stirrups. She didn't take time to wonder at the relief she felt before she reined in. Instead, she squared her jaw and concentrated on his motive for following her. If he insisted she return to Natchez, she'd put the man in his place faster than the jagged lightning streaking across the darkening sky.

He pulled to a stop, his forehead furrowed in concern.

His green eyes caught and held hers. "Jim said it's a day's ride to the plantation. Seeing as it's so late in the day, I'm hoping you don't mind if I ride along with you."

"I'll be fine." She lifted her chin, determined to show Mr. O'Shea that she could take care of herself.

A tight smile twisted his lips and he inclined his head as if it was all he could do not to argue. He dismounted and reached to lengthen the stirrup leathers. His gaze met hers over the back of the horse. "In good conscience, I feel obliged to accompany you. With your permission o' course. Many a man has lost his life along this stretch o' road."

Something akin to a knife twisted inside Isabella's chest. *Jonathan.*

One glance at the stubborn jut of his chin convinced her he wasn't turning back. "You're right. I wasn't thinking. My need to be with my sister-in-law overrode my common sense."

"O' course I'm right, mistress." A cocky grin swept over his face, banishing his earlier deference.

Isabella stiffened. She'd better set this one straight right away, or he'd never mind his place at Breeze Hill.

"Mr. O'Shea—"

"Might as well call me Connor, seeing as how I'll be working for you the next few years." He swung into the saddle, the stirrups set to accommodate his long legs. He jerked his chin toward the road before them. "After you, mistress."

She pressed her lips together. Somehow Connor O'Shea had taken control of the situation, and she didn't know how to wrest it back. But it didn't matter. Truth be told, she didn't begrudge his company. Without answering, she led the way deeper into the wilderness toward home.

They rode on, the shadows along the narrow path lengthening, darkening with the hour and the mist that turned to rain. Isabella wished for an oilskin cloak to turn the water as her garments became more soaked by the hour. Miserable and cold, she came alert when Connor grabbed her reins and jerked his head toward the shadowed woods.

"Riders."

He spurred his horse up a steep incline into the thick undergrowth beneath massive oaks and towering pines, the animal scrambling for purchase on the slick ground. Isabella didn't question but followed, vines and briars clawing at her skirts, the horses' hooves kicking up the smell of decay from the leaf-strewn ground. Well hidden in the forest, Connor jumped from his horse and reached for her, his hands spanning her waist.

Isabella kicked free of the stirrups and let him lower her to the ground. She peered through the mist, thankful for the shadows surrounding them.

"Where?" The word came out a whisper of breath between them, no more.

"There." He leaned in close and pointed. "Keep your mount quiet."

Isabella cupped her horse's muzzle, soothing the quivering animal with hushed murmurs. All too soon, the sound of jingling harnesses and the slap of hooves splashing against the rain-soaked road reached her ears.

"Don't move. Don't even breathe," Connor whispered, his attention fixed on the trail.

Heart pounding, Isabella searched the shadows. Moments later, she spotted movement along the serpentine roadway. A dozen or so rough-looking riders and three wagons passed along the sunken trace mere feet away. Her skin crawled when one man looked right toward the spot where she stood. But his gaze, hooded by a slouch hat, slid past without pause, and he rode on.

Gradually the thundering of her heart slowed to painful thumps, keeping time with the steady drip-drip of rain plopping against the underbrush. Might the party of men be law-abiding citizens? It was just as likely they were cutthroats and thieves preying on hapless travelers on their way north after delivering their goods downriver from the fertile Tennessee and Ohio River valleys. One never knew, so it was best to avoid the unknown if at all possible.

Isabella eyed the broad back of the man who stood between her and possible death. And what of Connor O'Shea? She knew nothing about him, other than what Mr. Bloomfield had told the crowd gathered at the auction. Would he protect her with his life should they be discovered? She shivered and closed her eyes. Would her determination to be at Leah's side get them both killed?

The urge to pray nagged at her conscience, but she pushed it away. Surely God mocked her pleas that only surfaced when she needed Him. Moments ticked by without any movement from her companion; then the tense set of his shoulders relaxed.

"They're gone." He led the way back to the road and

helped her mount. The rain fell harder, and Isabella pulled her light traveling cloak around her. But the garment did little to deflect the chill brought on by both the rain and the close encounter with the party of strangers.

Connor held her horse back, scowling as his gaze swept her from head to toe. "How far is it to the nearest inn?"

"An hour at most. But it's a rough place. Papa never stops there."

"We will tonight."

Isabella didn't argue, but she wouldn't set one foot in Harper's Inn. They'd press on when the time came.

The rain was falling in sheets by the time she spotted the inn in the distance. Connor stopped in front of the crude stable just as three men emerged and mounted their horses.

One man rode close, almost losing his seat when he swept off his tricorne and tried to bow from atop his horse. He grabbed at the saddle horn and urged his mount in her direction, grinning in a drunken stupor. "Good evening, madam."

Connor edged between Isabella and the man. She breathed a sigh of relief when the tipsy man went on his way without further comment. Connor slipped from his horse and reached for her.

"We'll keep going." Isabella clasped the saddle horn, having no intention of dismounting. "As you can see, Harper's has a reputation for attracting seedy characters."

"Ye'll catch a chill, Miss Bartholomew, if we go any further."

"And what of you, Mr. O'Shea?" Isabella eyed his soaked garments.

"I'm used t' it." He shrugged. "In Ireland, not many days passed without a wee bit o' rain. And Carolina had its share as well."

She wondered how long he'd been in the Natchez District. But now wasn't the time to ask. A round of raucous laughter came from inside the two-story building next to the stable. She shuddered. "We must press on. The accommodations at the next inn are much more suitable."

"How much farther?"

"Two hours, maybe more."

He shook his head. "Too far. We'll stay here."

The stable door cracked open, and a moonfaced lad peered out. "You want to stable the horses overnight, sir?"

"Aye, I do." Connor tossed the reins of his horse to the lad.

"Mr. O'Shea—Connor—I insist we travel on."

Connor turned, wide hands splayed against his hips, rain running in rivulets off the brim of his hat.

"Mistress Bartholomew, you may own my papers, but you are the most pigheaded lass I've ever known." He stabbed a finger at the tavern, frown lines pulling his brows together. "I'm going in that inn, finding something to eat and a place to sleep. And if you've got one lick o' common sense, you'll do the same."

He stalked off, leaving her sitting astride, the stable lad gawking at her. She glared at his retreating back.

Who was he to be giving orders?

She would ride on. The next inn lay a couple of hours north in the direction those men had taken. Three if the rain didn't let up.

Her gaze waffled between the rain-drenched road twisting northward and the disreputable tavern.

Connor knew the exact moment Isabella Bartholomew entered the tavern.

A wave of awareness coursed through the motley crew of men and the smattering of women, hardly ladies of Miss Bartholomew's station. The din barely subsided before it took up again. He'd felt the pause more than heard it, but no doubt about it, the patrons of Harper's Inn knew a lady graced their presence.

He scowled. There'd be trouble, sure as rain on the moors. But what else could he do? He didn't want the foolish lass catching her death out in this weather, and neither of them came prepared for being drenched for hours on end.

After placing the last coin in the proprietor's hand, Connor made his way toward her. She watched him cross the room to her side, her cloak clasped tight around her shivering frame. He leaned in close and motioned toward the stairs that led to the second-story rooms.

"Mistress, I've secured lodgings for the night as well as some nourishment."

Nodding, she lifted her sodden skirts and glided across the room toward the stairs. Hand on the hilt of his knife, Connor stayed close behind, praying they wouldn't attract any unwanted attention. His prayers didn't last long.

A hand shot out and snaked around Isabella's waist.

"*Ma chère*, looks like you need someone to warm—"

Connor's knife at the man's throat cut him off mid-sentence. "You can be takin' yer filthy hands off o' the lady."

Like a ripple of river water over a sandbar on the Mississippi, a deadly hush fell over the entire room. The man let go, lifting his hands in a gesture of submission. Cold black eyes stared at Connor.

"I did not know she was your woman, *monsieur. Pardon.*"

"Anybody else touches her, he dies." Connor's low voice carried across the room. He nodded toward the stairs. "Go."

After a moment's hesitation, Isabella continued on, looking neither to the right nor to the left. As soon as she reached the landing, Connor followed, cat-footed, his senses alert for any sudden movement. The din started up before he placed his boot on the first step, the confrontation already forgotten. He panned the smoke-filled room one last time and found the Frenchman staring at him with rage in his eyes.

Forgotten by all but one.

Seated in the shadows of the tavern, Nolan James Braxton III watched Isabella Bartholomew's progress up the stairs.

Interesting.

What was she doing in Harper's? And who was the Irishman?

Perhaps she wasn't the lady she claimed to be.

She wouldn't be the first. His own mother had stepped into the role of Mrs. Nolan Braxton II, and no one had been the wiser.

"I will kill him." Pierre Le Bonne slid into the seat next to him. He fingered the long knife strapped to his thigh. "Tonight. I will slit his throat and leave him on the banks of the river, flopping like a dead fish. *Oui?*"

"Leave it be."

"Non!" Pierre slapped the table and let loose a string of curses. "He made me to look like the fool."

The French-Canadian's face turned red, his black eyes popping fire, ready to do battle for an honor that was as dark and shadowy as the tavern they frequented.

Nolan drained the last of his ale. Pierre's explosive temper would be his downfall one day. He would be better served to stay calm and collected, unmoved and unruffled by things he could not control.

An art Nolan had perfected.

"You will do nothing. Understand? You should never have grabbed the girl in the first place."

Pierre glared at him, sullen and unrepentant. But the man would do as he said. Without Nolan, Pierre's life wasn't worth the swill left by a ravenous hog.

"Bah! She is nobody or she would not be in such a place as this."

Nolan pinned him with a look. "She is my future wife."

"Mon dieu." Pierre's expression became guarded. *"Pardon, monsieur."*

Nolan ignored him and eyed the stairs. From the deference the Irishman gave Isabella, Nolan didn't believe this was a lovers' tryst. A servant, if he didn't miss his guess. Interesting that she'd appeared in the tavern at all. Still, he could hardly approach her and offer assistance. Not here. Not now. But he would. Soon.

Snubbing out his cigar, he motioned for another tankard of ale. He'd given Isabella enough time for mourning. It was time to make his intentions known. If he waited too long, someone else would ride in and steal her and Breeze Hill right out from under his nose.

And he'd worked too hard to see that happen.

Everything was going according to plan.

Well, not everything.

He hadn't meant for the plantation house to catch fire or for Isabella's father to almost die trying to rescue that twit Leah. But even that could work in his favor.

Rumor had it that Bartholomew's health was precarious at best. If the man should take sick and die, no one would think anything nefarious was afoot, would they? The poor man simply hadn't recovered from his injuries after the fire.

As for Jonathan's widow . . . she was young and beautiful, if a bit fragile. Her mourning period would be over soon. Gentlemen callers would swarm Breeze Hill in droves, and she'd be married and whisked away before the end of the year.

Leaving Breeze Hill and Isabella to him.

Yes, everything was working out much better than planned.

Connor motioned Isabella into a room at the far end of the hall.

He stepped across the threshold and eyed the humble

quarters. A bed—small, but big enough for two in a pinch—took up more than half the space. A fireplace, a rickety table, and a chair filled the rest.

And a woman.

His heart pounded as Isabella faced him. He did not need to be here. Not with Isabella Bartholomew staring at him. Blindly, he turned toward the door and wrenched it open. He needed to leave.

Now.

He barreled straight into the innkeeper's wife, bearing a tray with cheese, a bowl of vegetables and stew meat swimming in grease, and a hunk of bread.

"Bread and cheese for you and the lady." She strained to see over his shoulder. "Will there be anything else?"

"That will be all. Thank you, and good night." Connor blocked the room from her prying eyes, grabbed the tray, and shut the door in her face.

He turned to find Isabella standing in the middle of the room, looking lost and frightened and a lot like a drowned kitten. His gut instinct told him to set the tray on the table, turn tail, and run.

And he would. As soon as he built up the fire.

Like a bull charging a split-rail fence, he strode across the room and dropped the tray on the table, the clatter loud in the silence. Isabella jumped and wrapped her arms around her waist.

Connor whipped the cover off the bed and held it out. "Here. Wrap up before ya catch a chill."

She clutched the quilt to her. He turned his back on her and fed the kindling in the fireplace. A rustling told him she'd finally come out of her stupor and done as he asked.

"You'd better eat." He tossed a log on the fire.

Anything other than stand and stare at his back.

Connor willed the fire to take hold so he could leave and find somewhere safe.

"Connor?"

He froze, the husky tone of her voice bringing back memories. Memories better left in the dark recesses of his mind. He risked a glance in her direction and wished he hadn't.

Curling strands of damp hair escaped their confinement and framed her face. "I apologize for taking off like that this afternoon. But you see, the babe is my brother's first child." She lowered her gaze, long lashes sweeping against pale cheeks. "Jonathan died five months ago."

Connor let his breath out in a rush. What had he expected? The woman to launch herself at him like Potiphar's wife? Like *Charlotte*? He shouldn't judge her by the actions of another. On the other hand, he didn't need to put himself in the way of temptation. What if Isabella Bartholomew turned out to be a temptress as well? Would he be able to withstand the lure of such a beautiful woman?

He bit back a groan. *God, help me.*

"I'm sorry for your loss. Losing a loved one is no' easy." He threw one last log on the fire and stood.

"It's too soon for the babe to be born. My father isn't

well, and my sister-in-law needs me." A sheen of moisture glistened on her lashes.

Tears. He'd lingered long enough. He edged toward the door. "Will you be all right? Do I need to call a maid?"

"I can manage."

"Good." He took three long strides and reached for the latch.

"Where are you going?"

The tremor in her voice nearly undid him. So much like Charlotte. Beautiful, beguiling, and utterly bewitching. And sweet, or so he'd believed. She'd baited her hook, caught and landed him.

Then gutted him when it suited her.

"I mean, those men." A shudder shot through her words, and she glanced at the door. "Downstairs."

He closed his eyes. He'd misjudged her again. All because of his own sordid past. *Forgive me.*

He'd insisted on stopping, but Miss Bartholomew had been right. They should never have entered the tavern, should never have mounted those stairs. He posed as much danger to her as the miscreants in the tavern below. He prayed they didn't get it in their drunken heads to storm upstairs and violate his mistress.

And mistress she was, in the purest sense of the word. She owned his papers, making him honor-bound to protect her as mistress of the house, same as he would the master.

"I'll be right outside the door, mistress. You'll be safe."

He prayed he could keep her safe.

Chapter 3

LONG BEFORE DAWN, Isabella was up, stoking the fire, donning her clothes, and wrapping the food she had been too worried to eat the night before. Cutthroats and thieves frequented Harper's, not gentlemen farmers and certainly not ladies. Walking into the tavern had been one of the hardest things she'd ever done. But common sense told her it was foolish to ride along the trace behind three drunken men.

The faint rustling of movement and a light knock had her hurrying to the door. She rested the palm of her hand against the rough-hewn planks. "Yes?"

"Mistress Bartholomew?"

Her heart gladdened at the comforting sound of Connor's Irish brogue, and she resisted the sudden urge to smooth her hair back. She'd done the best she could without a comb or other essentials for her toilet, but it couldn't be helped. And besides, what did it matter how she looked to her indentured servant?

She quickly undid the latch and flung open the door, relieved to see his broad-shouldered bulk on the other side. He stood solid, looking no worse the wear from having spent the night outside her door.

"Top o' the morning to ya, mistress." He gave a short bow. "Looks like the rain has gone, and we'll have a good day for travel. Are ya ready t' be on our way?"

"Yes." She grabbed the bundle of food, glad to be shaking the dust of the place off her boots. "I am more than ready."

He chuckled at her enthusiastic response, lines bracketing his crooked grin. "Let's be off, then."

Her indentured servant turned out to be an enigma. He'd bucked her on the trail, determined to have his way. But tough as nails, he'd defended her downstairs at the risk of his own life. Then he'd watched over her, standing guard in the hallway all night long. In addition to giving orders. She followed him down the stairs and out of the inn, where he helped her mount. She could do worse than having Connor O'Shea as her escort and protector.

An hour down the road, Isabella's stomach rumbled. Pressing a hand to her middle, she realized that if she hadn't eaten, Connor probably hadn't either. "Let's stop and eat a bite. I brought the bread and cheese from last night."

"You didn't eat?"

"I wasn't hungry." She shrugged. He didn't need to know

that the raucous laughter from the tavern and worry over her sister-in-law tied her stomach in knots for most of the night.

He led the way off the trail to a secluded spot and helped her dismount. She settled on a fallen log. The storm had blown the clouds away and the temperature had risen along with the sun, promising another blistering hot day. She unwrapped the bundle, broke the bread in two, and offered Connor the larger piece.

"Thank you." He hunkered down against a tree, facing the trail.

Isabella took a bite. The bread was a bit dry, but not bad, considering. She risked a glance at Connor. He ripped a piece of bread off with his teeth and chewed slowly, his eyes never leaving the trail, watching, always watching.

How long had it been since he'd eaten? It suddenly dawned on her that he'd paid for her room and her repast at the inn. He hadn't asked for coins from her for either. For the good it would have done. Her pockets were as empty as her head—she'd left her purse in the carriage. She lowered her gaze, grateful for his interest in the road and the dappled shade that masked the blush stealing over her cheeks.

"You're not eating."

"Just . . . thinking." So much for being ignored. "Connor?"

One eyebrow arched in question.

"I need to apologize. I shouldn't have rushed off toward home like I did." She tore a piece of bread from the chunk in her hand. "If you hadn't come after me, I shudder to think what might have happened."

He nodded. "My pleasure, mistress."

Isabella sighed, wishing he'd dispense with the formality. "Just because I'm admitting my mistake doesn't mean we should have stopped at Harper's, though."

He stared at her, then looked away, a muscle in his jaw clenching. "It was no' a place for a lady, that's for sure."

"Apology accepted."

"That was an apology?"

She shrugged, trying not to smile at his consternation. "If I choose to take it as such."

"Very well, then. You may take it any way that suits your fancy." He leaned down, offering her his hand. Dappled sunlight played across his sun-darkened features, and a mischievous gleam emanated from his eyes. "But don't be expecting such too often."

Isabella let him pull her up, her gaze searching his.

"I'll do well to remember that, sir."

Connor turned away, wanting to kick himself.

He'd trifled with Isabella Bartholomew. And an indentured servant did not toy with the gentry. Maybe the Bartholomews weren't gentry, such as those in Ireland and Carolina, and maybe Isabella wasn't anything like Charlotte, but he'd be willing to bet the Blarney stone her father was. There could never be anything between the two of them other than master and servant.

And he'd do well to remember *that*.

He helped her mount, being careful not to linger long.

In spite of the distance he tried to put between them, she chattered on about how they'd be able to make better time because of the break in the weather.

"I hope Leah is all right. It's her first child, you know."

Connor mumbled a reply and mounted his own horse, leading the way along the shadowed path. As soon as they reached the road, she rode up beside him, her horse keeping pace with his.

"I understand from the agreement that you have several brothers. Any sisters?"

"No."

She looked away, the hurt obvious. She grew silent when the trail dipped into a dark recess worn away by years of travel. They continued on without speaking.

Connor kept his focus on the trail and the dense under-growth closing in around them. He'd succeeded in pushing her away, but he didn't have to like it. She was simply trying to find out more about his family, and if the Bartholomew family was going to be responsible for bringing his brothers to America, the more sympathetic they were to his plight, the more likely they'd hold up their end of the agreement.

Inwardly sighing, he offered an olive branch. "*Mam* birthed the five of us lads before passing on."

"I'm sorry for your loss." Her voice had lost some of its friendly warmth. That's what he wanted, wasn't it? To push her away so there would be no confusion about where they stood.

"She's been gone seven years. *Da* followed her to his grave three months later."

"You miss them."

Shimmering pain slammed into him. He should have been there when his *mam* passed over. Should have been there when *Da* simply gave up and left his brothers to fend for themselves. Instead, he'd been banished to America because of his foolish dalliance with a woman above his station.

And just like the prodigal's father, *Da* had offered his forgiveness, but Connor couldn't forgive himself.

He shrugged, trying to make light of something that clawed at him daily. "Best to put it out o' my mind and forget about it."

He didn't offer any more about his past but guided his horse up a muddy incline, rife with slick mud. The animal slipped, scrambling to keep her footing. The incline leveled off, and Connor reined in, glancing back. "Careful here. Don't be breaking your horse's leg now."

When Isabella topped the incline, she paused, giving her horse a breather. Her gaze caught his, frown lines puckering her forehead. "I apologize if I've offended you by asking about your family. I was simply passing the day in a pleasant manner."

"Speaking o' the dead is not a pleasant way to pass time, if ya don't mind me sayin' so, lass."

Hurt slashed across her face. He'd been too harsh, but he didn't soften the words with an apology. He reined away, and they rode the rest of the way in silence, Connor putting more emotional distance between them with each passing mile.

The sun was high in the sky by the time they neared a cutoff. They passed over a wooden bridge spanning a gently flowing creek with pine and oak trees standing tall and true. He spotted a cluster of buildings in the distance.

"This is Breeze Hill?"

"Yes." Isabella nudged her horse forward and he followed.

Aptly named, a modest but stately plantation home sat atop the hill beneath the shade of a dozen or more moss-draped cedars. Painted white with black shutters, the home boasted eight, no, ten white columns supporting a smaller second story with its own gallery and a spindled widow's walk from one end of the house to the other.

A wide porch ran the length of the first floor, which had at least four rooms, two on each side of the front door with its fanlight and matching sidelights. From the front, Breeze Hill was an impressive sight, with no sign of the damage Miss Bartholomew had mentioned.

They rode right up to the front door, and her almond-shaped dark eyes rested on him when he helped her dismount, but he didn't make eye contact. Now that they were here, he'd probably rarely see her. It would be best in the long run. Better for him to stick to the role of indentured servant.

Starting now.

He took the reins of both horses. "I'll find the stables, mistress."

She nodded, turned, and hurried into the house without a backward glance. Connor watched her go. He should feel relieved that she thought him cold and unfeeling.

Instead, he felt lower than a sunken flatboat foundering at the bottom of the Mississippi.

"Isabella, dear, you look a fright."

"I came immediately." Isabella knelt by her sister-in-law's chair, taking both her hands in her own. "Are you all right? The babe? Are you in pain?"

"Susan says it was a false alarm." Leah eyed Isabella's travel-stained clothes and disheveled hair. "Surely the Wainwright party didn't ride home in that thunderstorm last evening?"

"No. We stopped at an inn on the way." Isabella looked away, hoping her sister-in-law wouldn't ask what inn or who all had been in their party. The whole incident with Connor O'Shea might not bode well for her if word got out that they'd made the trip together, alone, even though everything had been aboveboard and totally innocent.

He'd teased her about putting her life in danger by insisting they stop at Harper's, but then he'd grown colder as the miles passed, barely responding to her questions about his family. He'd shut her out completely when she tried to apologize.

"I'm glad the boys met you on the trail and that Mr. Wainwright decided to wait out the storm." She smiled brightly. "All's well that ends well."

Relief at finding Leah and the babe all right overshadowed the exasperation that her sister-in-law had sent for her at the first sign of a twinge. "I'm just thankful you and the babe are all right. How's Papa?"

Leah bit her lip, looking a bit like a lost child. "I'm sorry, Isabella. I haven't seen him since you left, what with the scare with the baby and all."

Isabella sighed. Leah blamed her avoidance of her father-in-law on her delicate condition. In some ways, Isabella sympathized with her, but her father's burns proved how much he loved them all. He'd saved Leah's life at the risk of his own. She loved her sweet sister-in-law to distraction, but sometimes she wondered exactly what Jonathan had seen in Leah.

Guilt assaulted her. She shouldn't second-guess her brother's love for Leah. What did she know of their feelings for each other? They'd enjoyed such a short time together, and it wasn't her place to judge whether he'd made a good marriage or not.

She patted Leah's hand. "That's all right, darling. The baby's welfare is the important thing."

"Thank you for understanding." Leah brightened, as if she'd been afraid of a reprimand. "Did you find a carpenter?"

"Yes, I did."

Leah clapped. "How exciting. I can't wait until the wing is repaired."

"I'm going to check on Papa now. Would you like to go with me?"

"I'm still feeling a bit queasy. Maybe later . . ." Leah placed a hand on her stomach. She'd been sick with grief over Jonathan's death, and so it had taken weeks to realize she suffered from a new, different malady: the nausea and vomiting that often accompanied pregnancy. Gradually the knowledge she carried Jonathan's child pulled her from the darkness she'd burrowed in for months.

"As you wish."

Isabella hurried upstairs to change before she saw her father. He had enough to worry about without wondering at her whereabouts for the last twenty-four hours. She could only pray the knowledge wouldn't reach him.

An hour later she eased into his bedroom, not wanting to wake him if he slept. To her surprise, she found him sitting up in bed, pillows supporting his back.

"Papa." She rushed to his side.

"You look tired." He reached out one hand, red, puckered, and drawn. She wrapped it in both of hers, being careful of the tender flesh. His eyes, bright and clearer than they'd been since the fire, stared at her from his ravaged face.

"I am. But nothing a good night's sleep won't cure."

"All went well? When did you get home?"

"I found someone to repair the damage to the house." A blush stole over her cheeks. She wouldn't lie to her father. She just hoped he wouldn't ask more questions about her trip home.

"I want to meet him as soon as possible," he rasped.

"Do you think you're up to it? Mr. Mews could—"

Her father's dark brows drew together. Pink scarring from the fire gave him a ferocious one-sided look, but Isabella knew he wasn't truly angry.

"I'm still the owner of Breeze Hill, and I'll oversee the repairs even if I have to do it from this confounded bed."

"Yes, Papa." Isabella ducked her head, barely able to contain the joy that leapt in her breast. She'd done the right thing by finding a skilled carpenter to repair the damage caused by the blaze. Papa's excitement over the coming renovations proved it.

"Bring him to me immediately. No, show him the damage first, then bring him here."

"What about Mews? He could show Con—Mr. O'Shea— what needs doing." She'd never dreamed she'd be spending more time with Connor once they arrived home. Couldn't he manage the repair job without her?

"Mews couldn't build a pigsty." Her father scowled. "No, you'll have to show the man around. O'Shea, you say? Irish?"

"Yes, sir." Would Connor's ancestry be a problem? Surely not. Her father judged a man on his work ethic, not his homeland, and she'd never known him to say an unkind word about anyone. "Mr. Bloomfield said he apprenticed with a master craftsman by the name of Benson."

"Ah. I've heard of Benson. Your Mr. O'Shea should be well qualified."

Isabella cleared her throat. "There's something else."

Her father speared her with a look. "What is it, Daughter?"

"Mr. O'Shea is indentured to Breeze Hill." She held out the papers that Connor had signed. "In exchange for passage for his four brothers from Ireland."

"Indentured?" Her father glanced over the papers. "Why would the man go to such extremes? Why not just save money to send for them himself?"

"Perhaps he felt that someone with connections would be better able to find passage for all of them."

"Perhaps." Her father reviewed the agreement, then nodded. "Very well. I'll send inquiries to Bloomfield. We can probably work something out after the harvest."

Relieved, Isabella stood.

"And bring the plans and your sketch pad when you return."

"But . . . you can draw so much better than I can."

The excitement left her father's face and his right hand curled into a claw. Isabella wanted to grab the words back, obliterate them from the sorrow-laden air surrounding them. "I'm sorry. I wasn't thinking."

"I know."

"You'll get better. You will. You're getting stronger every day. I can see it."

"From your mouth to God's ears." One side of his face tilted in a lopsided smile. "Now, be off with you. I want to meet this carpenter of yours."

"Yes, Papa."

Isabella kissed him and hurried to her room to grab her drawings, feeling more exhilarated than she had in months. Connor O'Shea might have been giving the orders on the way home from Natchez, but the tables were now turned. She'd be in charge of the repairs to the house, not her father and not Mews.

And she'd wipe that cocky grin off Connor's face once and for all.

Chapter 4

"I'll be taking orders from you?"

"Will that cause a problem, Mr. O'Shea?" Isabella arched one delicate eyebrow.

Connor clenched his jaw. Should it bother him that a woman bought his papers, a woman tried to order him around, then the same woman would be overseeing his work on the plantation?

It bothered him a great deal.

He needed to prove that he had the skills to construct a dwelling as finely as his former master, and he didn't need the distraction of sparring with Isabella Bartholomew day in and day out. But he'd deal with it.

For his brothers' sake.

He made a conscious effort to relax his jaw before he busted his teeth. "No, ma'am. No' a problem at all."

She smiled. "Good."

"After you."

He bowed low but caught a glimpse of the scowl that narrowed her pretty dark eyes before she turned away.

"Beggin' your pardon, but have I offended in some way?"

"No." She walked away. Suddenly she whirled to face him, her skirts billowing out like sails under a strong *gaoth*. "Yes. We don't stand on formality at Breeze Hill. No need to bow."

"Yes, mistress." Connor held himself in check, fighting the urge to bow just to see the fire in her eyes again.

Her eyebrows dipped in annoyance, and a slight tightening of her lips proved he'd needled her as expected. Perchance she didn't like being called mistress. He'd remember that.

"This way, then."

His lips twitched as he followed her through the front door and into a corridor flanked by rooms. Isabella walked the length of the hall, past a stairway that led to the second floor.

She opened a door and Connor was surprised to find himself outside once again, standing on a shaded porch of the U-shaped house with a one-story wing on his left and the burned-out shell of another wing on his right. Isabella moved down the steps to the expansive courtyard, and Connor followed.

He glanced at Isabella. "Do all the rooms in that wing open to the courtyard?"

"Yes."

"Interesting."

"My mother was from Spain and loved her courtyards. Papa built Breeze Hill to accommodate her wishes. We spend a lot of time on the galleries catching the breezes."

Connor blew out a deep breath, the heavy air already suffocatingly thick. "Yes, I can see how that would be a good thing."

"If you think this is bad, just wait until August." Isabella smiled, then turned to face the damaged wing of the house.

He moved closer, being careful of the charred remains. Hollow-eyed windows gaping at him revealed where the bulk of the damage lay. "What happened?"

Isabella stared at the house, her face filled with sorrow. Sparring with him would be better than that look of utter dejection on her face.

"The cotton caught fire right before harvest." She gestured toward the open fields in the distance, and when she did, he spotted clumps of charred trees between the field and the house. A few trees showed signs of new growth and might be salvaged, but others would not. Cords of firewood stood in silent testimony to the ravages of the fire.

"Before we could do anything, the fire raced toward the house. We let the fields burn. Papa . . . Papa did everything he could to save the house."

Connor wondered at the catch in her voice but didn't comment on it. He had yet to meet Mr. Bartholomew. "You did save most o' it."

"At a high cost." Pain laced her words. "Do you think we'll have to tear the whole wing down and start over?"

Connor smiled. She'd asked his opinion instead of ordering him around. It was a start. "Most of this will have to be torn down." He pointed to a spot past a massive fireplace where the roof was still intact. "There, closer to the main house, I think we can salvage some of the materials."

They walked around the perimeter of the wing, Connor looking inside. "Looks like two suites of rooms were destroyed. Do you want to rebuild them exactly as before?"

"I think that's what Papa has in mind. We have some drawings."

Back at the latticed porch, he stepped up, being careful of the charred flooring. He spotted a hastily erected barricade next to the blackened fireplace. "Does that lead to the main house?"

"Yes." Isabella grimaced. "Mews tried to block off the damage but didn't do a very good job."

Connor had to agree. "No need t' worry. I'll put up a more secure wall first thing."

"That would be wonderful." She gestured uncertainly toward the adjacent, undamaged wing. "My father would like to meet you. If that's all right?"

Connor couldn't imagine why she thought he wouldn't want to meet her father. Actually, he wondered why the man hadn't put in an appearance already and why he'd left it to his daughter to retain a carpenter to repair the house in the first place.

They retraced their steps through the courtyard and mounted the stairs to the first-floor gallery. There, Isabella paused, her teeth worrying her bottom lip.

"My father was badly burned in the fire." Her eyebrow arched in warning. "He hates pity."

Connor knew something about pride and pity. The incident that took his own father's ability to walk taught him about gathering the remnants of one's pride after a devastating accident. "I'll remember that."

She searched his gaze, love and concern for her father stamped on her features. Not a trace of the haughty plantation owner's daughter remained. Simply a woman intent on protecting someone she loved. The moment was fleeting; then she blinked and it was gone before she nodded and turned away.

Connor followed. There was something odd, something extraordinarily quiet about the house, about the entire plantation. Suddenly it dawned on him. It was the absence of servants. If he'd learned anything during his years of indentured servitude, he knew that when the very rich snapped their fingers, servants jumped. He'd failed to jump plenty of times and lived to regret it. Where were the servants? The slaves? Did the Bartholomews not have a horde of servants and slaves to see to their every need?

Were they any different? Might Isabella be different?

He wanted to believe that she was.

A tall, thin man shuffled across the courtyard, straw hat in hand. "Miss Isabella?"

Isabella stopped. "Yes, Mews?"

"Sorry to bother you, ma'am, but the lower forty is too muddy for planting after last night's rain. What do you want us to do?"

She hesitated a moment before answering. "Send Martha and Susan to the house. I could use some help with the cleaning today. Send a couple of men to haul more firewood. Also, see that someone mucks out the stables. We've been so busy in the fields, we've let that chore go."

"I'll get right on it." Mews nodded at Connor, then took his leave, looking relieved to have instructions for the day.

"That was Mr. Mews, Toby's father. He's the overseer here. If you need anything, see him."

"Yes, ma'am." Connor watched the man rush off, then turned to Isabella as she rapped lightly on a door next to the main entrance. Mews might have the title of overseer, but he took instructions from Isabella Bartholomew.

Not only would she be making decisions regarding the repairs to the house, she ran the plantation, too.

Interesting.

Did she have the backbone to juggle so many tasks?

Only time would tell.

A raspy voice bade them enter.

Connor stepped inside, his gaze taking in the sitting room first and foremost. A masculine room, large but simple and comfortable, situated in the corner of the main house to optimize the view. Tall, floor-to-ceiling windows graced both exterior walls, giving a panoramic view of the stables and the fields beyond. A door led to another room. A bedroom, perhaps. Across the room, a wingback chair and two spindly chairs faced a fireplace flanked by built-in bookcases.

Miss Bartholomew moved forward. "Papa?"

"Bring him in." A gnarled hand, streaked with pink-and-white welts, waved them forward.

Isabella Bartholomew's gaze met his, and her expression dared him to shame her father. Connor braced himself, not knowing what to expect but prepared for the worst. No matter how hideous the man appeared, he would do the honorable thing and ignore the injuries.

Connor rounded the chair and came face-to-face with a man who'd been through the fire, literally. The gnarled hands were the worst, as if Mr. Bartholomew had used his bare hands to put out the fire. Fire-damaged skin distorted his face into a grimace, and patches of soot-black hair covered his head, interspersed with spots of pink, puckered skin. Not willing to look away, Connor focused on the man's eyes.

Blue eyes stared back at him, bright, steady, firm. What kind of man had Master Bartholomew been before the fire that almost took his home, his family, and his life? Connor bowed slightly at the waist, enough to be deferential without becoming a simpering fool. "Good day, sir."

"Mr. O'Shea." Mr. Bartholomew cleared his throat. "Isabella tells me you've come to repair the damage to Breeze Hill." His words were low and raspy, his vocal cords as tortured inside as he'd been on the outside.

"Yes, sir."

"Have you toured the house?"

"Only parts of it. I've seen the damaged wing, sir."

"And your opinion?" He arched a brow, and Connor spotted the resemblance between father and daughter in that one look. "Are you capable of rebuilding the wing?"

Connor remembered Mr. Benson's confident response to such a question. "Yes, it would be an honor to take on the job, sir."

"Good. We have lumber on hand, but give Isabella a list of anything else you need. She'll see that it's ordered and delivered."

Connor flicked his gaze to Isabella. "Miss Bartholomew, sir?"

An amused expression twisted Mr. Bartholomew's face even further. "Isabella has a head for numbers. I wouldn't trust anyone else to manage my affairs. You'll need some assistance. Isabella, Jim and Toby should be a big help to him, and it won't hurt those two lads to learn a bit of carpentry. Mews, too, for that matter."

"I'll tell them, Papa."

"May I ask how you want the rooms fitted out, sir?" Connor glanced around the room again before coming back to rest on Mr. Bartholomew. "Do you want something along these lines?"

"Maybe something not quite as austere as this. I'll let Isabella help you with that." Mr. Bartholomew reached for a set of drawings. "Here are the original floor plans, but Isabella has been working on some new ideas as well."

"Very good, sir."

"Isabella, have Mews show O'Shea the sawmill."

"A mill?"

"It's primitive, but I cut the lumber off the surrounding land to build this house myself. In recent years, my—" Mr. Bartholomew cleared his throat—"my son, Jonathan, had taken over the saw pit and was in the process of securing contracts to supply lumber for new construction in Natchez when he met an . . . an untimely death. I'd hoped to continue—"

"Papa, I'm afraid that's out of the question now." Isabella put a hand on his arm. "We'll need all the lumber to repair the house."

"Maybe someday, eh?" He patted her hand. "There's ample lodging at the mill, or Mews can put you up in one of the cabins closer to the main house."

"I'm sure the sawmill will be fine." The thought of living alone, away from everyone else enticed Connor like no other. Having time to himself was a luxury he'd never enjoyed.

"What part of Ireland are you from, O'Shea?"

Connor paused at the sudden turn in the conversation. "Kilkenny, Leinster Province."

"Ah." A ghost of a smile twisted Mr. Bartholomew's lopsided features. "Would you be Protestant or Catholic now?"

"Protestant."

"What do they say of Cromwell there?"

Could this be where Bartholomew threw him out on his ear? If the man knew anything at all about Kilkenny, he'd know that they celebrated Cromwell's death every year.

A cackle erupted from Bartholomew's damaged throat, and he waved a gnarled hand. "You don't have to answer. Cromwell destroyed many an Irishman's hopes and dreams."

"Yes, sir."

"Now, if you don't mind, I think I'll rest awhile before dinner. And, O'Shea, stop by every evening with a report of how things are progressing."

"Yes, sir."

Connor followed Isabella out the door, her carriage as straight and regal as a queen's. The weight of this entire family—no, not just the family, but the plantation itself—rested on her slim shoulders.

No wonder about the desperation he'd seen in her eyes.

Chapter 5

ISABELLA JOINED her sister-in-law on the front porch, dropping into one of the rockers and resting her head against the
slatted back.

Exhaustion threatened to overtake her. She hadn't slept at
all last night at Harper's Inn, and she'd been busy with one
thing or the other all day. Had it really been just last night
that she and Connor stayed at the inn? It felt like a lifetime
ago.

The clattering of hooves on the drive roused her.

"Why, it's Nolan Braxton." Leah clapped her hands. "We
haven't seen him in ages."

Isabella sat up straight, smoothing her skirt with one

hand. Before she could gather her wits, their nearest neighbor pulled his spirited mare to a halt and dismounted.

"Good afternoon, ladies."

"Afternoon, Mr. Braxton. Please join us." Leah's gaze slid to Isabella's, eyes twinkling. "We haven't had the pleasure of your company in quite some time."

"My apologies for not calling on you sooner." Nolan braced his booted foot on the second porch step and rested his forearm against a sturdy post. "I had business in New Orleans and just returned to oversee the late planting."

"Please have a seat." Isabella motioned to a chair. "Would you like a cup of tea? Leah and I were just about to have some."

"Thank you, Isabella. That's most kind of you."

Isabella made her way to the kitchen, where Martha had the evening meal simmering on the stove. Little Lizzy Mews sat at the table eating a biscuit drenched with butter and syrup. Her red hair looked like it hadn't seen a brush in a week, not since Isabella had braided the child's hair herself before she'd left for Natchez.

"Miss Isabella, you're back! Did you get me something?" Lizzy jumped up from the stool and rushed toward Isabella, a grin on her face and her arms stretched out for a hug, sticky syrup and all.

"That I did. But you'll have to wait until Toby gets here." Isabella enfolded the motherless child in her arms. She turned to Martha. "We've got company, Martha. Are there any tea cakes left?"

"Yes, Miss Isabella. I do believe so. Who's here?"

"Mr. Braxton."

Isabella took three teacups from the cupboard, but Martha shooed her away. "You go on back to the porch. I'll bring a tray on out directly."

"I don't mind. You've got so much to do already." They'd let so many of the servants go after losing their crops last fall. Only a handful of faithful had stayed on.

"It don't look right for you to do it yourself, miss."

"I'll do it." Lizzy jumped up.

Martha shook her head. "I don't think that's a good idea, Lizzy."

"Please?" Lizzy turned toward Isabella, her gaze pleading. "I'll be really careful."

"Oh, what's the harm? But if you're going to serve tea, you must look presentable." Isabella dampened a kitchen towel and rubbed the syrup off Lizzy's face. Then she untied the leather strings on Lizzy's untidy braids and finger-combed her hair before braiding it again. "There."

Martha made a clicking sound with her tongue but went about preparing the tray. "A mobcap would do a lot of good."

Isabella smiled down at Lizzy. "Oh, that's an excellent idea. Do you have one, Martha? And maybe an apron that's not too big?"

"There should be something that would fit her." She nodded toward a corner cabinet. "There. Second drawer on your left."

Soon Isabella had Lizzy outfitted in a pristine white apron

with a mobcap covering her hair. Lizzy grinned at herself, holding the apron out. Then she frowned. "I don't have any shoes."

"Oh, that's nothing to worry about. It's hot enough that Mr. Braxton won't think a thing about it."

Martha plopped the tray on the table. "Shoo, young lady. Go on back to your young man, and I'll send Lizzy out directly."

Isabella frowned. "He's not *my* young man."

"Not yet." Martha accompanied her words with a smile before turning to Lizzy. "Now, child, you be extra careful. No running. And put the tray right on that little table. Then stand back and ask—Lizzy, look at me—and ask Miss Isabella if that will be all. Do you understand?"

Lizzy nodded, the mobcap bouncing. "Yes, ma'am."

"After that—"

Isabella left Martha to her endless instructions and hurried back to the front porch. Leah's laughter pealed out long before she reached them. At least Nolan made Leah laugh, something she'd done little of during the last few months.

"Martha's fixing tea."

"Wonderful." Leah fanned herself vigorously. "Nolan's been telling me about the ball he attended at the Dunbar estate this past winter. One of the gentlemen got a little tipsy and asked a potted palm to dance."

"Sounds like he enjoyed himself immensely."

"He was quite offended that the lady rebuffed him." Nolan chuckled.

"I'm sure. Ah, here's Lizzy with our tea."

Lizzy looked scared but excited to be given such an important task. Isabella caught her gaze, reassuring her with a nod that she was doing just fine. A tentative smile blossomed on the girl's face; then she bit her lip, carrying the heavy tray across the porch toward the table.

Seconds before she set it down, she tripped, and Isabella jerked forward. Cookies and the teapot started sliding forward, toward Nolan. Isabella grabbed the tray and salvaged the teacups, but not before the silver teapot tipped over the edge of the tray and plummeted to the porch with a crash.

Leah screamed and Nolan jerked to his feet as hot tea splashed onto his riding boots and his fawn-colored breeches. He took a step toward Lizzy, riding crop raised. "Why, you clumsy child. Look what you've done."

"I'm so-so-sorry, sir." Lizzy stepped back, a look of terror stamped on her freckled face.

Isabella stepped between Nolan and Lizzy, took the tray, and set it on the table. She gently clasped Lizzy by the shoulders, giving her a reassuring smile. "It was an accident, Lizzy. No harm done. Now run on back to the kitchen and ask Martha to brew us another pot of tea. All right?"

"Yes—yes, ma'am."

Isabella took a deep breath, then turned to face her guest. "I'm sorry, Nolan."

But instead of the rage she'd seen on his face moments before, the calm, complacent countenance she'd come to expect from him met her gaze.

"No need to apologize, Isabella. You were right. The girl meant no harm. I was just caught off guard." He exhaled a breath. "If anything, I'm the one who should apologize to you and the poor child. I'm afraid I might have scared her out of her wits with my crazed reaction to something so inconsequential."

Leah pressed a hand to her bodice. "You weren't burned, were you, Mr. Braxton?"

"No, no, I'm fine. Thank you."

But Nolan had no chance to apologize to Lizzy, as the girl didn't return. Instead, Martha brought tea, serving it with a careful, somber air as if nothing had happened.

"Ladies, thank you for the tea, but I'd best be going."

"So soon?" Leah pouted.

"I don't want to outstay my welcome." Hat in hand, Nolan addressed Leah. "Mrs. Bartholomew, do you mind if Isabella accompanies me for a short walk before I take my leave?"

"Of course not." Leah's lips twitched, and she fanned herself vigorously, her amused gaze darting to Isabella. Isabella wanted to pinch her. "Take all the time you need."

Casting mock daggers at her sister-in-law behind his back, Isabella joined Nolan, and they strolled across the lawn underneath moss-covered trees. Nolan clasped his hands behind his back, the perfect gentleman. Finally he addressed her. "How's your father?"

"Better, but he's a long way from being well." They walked

around the perimeter of the house toward the grape arbor. Nolan stood back and let Isabella precede him beneath the cooling canopy.

"I'll have to say hello before I leave."

"Please do. He gets so few visitors."

Nolan didn't seem the least bit put off by her father's scars, unlike so many of their friends and neighbors. Even her father's closest friends rarely stopped by to visit. Of course many of the plantation owners and their families had gone north to escape the intense summer heat, but a few remained, especially those who couldn't afford the luxury of a summer home in Virginia or Kentucky.

Through the latticework and twisting grapevines, she could see Connor, Toby, and Jim working on the house. Nolan followed her gaze and motioned toward the workers. "I see you've found someone to repair the house."

"Yes."

"What's his name? If he's a master craftsman, it's likely I've heard of him."

"His name is Connor O'Shea. I don't think he's a master craftsman, but he was indentured to John W. Benson."

"An indentured servant? And Irish on top of that?" An amused smile flitted across Nolan's face.

Isabella pursed her lips. What did Nolan find so funny about either? She continued walking. "He's indentured to repair the damage to Breeze Hill in return for passage for his brothers from Ireland. It seemed like a fair trade."

"I hope your father knows what he's doing. The Irish are a

shiftless lot, you know. You'll be lucky to get an honest day's work out of the man."

Isabella glanced at Connor, busy ripping charred boards off the worst of the damage. Connor had proven he could be depended on—to keep her safe if nothing more. "Thank you for your concern. He seems to be working out just fine."

"I didn't mean to offend you. I'm sure the indentured servant will do a splendid job." He paused beneath the shade of an oak unscathed by the fire, took her by the shoulders, and turned her to face him. A smile curled his lips upward. "But I didn't come here to talk about your indentured servant. Isabella, I've stayed away all these months to give you time to grieve, but now that your mourning period is almost over, may I come calling again?"

"Nolan . . ." She looked away, not ready to have this conversation.

"You're a beautiful woman, and it's only a matter of time before you'll have so many gentlemen callers you won't know which direction to turn." He tipped her chin up with his forefinger, forcing her to meet his gaze. "Forgive me for rushing you, but I had to say something. I can't risk losing you to someone else."

Isabella searched his features. Many considered him a good catch and a man whom she might have wed only a few short months ago, but he lived for the parties and the gay lifestyle of his cronies. His own plantation flourished, inherited from his father, who'd emigrated from England and died before his wife and son could arrive. It was rumored that Braxton holdings had tripled in the years since Nolan had come of age and taken over ownership after his mother also passed away.

Rumors of mistreatment of his slaves, unsavory business practices, and illegal activity had surfaced over the years, but she suspected the rumor mill to be rampant with jealousy over his success. If pressed, Nolan would tell her the truth was much less gory.

"You're forgiven, Nolan, but I need more time. I've got all I can do to take care of Papa and run the plantation."

"Marry me, and I'll take care of everything."

It would be so easy to say yes. A man as successful as Nolan *would* take care of everything. But Papa wouldn't move from Breeze Hill, and she couldn't leave him. Not yet. Maybe in time . . .

"I'm sorry, Nolan. It's too soon. Papa needs me here, and so does Leah. When the babe comes—"

"The babe?" His brow crinkled. "What babe?"

"You didn't know?" Isabella smiled, blinking back tears. "Leah is carrying Jonathan's child. Breeze Hill will have an heir after all. Isn't it a miracle?"

Nolan looked like he'd seen a ghost, and in some ways, she supposed he had. No one had known about the baby, not even Jonathan. She couldn't imagine Leah's pain and despair over losing her husband so soon after they'd wed. But their grief had turned to joy when they'd realized Leah was with child.

Nolan let go of her shoulders and glanced toward the house.

"Yes, a miracle indeed."

Chapter 6

CONNOR HELD the level in his hands, heart pounding.

A spirit level.

He'd heard of such but had never seen one. Carefully he wrapped the precious bubble level in a layer of cloth and placed it in the chest at his feet.

Pivoting, he eyed the myriad assortment of tools that made his own meager collection seem paltry indeed. Lathes, saws, planes, hammers, a brass square, hand drills, a caliper.

Master Benson's tools had been sold at auction. He'd hated to see them go, but there was nothing he could do. He couldn't afford to purchase any of them.

When Mr. Bartholomew had mentioned that he'd built

Breeze Hill with his own hands, he'd meant it. Connor had never seen so many fine tools. And Mr. Bartholomew had entrusted him with them all.

He pried himself away from the shiny tools and explored the dogtrot log cabin. Two rooms, roughly the same size, with an open, roofed passage connecting them, sat in a grove of oak trees that offered plenty of shade and a cooling breeze. The floors could do with a good scrubbing, and the roof needed repairing.

He set to work, organizing the toolroom, making a note to build a table and a couple of chairs for the room he'd chosen for his lodgings.

He'd repay Mr. Bartholomew tenfold for his generosity. When his brothers arrived, he'd teach them the proper way to fell a tree and how to use the pit saw. They'd learn how to draw a plumb, how to form a foundation, how to turn a lathe and build furniture. His brothers would be master craftsmen of the finest order. The future for the O'Shea brothers was as bright as the afternoon sun that burst on the clearing.

Connor spent the rest of the day organizing and oiling the tools, straightening the cabins, marveling at his good fortune. He found a box of shingles and put them to the side, intent on fixing the roof first thing.

Early the next morning, he reached for the ladder, the box of wooden shingles in one hand and a hammer tucked in his waistband. A young girl, red braids flying, came around the corner and barreled right into him, knocking the box out of his hand and scattering shingles all over the ground.

"Whoa, there." He reached out and halted the child's headlong dash.

"Oops. Sorry, mister." Green eyes stared up at him. "You gonna beat me?"

Connor frowned at her. "Now why would I do that?"

She shrugged, digging in the dirt with one toe. "Well, yesterday Mr. Braxton up at the house wanted to beat me when I spilled tea on his boots."

Connor frowned. "Who's Mr. Braxton?"

"He owns Braxton Hall." She pointed eastward, away from the trace. "That way. I don't like him, but he's sweet on Miss Isabella."

"He is, is he?"

"Yes, sir. Miss Isabella stopped him from hitting me. If she hadn't been there, I imagine he would've kilt me."

Lips twitching, Connor hunkered down and started picking up shingles. "Well, I guess it's a good thing Miss Isabella was there. You want to help me pick up these shingles?"

"Yes, sir." As they worked, she squinted up at Connor, green eyes sparkling with curiosity. "Toby says you're from Ireland. That true?"

"'Tis true."

"Really? Our ma was from Ireland. She died when I was borned."

"Sorry to hear that." Connor tossed the last of the shingles into the box. "So you're Toby's little sister? You got a name?"

"Lizzy. What's yours?"

"Connor."

Lizzy reached for one of his tools. "What's this?"

"It's a plane. You use it to make boards smooth."

"Oh. Can I try it?"

"Maybe."

Since she seemed intent on staying awhile, he handed her the box of shingles. "Here. Think you can carry this?"

"Yes, sir." She lugged the box around to the front of the cabin, watching as he climbed the ladder. "You got any brothers or sisters?"

"I've got four brothers in Ireland."

"Four?" Her eyebrows rose. "All I've got is Toby. Don't know how I'd manage four."

Connor laughed. The youngster couldn't be more than eight or nine years old, but she sounded like an old maid. "Hand me that box."

She reached as high as she could, and he grabbed the box from her and scooted on top of the cabin. Soon he was replacing rotten shingles, the sound of the hammer ringing out.

"Miss Isabella had a brother. He got kilt, though."

"I heard about that." He wanted to ask questions but didn't want to get information from the talkative youngster.

"Robbers kilt him."

"You don't say?" Connor pried off a shingle and tossed it to the ground.

"Yep. And they threw his body in the swamp. And the

wild animals had already gotten to him before Miss Isabella found him. Could have been alligators, but Toby says there ain't no gators around here."

Isabella had found her brother? Poor lass. Bad enough to lose her brother like that, but to be the one to find him . . .

"Toby said his legs were—"

"Lizzy." Connor stopped working and held up a hand. He needed to put a stop to the child's morbid fascination with Jonathan Bartholomew's death. "I think I've heard enough."

"Sorry. I wouldn't have taken you for being squeamish."

"I'm not, but I just spotted Miss Isabella coming this way. You wouldn't want her to hear you talking so disrespectfully about her brother, now would you?"

Lizzy's face paled, her freckles popping out like a million stars on a moonless night. "No, sir."

"All right, then." He nodded at a hoe leaning against the cabin. "The yard needs weeding. Think you can do that?"

"Yes, sir." She grabbed the hoe and went to work.

Isabella neared the sawmill and stopped dead in her tracks. The mill had been transformed in the few short hours since Connor's arrival.

The lumber that her father and brother had left to season had been restacked at the edge of the clearing to allow more air to get to it. Little Lizzy Mews was hard at work clearing weeds from the yard, and Connor was on the roof replacing shingles.

As she crossed the clearing, he lifted the box of shingles to his shoulder and descended the ladder, turning as she drew near. "Good morning, mistress."

"Connor." She inclined her head, skirted the saw pit, and entered the dogtrot. A cooling breeze blew between the two cabins. Connor's tools lined the wall of one of the cabins while her father's collection of saws and axes gleamed against the other. Each piece had been oiled and sharpened until they shone like freshly minted coins.

Clutching a leather-bound portfolio to her bosom, she nodded toward Lizzy, hoeing weeds as if her life depended on it. "Looks like you've enlisted some help."

"She's a little rounder, that one."

"She is, isn't she? She's nothing like Toby. He's quiet, easygoing, takes after his father. Lizzy takes after her mother, Irish temper and all."

"What makes you think the Irish have a temper?" Connor wiped his brow with the neckerchief knotted at his throat. His loose-fitting shirt, damp from hard work, clung to his broad shoulders.

"Don't they?"

"No. Some might be a little more easily riled than others, but I'm sure it has nothing to do with being Irish."

"I see. So you don't have much of a temper?"

"Not really." He shrugged.

"And I suppose you've never touched the Blarney stone, either, have you?"

He chuckled, shaking his head at her teasing. "Not that you'd ever know it."

A smudge of grease tracked down one lean cheek, and Isabella had a sudden urge to move closer and wipe the grime off. Either that or bolt before she made a fool of herself. She cleared her throat and held out the portfolio. "Here are the drawings Papa mentioned."

He took the packet and spread her drawings on a hastily constructed table, made of a few rough boards placed atop sawhorses. She waited nervously as he glanced through her sketches. Then, reaching for the originals that her father had given him, he compared the two. Tapping hers, he frowned at her. "These are new designs."

"I know. I thought since we—you—had to rebuild anyway, that maybe we could turn the entire wing into a private suite of rooms." Feeling self-conscious, Isabella blundered on. "The drawings aren't perfect and not to scale, but perhaps—"

"This is sufficient." He flipped through the drawings again, stopping at one. "For your sister-in-law, yes?"

She peeked over his shoulder. He'd selected her favorite. She'd completely redesigned the space, allowing for a master suite and sitting room, a private dining room, a nursery, and a separate bedroom for a nurse. "Yes. The layout of the old rooms wasn't suited to a young married couple with children." She coughed slightly against the thickening in her throat. "And—and perhaps a different design might not bring back as many memories for Leah."

Connor nodded, shuffling the papers. He pointed to a second-floor plan. "And these?"

"I thought they could be used for guests or for more

children should Leah remarry and remain at Breeze Hill." She hesitated. "I know the original was one story, but adding a second story shouldn't be too difficult, should it?"

"It's going to take a lot more lumber."

"And more time."

"Yes, but you've got plenty of resources." He motioned to the saw pit and the forest of trees surrounding them. "You could hire more men, maybe even fulfill some of those contracts your brother negotiated in Natchez."

"All in good time. After the house is repaired and the crops are in."

"Well, even if you don't start the mill up full-time, there's not enough lumber here to do the job at hand. Especially not if you add a second story. I'll need to scout out more trees to cut and saw into lumber."

"Will you be able to rebuild with just Toby and Jim?"

Contrary to what Nolan had said about the Irish, it seemed that Connor O'Shea wasn't afraid of a bit of hard work. Just like the rumors of abuse that circulated about the Braxton plantation, maybe rumors of Irish laziness had been blown out of proportion. So far Connor had proven he was far from lazy.

"The work would go faster with more men, but our biggest problem right now is lumber ready for construction. We need more lumber seasoning, and I can't be both places at once."

And they'd circled back to the need of more workers. Isabella fingered the drawings, trying to think of a way to speed up the process. There were a handful of day laborers working the fields, but Mews couldn't spare them to work in the sawmill. They desperately needed the income from the harvest this year. But after they sold the cotton, she'd have the funds to hire the men he needed, and the day laborers would need jobs.

"I'll have the extra men for you come fall."

"I see." His brow furrowed, and it was obvious he was disappointed with the delay.

"It can't be helped. I simply can't spare the men right now. The crops come first." Surely he understood that. She reached for the drawings, scooping them up. Pain lanced her palm, and she dropped the drawings, jerking her hand away from the rough table.

"What? What is it?" Connor closed the distance between them.

Isabella turned her palm up, wincing at the sight of blood welling up around a splinter. She stilled when Connor cupped her hand in his large work-hardened ones, his fingers warm against hers. He reached for the splinter. Isabella cringed. "No, don't touch it."

His moss-green gaze lifted and met hers. "It's got to come out, lass."

"I know." Isabella stifled a moan.

"This will make it easier." He reached for a jar of salve, dipped his fingers into the yellow substance, and rubbed it on the tender flesh of her palm. The tip of his finger glided across her skin as smooth as butter melting over steamed corn on the cob.

Breathless with the tenderness of his warm touch, Isabella resisted the urge to jerk away. "What—what does that do?"

Sharp pain stabbed her palm, and she yanked her hand out of his grasp, folding her fingers into her aching palm. Connor flicked the offending splinter away.

"You did that deliberately." She blinked back the sting of tears.

"Did what?"

"Distracted me so that you could take it out."

"Perhaps." He swept off his hat, held it to his chest, and bowed. "Forgive me, mistress."

"Don't do that."

"What?" His lips twitched. He knew exactly what to do to make her forget all about the pain in her palm, and it wasn't just applying a soothing salve, either.

"You know. Bow."

He cocked an eyebrow and held out his hand, palm up. "Let me see."

"No."

His gaze softened. "I promise not to hurt you this time, lass. I just need to see if I got it all."

Slowly she extended her hand, still curled into a fist. He eased her fingers open and smoothed them flat against his palm.

"See, it's barely bleeding. A bit more salve, and you'll be good as new."

He dipped a cloth in a bucket of water and wiped the blood away, then smeared on more salve. His touch did funny things to her insides. She pulled against his grip, but he held fast.

"I'm sorry I hurt you, lass." Lifting her gaze, she stared into his eyes, their green depths pulling her in, mesmerizing her. "It was never my intention."

He lifted her hand to his lips and placed a kiss to her palm. Then he bowed low and stepped back.

A wave of heat washed across her face. Was he mocking her? She whirled and marched away, her heart pounding at his audacity. Why must he tease her so with his bowing and scraping?

He knew how much it infuriated her.

And that's exactly why he did it.

Just to needle her.

She didn't slack up until the house came into view. And that's when she spotted William Wainwright's horse tied out front. She lifted the hem of her skirts and hurried forward.

Just as she reached the front porch, William stepped outside, hat in hand. He glanced up, caught her eye, and nodded a greeting. "Isabella."

"Good day, William. How was the trip from Natchez?"

"Uneventful. Just the way I prefer it."

"And the boys? They made it back all right? I told them to come home with your party."

"Yes. They arrived without incident." He motioned toward the main road. "I can't stay long. I decided to ride on out with the boys and make sure you made it home safely. Jim said you were worried about Leah and the babe. I just spoke with her." He glanced over his shoulder toward the front door. "She seems fine."

"It was a false alarm." Isabella bit her lip. "Did you see Papa?"

"Yes." His gaze narrowed. "Isabella, your father seemed to think that you came home with our party."

"You didn't—" she rubbed the tender spot on her hand— "tell him any different, did you? I don't want him to worry."

"I didn't tell him, but he's bound to find out." William squinted at her. "What were you thinking? Taking off like that, and with a stranger. A servant, no less."

"I didn't take off with him. He followed me."

"Well, it's a good thing he did."

Isabella plopped both hands on her hips. "You can't have it both ways, William. One minute you're upset because a servant escorted me home. The next you're saying it's a good thing he did."

William shook his head and took up the reins of his horse. "There's no reasoning with you, Isabella Bartholomew. You're just as pigheaded as ever."

Isabella smiled and called after him as he rode away. "It was good to see you, too, William. Fare thee well."

Chapter 7

ISABELLA WOKE EARLY, more plans for the new wing swirling in her head.

In her earlier drawings, she'd placed the nursery next to the stairs that led to the second floor, where Connor could build storage beneath them, but what if they had guests? Leah wouldn't want strangers traipsing through the baby's room.

No, that would never do.

Wishing she'd made a copy of the sketches to keep for herself, she tried to remember exactly how she'd planned out the rooms. Groaning, knowing sleep would elude her, she tossed back the covers, donned her wrap and slippers, and grabbed a piece of charcoal from the hearth.

Thoughts spinning, she bounded down the stairs to the first-floor gallery. The sun peeked over the horizon, bathing the new day with light. The smell of woodsmoke and bacon hung in the stillness and her stomach rumbled. She had just enough time for a quick sketch before breakfast.

She searched the pile of rubble and found a whitewashed board that would do nicely. She'd transfer the drawing to paper later, after she was sure her new idea would work. Walking through the courtyard, she eyed the burned-out wing, trying to visualize the rebuilt space. Maybe the nursery would be better at the opposite end of the wing, away from the stairs and the noise.

Then Leah's bedroom would need to be next . . .

Sketching as she went, she walked past the brick fireplace that had halted the fire long enough for the men to douse the structure with water. Without the fireplace, the whole house might have burned. She paused, her attention on the gutted space in front of her.

She'd grown up in this very room, right next to Jonathan's. After she'd grown old enough that the two rooms over the main house had held romantic appeal, she'd moved upstairs.

The rooms were gone, but the memories lingered. She could almost hear the shrieks of laughter as her brother chased her through the rooms, or when they giggled and refused to go to sleep on Christmas Eve even when their father threatened them with dire consequences.

Then just last year Jonathan had brought his bride home,

turning both rooms into a bridal suite. Now he was gone, and no amount of wishing was going to bring him back. But there was the babe. A bittersweet feeling of love and affection for the little one who would carry on her brother's name blossomed inside Isabella. She just hoped that the new rooms were completed before the babe came, but if not, they'd manage.

She stared at the new sketches, pleased with the changes. She couldn't wait to show Connor. Her fingers were black with soot from the charcoal, so she headed back toward her rooms. The household would be stirring soon and breakfast would be served.

Stepping around the large fireplace that stood like a sentinel between the destruction and the rest of the house, she ran headlong into Connor. She squeaked in alarm. He reached out and grabbed her, holding her upright.

Just as suddenly as he'd grabbed her, he let her go, his gaze raking her from head to toe. He pivoted and left her staring at his back. "Mistress Isabella, what are you doing here?"

He sounded strangled.

"I was—" Isabella clasped her neckline and backed away. "I couldn't sleep, and . . . I didn't think anyone would be here this early. What are *you* doing here?"

He shrugged, the movement pulling at the fabric stretched across his shoulders. "Trying to beat the heat o' the day."

"Of course."

He'd forsaken his hat and his dark hair glistened with moisture as if he'd attempted to smooth it down with water from the pump. But the effort had been wasted. His hair could no more be tamed than the purple wisteria that grew rampant throughout the wooded hills and valleys surrounding Breeze Hill.

She swallowed, clutching the charcoal-smeared board to her bodice. "Good day to you, Connor."

And with that, she fled to the safety of her rooms.

The swish of muslin, then the light sound of slippers on the stairs let Connor know that Isabella was gone.

He braced both hands against the wall. Hanging his head, he closed his eyes and expelled a lungful of trapped air.

She didn't have to be present for him to see her—the white muslin wrapper cinched tight around her narrow waist, dark hair tumbling down her back past her waist. Her pink lips puffy and her eyes still heavy-lidded from sleep were seared into his brain.

He focused on a knothole inches from his face, willing his pounding heart to slow. She'd been fully clothed, for sure, but much to his shame—and disgrace—he knew what a lady's dressing gown looked like.

Lord, give me strength.

He reached for a crowbar, jammed it between two boards, and pried, using the force to work off his frustration. Isabella Bartholomew hadn't come here to tempt him. She hadn't even known he was anywhere on the premises.

But tempt him she did.

He pulled a board off the wall, the early morning encounter with Isabella and the charred remains reminding him of the first time he'd seen Charlotte Young, the daughter of an English aristocrat with vast holdings in Ireland.

Charlotte rode a Thoroughbred mare, its shining coat as black as the board he held in his hands. Her hair streaming behind her, she'd raced the animal across the moor, laughing with exhilaration. She'd seen him watching from a distance and rode her horse right up to him.

And so it began.

She'd gotten him a job in the stables, and he'd been more than willing. Work was hard to come by for a poor Irish lad. He would have slopped hogs for a few pennies if it would mean food on the table for his brothers and his crippled father.

It never occurred to him that Charlotte would look twice at him or that she would use him for her own pleasure.

He tossed the board out the window, watching as it landed on the pile, slid sideways, and tumbled to the ground, broken, charred, not worth anything but to be burned to a crisp over the household fires this winter.

Much like he'd been when Charlotte had finished with him.

"Isabella, what's got you in such a dither this morning?"

Leah chided Isabella from her comfortable spot in the shade where she darned socks, checked for loose buttons, and made simple repairs to the family's clothing. Isabella shoved her own clothes in a basket out of sight, hoping to do her wash without too much fanfare. She'd be hard-pressed to explain why her petticoats were covered in mud.

"I'm not in a dither. I just wanted to get the washing done before it gets too hot."

"Well, you could have fooled me. You've been working like a fiend all morning. You've practically worn poor Susan out."

"Don't worry about me, Miss Leah. I can keep up with you young girls any day." Susan chuckled, and using a sturdy oak stick, she lifted one of Papa's shirts out of the hot water. Turning, she dunked the shirt in cold water and swished it around.

While Susan's back was turned, Isabella plunged her mud-spattered petticoat into the pot. She swirled the petticoat in the boiling water, glad to see the mud dissipating. She knew exactly what had her in such a *dither*, as Leah put it.

Her face flamed as she remembered the embarrassing predicament from earlier in the day. She'd been so focused on the plans for the new wing that she hadn't even thought about how shameless it was to be seen in her nightgown and dressing gown.

But goodness' sake! She'd been covered from head to toe. There was nothing indecent about her dressing gown, yet somehow knowing Connor had seen her in her nightclothes made her squirm. It was bad enough that she'd have to face him again, but Susan, Martha, and especially Leah would be scandalized if they knew.

Leaving the petticoat to boil a bit longer, she reached for a black mourning fichu and draped it over the clothesline.

They'd made great headway in the mound of clothes when Martha hurried from the house, skirts raised. "Miss Isabella, Miss Leah, you have company."

Isabella poked her head out from between the clotheslines. "Company? Again? Who is it?"

"The Hartfords, ma'am."

"The Hartfords? Mrs. Hartford?" Isabella lifted a brow. "Without sending a calling card in advance?"

"The very one."

Stunned, Isabella could only stand there. Mrs. Hartford had never shown up on their doorstep unannounced. Martha shooed Isabella toward the house. "Come on, Miss Isabella, I'll help you freshen up."

"But the laundry—"

"Pshaw on the laundry." Susan waved her away. "It's almost done. I'll finish while you and Miss Leah entertain your callers."

"Very well." She reached to untie the apron. "Just help Leah, Martha. I can manage on my own."

"Miss Isabella, come quickly!"

Isabella whirled around at the panic in Susan's voice. She stood with her arm around Leah's waist, holding her upright. All color had leached from her sister-in-law's face. She hurried toward them just as Susan lowered her to a chair.

"Leah! Are you all right? Is it the babe?"

"I'm fine. Just a little weak, that's all."

"Stood up too quickly." Susan fanned her with her apron. "She popped up at the first mention of company, then turned white as a sheet. If I hadn't been right beside her, she would've fainted dead away."

Isabella hovered over Leah. "I'll send them away, tell them we're indisposed."

"No. I'm fine, really. I just need a few minutes."

"Are you sure?"

"I'm sure. I'll join you shortly."

"What you should do, young lady, is take to your bed for the rest of the day." Martha helped her up, her arm securely around Leah's thickening waist. "Go on, Miss Isabella. I'll help Susan get Miss Leah to the house; then I'll come help you change."

"Very well. But first, show the Hartfords to the grape arbor. It's cooler there."

"Yes, ma'am."

Isabella joined her guests under the arbor, the slight morning breeze gently rustling the leaves overhead. She'd not seen the Hartfords at all in the months since her brother's death.

And to tell the truth, she'd been a bit hurt by their silence, but she didn't let it show as she greeted them. "Mrs. Hartford. Samuel. It's so good to see you both."

"Miss Bartholomew." Samuel Hartford removed his hat and bowed, his moist hand grasping hers. A stray lock of wispy brown hair fell across his brow. "My condolences on your loss."

Isabella wanted to tell him that her brother had been gone almost six months and that his platitude was too little, too late. But she held her tongue. "Thank you."

Some had come to pay their respects, but not the Hartfords. Isabella hadn't even thought of it at the time, her grief had been so great. But later, in the dead of night, when sleep eluded her, she'd suddenly realized that she hadn't seen Samuel, his mother, or his father when her brother had died or when her father had almost lost his life in the fire that gutted one-third of their home.

Not even a letter of condolence had winged its way to them.

"Miss Bartholomew." Samuel's mother stepped forward and embraced Isabella. "Forgive us for not calling on you sooner, my dear, but Samuel and I have recently returned from an extended trip abroad. I was horrified to learn of what had happened to dear Jonathan and to your father."

Isabella blinked. "You've been away?"

"Yes, dear. I sent a long letter of condolence as soon as I heard. I must say that I was a bit—" Mrs. Hartford hesitated—"surprised when I didn't receive a reply. Did you not receive it?"

"No, ma'am." Isabella regretted thinking ill of the Hartfords. She'd just assumed—

"Oh, I'm so sorry, dear." Concern etched Mrs. Hartford's face. "You poor thing. You probably thought the worst of me."

"No need to apologize." Isabella's face heated.

"How is your father?"

"Somewhat better." She motioned to a few chairs. "Please, won't you be seated?"

Samuel seated his mother, then hurried to Isabella's side.

"Allow me." He offered her his arm and escorted her the short distance to one of the rockers. Beaming, he seated himself next to her. "Miss Isabella, might I say that you look quite fetching this morning."

Isabella opened her mouth, then closed it, not sure how to respond. Martha had performed the fastest toilet known to woman and then stuffed her into her best day dress. There'd been no time to lace a corset, but Isabella had little need for the finery. The last few months had stripped her of any excess poundage she might have carried.

Fetching would be the last word she'd use to describe herself after spending the morning toiling over a pot of boiling laundry. She chose tact over truth. "Thank you, Mr. Hartford."

"Please, Miss Bartholomew, you must call him Samuel. After all, we're some of your nearest neighbors." Mrs. Hartford beamed at the two of them, fanned herself, then rocked back and forth.

She gaped at the portly woman. Mrs. Hartford loved to stand on ceremony and had always insisted that they be so very proper in their interactions with each other. Suddenly it dawned on her why the woman had relaxed the formalities. Mrs. Hartford had her sights set on Isabella as a bride for her son. With the mourning period almost over, it was to be expected, but not from Mrs. Hartford.

Samuel was quite foppish and hung on his mother's skirt, doing her bidding. Isabella had never even considered that he might come calling, at least not for that purpose. But as she sat across from Mrs. Hartford and Samuel, with his impeccable clothes, pale skin, and pompous mannerisms, both beaming at her as if they'd just discovered the crown jewels, she knew why they were here.

Martha's arrival with tea gave her something to do to occupy her hands and her mind.

William Wainwright had spoken to her father yesterday. Had he broached the subject of marriage? Surely not. She couldn't fathom marriage to her brother's closest friend. William seemed more like a brother than a future husband.

No, he was probably just making plans for another trip to Natchez. The Wainwrights headed up a party of travelers several times a year to Natchez, relying on the safety of numbers to thwart attacks from the outlaws who prowled along the trace. The plantation owners often converged at Mount Locust seven miles down the road and traveled together to Natchez to do business. In the fall, when the harvest came in, the trips would increase, sometimes as often as every fortnight. She prayed that Breeze Hill's crops would yield sufficient to make the trip several times this year.

But she couldn't ignore the coincidence of three eligible bachelors calling in such a short time. There would likely be more. Not that there were dozens upon dozens of young men who would seek her hand, but there were enough who would see the Bartholomews' misfortune and loss of a male heir as their gain—if one of them could win her hand in marriage.

Isabella bit her lip. As word got out about the babe, maybe the deluge of suitors would shift from her to Leah. Or possibly diminish altogether.

"Will there be anything else, miss?" Martha stood straight and tall, her black dress neatly pressed, her apron starched and white. Only Isabella knew that the moment she returned to the kitchen, she'd whip off her good apron and put on her old stained one and get back to work cleaning and cooking.

"No thank you, Martha. But if you don't mind, could you check on Leah?"

"Yes, ma'am."

"Oh, your poor sister-in-law. So young to be a widow. That poor, poor girl. How is she?"

"As well as can be expected." Isabella offered her guests tea. Samuel smiled his thanks.

"I don't believe I've met the dear girl. She and your brother married while we were away."

"Yes, ma'am, that's correct."

"Quite suddenly, if I recall."

Mrs. Hartford's tone invited Isabella to share details of Jonathan and Leah's courtship and marriage. Isabella shrugged. "Not so suddenly, really. Jonathan courted Leah a month longer than Papa courted Mama."

A funny little smile lifted the corners of Mrs. Hartford's mouth, and she looked as though she couldn't figure out whether Isabella had made a jest or if she was serious. "Yes, of course." She took a sip of her tea. "And how is the plantation doing now that your father is indisposed?"

"Mama, I'm sure Miss Bartholomew doesn't want to talk business." Samuel leaned back in his chair, looking bored with the conversation.

"I'm sorry, Samuel. I meant no harm." Mrs. Hartford patted Isabella's hand. "Forgive me, Isabella. Samuel thinks I'm an old busybody."

Isabella smiled. Mrs. Hartford could be quite nosy on occasion. She reached for the tray. "Would you like a tea cake, ma'am? Martha's are exceptionally good."

"Thank you, dear." Mrs. Hartford took a sip of tea and nibbled on her cookie. "Ah, that is delicious. It's so disgustingly hot, isn't it?"

"Yes, ma'am."

"I told Mr. Hartford that as soon I can pack my things, I plan to go north to visit my sister for the rest of the summer."

"Mama, you just got back from Europe. Don't you think you should stay home for a while?"

"Heavens, no, Samuel. No one stays in Natchez during these unbearable months." Her mouth rounded in a moue of discontent. "Well, almost no one. The heat is just unbearable."

Isabella breathed a sigh of relief when she spotted Leah coming across the lawn toward the arbor, her pregnancy more obvious than when she was seated.

"Leah." Isabella stood and linked her arm through her sister-in-law's. "I'd like to introduce you to some of our friends. This is Mrs. Caroline Hartford and her son, Samuel. Their plantation is a bit north of us on the west side of the trace. Samuel and Jonathan were of the same age."

"Pleased to meet you, madam. Sir." Leah extended her hand, and Samuel bowed over it.

Mrs. Hartford's eyes riveted on Leah's thickening waist. "Oh, my. I didn't know there was a babe on the way. Did Jonathan know?"

"No, ma'am." Leah lowered her gaze, and Isabella kept her arm wrapped securely around her sister-in-law's waist. It didn't take much for Leah to become distraught, and Mrs. Hartford wasn't known for her tact.

"Oh." Mrs. Hartford fanned herself, looking from one to the other. "What—what a happy surprise this has turned out to be. Your father must be beside himself with joy."

Isabella tugged Leah closer. "Yes, ma'am. We all are."

Chapter 8

CONNOR AND THE BOYS made headway clearing the charred boards in preparation to rebuild.

The closer they got to the main house, the more reusable lumber they found. He'd even spotted a few pieces of furniture that had been shoved into a storage room after the fire and could possibly be salvaged. Toby carried anything useful outside and piled it on a cart to haul to the woodshed behind the house.

Nothing would go to waste.

Toby shuffled back inside and grabbed another stack of boards, his hands black from soot. "The cart's getting full. You want me to take this load to the woodshed?"

"No, go the long way around and take it to your *da*'s cabin. Miss Isabella and Miss Leah have company today. No need to disturb them."

"Yes, sir."

Connor went back to work, trying to tune out the muted conversation coming from the grape arbor, but he couldn't ignore the soft lilt of Isabella's voice and the occasional sound of her laughter.

Memories of colliding with her in the hallway jarred his brain like an oak slamming against the earth after being severed from its moorings with a crosscut saw. Even several layers of cotton, muslin, and lace hadn't disguised the soft contours of her slender form. The shock of seeing her, holding her, would stay with him for weeks.

He'd pushed her away, intent on putting distance between them, but she'd sucked in her breath, dark-brown eyes widening, startled, capturing his for the space of a heartbeat. Her full mouth had parted and then she'd jerked free, but not before he'd felt the desire to swoop in and taste those beguiling lips for himself.

Male laughter rippled across the lawn, bringing his thoughts to a screeching halt.

Get hold o' yourself, O'Shea.

You're the hired help, the indentured servant, no' the gentleman caller who has a fortune, status, and a plantation home t' offer.

Just like before.

The reminder needed to be branded into his head so that he wouldn't forget it.

Ever.

He forced a crowbar beneath a board and pried. He'd been a young, foolish lad the last time he let a woman of the upper class get under his skin. Older and wiser by several years, he shouldn't even look at Isabella Bartholomew, let alone allow his thoughts to dwell on her.

If he didn't stay away from her, her father would give him his walking papers, provided the man didn't kill him outright. And then where would his brothers be?

Right where he'd left them eight years ago, even after he'd promised his father he'd take care of them. How could he take care of them after being shipped half a world away?

He hadn't received a letter from Quinn in over three years.

Three years of silence. It felt like a lifetime.

Toby returned with the cart and bounded up the steps. "My *da's* looking for you."

"Do you know what he wants?"

The youngster shrugged, a hank of hair falling over his forehead. "Don' know. He just asked where you were."

"Thanks, lad."

Connor stepped outside and saw Mews headed his way, a middle-aged man wearing worn breeches and a tattered overcoat at his side. Mews jerked his thumb toward the other man, who could have been his own brother they were so much alike in height and build. "This here's Zachariah Horne. Says he's a carpenter by trade, a preacher by calling. I thought you might be able to use some help repairing the house."

"Mr. Horne." Connor nodded at the stranger, then turned to Mews. "I don't have the authority to hire anybody. You'll have to talk to Mr. Bartholomew about that."

"I'll work for a roof over my head and food for my family." Horne twisted his battered hat in his hands.

"Family?"

"Yes, sir." He motioned with his hat toward where Toby worked. "Two strapping boys as big as that one. They know how to work, they do. And I've swung a hammer a few times." Horne's frayed shirt collar was buttoned, his wispy hair combed and parted. His clothes might be shabby but they were clean, and he'd made an effort to look presentable. "The wife's in the family way, and we need a place to stay until after the babe's born. Anything will do. Anything at all."

Mews spoke up. "She's a Natchez squaw. Not many of 'em left."

"If that's a problem, we'll be on our way." Horne held his gaze. The family probably wasn't welcome on most of the plantations. Being Irish, Connor knew something about being ostracized. If Mews wasn't concerned with the wife's ancestry, Connor figured Mr. Bartholomew wouldn't be. And the man said he'd work for a place to stay and food to eat.

"We could use some help at the sawmill." Connor glanced at Mews.

"That we could." Mews hitched up his breeches. "And we ain't had no preaching since last summer. I don't mind hearing a good sermon now and again."

"Very well. I could use some help here." Connor

motioned toward the charred wing. "Tonight we'll see how Mr. Bartholomew feels about keeping them on for a while."

"I told the wife that the Lord would provide." Mr. Horne smiled, his grin splitting his face from ear to ear. "The wife and girls can work, too."

"Girls?" Connor frowned. "You have girls, too?"

"Seven. My oldest can watch the babies, but the others are old enough to help out with hoeing, washing, mending—whatever's needed. My girls are hard workers. You'll see."

Seven girls? Connor cleared his throat. "I'll leave the girls up to you, Mews. But no promises, Mr. Horne. If Mr. Bartholomew says he can't use you, you'll have to pack up and leave come morning."

"Yes, sir." Horne nodded, his head jerking like a gobbler's on his thin neck. "Yes, sir. I understand. You won't regret this."

Connor turned away, afraid he already did.

Isabella tried to concentrate on seeing to the needs of her guests, but the noise from the west wing was distracting. How in the world did three men, two of them hardly more than boys, make that much noise? But she couldn't very well tell them to stop work because they had visitors.

Through the thick grapevine canopy, she saw Connor speaking with a man she'd never seen before. The man picked up a crowbar and started tearing away charred boards. She frowned. Who was that man and what was he doing? Breeze Hill couldn't afford—

"Sounds like the repairs are coming along nicely." Samuel noticed her distraction. "Did your father hire someone who's qualified?"

"I did."

"You did?" Samuel glanced at her, a surprised look on his face. "I find it hard to believe that a woman of your . . . gentle sensibilities . . . would stoop to hiring a carpenter."

Why did Samuel think she couldn't make decisions regarding Breeze Hill? Men thought women's brains were as soft and spongy as cotton. But no matter. She couldn't be concerned with what he thought. Right now she was more concerned with the stranger and where he'd come from. She shrugged. "It had to be done."

Half an hour later, she waved the Hartfords off and headed toward the construction area. The man was still helping with the house and she spotted two gangly young-sters about Toby's age working alongside him. She frowned. Who were these people? They didn't have any money to pay another soul. She approached Connor.

"May I have a word with you?"

"O' course." He wiped his brow with a handkerchief.

"In private."

She walked toward the grape arbor, turned, and faced Connor. "Who are those men?"

"Zachariah Horne. He showed up this morning looking for work. Mews and I thought he might come in handy."

"It's not your job to hire people." Isabella didn't want to tell him that she didn't have the cash to pay the man.

"How do you know the man knows anything at all about carpentry?"

"He's done well so far, and I'll know how hard a worker he is before the day is out." Connor leaned against a post, his moss-green eyes boring into hers. The sunlight filtered through the leaves, casting his face into shadows. "He has a family. Several children, from what he said."

More mouths to feed? What would they do with them? They could barely feed themselves. She straightened her back, crossed her arms, and stared him down. "You'll have to tell them to leave."

"Give them a chance to prove themselves. There's a lot of work to be done around here and few hands to do it." Connor held up his hands and started ticking off all the reasons they needed help. "The house. The fields. Gardening. Cooking and cleaning. Felling trees and sawing lumber. Rebuilding the west wing."

It grated that he was right. Isabella sighed. "I can't pay him. Not until after harvest."

"All he wants is a roof over his head and food to eat. His wife's in the family way. I told Mews I'd see what he could do today, then approach Mr. Bartholomew with it tonight."

Another child? She turned, watched the man and his sons, who seemed to work without complaint. "And how's he doing?"

"He hasn't let up all afternoon. The boys are quick learners. And look." He led her to the other side of the arbor and pointed toward the cotton field. Workers spread out over the field. She counted three, no, four girls she didn't recognize.

They were hoeing along with Mews and the handful of workers they'd retained after last fall's fire. Mostly elderly men and women who had nowhere else to go.

"Who are they?"

"Horne's youngsters. And his wife and the other girls are helping Martha in the garden. Just fell in and starting working without being asked."

Isabella swallowed. "Just how big is the Horne family?"

Connor gave her a sidelong glance. "I think he said there were seven girls in all and the two boys."

Eleven more people, with a baby on the way. How would she feed them all? But how could she turn them away? She looked over the fields, at the extra hands getting the work done. Maybe the Hornes would be a big help after all. Lord knew she'd worried how they'd manage everything with the few hands they had.

Had the Lord answered a prayer she hadn't even thought to pray?

"And he just wants a roof over their heads and food to eat?"

"That's what he said."

"All right." She turned to Connor. "But the minute they stop pulling their weight, they have to leave."

A broad grin split his face. "Ah, I knew you'd see it my way, lass."

Connor knocked on Mr. Bartholomew's door, and when the man bade him enter, he swung the door wide. Isabella's father sat in the same chair he'd been in the first time Connor had visited. He moved forward until he was facing the man.

"Good evening, sir."

"Connor. I was hoping you'd come. Would you like something to eat?"

"I've eaten, thank you."

"Very well." He motioned to a spindly-looking chair. "Please. Sit."

"Thank you, sir." Connor eased down, hoping the chair could bear his weight.

Mr. Bartholomew chuckled. "Not exactly suited for a man of your size, is it?"

Connor smiled. "No' exactly."

"So tell me—how are the repairs coming along?"

"We've made great progress."

"Are you able to salvage anything?"

"Nothing on the far end closest t' the fields. Everything was destroyed by the fire."

"I was afraid of that."

"But there is less damage as we get closer t' the central part o' the house." Connor sat forward, warming to his topic. "I've salvaged some o' the furniture. A carved headboard, some chairs, and an armoire. There are two matching pedestal tea tables made out o' red oak. Good sturdy pieces. There's some damage t' the surfaces o' both, but the bases and legs are in perfect condition."

"I remember those tables. I made them for my wife as a wedding present. You say the tops are damaged?"

"Yes, sir. But I believe enough materials could be salvaged from each to make a serviceable sideboard."

"Would you like to repair them?"

Connor sat up straighter. "You'd let me work on pieces you made for your wife?"

"I said I would." Mr. Bartholomew eyed him. "If you're up to the task."

"I—" Connor stopped, then nodded. "Yes, sir. I can repair them."

Mr. Bartholomew leaned back and smiled. "Very well, then. I give you leave to work on the furniture. In your spare time, of course."

"Yes, sir." Connor schooled his features, unwilling to let the excitement he felt at working with the beautiful wood show. To think that Mr. Bartholomew would entrust such a task to him.

"Is something wrong, Connor? You don't seem to be very excited about the prospect."

"It's no' that at all, sir." Connor shook his head. "Mr. Bartholomew, if I may be so bold . . ."

The master inclined his head, a smile of encouragement on his distorted features. "You may."

"You're being generous. More generous than I deserve. A cabin of my own. All those tools to use." Connor dropped his gaze and twisted his hat in his hands. "And now an opportunity to work with wood as fine as those oak tables. Tables you made with your own hands."

"'For unto whomsoever much is given, of him shall be much required.' I have faith in you, Connor."

Connor wanted to assure the man that he'd live up to his expectations, and he fully intended to, but he couldn't help but remember how he'd let his own family down when they'd needed him most. If he'd done as his father asked, walked away from Charlotte and worked in the mines along-side Quinn, he'd be in Ireland still. "I'll do my best t' honor your trust, sir."

For a long moment, Mr. Bartholomew was silent, until finally Connor glanced up to find the man staring at him, gnarled hands clasped like claws in front of him. "I'm counting on that very thing."

When he didn't add anything else, Connor fidgeted. "Will that be all, sir?"

"Actually, Isabella brought something to my attention earlier this evening." Mr. Bartholomew pinned him with a look, shrewd and piercing. "She mentioned that you and Mr. Mews had retained the services of one Zachariah Horne, along with his wife and a passel of youngsters."

"Yes, sir." Isabella hadn't been happy when she'd found out about the Hornes. Connor wasn't sure if it was because he'd once again overstepped his authority, or if she was worried about taking on the needs of an additional eleven people, soon to be twelve. He suspected it was a bit of both.

"And what's your opinion of them after today?"

Connor started. Master Benson had never asked anybody's opinion, especially not that of an indentured servant. But he was finding that Master Bartholomew walked to the beat of a different drummer than most men of position and power. "The whole family worked hard today. Horne and his two sons helped us clear over half of the damage today. The girls worked nonstop in the fields, and Mrs. Horne helped Martha in the garden and in the kitchen."

"I believe Isabella said Mrs. Horne is with child?"

"Yes, sir, I believe so."

"I see." Mr. Bartholomew nodded. "When Isabella came to me with the news, she was afraid we'd have to turn them away. She's right in that we haven't earmarked funds to pay day laborers. But we do have plenty of housing since we let so many go last fall. Like you and Mews, she noticed how willing the family is to pitch in and work. I think they'll be an asset to Breeze Hill, and we can do a good deed for them as well. Tell Horne that he and his family are welcome to stay—or, wait, better yet, send him to me first thing in the morning, and I'll tell him myself."

As Connor took his leave from Mr. Bartholomew, he pondered Isabella's turnabout. She'd not been happy with the arrival of the Horne family, but she had accepted throughout the day that they were pulling their weight.

It proved that she could consider what was best for Breeze Hill even when she felt he'd wrestled control from her.

Chapter 9

Visitors swarmed Breeze Hill.

Not exactly visitors, but travelers passing through. Isabella and Leah were ensconced with their guests on the upper veranda outside Isabella's sitting room. The view of the barns and outbuildings, the grape arbor, and the fields beyond was more open now that the burned-out shell of the west wing had been cleared. But she'd be glad when the new construction started. She hoped Leah would too.

More than fifty wagons were parked in the grove of trees down the hill away from the main house, close enough to draw water from the well, but not to infringe on the family's privacy. The Wainwright and the Hartford men were among the travelers, as they had business in Natchez.

Isabella turned to William's father. "Mr. Wainwright, I hadn't expected to see you and William again so soon. What a happy occasion."

"Yes. My factor sent word for me to come to Natchez. A ship has arrived from England and the captain is most anxious to fill his hold and be on his way before hurricane season."

"You're still warehousing cotton from last year?"

"It was William's idea to hold some back. And he was right. We've been able to sell at a premium by waiting until now."

"William has a good head for business."

"As do you. I heard about your agreement with the Irishman. Very shrewd, my dear."

A tingle of pleasure shot through Isabella. "Do you truly think so?"

"Of course." His eyes twinkled. "Once the cotton is harvested, you'll be able to fulfill your end of the bargain with ease."

"Thank you, sir. That's my hope as well."

Martha stepped outside and caught her attention. "Miss Isabella, Mr. Braxton has arrived and is waiting in the parlor."

"Oh. What a surprise."

William smirked, and she arched a brow at him. Well, it was a surprise. Nolan had visited less than a fortnight ago after staying away for months. "Please bring him out to join us."

Martha showed Nolan out to the veranda, and he greeted Leah, then Isabella. "Good afternoon, ladies." He inclined his head in greeting to the others. "Gentlemen."

"Braxton." William returned the greeting. "What brings you to Breeze Hill? Are you planning on joining our party heading to Natchez?"

"I'm afraid I don't have any goods to take to market. Maybe next time." He smiled at Isabella. "I'm simply here to pay my respects to these two lovely ladies."

William's mouth flattened into a thin line.

Leah's fan fluttered, but not before Isabella caught the blush that stole over her cheeks. Isabella was anything but flattered or amused. Three suitors at once—assuming her suspicions were correct—were simply too much for any woman to bear. And especially when two of them circled each other like a couple of banty roosters about to go head-to-head with each other.

Mr. Wainwright moved to the edge of the veranda and looked down toward her father's rooms. "Is that Matthew there?"

Isabella stood, moved to his side, and spotted her father sitting in a chair outside his rooms. How had he gotten out-side? He could barely walk without—

Then she spotted Connor, hovering nearby. She sucked in a breath. "Yes, sir, it is."

"Good to see him out and about. I know you're relieved that he's on the mend."

"Yes, sir." Outwardly, Isabella remained calm, but inwardly, her heart raced in a panic. Her father hadn't left his chambers in months, let alone ventured outside. His strength wasn't up to it, and he didn't want others to know just how weak he truly was. She touched Mr. Wainwright's arm. "Please, if you'll excuse me for a moment."

He stepped back. "Of course."

Isabella headed down the stairs toward the first-floor gallery. As she descended the last few steps, Connor stood at the base of the stairs. His gaze met hers, and he gave a slight bow.

Isabella spoke quietly. "Connor, what's Papa doing outside? He could catch a chill."

His forehead furrowed in confusion. "In this weather? I doubt it."

She shook her head, exasperated. If Connor couldn't make her father go back inside, she'd see to it herself. Lifting her skirt, she made to pass him. "Foolish men."

Connor shifted in front of her, his eyes on a level with hers. "Your father saw your guests and would like a word with them. He said it's a matter o' utmost importance and concerns them all."

She searched his face. "What's wrong?"

He shrugged. "He didn't confide in me."

"Very well, then."

Isabella passed the message along, and the men trooped down the stairs to the veranda where her father waited. All except Samuel. He declined the invitation and instead stayed behind to regale Isabella and Leah with tales of his adventures abroad.

Normally Isabella found Samuel's jack-a-dandy ways and affected British accent amusing, but today her attention turned toward the men on the veranda below. As she watched, she caught William scowling up at them, but he wasn't watching her. His gaze was centered squarely on Leah and Samuel. Her heart thudded against her rib cage. William? And Leah?

She looked away, hiding the smile that bloomed on her lips. What a delightful turn of events. While William was a good man, she didn't relish the thought of marriage to her brother's boyhood friend. But Leah was a different matter altogether. Leah didn't think of William almost as a brother. She'd never even met him before coming to Breeze Hill as Jonathan's bride.

Isabella strolled along the length of the porch. She paused next to a climbing rosebush, admiring the delicate blossoms but covertly watching William from behind the foliage. Sure enough, he was paying little heed to the men's discussion because his attention was focused solely on Leah.

This changed everything. She'd known—hoped—Leah would receive callers someday and would eventually remarry, but Jonathan's death was so new, so fresh in their minds, that she hadn't even thought it could be so soon. And they'd all been so consumed over the birth of the baby that everything else had paled in comparison.

So to know a fine, upstanding man like William Wainwright had his eye on Leah . . . Isabella couldn't be happier. She turned, content to go back to Leah's side and think about her secret. But before she took two steps, Mr. Wainwright's voice rose.

"I'm telling you, Braxton, if we don't do something, these cutthroats are going to become dangerously brash."

"I don't see how we can do more than we already are. Traveling together in large groups seems to be the best deterrent to attack, if you don't mind my saying so, sir."

"For now. But what happens when they become stronger, more daring, or more desperate? What happens when they attack one of the plantations or kill or kidnap our women for ransom? Some of these men have no compunction against using such tactics."

"You can't be serious. They'd be fools to be so brazen."

"Bah." Mr. Wainwright threw his hands up. "You know nothing of the desperation that drives men of this ilk."

"We should ask the governor for help."

A murmur of dissent rose up among the men.

"Gentlemen, I can assure you that Spain and Governor Gayoso have the utmost concern for all plantation owners," Nolan inserted. "But it would be foolish to try to police twenty or thirty miles of a wilderness road. Absolute folly."

"Well, Spain should never have wrested control from Britain if they weren't willing to provide protection for the people."

"I have to agree with you there, Wainwright. And there's something else." Isabella's father spoke up, his raspy voice silencing the others. "O'Shea relayed something disturbing, and I thought you should know."

As invariably happened when her father got excited, his gravelly voice lowered to almost a whisper. The Wainwrights and Nolan leaned in close, but Isabella heard enough to be alarmed. Riders on their land. Crossing in the dead of night. Using back roads and trails that only locals used.

"All the more reason for us to band together and flush out these highwaymen," Mr. Wainwright stated. "If I were you, Braxton, I'd keep an eye out. Anyone not staying on the main trail cannot be trusted. Mark my word."

Nolan nodded. "Point taken, sirs. But I'm afraid you're overreacting."

"Overreacting?" Her father's voice rose to an unhealthy squeak. "As someone who doesn't have family of your own, possibly you don't understand or appreciate the worry the rest of us face. My own son lost his life to these cutthroats."

"You can't know that, Matthew," Mr. Wainwright interjected, his tone placating, compassionate.

"I can, and I do. Jonathan took a chance traveling the trace alone, and it got him killed."

Worry knotting her stomach, Isabella peeked through the foliage. Should she go to her father? He was so easily excited. She was afraid he'd suffer an apoplexy if he became too agitated. Her father sat in his chair, the others standing around him, tense and stiff. Connor stood off to the side, arms folded, listening.

"My apologies, Mr. Bartholomew. I meant no offense." Nolan bowed slightly from the waist. "And you make an excellent point. Possibly I don't have the same fierce drive to protect what's mine, but—" he paused, glancing toward the upper veranda—"I hope to change that someday, with your blessing, sir."

Isabella caught Connor watching her, a sardonic smile tugging at his lips. Her face heated. Then he averted his gaze and stared straight ahead as if he'd never even spotted her behind the climbing roses.

She eased away from the railing and headed back to where Samuel and Leah sat, not daring to look toward the group of men again.

If there was one thing Nolan could thank his mother for, it was the ability to play whatever part he'd been given. London had never known a finer actress, and her exquisite skill had changed everything one fateful day on the voyage to Natchez.

He leaned against a post, having decided he'd said enough. He'd tried to downplay the threat of highwaymen, but Wainwright and Bartholomew fed off each other until they managed to create a mini hurricane in a teapot.

It was more prudent to either keep silent or to agree with them. But not *too* agreeable, or he'd be labeled a milksop like young Hartford, whom no one took seriously. No, better to assert an opinion but back off and side with Bartholomew in the end.

"William, what say you of this?" Mr. Wainwright addressed his son. "You'll be taking a wife someday, raising a family. Aren't you concerned about these lawless cutthroats roaming the country?"

Nolan shifted his attention to the younger Wainwright, only to find him staring at the second-floor balcony, where Isabella and Leah sat, listening to that puppy Samuel Hartford.

"William?"

The younger Wainwright started, turned, a flush heating his face. "Sorry, Father. I was woolgathering."

"Indeed." Wainwright glanced at the women, then chuckled. "Bartholomew, I think our conversation is boring these young bucks. They seem much more interested in your daughter's company than in ours."

Bartholomew's gaze bounced off William, then landed on Nolan. The man didn't smile, but it was hard to tell when he was amused these days. "I fear you are right. And I also fear I've overdone it. I'll bid you all good day. We'll talk of this another time. Connor?"

The Irishman stepped forward.

Wainwright bowed. "Good day, Matthew. Godspeed on your recovery."

"And Godspeed on your trip to Natchez, friend."

Wainwright slapped his son on the back. "Come, William. It's time we stopped talking about cutthroats and highwaymen so you and Braxton can pay those fair ladies some compliments before we take our leave for the evening. You don't want young Hartford to have all the fun."

Nolan and the Wainwrights traversed the length of the porch and mounted the stairs to the upper balcony. At the top of the stairs, he glanced backward. The master of the house and his Irish servant were gone. It suddenly occurred to Nolan that Bartholomew hadn't stood in their presence. Interesting.

Possibly he was as weak and sickly as rumors said he was.

Nolan bit back a smile as the other men said their good-byes to Leah and Isabella. His gaze landed on Isabella as young Hartford bowed low and kissed her hand. Did these gentlemen know that she'd spent the night in Harper's Inn with the indentured servant? Without a doubt, the elder Wainwright would be shocked to his core.

He watched young Wainwright and Hartford through heavy-lidded eyes. As much as Hartford liked to tell scandalous tales about his adventures abroad, Nolan suspected much of it was bluster and wishful thinking. And when it came down to it, Hartford would bow to his mother's whims. If even the hint of scandal attached itself to Isabella's name, Mrs. Hartford would whisk her sniveling brat of a son off to greener pastures.

William Wainwright was a mystery, though. Hardworking, bright, his own man. From all accounts, he'd been close to Jonathan Bartholomew. Their fathers were entrenched in the area and had both received land grants for serving in the king's army. Still, Nolan was willing to bet that if the winds of scandal blew hard enough, Wainwright would keep his distance from the lovely Isabella.

But Nolan didn't intend to spread rumors. Truth be told, he'd prefer that his future wife not be the subject of rumors or gossip. So he'd keep his little tidbit to himself for now. Should Isabella decide to accept an offer of marriage from another suitor, he could always use the information to gently steer her back to his way of thinking.

Regardless, he'd have to do something soon. As he

suspected, every eligible suitor north of Natchez was vying for Isabella Bartholomew's hand, especially those whose land adjoined the Bartholomew holdings.

It could be argued that Bartholomew hadn't made much of a success with his holdings, but most of the disasters weren't of the man's doing. Nolan smiled, a small, stiff grimace, before lifting his glass and taking a sip of his drink. No, Bartholomew hadn't run Breeze Hill into the ground alone. He'd had plenty of help.

He scrutinized the U-shaped house, the wing destroyed by the fire. Granted, from the front, none of that could be seen. But the gentlemen farmers paying their respects didn't care overmuch about the house anyway. Their own homes were of a much grander scale. No, it was the land they wanted. The land so they could send their hordes of slaves to cultivate it, bring the fruits of their labors to harvest, and then sell to the highest bidder in the overseas markets.

They wanted the land, pure and simple. The trappings of decaying buildings and a handful of servants—bond and free—were of no consequence.

Nolan also wanted the land, but for a different reason altogether. Cultivating it was a necessary drudgery that masked bigger things. He'd discovered there were more lucrative ways to line one's pockets than growing cotton and tobacco and being at the whim of the weather, pestilence, and the market.

But to the world and to these men who stood on the veranda making small talk, he was a prosperous gentleman farmer. And as soon as he took possession of Bartholomew's land, he'd become even more prosperous than these fools who toiled in the dirt day after day.

Once he achieved his goal, his vast possessions would be attributed to his business acumen and management skills. Unfortunately, he'd never be able to boast about his most lucrative way of keeping his empire afloat. Breeze Hill was just the beginning. But one step at a time. There was no need to rush. His attention settled on Leah Bartholomew. Except in her case.

It had been a shock to discover that Jonathan's widow was with child.

A child that could wreak havoc with all his plans. Plans that would be ruined if the child came into the world, a boy, heir to Breeze Hill.

What if—?

Nolan gave a minuscule shake of his head, dislodging the thought before it could completely form. No, it was unthinkable. Even he had his limits.

He lifted the glass to his lips, disgusted to see that his hand was shaking.

Chapter 10

Twilight was fast approaching by the time Connor entered Mr. Bartholomew's chambers. The day had been long and busy, and he'd burned every minute of daylight.

Lamplight flickered over the dark paneled walls, illuminating the bookcases and the drapes already pulled against the night. Mr. Bartholomew's rosewood chair had been moved to where it faced the windows instead of the fireplace. The spindly chair had been relegated to the corner beside the fireplace, and a sturdy settee sat across from the master's chair.

Mr. Bartholomew motioned him forward. "Connor. Good to see you, boy."

Connor moved to stand beside the couch. "Good evening, sir. I see you've been rearranging your furniture."

"Indeed. Isabella thought I'd enjoy the view from the

windows better than that cold, dead fireplace." He chuckled and nodded at the settee. "And I expect my visitors will be much more comfortable as well. Sit. Sit, and tell me how your day went."

"Thank you, sir." Connor sat, pleased that the furniture bore his long-legged frame without complaint. "We're making progress. The boys are almost done clearing the west wing, and Horne and myself have been working at the sawmill. We've got several stacks o' lumber drying. But . . ."

Mr. Bartholomew squinted at him, his lopsided face looking ghostly in the lamplight. "But what?"

"It's still a slow go." Connor twisted his hat. "We need more men."

Mr. Bartholomew sighed. "Not two years hence, Jonathan would have been in the woods harvesting trees, overseeing a crew of ten—sometimes twenty—men. I saw to it that Mews had plenty of workers for the fields, and Martha and Susan ran a tight ship here at the house.

"Now I can barely feed myself, and my poor Isabella is trying to patch things up that nature and the violent will of men have destroyed." His gaze focused on his gnarled fingers. "I've failed her, Connor. I've failed both of them and my grandchild. What's to become of Isabella, Leah, and the babe with Breeze Hill fast on its way to ruin?"

"Don't be discouraged, sir. You should see the cotton this year. Mews says it's the best crop he's ever grown. And even though it's going to take a while, we're slowly building up a nice cache of lumber. Breeze Hill will rise again."

A look of yearning creased his features. "You make me want to believe, Connor."

Connor sat silent, watching him. The yearning to be strong, to be able to walk more than a few steps and to be in charge of his domain once again was palpable, and Connor knew how the lack of strength could twist up a man to the point he just wanted to curl up and die. He'd watched his own father suffer from a life-threatening accident.

An accident that might not have occurred had Connor been pulling his share instead of living it up as a stable hand at the Young estate.

He shifted uneasily. Mr. Bartholomew had been more than generous with him, giving him the opportunity to prove his worth as a master craftsman. He owed it to the man to bring Breeze Hill back to its glory. And maybe provide some healing to the man who'd been so kind. All he could think of was Mr. Bartholomew's passion for working with lumber.

"Mr. Bartholomew, I've been working on that side table I told you about. But I've run into a bit o' a problem. Would you be willing to take a look?"

"What kind of problem?"

"There's not enough oak to refinish the top as I'd hoped, and I'd like your suggestions on how t' proceed. I can bring the cart around in the morning, if it's to your liking."

Mr. Bartholomew's gaze stayed fixed on the wide expanse of lawn outside his windows, at the faint outline of the well, then the trees and the fields beyond bathed by the fading sun. Finally he nodded. "I think I'd like that."

Her father was missing.

Where could he have gotten off to? He could barely shuffle across the floor, let alone wander out of the house alone. She'd made sure that someone was in the house at all times to see to his every need.

And now this.

"Martha?" Isabella pushed her panic down and hurried toward the kitchen. "Martha, where are you?"

Martha stepped out, her florid face ruddy from the heat of the kitchen. Concern knit her brows together. "What's the matter, child?"

"Have you seen Papa? He's not in his room."

"I thought you knew." Martha grinned. "That Connor came by this morning with the wagon and hauled Mr. Bartholomew off down to the mill. Mr. Bartholomew looked like a child on Christmas morning. He was that excited."

"The sawmill?" Isabella's heart raced. "Papa's in no condition to be down at the mill."

"Don't you fret none." Martha turned toward the kitchen, wiping her hands on her apron. "The fresh air will do him good."

Ignoring her, Isabella headed toward the mill. This was the last straw. Connor O'Shea had hired Mr. Horne and his family without consulting her, and now he'd taken Papa out of the house.

Did he intend to put Papa to work too?

Isabella gritted her teeth. Next thing she knew, he'd be ordering her around, rushing to get the job done faster in order to send for his brothers. If he wanted his brothers brought over from Ireland, this was not the way to go about it.

By the time she strode—rather stomped—the half mile to the mill, she'd worked herself into a frenzy. She saw Connor stripping bark from a freshly cut tree and marched right up to him, her anger fueled all the more by the distance she'd walked.

"Where's my father?"

"Behind the mill with Lizzy." He kept working.

"Connor, he's a sick man. He needs to stay inside." She plopped her hands on her hips. "What if something happens to him?"

"Nothing's going t' happen, mistress."

"That's easy for you to say. You didn't have to endure his screams of agony in the weeks after the fire."

"No, I reckon you're right about that, lass. But I didn't force him to come."

He was the most insufferable servant they'd ever had at Breeze Hill. She was of a good mind to put him in his place, even though her father would chastise her if she did. He'd never talked down to the indentured servants or the day laborers, saying that men—and women—regardless of their station, should be able to prove their worth with honesty and hard work.

But still, Connor O'Shea tried her patience to the utmost.

"My father's health is too precarious to take lightly. He

could sicken and die from this little . . . jaunt . . . you've taken him on."

Connor stopped working, pushed his hat back, and looked off into the distance, brow furrowed. "He *is* going to die, sure as rain, if ya don't let him live a little."

Isabella's breath caught in her throat, the shock of his words rendering her speechless.

"You keep coddling him like a child, and he's going to wither up and die. He needs something to keep him busy, to give him purpose, to make him want t' live again."

"I am giving him purpose." She threw out her arms, then pointed toward the house. "That's what you're here for—to rebuild the house, to give him purpose and pride and the will to live."

He pinned her with a pitying look that made her squirm over her outburst. "It's not my work that'll do that, lass. It'll be his and his alone."

Tears stung her eyes. "What do you know of it?"

"My *da* lost all feeling in his legs in a mining accident. There was no work for a cripple to be had. There were four of us boys at the time, and we managed to keep a roof over our heads, but it wasn't enough. He couldn't work, so he lost the will t' live. If there had been a way to give him back his pride, his ability t' work at something, it might have turned out differently."

"You were the oldest? And you took on the burden of caring for your family?"

"I was the oldest. But I didn't do a very good job of caring for them. I—" He picked up the drawknife and swiped it down the log, shaving off a long layer of bark. "If anything, I made things worse."

Her anger dissipated like steam rising from a kettle. He felt the same responsibility for his brothers as she did for her father. Almost as if they were the parents instead of the children. She sighed and shrugged. "I'm afraid that any little upset will cause him to take a turn for the worse. He's come so far."

"Give him a chance. That's all I'm asking." He jerked his head toward the dogtrot between the cabins. "He's fine. Go see for yourself."

Isabella swiped at her cheeks, turned, and walked toward the mill. She stopped at the edge of the trees and stared. Her father sat in a chair in the shade of the dogtrot. Lizzy helped him hold a board as he sanded the imperfections from the wood.

Her father's tender flesh was covered with heavy leather gloves, the roofed passage kept the sun at bay, and he looked none the worse for wear. He leaned down and blew away the dust from the board. The fine wood particles danced away on the breeze. Lizzy grinned at him, said something that Isabella didn't quite catch, and her father laughed.

How long had it been since she'd heard that laugh, full of life and joy?

And purpose.

Fresh tears pricked her eyes.

Too long.

Connor came and stood beside her, arms crossed over his chest. They watched her father and Lizzy, not saying anything.

"He's smiling. Laughing." She wrapped her arms around her waist, pressing against the worry that knotted her stomach. "But he's still so weak; the smallest injury could—"

"Just let him be happy. Let him prove that he's still man o' the house." He jostled her shoulder. "And quit coddlin' him so much. He's a man, not a puppy."

She giggled, swatted at her eyes with the tips of her fingers, tilted her head, and looked up at Connor. He winked, and her insides turned to mush.

Chapter 11

Isabella walked along the gallery outside Leah's rooms and knocked.

"Leah?"

No answer.

When she didn't find her sister-in-law inside her sitting room, bedroom, or even in the smaller room turned nursery, she returned to the gallery and scanned the courtyard. Empty, and nothing stirred in the grape arbor but half a dozen brown birds flitting from vine to vine, their chirping filling the evening with cheerful noise.

She headed back toward her rooms, the crisp white lawn baby gown she'd embroidered dangling from one hand. She mounted the stairs, then entered the hallway that led to her sitting room. She fingered the tiny garment, smiling. She'd just finished it and couldn't wait to show Leah.

But tomorrow would be soon enough, she supposed.

She folded the gown and left it on the side table before opening the wide French doors to take advantage of what little breeze June offered. Hanging moss dripped from the cedars her mother had planted years before. The scent of azalea blossoms and honeysuckle wafted on the evening breeze, and she stepped outside onto the front porch and breathed in deeply.

A flash of a dark skirt among the oaks that led toward the road and the creek caught her attention.

Leah?

Leah hadn't taken a stroll in weeks, and especially not since the scare with the baby. Isabella whirled and hurried inside, down the stairs, and out the front door. Her sister-in-law didn't know that Connor had seen evidence of a band of riders in the woods. If the rumors of the things some of these horrible men did were true, they would have no mercy on Leah or any other woman.

She saw Leah turn off the main road onto the path that meandered along the edge of the creek. She hurried to catch up with her. It wasn't hard, as Leah strolled aimlessly along, stopping to pick a pink azalea blossom before moving on.

"Leah."

Her sister-in-law glanced back, then paused, waiting for Isabella to catch up. As she neared, she realized how foolish she'd sound if she insisted Leah return to the house. Maybe she shouldn't tell her about the riders. It was probably nothing and would only serve to remind her of Jonathan's death at the hands of such men. Instead, they'd walk together, then return to the house.

Out of breath, she linked arms with her sister-in-law. "Mind if I join you?"

"Not at all." Leah's tender smile didn't quite reach her eyes, puffy and red. "I would be glad for the company."

Isabella stopped, turned toward Leah, and searched her pale, splotchy face. "You've been crying. What is it, dearest?"

Fresh tears welled up in Leah's eyes, and she sniffed. "I'm sorry—" Her voice broke, and the tears spilled over.

Alarmed, Isabella drew her into her arms. "Are you in pain? Is it the babe? Maybe we should get you back to the house. I'll fetch Martha—"

"No. It's nothing like that." She sucked in a deep, fortifying breath. "It's just that Jonathan and I wed one year ago today."

Isabella's heart plummeted to her stomach, where it lodged like a stone.

"Oh, Leah, I'm so sorry." She took her sister-in-law's hands in hers, searching her gaze. "Why didn't you say something? I could have . . ."

She trailed off when Leah's attempt to smile dissolved into nothingness and the grieving widow shook her head. "There's nothing you could do. I've spent the day reminiscing, remembering the short time we had together."

And where it should be Isabella comforting Leah, Leah wrapped her arm around Isabella's waist and continued on down the path. She squeezed her close to her side.

Isabella remained silent, wishing she'd known. She would have done something to keep Leah occupied today, to keep the bittersweet memories at bay.

Leah chuckled, and Isabella glanced at her. "Do you remember last summer when Jonathan first brought me home?"

"Yes. You were extremely shy around us all."

"Yes, and very shy with Jonathan as well." A becoming blush stole across her pale cheeks. "As a matter of fact, he courted me along this path."

"Courted you?" Isabella frowned. "But you were already married."

"We might have been married, but we hardly knew each other. Jonathan promised me that if I'd marry him, he'd wait until—" Leah broke off. "I shouldn't be talking about this with you."

Isabella cleared her throat. "I agree, it's scandalous. And a bit unnerving, considering you're talking about my brother."

Leah's laugh rang out. "Truly, the first two months after he brought me to Breeze Hill, he stayed in the master suite, and I slept in your old bedroom next door. I'm surprised Martha and Susan weren't aware of it."

"I'm sure they were, but they would never say anything."

"Those were the most glorious months I've ever known." Leah sighed, and they continued on, each lost in her thoughts.

A rustling in the bushes brought Isabella back to the present, and she glanced around at the lengthening shadows. "We'd better head home. It'll be dark soon."

"Let's keep going." Leah pulled her along. "The wagon road that leads to the sawmill is just up ahead. The road will be brighter than the path, and it's probably shorter."

Isabella nodded, relieved that they didn't have to make the trip back along the shadowy pathway. When they reached the wagon road, she could see the outline of the sawmill off to her right, the glow of a single lantern sending out a beacon of light, letting her know that Connor had settled in for the night. Without speaking of Connor, they turned left and headed toward home.

"Isabella?"

"Hmm?"

"You know why so many gentlemen are calling on us these days, don't you?"

"How could I not know? With Jonathan gone and Papa's health so shaky, they've got their eye on Breeze Hill."

Leah laughed. "Don't sound so cynical."

"I'm only speaking the truth." Isabella shrugged.

Twilight fell quickly. Crickets began chirping in earnest, and a bullfrog croaked in the distance, but at least Leah had been right about the road. The way back would be easier than the shadowy, root-filled pathway along the creek bank.

"And have you decided on anyone in particular?" Leah threw her a glance, the evening shadows doing little to mask the interest on her face.

Isabella pursed her lips. "What makes you think I'm going to marry any of them?"

"You have to. We'll lose the plantation if you don't."

"Who says? The men who are calling on me?"

Leah looked confused. "It's common knowledge that a woman needs a husband to manage her affairs. None of the exchanges will do business with a woman."

"They might if they thought they were still doing business with my father."

Leah's mouth dropped open, and she whispered, "You wouldn't."

"Don't worry. I won't lie to them." Isabella looked up at the sky and sighed. "To tell you the truth, Leah, six months ago I would have considered marrying one of them, but—"

"Who?" Leah squeezed her arm.

"I'm not telling."

"I think William Wainwright is very nice, don't you?"

"Yes, he is." Isabella laughed. "But he was also Jonathan's best friend when we were children. I can't picture being married to a man who used to put frogs down my dress. Maybe you should consider William."

Isabella waited for Leah to deny that she'd ever even consider marrying again, but her sister-in-law either didn't hear her or chose to ignore her. "So if it's not William, then it must be Nolan or Samuel."

Samuel? Isabella shuddered. As for Nolan, Isabella didn't want her sister-in-law to know that she had entertained thoughts of marrying Nolan six months ago. But things had changed. She'd changed. She wasn't the flighty young girl she'd been then. The responsibility of her family and livelihood rested squarely on her shoulders. Until her father's health returned and Leah's future was settled, Isabella didn't intend to marry at all.

She couldn't help but compare the gentlemen farmers who were calling on her to Connor or to the hardworking man her father had always been. Papa wouldn't expect anyone at Breeze Hill to do work he wouldn't do himself.

And neither would Connor if he owned a plantation.

She frowned. Now where had that thought come from? She didn't know what kind of man Connor would be if he were a wealthy landowner. He was being paid to do his work. Well, not exactly paid, but he would be when the crops were harvested and they could afford to send for his brothers.

Regardless of his station, he put in the effort of three men, making sure the others did their share as well. She'd seen how much Mews deferred to him in decisions. On one hand, she was relieved. Mews asking Connor's advice relieved her of having to make everyday decisions regarding the plantation, but on the other hand, she couldn't shake the feeling that she was relinquishing control of Breeze Hill inch by inch.

"You know that everybody thinks I will inherit Breeze Hill now that Jonathan's gone, but that's not true. If your babe is a boy, he will be the rightful heir."

"Truly?" Leah placed her hand on her abdomen, then lifted her gaze to meet Isabella's. "I—it hadn't even occurred to me."

"So you see, there's really no reason for me to rush into marriage. If I married, I'd move away, and you and Papa need me here, so that's where I'll stay for the time being."

By the glow of a single lantern and the fading sunlight, Connor sanded the top of the double pedestal table he'd cobbled together from the damaged tea tables.

Mr. Bartholomew had suggested using the original top to create an inlay, then framing it with walnut. The contrast was pleasing to the eye, and he hoped Mr. Bartholomew liked the table as much as he did.

His next step was to perfect his varnish, and he'd been tapping pine trees for the sap, collecting wood ash, and had a good supply of linseed oil on hand. He'd been surprised to find walnut oil, mastic, and shellac in one of the cabins. He'd mix the varnish and try it on scrap pieces of lumber before he tackled the table.

But that task would have to wait for the light of another day.

He put away his tools and picked up the lantern. As he unlatched the door, a horse's whinny brought him up short. Quickly dousing the flame, he reached for the flintlock. As he lifted the gun from over the fireplace, he heard a yell and the sound of horses galloping away.

He rushed outside, determined to give the interlopers a taste of lead. Half a dozen mounted riders raced along the tree-lined path toward the main road. Connor jerked the gun to his shoulder and fired, knowing they were too far away for him to do much damage, but at least they'd know the sawmill wasn't left unattended at night.

"Leah!" A woman's scream caused his heart to stop beating on the spot.

Isabella? And Leah?

He tossed the useless gun aside and took off at a run.

The next few moments were a blur as he ran toward the sound of the scream. Yelling and cursing ensued, and the riders spurred their horses away. Connor let them go, his only thought to get to the women.

"Isabella! Where are you?"

"Connor, is that you?" Isabella's frightened voice rang out in the night.

There, huddled next to the tree line at the edge of the narrow wagon road, Isabella cradled Leah in her arms. Connor's heart gave a sickening twist. Dear saints above, had Leah been trampled in the melee or, heaven forbid, shot? He skidded to a stop and dropped to his knees.

"Leah." Isabella stroked Leah's face. "Are you all right?"

"Is she hurt? Was she hit?"

"I don't think so." Isabella shook her head. "We were walking toward the house; then we heard the—the horses and then the gunshot. We ran, but there was nowhere to go. No time—"

Leah groaned.

"Leah, talk to me."

"The babe." Leah curled around her stomach. "Home. Please."

Isabella looked toward Connor, pleading in her gaze.

"Get Martha." Connor moved closer, gathered Leah into his arms, and jerked his chin toward the house. "Hurry. I'm right behind you."

Isabella picked up her skirts and raced away. Connor moved as fast as he could, fighting the urge to run. Running wouldn't do Leah or her child any good.

Leah grasped his shirtfront with one pale hand, her pain-filled gaze on his. "I fell. I fell and now I've killed my baby."

"No, mistress. Don't think like that."

"No," Leah moaned. "No. I've killed him. I've killed Jonathan's baby."

"Shh. The babe will be fine." Connor prayed it was so.

Martha met him on the front lawn, and Susan had the door wide-open. "Take her to her room."

Connor hurried through the front hall straight to the out-door courtyard, turned left past Mr. Bartholomew's rooms. Mr. Bartholomew and Isabella were standing in his doorway, both as pale as the woman in his arms.

Chapter 12

THE NEXT EVENING, MR. Bartholomew stared out the window of his study at the darkness creeping over the land. Connor waited, hat in hand.

In spite of the pall and worry that hung over the house, it didn't escape Connor's notice that Mr. Bartholomew was standing on his own two feet. Granted, he had a death grip on the wingback chair, but somehow he'd found his strength yesterday and seemed determined to hold on to it.

Connor shifted his feet. "May I ask how Miss Leah is doing, sir?"

Mr. Bartholomew sighed. "Martha says there's nothing wrong with the babe, but Leah is terrified to leave her bed.

She insists that something terrible will happen to the child if she does."

"That's—" Connor broke off what he was about to say. Who was he to question the workings of a woman's mind? Especially one with child who'd been through what Miss Leah had been through. His own *mam* had taken to her bed with Caleb—or was it Rory? He couldn't remember. And she'd died after birthing Patrick, and he'd not been there to say good-bye to her.

Mr. Bartholomew took a deep breath, moved to his chair, and sat. "Tell me what happened."

Connor relayed his part in the events of the night before. "I had no idea Miss Isabella and Miss Leah were on the road, sir. I would never have fired off that shot had I known."

Lopsided scowl firmly in place, Mr. Bartholomew tapped his fingers against the arm of his chair. "No, it's probably good that you did."

"Good?" The shock that had shot through him when he'd heard that scream rose up to choke him again. "But I could have killed them. And Miss Leah—"

"Martha said Leah and the babe are fine," Mr. Bartholomew growled.

"Yes, sir."

"But if you hadn't heard those men and hadn't chased them off, it could have been much, much worse. They might have killed Isabella and Leah."

Stunned, Connor could only stare at him. Surely Mr. Bartholomew didn't believe that.

"Connor, sit down. I need to tell you something."

Connor sank down onto the settee and waited. Mr. Bartholomew would get to the point when it suited him.

"I'm about to tell you something I have never told another human being, not even Isabella." Mr. Bartholomew leaned back in his chair. "Do I have your word that you will keep my confidence?"

"Yes, sir."

"For months after the fire, the pain was so great I begged God to let me die. And then just about the time the fog lifted, Jonathan died." Mr. Bartholomew shifted in his chair, a grimace on his face. "Jonathan's death wasn't an accident."

Connor grew still. Had the man gone daft? Of course Jonathan's death wasn't an accident. Lack of sleep and grief must have addled Master Bartholomew's mind. "Sir, if you'll permit me, it's common knowledge that it wasn't an accident. He was murdered by highwaymen on the way home from Natchez."

"Pshaw." Mr. Bartholomew waved a hand. "Yes, he was murdered by highwaymen, but not for his *purse*. He was murdered because of who he was. The heir to Breeze Hill."

"Sir?" Connor sucked in a breath.

"It might not look like much, but there's four hundred acres of cleared land and six hundred acres of trees on this side of the Natchez Trace. There's another four square miles of pine and oak on the west side of the trace that joins Wainwright's land. Half the plantation homes around here were built from lumber I cut at my own mill."

Connor sat perfectly still, trying to take it all in. Could there be any truth to what Mr. Bartholomew was saying?

"Whoever is after my land expected me to die in that fire and leave my holdings to my heirs." He held up his hands, curved into claws. "Getting rid of Jonathan was the next move in a macabre game of chess with the goal of destroying my family."

"But why attack now? And why try to kill Isabella?"

Bartholomew's pale-blue eyes sparked fire. "They weren't after Isabella. They were after Leah."

"Leah?"

"Not just Leah, but the babe as well." Mr. Bartholomew's face hardened. "My heir."

"Papa?"

Connor jerked to his feet at Isabella's strangled cry. She stood in the doorway, her hand on the latch, face drained of color.

"Isabella." Mr. Bartholomew struggled to stand, holding his arms out in invitation.

"No, Papa, that's not true. Nobody would—" She broke off as a sob tore from her, her gaze ricocheting from her father to Connor and back again.

"No." She pried herself from the door and fled.

Connor took a step toward the empty door where she'd stood, before duty rooted him to the spot.

"What have I done?" An ashen tinge blanched the man's features, robbing him of the pink splotches left by the ravages of the fire. He slumped in his chair, waving a hand toward the door. "Go. Go after her. See that she's all right."

"Yes, sir."

Connor bolted. He didn't have to be told twice.

He spotted Isabella running toward the grape arbor. He followed, her pain drawing him like a beacon in the night. The arbor sat in darkness, vines trailing about the rough-hewn beams, cloaking the structure in shadow and tranquility.

But peace could not be found here tonight. Only heart-rending sobs that tore at Connor's insides.

He reached for her, and she jerked at his touch, her cries all the wilder.

"Shh, lass." Connor tucked her head under his chin and wrapped his arms securely around her, cocooning her against him. The scent of her hair assaulted his senses, and he closed his eyes, breathing in deep.

She stopped resisting and let him hold her, great gulping cries tearing from her mouth as if she'd lose her breath completely.

"It's all right, Isabella." Connor rubbed her back with one hand. "The fright o' nearly losing Leah and the babe upset your father. I'm sure none of that was true."

She groaned but didn't answer. How long they stood there, he didn't know. He held her, letting her mourn. Gradually her sobs slowed, became an occasional deep, shuddering breath, then quieted to a sniffle.

Connor held her away from him, his hands gentle on her shoulders. He searched her face in the pale light from the moon. She gazed up at him, eyes large and luminous, her lashes spiked with tears.

"Oh, Connor, what if it's true?" Her voice trembled. "What if someone killed Jonathan just for Breeze Hill? And tried to kill Papa? And now they're truly after Leah and the babe?"

"For a fact, you don't know that." Connor lowered his face to hers, willing her to believe him.

"I found him, you know. His horse came home without him, and the men searched the trace for days. Papa wanted me to stay home, let the men look for him. But I couldn't." She shook her head, her eyes taking on a faraway look. "The hogs or coyotes, something . . ."

"Hush." Connor cupped her face in both hands, one thumb pressed against her lips, silencing her. "It does no good to make yourself sick thinking about it."

"He was on his way back from Natchez and had coin from the sale of some lumber. It's no secret that the trace is a dangerous place, but that someone intentionally killed Jonathan for our land? It's unthinkable." Fresh tears swam in her eyes. "Why would anybody kill all of us for Breeze Hill?"

"Nobody's going t' kill you, lass."

A strangled laugh escaped her. "You're right. It's not me they want to kill. It's the rest of my family, including an unborn child. A *baby*. What kind of monster would do that?"

"I don't know." Connor rubbed his hands up and down her arms. "Let's pray your father is wrong."

She pulled away, wrapped her arms around her waist, and moved to the other end of the arbor, haloed by the moon.

"Prayer didn't keep my mother here. Or save Jonathan's

life, or keep the fields from burning last fall. It didn't even keep my father safe from the fire that swept through the house." She lifted her chin, a challenge in the firm jut of her jaw. "Why should I expect prayer to protect Leah, the babe, and my father now?"

She'd lost her faith in God. He could see that clearly. So many tragedies heaped one upon another had broken her to the point she didn't feel that God was listening to her, that He would answer her. And from the defiant look she threw Connor's way, she wasn't ready for him to refute her claims.

"What happened to your mother?" Connor moved closer.

She sucked in a sharp breath, her gaze boring into his. "What? No lectures about God?"

"No." Connor stared out at the cotton field. Just enough moonlight shone that he could see the clumps of plants marching away into the distance in perfect unison. Small, but growing bigger every day. Like her faith would have to do. "You're not ready to hear it. But I am ready to hear about your mother."

"My mother." Isabella sighed, then turned, the two of them facing the fields, side by side. "My mother came to New Orleans with her father, Don Esteban Salgado Valadez. She met my father, and they fell in love. My grandfather wouldn't give his permission for her to marry an American colonist with no title and little prospects for a future, so she ran away, married him anyway, and came to Breeze Hill. Her mother, my grandmother, grew ill when I was two years old.

She begged my mother to return to Spain for a visit. She went and never returned.

"Some—including my father—believe the ship went down at sea. Others say my grandfather had the marriage annulled and married her off to some Spanish crony of his."

"And you? What do you believe?"

"It doesn't matter what I believe."

"I think it matters to you." Connor leaned against a post and studied her shadowed face. "And it matters to me."

She gave him the ghost of a smile. A faint breeze blew a strand of hair across her cheek, and she brushed it away. "For a long time, I believed she was alive and would return. I waited, but she never did."

"And now you've given up hope?"

"What else was there to do?" Isabella shrugged, feeling like a lonely little girl again, longing for her mother.

"You're right, lass. There was nothin' else t' do." He reached out, smoothed her hair back, a faint smile playing on his lips. "But I have a feeling she loved you and Jonathan. How could she not?"

Warmth whooshed over Isabella, followed by a tingling chill. Not from cold, but from the sweet allure of Connor's presence, his concern and compassion for the little girl she'd once been.

His thumb brushed softly along her cheek and lingered at

the edge of her mouth. Isabella's heart thundered in her chest, and time stopped. Was she breathing? She needed to breathe.

She needed to run.

His eyes flickered upward, caught her gaze, and he blinked. She felt the subtle shift as he pulled back, putting some distance between them.

"You should go check on your *da*. He's probably worried sick by now."

Isabella nodded, then fled the arbor, knees shaking.

Somehow she managed to make it to the first-floor gallery, hurried past Leah's rooms and on to her father's rooms. She stopped at her father's sitting room door, took a deep breath, and looked back toward the grape arbor. Connor was gone. Disappointed, she lifted the latch and entered the room.

"Papa?"

Her father lifted his head, his expression full of anguish, then opened his arms. She rushed across the sitting room and flung herself at him, clutching his gnarled hands between hers.

"I'm so sorry you heard what I said to Connor. I never meant to cause you distress." Tears shimmered in his blue eyes.

"Do you really believe what you said?" She searched his face, looking for assurance that all would be well. Her heart skittered with fear. She couldn't bear it if someone tried to kill her father. Leah. And the babe.

"I have to consider it for Leah and the babe's sake."

"What will we do?"

"I don't know. But I've taken Connor into my confidence."

"Why Connor? Why not Mr. Wainwright or Mr. Hartford, even?"

"Having just arrived in Natchez, Connor couldn't have been party to any nefarious doings the last six months."

And more than once he'd come to her rescue, hers and now Leah's.

"That's why you told Connor? Because you don't trust anyone else? Not even Mews?"

"Mews is prone to talk when he's had a bit too much ale. I had to tell someone, someone who could look after you and Leah should something happen to me."

"Nothing's going to happen." Isabella knelt at his side, his hands clasped in hers.

"Maybe I should send you and Leah away."

"No, Papa. Send Leah somewhere safe if you must, but I won't leave you."

"I won't make any decisions tonight. Maybe things will look better in the light of day."

Isabella rested her head on his knee, content to feel his gnarled hand stroking her hair. Things always looked better in the morning. Maybe not perfect, but better.

She'd woken up every morning for the last six months to the reality that her brother was dead and was never coming back. And years ago, she'd stopped hoping and dreaming that her mother would return. She sighed and rubbed her cheek against her father's knee.

"Papa?"

"Yes?"

"Why did Mama go away?"

His hand stilled against her hair. "We've discussed this before."

"No, we haven't." She lifted her head. "You've told me that she went to visit her mother in Spain, but—but I've heard rumors."

"Who?" A ferocious scowl screwed up her father's misshapen face.

"It doesn't matter who said it or where I heard it. I'm old enough to know the truth."

Her father let out a long sigh, as if the very breath of life were being forced from him. He sat so still, Isabella thought he was going to refuse her request once again. Finally he gave her a little half smile that reminded her of the way he'd looked before the fire.

"You're right." He reached out and touched her face. "Have I ever told you how much you look like your mother?"

"Yes." She smiled. "Constantly."

"I fell in love with her the first time I saw her. She was the most beautiful woman I'd ever seen." Her father tapped his chest, right over his heart. "Not only was she beautiful on the outside, her heart was beautiful.

"When your grandfather realized that she felt the same way about me, he forbade her to see me, but nothing could keep us apart. Less than a month after we met, we ran away and got married."

"A Catholic wedding?"

"No. That was the one thing that pained your mother greatly. I was young and not as committed to my faith as I should have been, so I was willing to convert, but without her father's blessing, no Catholic priest would perform the ceremony. We were married in the Protestant faith by an itinerant preacher by the name of Fisk.

"We lived peaceably enough for a while, and I avoided New Orleans. Your grandfather was busy with his duties there and on infrequent trips to Natchez and mostly left us alone. When your grandmother became ill and your grandfather was called back to Spain, he asked your mother to come to Natchez and see him off. It was during harvest, and I didn't feel I had time to go. Your mother went, leaving Jonathan and you here with your nurse. I thought he'd had a change of heart, but that wasn't the case."

"She left us here?"

"It was to be a short time. A week, maybe two. That was all. She would never have left you otherwise." Her father's crippled hands curled into fists. "She didn't come back, and Don Esteban didn't even have the decency to send word that he had taken her."

Isabella frowned. "What do you mean? Taken her?"

"When she didn't return at the appointed time, I journeyed to Natchez, but it was too late. He just took her, forced her on board." He scowled. "Busybodies who like to stir the pot insist that she left willingly, but it's not true."

"How do you know?"

He glared at her. "She would never have abandoned you and your brother. Never."

Isabella searched his gaze. How could he be so sure? "Papa, why didn't you go after her?" She held her breath, waiting.

"I tried. I begged, cajoled, and threatened every ship's captain in port. But a terrible storm was brewing and no one would leave the harbor. And then word came from your grandmother that the ship your mother was on had sunk and all on board were lost."

"Did you believe her?"

"I didn't have much choice, did I?"

Chapter 13

NOLAN JERKED to his feet and slapped his hands against the polished sheen of his mahogany desk, imported from France. Fifty candles illuminated the room, reaching out and banishing the darkness. But the glow didn't brighten his foul mood tonight.

He glared at Pierre.

"You did *what?*"

"We set out to burn the sawmill just like you said, but someone was there. He shot at us, and when we were trying to get away, we almost ran down two women."

Pierre sat on the edge of Nolan's desk, toying with the clasp on a cigar box. Irritation swamped Nolan, and he narrowed his gaze. Pierre loved to goad him, and experience had taught Nolan that if he ordered the Frenchman to move, he'd smirk, looking like he'd gotten the upper hand by prodding him. But Nolan wasn't in the mood for playing games. "Get off my desk."

Just as Nolan expected, Pierre grinned, but he moved, slumping down into an overstuffed chair. He took out his knife and started cleaning his nails, deliberately goading Nolan with his uncouth habits.

"Looked like Mademoiselle Bartholomew and a blonde. A bit plump for my taste." Pierre snapped his fingers as if he'd just thought of something. "There is a sister-in-law, no? And if the rumors are true, she is *enceinte*."

Nolan scowled. How did Pierre know these things? Nolan had only found out less than a fortnight ago. But then Pierre ran in circles that Nolan avoided. Servants and sharecroppers frequented taverns like Harper's Inn and talked freely about their masters. It wasn't surprising that Pierre knew of the babe. "Were the women harmed?"

"Non." Pierre shrugged, inspecting his nails. He cast a sly glance at Nolan, his dark eyes gleaming. "But if they were, or even if she lost the child because of such an unfortunate accident, it would be to your benefit, no?"

Nolan ignored the Frenchman's question. Not only had Pierre failed to destroy the sawmill, he'd tipped their hand to Bartholomew and almost killed Isabella and Leah in the process. "Tell me, Pierre. Would you have felt any remorse had you killed the women, even by accident?"

"It would have been a pity but would have neatly solved your problem." He leaned forward and opened the cigar box. He took out a Havana, struck a match, and pulled on the cigar.

Nolan slapped the lid shut on his cigar case. "What's that supposed to mean?"

"The young widow. The one with child." Pierre leaned forward, abandoning all pretense of the devil-may-care French thief and highwayman. "You'd like to see her gone, wouldn't you?"

"No." The denial sounded weak even to his own ears. "No. There will be no more killing."

"As you wish, *monsieur*. But we both know that a male child born to the Bartholomew woman will destroy what you've worked for."

"And what do you propose we do, Monsieur Le Bonne?"

"We eliminate the problem, *non*?" Pierre leaned back, puffed his cigar. As the smoke curled, distorting his features, he smiled.

Nolan opened his mouth to forbid Pierre from harming Leah Bartholomew and her unborn child but snapped it shut instead.

What Pierre did was his own business.

Sunday morning, Isabella carried a small tray and joined Leah on the gallery outside her rooms. Leah, pale and sickly looking, a lap quilt draped over her in spite of the heat, barely acknowledged her presence.

After the accident last week, she'd withdrawn, venturing no further from her rooms than this porch. She'd even declined invitations to the dining room, choosing to take her meals in the safety of her sitting room.

Sighing inwardly, Isabella motioned to the tray. "I brought some refreshment." Without giving Leah an opportunity to refuse, she poured two cups of tea and handed one to her sister-in-law.

Leah held the tea up to the light, a faint smile softening her features. "Remember the lemons Jonathan brought from Natchez to celebrate our marriage?"

"I remember. I think he thought we'd be so enamored of the lemons that we wouldn't even notice he'd brought home a bride."

"It was the next trip that he—" Leah broke off, tears filling her eyes. "I'm sorry. I shouldn't talk about Jonathan's death."

"Leah, holding in your grief isn't good for you or the baby. You should talk about Jonathan if you wish. Share your happy memories, your hopes and dreams. Jonathan would want you to be happy, to move forward with your life."

"But that's just it, Isabella." Leah bit her lip, her gaze straying to the burned-out shell where she'd spent such a short time as a young bride. "My life is like the west wing. Charred and empty. Everything we had together was destroyed in that fire."

Pain radiated from Leah's blue eyes, and Isabella reached out and clasped her hand. "Not everything, dearest. You're carrying Jonathan's babe. Everything else was just possessions, trinkets with fond memories, but this—this child is a part of him. Just focus on that and the rest doesn't matter."

Leah's hand gripped hers, her gaze searching Isabella's. "I'm frightened."

"There's no need to be afraid. Martha and Susan will be here with you every step of the way. And Mrs. Horne has birthed almost a dozen children of her own. You'll be perfectly safe with them."

"No, I'm not afraid for myself." Leah pulled away, her hand gently cradling her rounded stomach, comforting her unborn child. "I'm terrified that something will happen to the baby." Her eyes filled with fresh tears, and she whispered, "This child is all I have left of Jonathan."

A chill ran down Isabella's spine. Not only did her father fear for the child's life, but now Leah did as well. Were they all just a little bit crazy, or did they really have reason to fear?

And how did she answer her sister-in-law? How did she assure her that there was nothing to fear, when the same fear clawed at her own thoughts?

A measure of relief rolled over her as Lizzy ran across the courtyard and bounded up the steps. Lizzy's eyes shone with excitement. "Miss Isabella, we're going to have church this morning. Wanna come?"

"Church?"

"Yeah. I mean, yes, ma'am. Under the grape arbor. Mr. Horne's gonna preach and Papa's gonna play his fiddle." She grinned. "Then afterward, we're goin' fishing."

Isabella glanced at her sister-in-law, hoping to draw Leah off the porch. "Leah, would you like to go? It's a short walk to the grape arbor."

"No thank you. I think I'll stay here."

"Well, maybe you'd like to go fishing with us later?" Lizzy leaned over the railing, pigtails swinging. "Me and Toby found some grubs this morning."

If possible, Leah paled even more. "No, no thank you."

"Thank you for the invitation, Lizzy." Isabella looked pointedly at the girl. "Run along, now. Miss Leah and I can hear the singing and preaching just fine from here."

"Yes, ma'am."

Isabella fanned herself and pushed her rocker into motion, watching as everyone gathered around the grape arbor.

The Horne family walked from their cabin, the older children helping with the younger ones. Mr. Horne, his tall, thin frame impressive in a worn black coat, escorted his wife to a straight-backed chair. The children sat obediently at her feet.

Out of the corner of her eye, Isabella spotted Connor as he rounded the bend on the wagon road that led from the sawmill. No coat, but he'd donned a green jerkin over a fresh cotton shirt, and she couldn't help but think about how the green would complement his eyes. He joined the others, leaning against a tree as Mews tuned his fiddle.

The next hour was filled with singing, followed by a rousing sermon by Zachariah Horne. Isabella wouldn't have believed the quiet, mousy Mr. Horne capable of such enthusiasm if she hadn't seen it with her own eyes.

The longer he preached, the more animated he became. He paced the length of the grape arbor, turning only to retrace his steps and repeat the process time and again.

"And then Mistress Job told her husband to curse God and die. What height of folly! That the woman would taunt the very God of heaven in such a manner."

Mr. Horne paused, the sudden silence just as unnerving as his shouting. He pivoted, his intense gaze landing on each and every one of his listeners. Isabella felt that his gaze even stretched so far as to include her on the gallery.

"But as she goes, so go we." His voice rose once again. "What man or woman among us hasn't questioned God in our hour of sorrow? Mistress Job had just lost all her children. Her husband's cattle, sheep, goats, camels—all gone. Methinks Mistress Job was in the pit of despair. But—" one bony finger stabbed skyward—"Job said, 'Thou speakest as one of the foolish women speaketh. What? shall we receive good at the hand of God, and shall we not receive evil?'"

Isabella fanned faster as the man's unorthodox preaching pierced her heart. She'd never seen a man of God become as passionate over his topic.

Before his injuries, her father had read Scripture and led them in a prayer every Sunday, and upon occasion they'd attended church when in Natchez, but Mr. Horne's boisterous preaching was unlike anything she'd ever heard.

She was relieved when he finally wound down and motioned for his wife. Mrs. Horne stood and, joined by her three oldest daughters, started singing.

The haunting melody of a familiar hymn rang out over the clearing, the woman's and her daughters' voices blending in perfect harmony.

By the time they reached the end of the first refrain, Mr. Mews had joined in with his fiddle, the gentle glide of his bow across the strings buoying the words and lifting them heavenward, where they lingered on the breeze.

Jesus, my all in all Thou art,
My rest in toil, my ease in pain;
The medicine of my broken heart,
In war, my peace—in loss, my gain.

A sob from Leah had Isabella out of her rocker in an instant. Alarmed, Isabella knelt by her sister-in-law's side and clasped her hands. "What is it?"

"Oh, Isabella. It's as if they're singing *to me, for me.* Straight from God's heart to mine." A tremulous smile blossomed on her face even as her tears spilled over and ran down her cheeks. "Listen to the words.

"'Jesus . . . my rest in toil, my ease in pain.'" Leah whispered the words along with Mrs. Horne and her daughters. "'The medicine of my broken heart, in war, my peace—in loss, my gain.'"

Leah's gaze met Isabella's, her eyes shining. "How could I have been so blind to try to carry my burdens alone? Why haven't I called out to God before now?"

Isabella blinked back her own tears, fighting the heaviness

that weighed her own heart down. Blindly she whispered, "I don't know."

⌇

After Leah retired to her room for an afternoon nap, Isabella walked toward the creek, where everyone had gone fishing. Even her father had asked Toby to bring the pony cart around for the outing.

Grateful for the gentle breeze ruffling the leaves overhead, she followed the path along the edge of the creek. Birds chirped overhead, and a squirrel scampered across in front of her, darting up the nearest tree. The milk cows lay in the shade, chewing their cuds, avoiding the heat of the day. The possibility of someone trying to kill her father, Leah, or the babe seemed far-fetched indeed on such a sunny Sunday afternoon.

Surely her father had just been overwrought and worried. And all mothers worried needlessly in the weeks before the birth of their child, didn't they? Once the babe was born, everyone's fears would be laid to rest.

Isabella found herself humming the tune to the hymn that had touched Leah's heart. *"Thou hidden source of calm repose; Thou all-sufficient love divine."*

Quickly she shut off her thoughts. She wasn't ready to hand over her sorrows, her grievances. How could God justify all the wrongs that had befallen her family? She'd grown up without a mother. Leah's babe would be bereft of a father.

How could one sermon, one song, heal the wounds

festering in her heart? But if the peace and joy on Leah's face were any indication, she'd embraced Jesus as her source of comfort. A longing to do the same washed over Isabella like a cooling spring rain, but she pushed it away. She couldn't let go of her hurt so easily. She . . . she just couldn't.

Lifting her skirts, she hurried down the path toward the fishing hole. She'd spent too much time with her own maudlin thoughts today. Lizzy's joyful countenance and one of the child's fishing poles was just what she needed.

Everyone, from the oldest to the youngest, lounged along the bank, poles dipped in the water. Lizzy spotted her first, hopped up, and ran to her side, red braids flying. "Miss Isabella, I caught a big fish. Come see."

She pulled Isabella to the bank and lifted the string of fish from the water. Isabella dutifully admired the walleyed creatures gaping up at her.

"We're going to have fish tonight."

"Hmm, that sounds delicious."

"You wanna fish?"

"Do you have an extra pole?"

"Yes, ma'am." Lizzy took her by the hand again. "Come on." She led her to where Connor sat and handed her a pole. "Sit here, Miss Isabella. It's the best spot in the whole world. It's where I caught the big fish."

"I couldn't take your spot, Lizzy." Especially since it was about as close to Connor as one could get. She avoided his gaze. She hadn't seen him since the night she'd rushed out of her father's rooms to the grape arbor. In spite of the heat of the day, she shivered remembering the touch of his thumb lightly tracing her lips.

"It's all right. There's plenty of room." Lizzy reached for her hand and tugged her down. Chattering like a magpie, the child plopped down beside her, grabbed another pole, and expertly threaded a worm on the hook.

Isabella tried to concentrate on the small cork that bobbed in the water but found it impossible with Connor so near. He sat to her left, one forearm resting on a raised knee. Lizzy sat to her right, keeping up a running monologue on how best to catch a fish.

She felt a tug on her line and jerked the pole, being careful not to pull too hard. Confident she'd caught a fish, she lifted it out of the water, but an empty hook was all she had to show for her efforts.

"Your bait's gone, Miss Isabella." Lizzy sounded disappointed.

"That it is."

Connor reached for a wooden bucket, fished out a worm, and baited Isabella's hook. He shook the bucket, then held it out to Lizzy. "Think you can find some more bait?"

"Yes, sir." Lizzy gave him an adoring look, grabbed the bucket, and took off.

Isabella tossed her line back in the water, smiling as the child ran for the woods. "She's smitten."

"I guess I just have a way with red-haired lasses." Connor grinned and then winked.

Isabella focused on her cork again, his teasing setting off

a fluttery feeling in her stomach. They fished in silence for a while; then Connor asked, "How's Miss Leah?"

"Worried about the babe." Isabella jiggled her line. "I should have insisted she go straight back to the house that night. I knew it wasn't safe."

"How so?"

"The day the Wainwrights were here, Papa said you'd seen riders on our land. Is that true?"

"Horne, his two older boys, and I have been snaking logs out all along the bluffs on the other side of the sawmill, and we've seen evidence of riders crossing that part of Bartholomew land."

"But you haven't seen anyone?"

"No one." Connor shook his head. "And neither has Mews, Horne, or any o' the others. Just this past week, we saw evidence of horses passing through, but we were in the woods all day every day and never saw anyone."

"There are plantations behind us who have to cross our land on their way to the trace. As a matter of fact, Nolan Braxton owns most of the land on that side of us. There's nothing wrong with his workers crossing our land."

"'Tis true. But you'd think we would have encountered someone. As it is, we've seen nothing but the signs of their passing. And moving fast, too."

"What if it's highwaymen?" Isabella frowned at her cork.

Connor arched a brow at her. "No need in borrowing trouble."

"I'm not borrowing trouble, but—"

Lizzy came running with the bucket of worms, and neither Isabella nor Connor said anything more about bandits and robbers.

An hour later, Mews declared they had enough fish for supper, and the children piled into the pony cart with her father and Toby. Lizzy grabbed the string of fish she and Connor had caught and ran to the cart. "I'm gonna help my *da* clean the fish."

"Do you want to ride?" Connor helped Isabella to her feet and motioned toward the cart.

She shook her head, not seeing room for one more body in the small cart. "No, let the children go on. I don't mind walking."

Toby slapped the reins, and the pony plodded off, carrying its load of children and fish. Mr. Mews and Mr. Horne walked along behind, discussing the best way to clean the fish. As the pony cart disappeared around the bend along with Mews and Horne, Isabella realized that she and Connor were alone.

Butterflies danced in her stomach. More than once, she'd been invited to take a stroll around Breeze Hill by first one, then another suitor, and never had she been as aware of being alone with anyone as she was with Connor O'Shea.

It was the strangest, most wonderful feeling in the world.

And the scariest.

She cast about for something to talk of, anything to break the silence that grew louder with each passing step. She pointed to a stand of oaks in the ravine to her left. "Have you inspected those trees? Jonathan and I used to play here, and some of them were so big we couldn't even reach around them holding hands."

Connor nodded. "I'd noticed them, but I would hesitate to cut this close to the house and the creek bank."

"Why?" Isabella frowned.

"These trees provide a windbreak for the house and outbuildings."

"I hadn't thought of that." Isabella nodded. "Papa says it's possible to look at the rings and patterns on a tree and tell how long ago it was damaged by a hurricane or a tornado."

Connor laughed. "I'm no' that good, I'm afraid. But I have cut into some o' these trees and found the grain t' be twisted and gnarly. So I suppose it's possible."

They rounded a bend and half a dozen cows grazed along the path, slowly making their way back toward the barn. Isabella picked up a stick and prodded one of the stragglers along. "Get on up there, Bessie. Toby always has to come looking for you."

The boom of a musket rang out, followed by an inhuman shriek. Connor and Isabella froze. The cows' ears perked forward, their attention focused on the ruckus up ahead. Another explosion of sound signaled a second shot, and the one shriek became many and grew louder.

Isabella's heart thudded. "That sounds like wild hogs."

"It is, and they're headed this way." Connor grabbed her hand. "Come on."

He hurried down the path toward home, but as soon as they rounded the bend, the herd of hogs rushed across the open field straight toward the narrow pathway.

Connor pulled Isabella off the path toward a half-rotten log. It wasn't the best place to seek shelter, but it was their only option. He grabbed her by the waist and threw her over the log. She hit the ground, the breath nearly knocked out of her, but fear overrode her discomfort. She rolled toward the log, just as Connor vaulted over it himself.

"Dig in tight, lass."

The pungent odor of decay rose up to meet her as she wedged herself into the depression next to the log. Connor dropped down behind her, cocooning her with the length of his body. She closed her eyes and prayed that the hogs would be so terrified they'd just keep going. The animals would tear them to pieces if they got a whiff of them.

Moments later, the squealing, grunting mass careened down the path, some passing around and over the log, the entire thing shaking with the force of their passage. Connor jerked against her and let out a low moan.

She tried to twist around to see, but his strong arms tightened around her like a vise. He squeezed in even closer, his shoulders hunched protectively over her, his head nuzzled against the crook of her neck.

In moments, it was over.

The hogs were gone, disappearing into the wilderness as if they'd never been there. The only evidence was the churned earth and the choking dust billowing all around them.

Connor touched her shoulder, urging her to look at him. Isabella opened her eyes and squinted through the dust.

"Are you all right, lass? Are ya hurt?"

"I'm fine. Just a bit scared."

She sat up and pushed her hair back, then sucked in a quick breath when she spotted a smear of blood on Connor's temple. She reached out trembling fingers. "You're hurt."

"I got clipped on the skull, but I'll live." Connor sat up and leaned back against the log.

"Let me look at it."

She rose to her knees, jerked up a fold of her skirt, and dabbed at the blood. With shaking fingers, she pushed a lock of hair out of the way, breathing a sigh of relief when she realized the cut was small, barely bleeding.

Connor watched her, his eyes half-closed and looking slightly dazed. Panic swept over her. Maybe the injury was worse than she'd thought. Her hands fluttered against his chest. "Connor, are you all right? Should I get Mews?"

She started to stand, but he grasped her by the wrist and stopped her flight. He shook his head. "I'm fine. Just—"

Isabella faltered, then sank back to the ground. She let her hand drop to her lap, her heart still pounding from their near miss. He reached out and tucked a strand of hair behind her ear. She shuddered at the brush of his fingertips against her sensitive skin. His gaze flickered, dropped to her lips, then swept back to meet hers again.

Questioning.

Asking permission.

She closed her eyes, trembling with an emotion she didn't dare try to examine. His hand lingered, then cupped the back of her head. She couldn't summon the power to resist. Didn't even want to try.

His lips were firm and warm. She rested her hands against the soft cotton of his shirt and melted into his kiss. He groaned, then wrapped both arms around her and caught her against him, slanting his mouth over hers.

Isabella's arms slid around his neck, her fingers digging into his hair, as he devoured her mouth with his. Did a near brush with death make her heart pound like this, or was it just Connor's kiss that put her heart to flight as sure as the gunshot had startled the hogs?

He pulled away, his eyes at half-mast. Isabella gazed at him a moment before embarrassment heated her cheeks. He tucked her head against his chest, and she felt the rapid thud of his heart through the thin cotton of his shirt.

"Lass, what's happening between us?" A deep breath shuddered through his chest.

"We got one!" Mews yelled out.

Isabella jerked away, eyes wide as she stared at Connor.

He straightened, and they both peered over the log.

Two hundred yards hence, Mews and Mr. Horne stood next to an oak tree, grinning at the massive hog lying dead at their feet.

Connor slumped back against the log, closed his eyes, and ran one hand through his hair.

"You almost got more than a hog, you *eejit*."

Chapter 14

MEWS ALL BUT SUFFERED an apoplexy.

Connor was sorely tempted to strangle the man himself.

"I thought everyone had already headed toward the house, so Horne and I circled back around. Them hogs have been after them acorns of an evening, and I was hoping to get one." He twisted his hat in both hands, smashing the straw as effectively as if the hogs trampled it themselves. "I'm so sorry, miss."

Connor eyed Isabella as he and Horne hoisted the hog on a pole between them and headed home. She and Mews walked on ahead, Mews still apologizing for nearly getting them killed.

She patted the older man's arm. "It's all right, Mr. Mews. You couldn't know we'd lingered, searching out trees for the mill."

Connor tuned out Mews's response, focusing on Isabella as she walked ahead of him. Had Isabella only stayed behind to talk about trees and hurricanes and such? He'd participated in the conversation, but neither his heart nor his mind had been on it. That's why, the moment the danger had passed, he'd given in to the temptation to taste her lips.

What had possessed him to kiss her?

Oh, he didn't have to ask himself that question. He'd been thinking of little else for the last week.

Her lips tasted as sweet as wild honey, her skin soft as rose petals, her hair like black corn silk, and her eyes liquid darkness he could drown in. He shouldn't have given in to the adrenaline of the moment, the fear that she'd been hurt, the fear that he could have lost her in that instant.

Because now he would dream of the taste of her lips.

A better question would be why he couldn't stop himself. He should know better. He *did* know better.

Nothing good could come of pursuing a relationship with Isabella. She was the master's daughter, and he'd learned the hard way to stay away from a woman who chose suitors to line their pockets or their lineage. Commoners like him were simply playthings to be discarded when something bigger and better came along.

Things seemed different here in America, for sure. Isabella herself had said so, but he wagered it wasn't that much different from Ireland when all was said and done. Money and station still ruled everything, regardless of which side of the world they were on.

But might the Bartholomews be an exception? It hadn't escaped his notice that there were no slaves at Breeze Hill, only indentured servants and day laborers. What had Isabella said the first day? Something about not dealing in slaves?

Scowling, he hoisted the pole higher on his shoulder. Who was he trying to deceive? He had two good eyes and two good ears. The parade of wealthy planters and their progeny through Breeze Hill had been nonstop since he'd arrived. Anybody with one eye and half sense would know why they were calling.

They stepped into the clearing, Breeze Hill spread out before them. Isabella and Mews were a bowshot ahead. She glanced back, her gaze meeting his; then she looked away, a blush on her cheeks.

Connor groaned. He'd been here only a few months, and he'd already jeopardized his brothers' passage from Ireland.

With a woman, no less.

A woman who had no clue that she was leading him down a path as dangerous and forbidden to the two of them as the devil's backbone itself.

Charlotte had known exactly what she was doing. As a matter of fact, he'd been cautioned several times that Charlotte Young was only using him, but he'd ignored the warnings as jealous ramblings from the other stable hands. He'd even beaten a few of his friends to a pulp for daring to besmirch her character.

When rumors of their illicit relationship reached his father's ears, *Da* had tried to talk sense into him, had tried to convince Connor to return to the mines. But Connor had refused, insisting that he could make thrice as much working for Mr. Young as he could in the mines.

He'd been so besotted, he thought she really loved him. That in good time, she would tell the world of her true feelings. If her family threw her out, so be it. Their love would see them through. His family would take them in.

He'd been young, he'd been an *eejit*, and when the time came to pay the piper, she'd laughed in his face.

Isabella was not Charlotte, though. Charlotte had never loved him, and she'd never had any intention of marrying him. The whole year had been a diversion to her, nothing more.

And as he watched Isabella walk along the path ahead of him, doing her best to put an old man's worries to rest, he knew she wasn't playing games. But just as surely, he realized she didn't know where their attraction could lead, that they couldn't explore this tender, budding passion flaring between them.

But he knew.

He knew all too well.

And he wouldn't jeopardize her reputation—or his brothers' lives, their freedom, and his own convictions—knowing there could be no future between them.

Connor's breath hitched when he saw Isabella walking toward the mill the next morning, a basket draped over her arm. Her hips swayed with the rhythm of her movement, her skirts switching against the short grass.

She stopped in front of him, basket in hand. "Good day, Connor."

"Good day, mistress."

Instead of the usual ire that resulted from his use of the formal greeting, her features softened, and a shy smile tugged at her full lips.

He forced himself to concentrate on peeling bark off the oak he'd felled before dawn, even as his stomach rumbled when he caught a whiff of succulent fried meat and bread fresh from the oven. But he would not be swayed, not this time. Isabella was playing with fire, but she didn't know the danger like he did.

If he ignored her, she'd leave, and he wouldn't make a fool of himself.

"Where's Papa?" She looked around, her brown eyes wide and much too enticing.

"Mews and Horne are finishing butchering the hog, so Toby took him over to the smokehouse in the pony cart."

She rested the basket on the end of the log, right in his line of sight. Her slim fingers fiddled with the handle, and his thoughts shot back to the feel of her hands running through his hair. He jerked his attention back to the job at hand and jabbed the peeling iron against the log, grunting with the effort. "Your trip here was wasted."

A soft laugh escaped her. "No. Not wasted entirely. Martha baked fresh bread this morning." She lifted the corner of the cloth, and the aroma assaulted his senses. His mouth watered.

"Would you like some?"

Connor motioned to the table in the dogtrot. "Just leave it there. I'll take a break directly."

After a long pause, she picked up the basket. "Very well."

He heard the disappointment in her voice, the confusion at the way he was acting, but he didn't relent. He couldn't.

"There's leftover fish, too." She pulled meat, bread, and cheese from the basket, then turned to leave.

The scrape of iron against wood filled the silence, but nothing could fill the ache in his chest as he sent her away. It occurred to him that he was rejecting Isabella just as Charlotte had rejected him, but for totally different reasons.

He was doing it to protect her. To protect himself. He wanted to call her back, ask her to share his meal, make her smile, try to make her understand.

And if he was completely honest, taste her lips again.

But he didn't. Instead, he pushed the peeler harder, but out of the corner of his eye, he watched her walk away.

Suddenly she turned, caught his furtive glance. She stood there, their gazes locked on each other. Then she blinked, plopped the basket down, and drove forward, hands on her hips.

"I may not know a lot about men, Connor O'Shea, but . . . but something is wrong, and I want to know what it is."

Connor steeled his heart against her plea. "There is nothing wrong."

"I don't believe you." She raised her chin and glared at him, her Spanish eyes flashing fire. "I insist that you tell me."

"And I'm expected to obey since Breeze Hill owns my papers?" Connor lifted a brow.

A rosy hue that rivaled the rising sun dewed her cheeks, and whatever rejoinder she'd been about to say died on her lips. She looked away, appearing contrite. Charlotte had never been contrite, embarrassed, or unsure of herself in any way, fashion, or form. "That's not what I meant."

"Isn't it?"

She bit her lip, the action so sweet and innocent that he wanted to relent. "After yesterday, I thought you would be glad to see me."

"Yesterday was a mistake, and it should never have happened. Just so we're clear, Miss Bartholomew, I'm here to work to bring my brothers over from Ireland. Nothing more and nothing less. I won't be toyed with."

Her mouth fell open, and a flush of scarlet swept over her cheeks. "Toyed with?" she sputtered. "How dare you! You . . ." She glanced around and lowered her voice. "*You* kissed *me*. Not the other way around."

"That's exactly why I'm putting a stop to it. Now." He dropped the peeler and stalked toward her. "Nothing good can ever come o' letting a servant take liberties, mistress. You can be sure o' that."

The flush on her face blanched to white, and the fire returned to her eyes, hotter than ever. "It won't happen again. You can be sure of *that, Mr. O'Shea*."

She turned, lifted her skirts a good half inch off the

ground, and stormed away, leaving her basket where it lay, discarded and forgotten.

Isabella stomped away, her heart pounding with hurt outrage.

Connor—no, *Mr. O'Shea*—had humiliated her. She'd fallen asleep with a smile on her face, thinking of the sweet, torturous pressure of his lips on hers, his strong hands holding her, shielding her from the slashing hooves of the wild hogs bearing down on them.

Then this.

She blinked away the sting of hot tears. She wanted to die right there on the spot. But she wouldn't allow herself that luxury. Not with his eyes boring a hole in her back. No, she'd wait until she arrived at the safety and privacy of her room before she melted into a puddle of misery and embarrassment.

The closer she got to home, the more she embraced her anger instead of her heartbreak. Did he find her so repulsive?

She dashed her tears away with the tips of her fingers, growling low in her throat, so mad she could toss him to the hogs herself if she could pick him up. She couldn't believe she'd been so gullible as to let him take such liberties. But in the heat of the moment, she'd not had the presence of mind to push him away, to reprimand him for even thinking of touching her, of kissing her.

In hindsight, she should have slapped his face.

Screamed for help.

Had him put in stocks and flogged.

But she'd enjoyed his kisses.

Immensely.

And she'd thought he had too. How could he hold her so close, so tenderly, moaning with the pleasure of the contact, and not feel anything?

Oh, he pretended that he was pushing her away to save her from the shame of being involved with a servant, someone of a lower class. That was just an excuse to extricate himself from an unwanted situation.

A fresh surge of embarrassment, anger, and hurt flooded through her. Today's rebuff showed her what kind of man Connor O'Shea truly was.

But he didn't have to worry. She wouldn't *toy* with him again.

Chapter 15

THE SUN HUNG LOW on the horizon when the clink of chains drew Connor from the back of the house, where he'd been using the last bit of daylight to square off the foundation for the new wing.

He stopped at the corner of the house, the sight that met his eyes turning his stomach. Fifteen—no, at least twenty slaves, mostly men, shuffled along, iron bands on their ankles, a length of chain suspended between each stirring up puffs of dust where it dragged across the ground.

The slaves' ankles were chafed, but they didn't utter a sound, just kept moving forward, one step at a time, keeping pace with the men herding them along like a string of pack animals. A heavily armed bearded man rode at the head of the party, two men flanking him and two more bringing up the rear.

The leader waved his men away. "Stay here. I'll see about lodging for the night."

The guards dismounted, ground-hitched their horses, and moved to hunker down in the shade of one of the cedars that marched along the circular drive in front of Breeze Hill. Ever so slightly, a tall, muscular slave in the middle of the pack moved away from the guards, easy-like, not making much show or commotion or drawing attention, but seeking shade away from the men who held them captive. The others, tethered to the big man, all moved in unison with him like a team of mules harnessed together.

Once in the shade, several of the slaves sank to the ground, their heads hung low. More than one, including the one who'd shepherded his fellow captives to a bit of comfort, stood stoic, facing the slave traders, waiting.

Connor's attention shifted when the front door opened and Isabella stood silhouetted there. The slave trader's eyes swept Isabella from head to toe; then he grinned, jerked his hat off, and bowed low. Connor stepped onto the porch and moved closer, a feeling of foreboding twisting his gut. He didn't like the way this man treated his slaves, and he didn't like the familiar way he devoured Isabella with his gaze. It wouldn't hurt for him to be close by in case she needed him.

Her gaze flickered toward him, a hint of relief on her face. They might have avoided each other like the plague the last few days, but that didn't mean he wouldn't protect her with his very life. He hoped she knew that.

"Good day, madam. Cecil B. Turnbull at your service."

"Mr. Turnbull."

"May I be so bold as to inquire how far it is to the next inn?"

"Toward Natchez?"

"Yes, madam."

"It's seven miles to Mount Locust."

"Seven miles?" Turnbull clasped his hat against his chest. "Perhaps I could impose upon the master of the house to allow us lodging for the night?"

"I'm sorry; we don't have adequate housing for your party."

"Not to worry, madam. We'll be perfectly fine out in the open."

"As you wish." Isabella's gaze sought Connor's. "Connor, could you show these men to the well? If you need anything, Mr. Turnbull, ask Connor or Mr. Mews. Either can take care of you."

"Yes, madam. I am indebted." Turnbull bowed, hand outstretched as if to take hers.

Connor moved quickly, inserting himself between Isabella and the insolent slave trader. Isabella stood so close to his back, he could almost feel the heat of her touch. Faster than a striking rattler, the leer on Turnbull's face turned to a hard scowl.

"This way, sir." He motioned toward the well, situated a hundred yards downhill from the house.

"Thank you, Connor." The tips of Isabella's fingers rested against his back for an instant, so fleeting he might have imagined her touch; then it was gone, and the door clicked shut behind him.

"Bring them Negroes on over here. We'll camp here for

the night." Turnbull dropped the affected social graces and yelled at his men. Connor heard the rattling of chains as the guards prodded the slaves across the yard.

Turnbull turned back to Connor. "Is the master of the house in? I'd like to talk business with him."

"He's home, but he's indisposed. I'll gladly give him a message, if you like." If Isabella didn't see the need to fetch her father, Connor wouldn't either.

Hands clasped behind him, Turnbull rocked back on his heels, looking down his nose at Connor. "I've got slaves for sale. I figure the master might want to take a look at 'em while we're here."

"I'll tell him, but it is late and it might be best t' wait until morning."

"I'll be here."

"Very well."

Connor dipped his head with as much deference as he could manage, then turned away, leaving Turnbull and his men to make camp as they saw fit. He strode past the wide, panoramic windows lining Mr. Bartholomew's sitting room situated on the corner of the house. Faint candlelight spilled from windows, and Connor caught a glimpse of Isabella's father watching the strangers from the shadows.

"I'm not interested." Mr. Bartholomew scowled.

"I'll tell him, sir."

The coffers here at Breeze Hill didn't extend to buying slaves. Connor had figured that out shortly after Isabella had bought his papers in Natchez, and each day brought home to him how desperate Breeze Hill's financial situation was. From the rumors circulating among Mews and the other men, they needed one good harvest to put them over the hump this year.

And from bits and pieces he put together, Jonathan's dreams to expand the lumber business had been a big part of the plantation's plans to turn a profit.

Mr. Bartholomew turned from the window and speared Connor with a look. "This might be some of the men who've been crossing Bartholomew land at night."

"I don't think so, sir. Those men travel fast. They're not transporting slaves."

"But they could be some of the same. Have you seen any more evidence of riders passing through?"

"Nothing that went unaccounted for. Mr. Braxton rode through here a couple of times heading toward his plantation, but other than that, the last week has been quiet."

"Braxton came by? Alone?"

"Yes, sir. He was on his way home from Natchez."

"The fool's going to get himself killed. He should know not to ride the trace alone. Wainwright's got the right idea by traveling with a large party. There's safety in numbers."

"What about his idea of forming a vigilante group to flush out the cutthroats?"

"Bah!" Mr. Bartholomew waved his hand in dismissal. "None of us have the resources or the manpower for such an undertaking. Every available man, woman, and child is needed in the fields. Without the backing of Gayoso and his soldiers in Natchez, we wouldn't stand a chance. As much as it pains me, I have to agree with Braxton on that."

Master Bartholomew peered out the window, silent, watchful. "I want you to find Mews and the rest of the men and keep watch. Nothing good will come of Turnbull's presence, mark my words."

"Yes, sir."

He faced Connor, turning his back on the strangers. "Now tell me how the repairs are coming along."

Hours later, a shot jarred Isabella out of an uneasy sleep.

She lay in bed, her heart pounding, listening. The haunting strains of a fiddle rolled throughout the house. She frowned. Mews's cabin was on the other side of the barn, and he never played his fiddle so late at night.

Had she really heard a gunshot? Where had it come from? She jerked as another shot tore through the night, followed by the sharp bark of taunting laughter.

A chill twisted her insides. *Turnbull's men.*

Be my help and refuge from my foes.

She sucked in a deep breath. A prayer? No, she was simply repeating a line from the song that Leah had been singing all week. So be it. Perhaps God would have mercy on her family this night.

Startled by the sound of another gunshot, she slipped from bed, lit a candle, and pulled her dress over her nightgown. She hadn't wanted to give the strangers leave to stay, but what else could she do? One didn't turn away travelers who came seeking asylum along the trace. It just wasn't done. Even if the travelers themselves might seem of a suspicious character. The best she could hope for was that they'd take their rest and be on their way come morning.

But it seemed that would not be the case with Turnbull's party.

She hurried down the stairs toward her father's rooms. He'd know what to do. The closer she got, the louder the music. Yells interspersed with sporadic gunfire had her heart pounding so hard she thought it would beat right out of her chest.

Susan and Martha, with Leah in tow, met her at the base of the stairs, Leah looking like she was scared out of her wits. The dim light of a candle flickered over her face, ghostly pale.

Leah clasped Isabella by the arm. "What is it? What's happening?"

"I'm not sure. I'm headed to Papa's rooms. I'll be able to see what's happening from there without going outside."

Isabella moved farther down the hall toward her father's rooms.

"Isabella, don't leave me. I'm frightened."

"I must check on Papa. Take Leah to my sitting room upstairs. It's the farthest away from this madness. Stay there."

"Yes, ma'am." The women shooed Leah up the stairs, and Isabella hurried to her father's rooms. She knocked softly on his sitting room door, not wanting to be on the business end of his pistol.

"Papa?"

No answer. Alarm washed over her. Had her father been shot? *Dear heavenly Father, what kind of men have I allowed to stay in our midst?* She wrapped her trembling fingers around the latch and twisted.

"Papa?" she whispered. She pushed and the door swung open, revealing an empty room, dark and silent.

Where was her father? She turned to the sitting room windows, her gaze landing on the slave traders' campfire. Someone threw another log on the fire and the flames shot higher.

A slave stood in the midst of the circle of men, his black skin glistening in the night. A shot rang out. A spurt of rocks and dirt kicked up at the Negro's bare feet, peppering him with tiny particles.

The fiddle twanged. A man laughed.

"I told you to dance. Now dance." Turnbull aimed his pistol at the captive's feet and pulled the trigger.

And yet the Negro stood, straight and still as a statue.

Isabella's heart burned. She wanted these evil men gone from Breeze Hill. She glanced around the room. Where was Papa?

She would find Connor. And Mews. She'd gather all the men, and they could make a stand against Turnbull, tell him he had to leave. There was little they could do to help the slaves, but her father didn't have to allow such vile behavior here at Breeze Hill.

Out of the corner of her eye, she saw a form lurching with a peculiar gait toward the interlopers, a bullwhip in one hand, a pistol in the other. Her eyes widened in horror.

"Papa!"

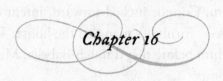

Chapter 16

MEWS GAZED AT CONNOR, his Adam's apple bobbing. "What are we going to do?"

Connor rubbed a hand over his chin. Mews was a good man, loved the land and growing things, but he was as timid as a field mouse when it came to facing a fight.

"Can you shoot if you have to?"

Mews swallowed, then firmed up his jaw. "Yes."

"Toby, you stay close to your father now. If it comes to a fight, keep his pistols primed for him. We're not going to confront them unless we have to. We're just going to wait them out. Sooner or later, they're going to get drunk enough to pass out; then we'll keep watch until morning. They'll probably leave peacefully then. You two stand watch over by the summer kitchen."

Toby followed his father, the two of them making a wide arc around the slave traders, keeping to the shadows. Horne faded into the darkness in the opposite direction, taking his sons with him. Connor inched forward, intent on placing himself between Turnbull's men and the house. They'd have to deal with him before they'd touch Isabella, Miss Leah, or Mr. Bartholomew.

"Papa!"

Connor's heart lurched in his throat at the sound of Isabella's scream. He spotted her running from the house at the same time he caught a glimpse of Mr. Bartholomew rushing toward the slave traders. He sprinted, catching Isabella around the waist, pulling her back into the shadows.

"Let me go." She kicked and clawed, and it was all he could do to hold on to her and the pistol at the same time.

"Quiet, lass."

Mr. Bartholomew's bullwhip cracked, the tip jerking the pistol from Turnbull's grasp. Isabella froze, shocked into immobility at her father's brazen daring.

Turnbull's men barreled to their feet. Connor pushed Isabella behind him and surged forward, praying the night wouldn't end in bloodshed. The whip snapped, and another slave trader screeched in pain, the knife he'd pulled flying into the darkness to land with a thud on the ground. Mews, Horne, and the others stepped into plain sight.

Mr. Bartholomew stalked into the circle of light cast by

the fire. Turnbull's men, as well as the slaves, fell back as the light played across his distorted features. Isabella's father didn't pay them any attention. He kept going until he was nose to nose with Turnbull. The slave trader backed away, looking as if the very devil had materialized before him.

"I'm Matthew Bartholomew, master of Breeze Hill." Mr. Bartholomew bowed, every inch the stately plantation owner. "My daughter gave you leave to stay here tonight, sir." He pointed the whip at Turnbull, his hand trembling. Connor knew it to be from lack of strength, but to the slave traders, it seemed to stem from a terrifying rage. "And you saw fit to abuse that privilege by treating your slaves like dogs. I will not put up with such treatment on my property."

Turnbull recovered himself and held out both hands. "We meant no harm. We were just having a bit of fun."

"Gather your belongings and leave at once. All of you."

"As you wish." Turnbull bowed, but not before Connor witnessed the pure hatred that rolled over his features. Isabella's father had made an enemy out of Turnbull tonight.

Mr. Bartholomew shifted his attention to the tall, stoic slave who stood between his fellow captives and the violence before them. For a long moment, he stared. "I'm sorry there is nothing I can do for you and the others. But know that your plight is not what God intended for man."

The two men measured each other, the Negro's eyes wide as he assessed Mr. Bartholomew's puckered face. Finally he nodded, indicating that he understood. Mr. Bartholomew turned, shoulders slumped. The night's rage had taken its toll on him, and he shuffled toward the house.

"Connor, Mews, see that they leave the property."

"Yes, sir."

Isabella's worried gaze met Connor's before she took her father's arm and escorted him inside.

Isabella's father sank into a chair in his sitting room, his head in his hands.

She lit a candle and knelt in front of his chair, waiting for him to acknowledge her presence. He shook, whether from anger or weakness, she couldn't tell. Had he been injured?

"Papa, are you all right?"

"I'm fine." He took a deep, shuddering breath before pulling his hands away from his face and gripping the arms of his chair. The candle cast shadows across his haggard face, but to Isabella, each welt, each pucker, was a testament to his love for his family.

His battle scars.

Isabella clasped his hands, feeling the chill from his damaged skin. "Are you cold? Do you want a blanket?"

"No." He looked past her, his vision turning inward, seeing something only he could see. "I watched that slave stand there holding on to his dignity. And I watched Turnbull goad him. Then he started shooting. I knew it was only a matter of time before Turnbull lost all reason and shot the Negro out of pure rage. I couldn't let that happen. Not here, not at Breeze Hill."

"Of course not, Papa."

"I wanted to help them, but there was nothing I could do."

Isabella remembered the look in the slave's eyes. "He understood, Papa. He knew you wanted to help."

Papa had never said much about slavery, but she remembered traveling through Natchez with him once. He'd viewed the auction block with distaste and made an effort to avoid the area ever since. What drove his aversion to slavery? What made him different from most of their neighbors, who felt the only way to prosper was on the backs of others?

"Papa?" She tried to think of a way to broach such a delicate question. "What makes one man embrace slavery while another shuns it?"

"Short of greed?" He arched a brow, the look ferocious on his lopsided face.

"Yes."

"I don't know, Daughter. Some have probably never thought about it. They were born with slaves at their beck and call, and they don't know any different. It just is, and it's never occurred to them that it's wrong to own another human being."

"When did it occur to you that it's wrong?"

Her father looked at her, his eyes glittering in the light. "The day I found out my grandmother was born into slavery."

Isabella withdrew her hands from her father's and searched his face. How could her father have descended from a slave? His pale skin and blue eyes belied the fact. And she'd gotten her dark skin from her Spanish mother. Or so she'd always been told.

"A slave? But—"

"An Irish slave."

Connor's thick brogue came to mind, how the cadence of his words wrapped themselves around her heart every time he drew near. Even though she hadn't known she carried the blood of an Irishman, did her heart yearn for that connection? Or maybe she just yearned for Connor.

"I don't understand."

"English warlords captured thousands of Irish children in the 1600s and shipped them off as slaves to Barbados. My great-grandmother Maggie McKinnion was one of them."

Isabella struggled to understand. Since they owned no slaves and she'd visited the other plantations on rare occasions, she'd never thought much about it. The balls she had attended hadn't brought to light the plight of slaves with cruel masters. The house servants were well dressed and spoke respectfully. She'd heard stories, whispers of cruel masters and overseers, but she'd had such little contact with anyone other than a few house slaves that she hadn't seen much difference in them and the men and women who worked at Breeze Hill.

Until tonight. Until Turnbull had tried to force a man to choose between indignity and death.

"Great-Grandma Maggie had one child while in the bonds of slavery. A girl. My grandmother. Sadie McKinnion." Her father's eyes took on a distant hue. "When Sadie was a young girl, she was sold off and never saw her mother again. She became her master's mistress and bore him three daughters. In exchange for his name and protection, he forbade her to speak the McKinnion name ever again. She complied to gain her freedom and that of her daughters. But that didn't stop her from filling her daughters' heads with tales of Ireland and where they had come from."

"And your mother, my grandmother, passed the stories down to you?"

"Yes."

"Then why wasn't I told?"

Her father reached out and rested a hand on her hair, his eyes filled with sadness. "Cruelty isn't just confined to slavery, Daughter. My father was a hot-tempered British soldier, and my mother a redheaded half-Irish wench who gave as good as she got. They fought like wild dogs from as far back as I could remember. It could start over anything, but it always ended the same. He hated that she was Irish. She hated that he was British.

"When they both died of a fever epidemic, I joined the militia and never looked back. This is my country. I won't be labeled British or Irish or any other blood that I have in my veins. I was born here in the New World, and their fighting means nothing to me. Every man has the right to prove himself regardless of race or creed or his bloodline."

"Or the fact that he's a slave or a descendant of one?"

"That too." He gave a short bark of laughter. "I'm not sure what my father hated worse: that my mother was Irish or that she was descended from a slave."

"Were you ashamed? Is that why you never told me?"

"It was over a hundred years ago. I didn't think it mattered.

I wanted the Bartholomews to start fresh here at Breeze Hill, be respected, and not be looked down on because we were once slaves or Irish or, in your case, Spanish. We are the Bartholomews of Breeze Hill. I thought that was enough." Her father clasped her hands in his. "Please forgive me for not telling you."

"There's nothing to forgive, Papa. You did what you thought was right."

He kissed her forehead. "You're a good daughter."

A knock sounded at the door. Isabella's father rested one hand on his pistol. "Who is it?"

"It's Connor, sir."

"Come in."

Connor entered the room, tall and commanding. His gaze landed on Isabella, moved across her face, then swept over her as if to assure himself she was unharmed. A wave of awareness shot through her, and she looked away.

"I just wanted to let you know that Turnbull and his party are gone, sir."

"Thank you. Do you have guards posted?"

"Yes, sir. I doubt they'll return, but the men thought it best to be prepared just in case."

"I agree. Thank you. Isabella, could you ask Martha to make some coffee for the men?"

Isabella struggled to her feet. To her embarrassment, she discovered that both feet had gone to sleep. She braced herself against the table, trying not to grimace at the tingling sensation shooting up her limbs.

"Coffee, Papa?" Procuring and grinding coffee was expensive and time-consuming, and Papa only indulged on rare occasions.

"Yes. They'll need the fortification for the long night ahead. And use the coffee beans, not that awful cornmeal concoction Martha drinks."

"Yes, Papa."

Isabella forced her feet to move. Connor opened the door for her and followed her out into the hallway, holding a candle to light the way. She focused on walking, not wanting to make a fool of herself in front of him. She eased her right foot down and winced. Then the other. The feeling was gradually coming back, and it felt like ten thousand tiny ants were attacking her feet.

Connor reached out a hand to steady her, his brow furrowed in concern. "Are you all right?"

"I'm fine." Heat surged up her neck.

"You're limping." He turned her to face him, the candle held high so that he could see her clearly. Eyebrows lowered, forehead creased, he searched her face. "Are ya hurt, lass?"

"No." She pulled her arm away. Would the man not allow her a morsel of dignity? "My feet are asleep. That's all."

"Oh. Sorry, lass." A hint of laughter threaded through his voice. "I could rub the feeling back into them, if ya like."

Heat flooded her cheeks at his teasing comment, and she took the candlestick from him and pointed to the door. "Out. We'll bring the coffee when it's ready."

He left, the sound of his chuckle teasing her ears.

Isabella mounted the stairs to her rooms to find a barricaded door. She knocked. "Martha?"

A scraping, bumping sound greeted her and Martha opened the door, her round face pale under her mobcap. "Is all well?"

"All is well."

"What happened?" Leah sat on the settee, Susan's arm around her.

"The slave trader and his men were drinking and it got out of hand. They're gone now. Papa told them to leave."

Martha plopped her hands on her hips. "Good riddance. It was obvious from the outset they were an unsavory lot."

Isabella couldn't agree more. "Papa wants the men to stand watch. Martha, I'll need your help in the kitchen."

"Does he think they'll come back?" Leah's voice wobbled.

"No, but it's best to be prepared."

Leah expelled a shaky breath. "What a fright."

"Yes, it was frightening, but it's over now." She turned toward the door.

While Martha ground the coffee beans, Isabella stoked the fire and assembled an array of tin cups, all the while wrestling with what her father had told her.

He'd never said much about his past or where he came from, other than that his parents were dead. She knew he'd been a soldier and was awarded a land grant here in Natchez. She'd been so focused on her Spanish heritage to wonder about her father's side of the family.

Somehow, she'd assumed Papa just . . . was. That his parents had immigrated to the New World, produced a son, then left him to fend for himself after they died. It wasn't such an uncommon occurrence.

But being descended from Irish slaves was uncommon.

Or at least she thought it was. She'd never heard of such a thing. Maybe it was more common than she thought, but no one mentioned it because they were ashamed.

She reached for another cup, but her hand paused in mid-air as something her grandfather had said about her grandmother came back to her.

What bothered Papa the most about his heritage?

The fact that he was part Irish or that he'd descended from a slave?

A candle flickered on the front porch, and Connor saw Isabella and Martha setting out a tray. He hung back as they poured steaming cups of coffee for Mews, Horne, and the boys.

"Coffee, miss?" Horne's voice was incredulous.

"Papa insisted. He's grateful." Her gaze swept the men, landing at last on Connor. "To all of you."

Horne raised the cup to his mouth, sipping the hot brew appreciatively. He closed his eyes, savoring the flavor.

Toby sat on the porch steps, sniffed the coffee, then took a tentative taste. His mouth twisted. "'Tis bitter."

"Drink it anyway," Mews instructed. "Mr. Bartholomew has bestowed a rare gift on us, and it shan't be wasted."

"Here." Isabella added cream and sugar to Toby's coffee, and he tried it again. "Better?"

"Yes." The boy grinned. "Thank ya, Miss Isabella."

"You're welcome."

She ruffled Toby's hair, then headed Connor's way, cup in hand. His fingers brushed hers as he took the coffee. Connor lifted the cup, savoring the dark, earthy aroma.

"Should I fetch the cream and sugar?" Teasing laced her tone.

"No cream and sugar." He winked at Toby. "I'm no' a milk-faced lad."

Isabella laughed, then moved away, refilling cups. Connor strode to the end of the porch, attention on the shadowed tree line that bordered the property. All was calm and peaceful, as if Turnbull and his men had never been here.

One by one, the men finished, thanked Isabella and Martha, and drifted away, going back to their posts keeping watch over the main house and the outbuildings. Martha picked up the tray and headed inside just as Connor drained his cup and returned to the center of the porch. Isabella held out the pot. "There's a small amount left. As Mews said, it shan't go to waste."

Connor held out his cup, and she refilled it.

"Isabella?" He willed her to look at him.

She glanced up, wary, one eyebrow lifted in question.

"I'm sorry for what I said the other day. It was uncalled for." He looked away, then berated himself for being a coward. He turned, faced her head-on. "You did nothing wrong. The problem is with me, not you. Please, will you forgive me for acting like an *eejit*?"

She wiped down the table, studiously ignoring him.

"Truce?" He dipped his head, trying to catch her eye.

Finally she nodded. "Truce. And you were an *eejit*."

He laughed, drained the last of the tepid coffee, and held out the cup. "Now that we've established I'm an *eejit*, you'd better head back inside and get some sleep."

"Connor?" A frown marred her forehead. "What was life like in Ireland?"

Connor thought back to the nights so cold they all huddled together for warmth, to the days he and his brothers foraged for peat to keep the fire going.

"It was a hard life, but we had each other." He shrugged. "Winters could be harsh, but we always knew the long summer days would come. The sun would still be shining this time of night."

"Truly?"

"*Fíor.*" He nodded. "Mews would be in hog heaven with eighteen hours of daylight to work the fields."

"I don't think Lizzy and the Horne girls would like that overmuch." Isabella walked to the edge of the porch, wrapped her arms around her waist, and stared at the sky. Her attention shifted back to him. "If Ireland is so wonderful, why did you leave?"

Her question twisted like a knife in his gut. He couldn't tell her the truth. But what could he tell her? That he'd sacrificed his family for a woman who wouldn't wipe her dainty kid boots on him in public?

"Everything is no' so rosy in Ireland. 'Tis a beautiful land,

and roots run deep, but for the poor, the only opportunity lies in the New World." He frowned. "And what, pray tell, has brought on this sudden interest in me homeland?"

"Something Papa said." She shrugged and turned away. "Never mind. I shouldn't have pried."

"It's all right." Connor breathed deeply, enjoying the slight breeze that stirred the moss trailing from the cedars. "What did he say?"

"He said that many poor Irish were sold into slavery, just like the Africans." She fiddled with a tea towel. "Children, even. Is that true?"

"'Tis true." Connor clenched his jaw, then nodded. "Ireland has a long history o' violence and fighting."

"Will you ever go back?"

"No. There's nothing for me there, except a postage-size plot o' rocky ground that the British crown says the O'Sheas have no legal claim to." Connor leaned against a porch column. "While I miss Ireland, it's me brothers I long for. I should've . . ."

"Should've what?"

"I should've been there all these years. With *Mam* and *Da* gone, the boys are my responsibility. It's been three years since I heard from Quinn. What if—?" He broke off, unable to voice his fear that something had happened to his brothers.

"Three years?" Isabella's voice filled with compassion. "I'm sorry, Connor. Do your brothers know you're no longer in the Carolinas?"

"I asked Bloomfield t' post a letter." He didn't tell her that

Bloomfield had also penned the missive. It would've taken Connor a month of Sundays to write everything down, and even then, Quinn would've had a hard time figuring out his chicken scratch. He shrugged, gave her a joyless smile. "Quinn, Caleb, Rory, Patrick—the lads are all I've got left in this world. It would be a fine thing t' lay eyes on them."

Her mouth curved into a smile, and she laughed quietly. "Do you know why I bought your papers that day in Natchez?"

What kind of question was that? "Because Breeze Hill needed someone to rebuild the west wing?"

She leaned against the column opposite him. "Yes. And no. I bought your papers because you were willing to do whatever it took to be reunited with your brothers. I knew—" her lips twitched—"or at least I hoped someone who cared that much about their family could be trusted and would fit in here at Breeze Hill. I thought it was admirable that you were willing to sacrifice your freedom for theirs."

Connor scowled. She talked as if he were some kind of saint. "You give me too much credit, mistress. There are some that would say I'm the reason my brothers are in the dire straits they're in."

"How so?"

He lifted a brow at her, and she had the grace to blush.

"I'm sorry. I'm prying again. But—" she paused, then continued softly—"it's never too late to make amends."

"For some it is." For *Da*. For *Mam*.

"As long as there's breath, it's not too late." Tears

shimmering in her eyes, she turned and faced the long, winding drive that led to the main road. "I'd give anything to see
Jonathan come riding up to Breeze Hill once again."

She closed the short distance between them and placed a
hand on his arm. Her touch burned through the thin cotton
of his shirt. "That's never going to happen for me, but for
you and your brothers, it will. Someday."

Chapter 17

NOLAN INSPECTED the slaves that Turnbull lined up before him.

Truthfully, he wasn't the least bit interested in purchasing yet another slave, and his overseer was off somewhere doing who knew what, leaving him to deal with the slave trader.

Turnbull, his hand bound in a bloodstained neckerchief, motioned to a tall, muscular slave. "Master Braxton, this here's Abraham. Abraham is the man for any job you need done. Fieldwork, handy with a hammer and the forge. See those muscles? He's got the strength of an ox and the stamina of one too."

Nolan eyed the slave, not liking the surly way he looked back at him. Apparently Turnbull noticed the lack of respect as well.

"Mind yo' manners, boy."

Abraham shifted his flat gaze toward Turnbull. "Yes, suh."

"He can operate a forge, you say?"

"Good as any."

Nolan made a circle around the merchandise. He could use a smithy to keep the horses shod. A lame horse and a captured highwayman could lead to disaster. He made Turnbull an offer.

"For that price, I could've left his carcass with Bartholomew." Turnbull's laugh was cruel. "A gift, if you will."

"Bartholomew? What happened there?"

Turnbull rubbed his fingers across the bandage on his right hand. "Bartholomew stuck his nose in where he wasn't wanted. Used a whip on me and my men. I could've killed him on the spot—once I realized he was human—"

Turnbull broke off, seeming to realize he was talking to one of Bartholomew's peers. He shrugged. "My apologies for speaking ill of Master Bartholomew. It was the shock and all. He like to scared me spitless."

Nolan chuckled. "No harm done, Mr. Turnbull. I can see how that could happen."

Turnbull looked relieved. Nolan made another turn about the slave, thinking. Turnbull had a reputation for murder and mayhem that Nolan doubted Pierre could even touch. The man might come in handy. Very handy indeed.

He pivoted. "Mr. Turnbull, I've reconsidered my assessment of the merchandise. I'll triple my offer if that's acceptable."

Turnbull's eyes narrowed; then he bowed, a delighted grin sweeping across his pockmarked face. "I accept your offer, sir."

"Good. Now that we've got that out of the way, would you join me in my study? I have other business to discuss."

Connor tilted his head back and looked up, up, up into the branches of a mighty oak, straight and true.

Circling the tree, he admired it from all angles. Big and impressive but completely inadequate for his needs. The crosscut saws back at the sawmill couldn't handle a tree of that size. He moved on, looking for smaller trees not twisted by the hurricane-force winds that roared through the area during the fall months. After he marked two dozen trees, he mounted the horse he'd borrowed from the stables and headed back toward home.

Thinking about the trees he planned to cut, he considered the idea of digging a saw pit in the woods. The earth was loamy enough that the job shouldn't be too backbreaking. And cutting and sawing those trees right on the spot would save days of snaking the logs home.

As he neared the trace, he pondered the merit of snaking the logs out to the road, then loading them on wagons and hauling them home. It was probably three miles home as the crow flew, but closer to four or five on the winding trace. He'd discuss it with Mr. Bartholomew tonight.

The sound of jingling harnesses and creaking wheels interrupted his musings. Shortly a garrison of Spanish soldiers riding close to a fancy enclosed carriage the likes of which he'd never seen rounded the bend heading northward along the trail. Whoever was in that carriage must be important to warrant an escort from the Spanish fort in Natchez.

When they passed, he faded into the shadows to find another route home. He had no quarrel with the Spanish government or its soldiers, but still, he had no desire to be questioned or detained either. The trail twisted and turned along the ridges that populated the area. He urged his mount across a wash, hoping to reenter the trail a half mile ahead of the travelers and be long gone before they got there.

Ten minutes of riding through dense undergrowth, having his jerkin grabbed by thorns, and fighting mosquitoes the size of bumblebees, he spotted the serpentine trace ahead. Moments before he descended to the trail, his horse's ears perked forward, and he sawed back on the reins. Movement on the trail caught his eye.

Had the Spanish garrison made it this far already? Surely not.

More than a dozen mounted men eased along the roadbed, keeping their mounts quiet. They were a rough lot, armed to the teeth and looking for trouble. Long years of travel had worn the road down to where high banks ascended on each side. One man rose up in the saddle, turned, and motioned to his compatriots. One by one, the group disappeared, urging their mounts into the woods. Even as Connor watched, some of the cutthroats embedded themselves along the high banks overlooking the trail.

An ambush? Against the soldiers?

Connor crept back into the trees, careful not to make any sound. As soon as he'd put enough distance between him and the ambush, he urged his mount through the dense underbrush, hoping to warn the Spaniards in time. He was still twenty yards from the trace when the carriage came into view, moving along at a good clip. He broke from cover and hit the roadbed between the ambush and the soldiers, shouting out a warning.

"Ambush!"

The entire garrison took cover as a barrage of shots rang out. Connor threw himself off his horse and dove toward a fallen log. A clean-shaven officer not much older than Connor hunkered down behind the same log. "How many of them are there?"

Connor didn't have time to ponder the fact that the man spoke English, and not with a Spanish accent, but as someone born in the colonies. "I don't know, sir. Fifteen. Maybe twenty."

The man took careful aim and fired on their attackers before barking orders in Spanish to his men. The soldiers took care to unload their pistols in groups, giving the rest of the party time to load again.

A volley of shots peppered them and one group of soldiers surged forward while others fell behind the lines and reloaded, the group steadily advancing on their attackers. As suddenly as it began, the attack ended, and with yells and bone-chilling screeches, the highwaymen caught up their horses and fled.

Connor stood next to the log, looking at the carnage. Two

men lay dead; another one pressed a compress to his shoulder while blood seeped through his fingers. The officer barked orders in rapid-fire Spanish, and several soldiers mounted their horses and gave chase.

Others took up positions around the perimeter, watching for a counterattack. The remaining party made quick work of bandaging the wounded and hoisting the dead onto horses. The officer approached Connor.

"Captain Stephen Minor, at your service." He bowed, showing Connor a deference that would have been ludicrous under any other circumstances. "I'm beholden to you. If you hadn't come along, that bunch of cutthroats would have had us right where they wanted us."

"Think nothing of it, sir."

"I beg to differ." The officer nodded toward the carriage. "Miss Watts is a personal friend of the governor, and he would be grieved to learn of any assault on her person."

"Stephen?"

The captain turned as the woman in the carriage beckoned. "Excuse me."

Connor dipped his head in reply, and as the officer walked away to tend to his charge, he went looking for his horse. It was time to be on his way if he wanted to get home before dark. He'd just caught up the reins when Minor approached him again.

"Just a moment, if you would be so kind."

Connor stopped, turned back.

"The lady inquires your name."

"Connor O'Shea, sir. Indentured servant to Matthew Bartholomew of Breeze Hill Plantation."

"Ah, Bartholomew." Minor nodded. "I knew his son, Jonathan. Such a pity. And the fire, as well. How fares Bartholomew these days?"

"Some better, sir."

"Good to hear."

The soldiers returned, their attempt to chase down their attackers unsuccessful. Minor mounted his horse and ordered his men to fall in. "We'd better get on before dark falls. Will you accompany us to the inn?"

"No thank you, sir. I must get back to Breeze Hill."

"Are you sure?" His horse pranced as if anxious to put some distance between itself and this place.

"Yes, sir."

"Very well, then. Godspeed to you, O'Shea. And give Bartholomew my regards."

"Miss Isabella! Miss Isabella!"

"That Lizzy, always caterwauling about something." Martha tsked and shook her head. "Somebody needs to teach that girl some manners."

Isabella chuckled, knowing that Martha was just as fond of the motherless child as the rest of them. Most nights— every night, if truth be told—Martha made sure to cook enough food for the Mews family.

Lizzy rushed headlong onto the porch of the summer

kitchen, where she and Martha sat peeling potatoes. "Riders." Lizzy's face was almost as red as her hair. She pointed. "They're tearing up the cotton."

Isabella ran for the dinner bell and pulled the cord, summoning the men to the house. Mews and the other field hands came running, followed quickly by Horne and the boys who'd been working at the sawmill.

"Lizzy saw riders in the cotton."

Mews addressed his daughter. "Which field, girl?"

"The one next to the trace."

Anger rumbled through the workers. They'd just finished plowing it last week. And to think that someone cared so little as to trample it.

The men rushed to drive the interlopers out, some with guns, others with hoes, axes, whatever came to hand. Isabella hurried toward the house. She was halfway to the field with her father's musket when he and Jim arrived in the pony cart.

"I heard the bell." He eyed the gun in her hand. "What's wrong?"

She explained quickly, then hiked her skirts and took off toward the field.

"Isabella, come back here. Let the men handle it."

But Isabella didn't stop. Her family's livelihood was at stake here. She gripped the cold steel in both hands, anger warring with common sense. She'd blow these highwaymen away before she'd let them destroy her family.

Tears blurred her vision as she ran, the gun growing heavier with each step.

She couldn't deny that someone wanted to destroy her family. Her father was right. Somebody wanted to lay spoil to everything they'd worked for.

They'd burned the cotton last fall, almost killing her father and Leah in the process, murdered Jonathan, and most recently put Leah and the babe's life in danger. No one with any respect for human life would try to run down a pregnant woman.

She could see the field in the distance when Mews and the others fired their first shots. Sporadic gunfire answered them; then the riders spurred their mounts away, angling across the field toward the trees to Isabella's left.

White-hot anger arched through Isabella as the slashing hooves tore up even more of the precious plants, and without thought to her own safety, she jerked the gun to her shoulder and squeezed the trigger. The recoil of the heavy gun knocked her on her backside, but she didn't care. Whether she hit anybody or not, she couldn't tell, but satisfaction coursed through her as they ducked low over their mounts and raced toward the cover of the trees on the opposite side of the field.

She struggled to her feet just as the little pony cart came bouncing along the wagon trail. Her father gripped the reins in his gnarled fists, his fire-ravaged face mottled with pent-up rage. Jim held on to the cart with both hands.

"They're gone? Did we get any of the blackguards?"

"I don't know." Isabella placed the heavy musket in the cart, lifted her skirts, and hurried toward the field.

Row after row of crushed plants littered the ground, pounded by the horses' hooves. Not just sporadic, but deliberate attempts to destroy the cotton. It was too late to replant. Either they'd have to pick the cotton bolls that survived and managed to bloom out, or let the entire field go to waste.

Regardless, they didn't have time to spend in such a way, and the yield would be a fraction of what they'd hoped for.

Isabella glared in the direction the riders had gone, anger clutching her in its iron grip.

They would pay for this.

Connor headed straight to Mr. Bartholomew's quarters. The plantation owner needed to know what had happened on the trace today. He knocked and Mr. Bartholomew bade him enter.

He stepped through the door and came face-to-face with Isabella. Splotches of color gave her cheeks a rosy glow, and she looked fit to chew nails.

He glanced at Mr. Bartholomew. "Excuse me, sir. I'll come back later."

"No, Connor, come in." Isabella's father waved him into the room.

Connor glanced at Isabella. Her hair was disheveled and dirt smudged her cheek. Mr. Bartholomew looked a bit ragged as well. Had something happened in his absence? A niggling worry grabbed him. Had the thieves come to Breeze Hill after the Spaniards had routed them?

"Forsooth, man, what happened to you?" Mr. Bartholomew eyed Connor's dusty, sweat-stained attire, the powder burns on his frayed shirt. He'd forgotten his own bedraggled appearance in his concern over Isabella and her father.

"Highwaymen attacked a band of travelers about two hours ago. Spanish soldiers led by an American named Stephen Minor."

"Minor, you say?"

"Yes, sir."

"Was anyone injured?"

"Two soldiers were killed, but the others were able to thwart the attack."

Mr. Bartholomew scowled. "I'll wager the ruffians are the same ones that destroyed the cotton field. They were probably trying to escape the militia."

"The cotton field, sir?"

"Yes. A party of riders, fifteen or twenty in all, trampled the cotton in the new ground not long ago. We fired shots but didn't kill any of the blackguards. A pity."

"But why trample the cotton field?"

"With these men, it's more a matter of 'why not' than 'why.' They seem to thrive on creating havoc. I'm also concerned that they would attack a group of Spanish soldiers. Were they escorting a payroll of some sort?"

"Not that I know of. There was a fancy carriage and a lady. A friend of the governor. A Miss Watts, I believe."

"Ah, the lovely Elizabeth. What if they were after the

carriage or Miss Watts? Possibly for ransom as Wainwright feared? Surely they wouldn't be so brash." Mr. Bartholomew tapped his fingers on the arm of his chair. "Isabella, get some paper and a quill. I need to send a letter to Wainwright. These attacks are getting out of hand, and something needs to be done."

"You attacked a party of Spanish soldiers led by Stephen Minor? Along with the governor's lady friend? Of all the dull-witted things to do."

Nolan stared at Pierre. One more error in judgment of such magnitude, and Nolan would be tempted to put a bullet in the man himself. Or maybe have someone of Turnbull's ilk do it. But right now he needed to find out exactly what mischief Pierre had gotten into.

"What happened?"

"We had them in our clutches, and then someone warned them." Pierre swore in French. "It was the Irishman from the inn. The one with the Bartholomew woman. I heard him yell out."

"O'Shea? He's nothing but an indentured servant. Nothing to be concerned about."

Pierre rubbed his head. "He put a crease in my skull, and I aim to make sure he pays for it."

Pity the bullet didn't do more than graze the numskull. "Never mind about O'Shea. Why in heaven's name did you attack the soldiers in the first place? For the woman? I'll not have you plundering and killing women and children. We want people to travel the trace, not avoid it. Do I have to remind you the coin flowing along that road is what's lining both our pockets?"

Pierre looked at him like he'd lost his mind, his flat black eyes as unemotional as a rattler's. "*Oui*. The coin. The lovely Mademoiselle Watts was a decoy for a transport of Spanish gold hidden in a false bottom of her carriage."

Nolan kept his surprise from showing by sheer force of will. How did Pierre know these things? He scowled. "And you knew this but executed a half-baked idea that failed?"

"It only failed because the Irishman was there."

Nolan stood, sauntered to the edge of the porch, and spotted Turnbull readying for his departure. But he'd be back as soon as he delivered this last batch of slaves to Natchez. Nolan's instincts about the man's character had proven true. He'd do anything for money.

And being a slave trader gave him reason to travel from plantation to plantation without being questioned. Just the kind of man Nolan could use. And one who would follow orders, unlike the hotheaded Frenchman standing behind him.

"You need to lay low for a while. Bartholomew is on his guard now, as well as Minor and the governor. They'll have the militia swarming the bluffs for days to come, looking for the men who waylaid those soldiers." He turned from the window. "And, Pierre. Don't come to Braxton Hall again. Your presence here puts us all at risk. Should you need to contact me, send word through Turnbull."

"The slave trader?" Pierre sneered. "You've changed, Monsieur Braxton, since your sainted mother died."

"My mother was no saint."

"Maybe, maybe not. But she was loyal to a fault and generous." Pierre's gaze panned the well-appointed office, the heavy oak desk and the plush upholstered chairs. "I have wondered how the Braxtons came about Braxton Hall. Neither you nor your mother strike me as English aristocrats." His scan stopped on the oil portrait hanging over the fireplace. "Of course I never met your father."

Nolan bristled. "What are you getting at?"

"Nothing." Pierre opened the door. "I was just making an observation. But one does wonder."

Nolan glared at the door after Pierre left.

Yes, it was time to sever all ties with Pierre Le Bonne.

Chapter 18

CONNOR STOOD ON TOP of the log suspended over the saw pit, pulling the whipsaw upward. Jim pulled it back down.

Up. Down. Up. Down. The seesawing motion became monotonous after a long day.

Horne and his boys were snaking more logs in, and after Connor and Jim finished sawing this one, he'd let Jim try his hand as top dog. The boy had the strength for it and the concentration to make a straight, clean cut. With Jim and Toby working the pit saw and Horne and his boys felling trees, it would free Connor up to work on the house more.

Truth be told, he wanted them all to be able to work the saws as well as wield a hammer. Skills they could use no matter where they were.

Lizzy came tearing along the wagon road from the big

house. She skidded to a stop at the saw pit and squinted up at Connor. "Mr. Bartholomew wants you right away."

"Jim, I'll be back soon. You can stack some of that lumber while I'm gone."

"Yes, sir."

Connor jumped off the log and headed toward the house. "Something wrong?"

Lizzy hurried to keep his pace. "Nope. Don't think so. Leastwise, nothing really bad. Mr. Bartholomew wasn't yelling or nothing like that."

Connor grinned. "I see."

"But there was a whole passel of soldiers at the house about an hour ago, all smartly dressed in their uniforms."

Connor's amusement fled. "Soldiers?"

"That's what I said, didn't I?"

Connor stopped at the well, brushed sawdust off his clothes, and used his neckerchief to wipe the worst of the dirt and grime off his face. He hurried through the courtyard, bounded up the gallery steps, and rapped on Mr. Bartholomew's sitting room door.

"Come in."

"Mr. Bartholomew, sir. Lizzy said you wanted to see me?"

"Yes, Connor. Come in. Have a seat." Mr. Bartholomew motioned to the settee, waving a piece of parchment in the air. "I received this letter from the governor this morning about the incident with Captain Minor and Miss Watts."

"Sir?" Connor sat on the edge of the settee, pressing his damp palms against his breeches.

"At ease, man. It's not bad news." Mr. Bartholomew chuckled. "The governor sends his deepest gratitude for what you did to warn Miss Watts's traveling companions of the danger they were in. He says, and I quote, 'Without Mr. O'Shea's presence of mind, I fear that dear Miss Watts might have been accosted or lost to us forever. It is with deepest gratitude that I extend my undying regard to Mr. O'Shea.'"

Connor swallowed. "It was the least I could do."

"Of course. I wouldn't expect anything less of you, Connor." Mr. Bartholomew placed the letter on a side table and folded his hands together. "However, expressing gratitude isn't the only reason the governor sent a message posthaste. It seems he and Captain Minor believe the highwaymen are led by someone in a position of power with possible access to government secrets. So naturally he's quite concerned."

"Someone from this area, north of Natchez?"

"Yes, that seems likely as attacks on travelers have been more prevalent in this area in recent years."

The possibilities ran through Connor's mind like quicksilver. Wainwright, Hartford, Braxton. Five men, including the younger and elder Wainwrights and Hartfords. He'd heard tell of a handful more plantation owners, though he hadn't met them. Even the proprietors at Mount Locust or Harper's Inn could be suspect.

"What does the governor propose?" Under other circumstances, Connor wouldn't have dared to ask his master such a question. But Mr. Bartholomew had taken him into his confidence, so he felt the question was justified.

"The governor requested my presence in Natchez. Regretfully, I had to decline the invitation. My health makes travel impossible. We'll keep our eyes and ears open and try to ferret out the guilty party. And that's where you come in."

"Sir?"

"You're aware of the misfortune that has befallen me and my family, so I won't belabor the point. I am confident you had no hand in any of what occurred. I also believe you have the utmost integrity, and now Captain Minor and the governor himself are also indebted to you."

Connor kept silent and waited, unsure what Mr. Bartholomew wanted of him.

"I'll speak plainly." Mr. Bartholomew leaned forward, a guarded look on his scarred face. "Connor, if something happens to me, I need to know I can depend on you to look after Leah and Isabella."

"Nothing's going to happen——"

"We don't know that." Mr. Bartholomew held up a hand, then turned both hands, palms up, his fingers curled like claws. "Who would have thought a year ago that I'd be this helpless?" His gaze lifted to Connor's. "Do I have your word?"

Connor nodded. "Yes, sir. You have my word."

A cool breeze blew across the porch, lowering the temperature from the sweltering heat of the day. The sun sat on the horizon, ready to dip out of sight any minute. Isabella and her father relaxed on the porch right outside his room.

"Papa, what are we going to do?" Isabella asked. "If they destroy all the cotton this year, we won't have enough to pay our creditors or enough to see us through the winter months."

"Or enough to send for Connor's brothers."

"We won't have the coin to send for *any* of his brothers, let alone all of them." A twinge of concern hit Isabella. "Has he said anything?"

"No. Nothing. But he almost has enough lumber to start the repairs, and he should be finished after harvest. He'll expect me to follow through on our agreement." Her father set his rocker into motion. "As I should. He's been a huge help to us. To everyone. You did well in choosing him."

She sighed. "Seems like things have only gotten worse instead of better since he arrived."

"I'm convinced our troubles have little to do with Connor's arrival." Her father frowned. "Mews says the cotton was damaged beyond repair. At most, we'll pick a third of the crop we hoped for."

Isabella suspected as much. While she couldn't gauge the yield to the extent Mews could, she'd been by the field several times in the last few days, and she'd come to the same conclusion on her own. There had to be a way to bring in extra cash to see them through the winter months. She bit her lip as an idea formed.

"We could sell the lumber. You and Jonathan were building up a reputation in Natchez. When I visited back in May, there was construction everywhere." She warmed to the subject. "They're desperate for lumber."

Her father tapped his fingers against the arm of his chair. "It would delay the repairs on the house."

"If we don't have money to buy staples and seed for next year, we'll lose the house and everything else anyway."

"True. It's too late to plant more cotton, but we *could* sell some of the lumber. I can send Connor to Natchez with a list of contacts—"

"You'd send Connor to do your business?"

"Who else is there? I can't go, and Mews hasn't the head for business."

"Send me, Papa."

"Ah, Isabella, it's too dangerous. And you're a—"

"A woman. But please let me go. I can travel with the Wainwrights and stay at Wainwright House, and your contractors can meet me there. They'll understand, knowing your health prevents you from making the journey."

Her father shifted, pushed his rocker into motion with one foot. She waited, hardly daring to breathe. Finally he nodded.

"Yes, that might work. I have some letters to send that can't wait. Wainwright's party is sizable enough that you should be safe." He smiled. "You've got your mother's beauty and your father's business sense, so it stands to reason that you should go along. Connor can select the best lumber to send."

"You'll send lumber this trip, without a contract?"

"Only a wagonload, or maybe two or three. There's nothing like a small taste to whet the appetite. I'm confident you and Connor will negotiate the best price."

"Connor? You're sending Connor?" Isabella's heart sank. The trip would take four to five days at least. How would she manage being in close proximity with him for that long? "Why not send Mews?"

"Connor knows lumber, and I'd feel better if he were along. Mews and Toby can help drive the wagons."

"But—"

He held up a hand. "I've agreed to let you go. But if you insist on arguing with me, I'll revoke my permission and let Connor handle it." His countenance softened. "It's for your own good. I trust Connor with your life."

"Yes, Papa."

"Good." Her father regarded her, his expression filled with concern. "Isabella? Is something wrong between you and Connor?"

"What do you mean?" Heat rushed to her face, but she held her father's gaze, hoping the shadows hid her embarrassment.

"You think I haven't noticed? Your eyes flash just like your mother's used to when I mention his name. You leave the room when he comes to give me a report. And he won't even look at you." His scarred face hardened into a scowl of terrifying proportions. "Has he taken liberties or offended in some way? If he has, I will have him hanged, drawn, and quartered."

"No." Isabella wished for the ground to open up and swallow her. If her father knew that Connor had kissed her, he might very well do as he said. She looked down, her voice dropping to a whisper. "No. It's not like that."

"Isabella, look at me." His voice was soft, tender.

She bit her lip and looked up.

"You're a woman grown. Many women your age are already married with children. But I can tell from the look on your face that you're affected by talk of our indentured servant. Do you think he's not good enough for you because he's a servant?"

"No, Papa. You taught me to never judge a man by his station in life or his material possessions."

"Yes. And now that you know a bit about your family history, you know why I'm willing to give any man a fair chance." Her father looked across the gathering twilight at the fields in the distance. "I had nothing but the clothes on my back when I came here, and I hacked this plantation out of a canebrake, fought off snakes and wild hogs, attacks from the natives and the highwaymen. It wasn't easy, but I persevered."

"And somebody seems determined to take it all away."

"I don't understand why. It's common knowledge that I won't sell Breeze Hill. I'll die here." Her father reached out and took her hand, tears shimmering in his eyes. "Perhaps I'm a foolish old man, grasping at hidden menace in the shadows where there is none."

He gestured toward the quiet fields, the lights flickering on in the cabins nearby. The occasional sound of laughter floated on the breeze as the handful of tenant farmers and indentured servants enjoyed their supper before bedtime. Soon, Mews would play a lively jig on his fiddle before shooing Toby and Lizzy off to bed.

"On nights such as this, I think that maybe I imagined it all. What if Jonathan's death was random? What if he was simply at the wrong place at the wrong time? What if lightning struck the cotton and caught the house on fire by chance? What if it was a coincidence you and Leah just happened to be taking an evening stroll when those riders came through?"

"And the cotton fields? Do you think it was a coincidence those men trampled half the cotton?"

"No. But they were being pursued by the governor's militia. Mayhap they took their anger out on the nearest victim—our cotton." He shook his head. "But I can't help but worry. I just wish . . ."

"What?"

"I wish you'd take Leah with you."

"To Natchez?"

"Yes. I could make arrangements for her and the babe. I'm sure Wainwright—"

"She won't go. And besides, Martha would never allow it—it's too close to her time."

"I suppose you're right. I can't help but wish that the two of you—and the babe—were tucked safely away in Natchez."

Isabella clasped his hand in hers. "Papa, we're as safe here with you as we'd be in Natchez. If trouble is going to find us, it's going to find us wherever we are."

"Natchez?"

Connor gripped the adze and gaped at Isabella. Surely

he hadn't heard correctly. "What about the terms o' my indenture?"

"All in good time. I've got business in Natchez, and Papa insists you go along as my escort." Isabella's gaze shifted, avoiding his. There was something she wasn't telling him.

"You? And me?"

When he agreed to Mr. Bartholomew's request to protect Isabella and Miss Leah, he'd never dreamed that meant traveling along the trace with them. He scowled. "Don't tell me that Miss Leah is going too."

"Don't be ridiculous. She's in no condition to travel." The way she jutted her chin and the two bright spots of color on her cheeks told him the idea had been discussed but apparently discarded.

She crinkled her nose as if she smelled something tainted. He narrowed his eyes. Well, she wasn't the only one who detected a foul odor in the air. If he didn't know better, he'd think she'd orchestrated this whole trip to spend time with him. It was the kind of thing Charlotte would have done.

But he couldn't believe she'd want to spend that much time with him after he'd kissed her, then promptly insulted her by keeping his distance. He'd managed to avoid her quite successfully the last few days. But heaven help him—being thrust into close proximity with her for days on end might dismantle the carefully constructed wall he'd built around his heart.

"There's nothing in my contract stating I would be traveling back and forth to Natchez." Connor hacked away at the log resting on a pair of sawhorses, taking his frustration out on the hapless beam. Chips of fragrant wood curled off the timber and landed at his feet. "That'll take two or three days."

"Four. At least."

He forced himself to relax his death grip on the adze. He might as well accept the inevitable. "Why am I being ordered t' Natchez?"

"It's not an order."

"It might as well be. You'll be with the Wainwrights. Surely your father trusts them enough to look after you."

"That's not the only reason you're needed. We're—um—" she paused, looking uncertain—"we're going to secure some lumber contracts."

Connor bit back the urge to ask if she was daft. "That lumber is earmarked for repairs. I won't be party to hauling it off to Natchez."

"If I had my way, you wouldn't be going, but Papa insists. He says I need you to help set up the accounts with the buyers." She crossed her arms and gave him a look that said she was fully capable of handling the negotiations on her own. "But after this trip, you won't have to worry about it. Mews and the boys can handle the deliveries and you can stay here and move forward with the repairs on the house."

He dropped the adze and moved to stand toe-to-toe with her. "And what will I use for those repairs if you sell the lumber? Tell me that, mistress."

"We won't transport all the lumber to Natchez." She inclined her head, lifted her skirts, and turned away. "You'll have plenty of lumber to finish the repairs here."

"This was not part o' the terms, lass."

She whirled to face him. "I know it is not what we agreed on. Do you think I like it any more than you do? Do you think we wanted to lose part of the cotton to those men? This is the only solution I can think of, and if you have a better one, I'd like to hear it."

Connor ran a hand through his hair. She was right. There was no other solution.

"I'll start gradin' the lumber, then."

Chapter 19

TRAVELING THE TRACE made even the horses nervous.

"Whoa." Connor kept a tight rein on his team, which seemed inclined to bolt any minute. He glanced at Isabella, seated next to him. "How likely are we to be attacked on this journey?"

"Not likely. Not with such a large party as this. And definitely not on the way toward Natchez."

"And why is that?"

"The thieves aren't interested in the goods we're carrying to Natchez."

"Ah. But they would be very interested in the jingle in our pockets on the return journey?"

"Exactly."

"I see."

Connor kept an eye out regardless. They'd left before daybreak and, if they didn't have any problems during the journey, would arrive in Natchez before dark. The sooner they got to Natchez, the sooner they could sell the lumber, and he could get back to Breeze Hill, back to the job he'd been hired to do.

A commotion at the head of the column had him reaching for his pistol. Isabella craned her neck. "What is it?"

"Riders."

The call to halt echoed down the line. Connor could see Mr. Wainwright speaking with the head of the other party. The men nodded, and Wainwright's son wheeled his mount and started down the column.

When he drew abreast of them, Wainwright pulled his mount to a halt and doffed his hat. Isabella leaned across Connor, close, and he got a whiff of something tantalizingly sweet.

"Who are they, William?"

"Travelers returning to Tennessee. They ferried their goods downriver, and now they're headed back. They're probably just as wary of us as we are of them. They have horses, no wagons, so we're going to stay put and let them pass." His steady gaze rested on Connor. "But keep your weapons handy. They might not be who they say they are."

The strangers moved single file alongside the wagons. Connor pulled his pistol and rested it against his thigh. Their party might be strong in numbers, but they were spread out like butter on a piece of crusty bread. His horses rolled their eyes and snorted. "Easy."

He glanced over his shoulder at Mews and Toby in the wagon behind theirs, also loaded down with lumber. They were in a tight spot for sure. Sloping banks of soft, loamy dirt lifted high above his head on both sides of the wagon, leaving them vulnerable to attack from all sides. There was barely room for one wagon to make it through this bottleneck, let alone for two parties to pass each other.

Connor's eyes met and held the leader's as he drew near, so close they could reach out and shake hands if they chose. Instead, Connor kept one hand on his pistol, the other holding the horses in check.

The man's attention moved to Isabella, and he tipped his hat. Connor shifted, blocked the man's view, and his gaze slid past Isabella back to Connor. No words were spoken, no greeting. He gave a short nod and continued on.

Then came another and another, the tension mounting as the men rode past, all with their guns held at the ready. Thankfully, they passed without incident, and the call came from the front to head out.

Soon the whole party was moving forward again, and Connor breathed a sigh of relief.

"That went well." Isabella's voice came out high-pitched.

Connor urged the horses forward. "We might not be so blessed next time."

They arrived at Wainwright House in Natchez as darkness fell, and none too soon. Lightning flashed and thunder rolled across the river. Isabella allowed Connor to lift her down from the wagon.

William walked up to them and eyed the encroaching storm. "Looks like we arrived in the nick of time."

Connor plopped his hands on his hips. "Where's the best place to find contractors and craftsmen?"

"I'd say Brice's Tavern."

"Mistress Bartholomew, with your permission, I'll go immediately and put out the word that Breeze Hill has lumber for sale. Hopefully by the morrow, you'll have your contracts in hand."

"I'll accompany you."

Connor glared at her. "Brice's Tavern is no place for a lady."

William crossed his arms and regarded them, an amused smile on his face. He didn't believe she had control of her indentured servant. Isabella lifted her chin. "My father wouldn't have sent me if he didn't want me to be involved in the negotiations."

"There will be no negotiations tonight, mistress. I'll simply make some contacts and have them come visit you here at Wainwright House." His gaze cut to William. "Assuming that's all right with you, sir?"

William's lips twitched. "Quite all right."

"You're new to Natchez and don't even know where the tavern is."

"O' course I can find it. I landed in Natchez months ago, lass."

"Still—"

"Begging your pardon, Mistress Bartholomew, but your father asked me t' protect you, and I don't think allowing you t' accompany me t' a tavern of ill repute would suit."

Her face heated at the reminder of the night they'd spent at Harper's Inn. He arched a brow. "And besides, it's beginning t' rain."

"Isabella." William stepped forward and gave a slight bow. "I'll be glad to accompany Mr. O'Shea to the tavern. You'll be quite comfortable here at Wainwright House until we return."

They were right on all counts, which irritated her no end.

"Very well, then. You may go."

A gleam of triumph sparked in Connor's gaze, and she wanted to kick him in the shins.

Thankful for the rain that cooled his ire, Connor barreled down one street, then another. Isabella Bartholomew was the most stubborn woman he'd ever met. If he—

"Hold up there, my good man."

Connor blinked. He'd forgotten about Wainwright. He slowed his pace, gave a slight bow. "My apologies, sir. I didn't mean to rush ahead like that."

"No harm done." Wainwright ducked under the nearest stoop as the rain began to fall harder than before. Connor joined him. "I enjoyed seeing you put Isabella in her place like that. However, are you sure you know where Brice's Tavern is?"

Connor glanced one way, then the other, then shrugged. "T' tell you the truth, I have no idea. I've been in Natchez twice: the day I arrived and the day Isabella—Miss Bartholomew—bought my papers."

"But you told Isabella you'd been here for months."

"I've been in the *district* for months, just not in Natchez. As soon as we arrived, we made our way t' the outskirts of Natchez to build a country estate for Mr. Bloomfield and remained there until Master Benson died of the fever."

"Let's hope Isabella doesn't find out, then." Wainwright chuckled and clapped Connor on the back in a friendly manner. "Follow me, and I'll lead you to Brice's Tavern."

The streets had turned into a muddy quagmire by the time they arrived at the tavern. The place was packed as everyone attempted to avoid the nasty weather outside. Most ignored them, except for a beady-eyed man whose gaze followed them as they wove through the crowd.

Wainwright approached the proprietor. "Mr. Brice, how fare you these days?"

"Fair to middlin', sir. Fair to middlin'."

"This is Mr. O'Shea." Wainwright motioned to Connor. "He's here on behalf of Breeze Hill Plantation with seasoned lumber to sell. Might you know of any new construction going on?"

"Aye. There's new construction all along Wall and Jefferson Streets." He nodded at a man seated in the corner. "See the man with the pipe. He's overseeing several building projects as we speak."

"Thank you, Brice." Wainwright ordered a tankard of ale and approached the stranger. "Good afternoon, sir. Mr. Brice informed us you might be interested in some lumber."

"I might at that." The man removed his pipe. "Name's Wicker. And who might you be?"

Wainwright bowed. "William Wainwright of Wainwright Hall, north of Natchez."

Wicker's eyes slid to Connor, begging an introduction. Wainwright complied. "And this is Connor O'Shea, master craftsman, serving Mr. Bartholomew of Breeze Hill Plantation. O'Shea is representing Mr. Bartholomew, as he is indisposed."

"Yes, I heard about Bartholomew. Nasty business." His attention turned to Connor, and a smirk crossed his face. "Master craftsman, you say. And who did you learn the trade from?"

"Benson, sir."

"I've seen some of Benson's craftsmanship." Wicker stuck his pipe in his mouth, took a long draught, and nodded. "Excellent work."

"Yes, sir."

"Can you offer a steady supply of lumber, O'Shea? I've contracted to build three magnificent homes to rival the governor's mansion in the next two years. I'll need lumber. Lots of it."

Connor squelched his panic. Mr. Bartholomew would have to hire more laborers. But wasn't that why they'd come to Natchez—to find a way to generate revenue for Breeze Hill, to rebuild, to plant crops, and—God willing—to send for his brothers? He nodded. "Yes, sir. Breeze Hill can and will supply the lumber you need. We have two wagons at Wainwright House awaiting your inspection."

"Tell you what, O'Shea, I'll take a look at that lumber of yours. If it's of the quality I require, we might be able to strike a deal."

"Thank you, sir. Mistress Bartholomew is residing at Wainwright House and can receive you on the morrow if you're agreeable."

"Bartholomew's daughter? What does she have to do with this?" Wicker scowled at Wainwright. "This is business, not a tea party."

"Mr. Wicker, agreeing to let Miss Bartholomew have the last say in the negotiations was the lesser of two evils." Wainwright chuckled. "A compromise to save our sanity, if you get my meaning."

"Ah, a difficult chit, then?"

Wainwright tossed a glance at Connor, his lips twisting in amusement. "Some would say so."

"I'll call promptly at ten then, but make sure that girl keeps her place." Wicker rose. "Good day to you, sir."

When they were alone, Wainwright took a draught of his ale. Connor waited, watching patrons enter and leave. Wainwright motioned for a refill. "How about a pint, O'Shea?"

"No thank you, sir." Connor remained watchful. He didn't like the looks of this place. Didn't like the looks of the beady-eyed man across the room. Something wasn't right, even though Wainwright didn't seem the least bit fazed. Besides, Connor didn't have enough coin in his pockets to waste on stale ale.

An hour later, Connor helped an unsteady Wainwright to his feet.

"You've had enough, sir. We'd best be goin'."

"Just one more." Wainwright reached for the tankard and drained the last drop.

Before the man could ask for more of the strong drink, Connor propelled him toward the door. They'd barely left their chairs when two men slid into the vacated seats. More men crowded the low-ceilinged building, squeezing into every nook and cranny, some standing, some hunkered against the walls or loitering on the stairs.

Someone shifted, bumped Wainwright, and he jostled a stranger who stood between him and the door. A hand shot out and grabbed a fistful of Wainwright's waistcoat. "Watch where you're going, mister."

Instantly Connor came alert. It was the same man who'd watched them when they first arrived.

"My apologies, sir. It was an accident." Wainwright pushed the man's hand away. "If you'll kindly move aside and let me pass."

"And what if I don't?" Small beady eyes flickered to Connor, then back to Wainwright. "Move aside, that is?"

"Are you challenging me?"

"Challenging you?" A snort not unlike that of a pig escaped. "To what? A duel?"

"You're challenging me to a duel?" Wainwright wove, unsteady on his feet. He took a deep breath, his bloodshot eyes bulging. He leaned forward, scowling. "Knives or pistols?"

"We'll settle this right now. No need for a duel." The man took a swing at Wainwright.

After the first punch, Wainwright's head seemed to clear, and he threw two punches at his assailant.

Connor plunged into the fray, swinging his fists, trying to get a good lick in. But the room was too crowded, too many people everywhere, to make contact anywhere that would do much damage. And besides, even a bit unsteady on his feet, Wainwright seemed to be holding his own.

Like a cascade of falling cordwood, arguments ensued and fists flew as those close by joined in the melee. A flash of metal glinted in the lamplight, and Connor jerked back just in time to avoid being stabbed.

Wainwright wasn't so lucky. The knife caught him in the stomach.

Connor dove at the knife-wielding man, grabbed his arm, and jerked it upward with such force he heard the shoulder bones crack. A scream of pain tore from the man's throat, lost in the roar of the dozen or so men pushing and shoving, shouting and throwing punches at each other.

Connor shoved the man into the throng and reached for Wainwright, slumped over the nearest table. If he could make it to the door before the beady-eyed man's companions got to him, they might get out of here alive.

Only a few more feet and he'd make it.

A chair slammed into his head and shoulders from behind, splinters raining all around him. He pushed Wainwright toward the door, grabbed a piece of splintered wood from the chair, and drove it into his attacker's stomach. The man fell back with an oomph.

Beady Eyes filled his spot, rushing at Connor.

Whatever these men had against Wainwright, it was obvious they weren't going to let him live. Wainwright wrenched the door open, lurched outside, and fell against a rain barrel, clutching his middle.

Halfway out the door himself, Connor caught a glimpse of the man's face, pain-filled and pasty white.

Beady Eyes charged. White-hot anger exploded in Connor's chest. Enough of this. Instead of dodging, Connor grabbed him and propelled the man right out the door with him. They landed in a heap, Connor's knife at the man's throat.

"One move, and I'll slit your throat."

The man went limp. "We didn't mean nothin', mister. It was just a little misunderstanding, that's all."

"I don't believe you. You had your eyes on my friend from the moment we entered the tavern." Never mind that he and Wainwright weren't exactly friends. Right now he just wanted to know why Wainwright had been singled out, and not just for a beating, but a gutting. Connor pressed the knife against the man's throat. "Talk. Why were you after Master Wainwright?"

"Connor, I don't think they were after me. They were . . ." Wainwright trailed off, then let go of the barrel and rolled to land on his back in the mud-logged street. Blood covered his torso.

Connor let the man go and knelt in the mud, feeling for a pulse. "Master Wainwright, can you hear me?"

"Wainwright of Wainwright Hall?" The man's eyes bugged out, and he backed away. "Truly, sir, we didna mean no harm to a Wainwright. It was you we was after. You tell 'em that, ya hear?"

And with that the miscreant fled.

A clatter woke Isabella.

"Finally," she whispered, reaching for a candle.

Long after Mr. Wainwright and the housekeeper had retired, she'd stayed up waiting on William and Connor but had fallen asleep on the settee in the parlor.

The door burst open and Connor and William fell into the room, Connor's arm wrapped around William's waist. William was barely conscious, one arm draped over Connor's shoulder.

"Merciful heavens, what happened?"

"He's been stabbed."

"Stabbed?" Horror swept over Isabella.

"Which room is his?"

"Upstairs. Second door on the right. I'll ring for Mrs. Butler."

"What's going on down there?" Mr. Wainwright poked his head over the banister, candle held high. "William!"

In a daze, Isabella watched as Mr. Wainwright called for their stable hand. Mews and Toby came running as well.

Within minutes, the men had William in a bedroom on the main floor, as carrying him up the stairs proved too difficult.

The men closed the door behind them as Mrs. Butler bustled to the kitchen to boil water. The stable hand—she learned his name was Jack—rushed out of the house in search of the doctor. Then, suddenly, Isabella found herself alone, standing in the middle of the parlor, everyone with a job to do.

Everyone except her.

Indecision warred within her. She should go help Mrs. Butler. Anything to keep busy, and the poor woman was distraught. She took one step in that direction and spotted a prayer book on a side table next to the door.

Tears stung her eyes, even as an irrational anger swept over her. She'd prayed for her mother to return, and she never had. She'd prayed for Jonathan to be found safe and sound, but it wasn't to be. They'd lost their crops. Her father had almost lost his life. And now William lay on a bed in the next room, at death's door.

She grabbed the prayer book and held it up, her gaze beseeching heaven. "What next, God? Will You take the babe as well? Like Job, will I lose everything I hold dear?"

"Thou speakest as one of the foolish women speaketh."

The words Job flung in his wife's face pricked her conscience. Hands shaking, she stared at the prayer book. Job had been righteous, but even he had been contrite over questioning God's sovereignty. She was nothing, nothing but a speck compared to Job and even less compared to God Almighty.

That she'd dare to shake her fist at Him, to question His

judgment, His decision over who prospered and whose crops failed, over who lived or died.

She trembled at the realization that God had been merciful to her even as she wallowed in her grief. Even as she'd lashed out at Him, blaming Him for everything that ever happened in her life, when she should have run toward Him, just as Job did.

"Curse God, and die."

"No," she whispered, heart pounding. "No. Please forgive me."

Shame filled her. She hadn't said the words out loud, but her actions had told her father to curse God, Leah to curse God. They were the ones who suffered the most, not her.

In my grief over Jonathan, I wanted to lash out, to blame someone. I pushed You away when I should have drawn closer to You than ever before. God, I'm sorry.

As her tears overflowed, she collapsed on the settee and asked God to forgive her foolishness, asked Him to give her the peace Leah had found, the peace that Mr. and Mrs. Horne enjoyed.

And when she'd cried until she had no more tears and the weight of her past mistakes lifted, she turned her attention to petitioning God for William's life.

Prepared to accept God's will, no matter the outcome.

Sometime later, she jerked awake to soft candlelight and the feel of a blanket draped over her, the prayer book still clutched against her.

Connor slumped in a chair across from her, legs splayed,

head lolling against the back of the chair. Somewhere in the house, a clock struck three. Isabella sighed, watching Connor sleep. His chest rose and fell with the gentle rhythm of slumber. She smiled when a soft snore escaped his lips.

He stirred, and she closed her eyes, pretending to be asleep. All was quiet for so long that she risked peeking at him, only to find him watching her, his gaze heavy-lidded from sleep.

She said the first thing that popped into her mind. "You snore."

One side of his mouth lifted. "So I've been told. But I don't believe it. I've never heard me snore."

Isabella laughed softly, then glanced toward the hallway that led to the bedroom where William lay, the doctor fighting to keep him alive. Her stomach clenched with worry. "How does William fare?"

"Holding his own for now."

"This is my fault." She caught Connor's gaze. "If William hadn't gone to Brice's Tavern on my behalf, none of this would have happened."

Connor shook his head, looking as weary as she felt. "It's no' your fault, lass. If anything, it's mine."

"Your fault? There's no need to blame yourself."

"There is when that knife was meant for me."

Chapter 20

THE DOCTOR TOOK his leave just as the sun rose over the horizon. Connor let him out, then spotted Isabella seated at a secretary in the parlor, papers strewn all over the desktop.

She looked up, saw him standing there. "How's William?"

"The doctor says he'll be fine. No vitals were injured."

"The Lord has blessed indeed."

"Yes, he has." Connor chuckled. "The doctor suggested he stay abed for another week, but Master William vetoed that idea right away."

"I'm afraid this will delay our return trip. I'm sorry, Connor. You didn't want to come in the first place, and now this."

"Ah, lass, it can't be helped. I'm just thankful it wasn't worse."

"Amen to that." She spoke softly, studying the prayer book on the edge of the desk. A tiny smile played over her lips.

Connor lifted an eyebrow. Something was different about Isabella this morning. He couldn't quite put his finger on it, but she seemed more relaxed, softer.

The hall clock struck six. Connor snapped his fingers. "In all the uproar, I forgot to tell you that a Mr. Wicker will be here at ten to look at the lumber."

"Wicker?" Isabella scrunched her forehead. "The name's not familiar."

"He's overseeing the construction of several homes here in Natchez. He said he would stop by this morning to look at the lumber. Should I send word for him to wait another day?"

"No. I see no reason not to meet with him."

Connor stood, waiting. For what, he didn't know. He'd never been one to just sit or stand and do nothing. But what could he do? His work was back at Breeze Hill. And the longer it took to complete that work, the more time it would take to bring his brothers over.

He spotted Isabella's papers, the fresh quill and ink. He could cipher in his head and could sketch and figure measurements to the nth degree, but he could barely read and write, not enough to compose a letter to Quinn. He cleared his throat, wishing for the skill with pen and paper to let his brothers know his whereabouts and that he was working toward bringing them to America. Maybe he could impose on Isabella—

"Was there something else?" She smiled, looking at him with a quizzical expression.

He motioned toward the inkwell. "Would you mind writing a letter to my brother back home in Ireland?"

"I would be honored. His name is Quinn, correct?"

"Yes. Quinn."

She pulled out a fresh piece of paper, dipped the quill, and waited with it poised above the paper. "What would you like to say?"

Connor paced, trying to think what to tell Quinn to keep the letter to one page. "Tell him that I'm indentured to Breeze Hill as a master carpenter and that your father will send for him as soon as he can."

"Shouldn't I tell him how you fare?"

Connor glanced at her. "I thought that's what I just said."

She laughed. "No, you didn't. You told him what you *do* but not how you *are*."

He waved a hand at the paper. "Well, just add that part in wherever you want to."

"As you wish."

Isabella's pen scratched along the paper, her penmanship delicate and flowing. Connor studied her handwriting. He could barely make out the words hidden in the flowery whirls. Fancy flourishes should be reserved for scrollwork on wooden balustrades, not when putting words to paper.

Isabella glanced at him, one eyebrow raised. "What do you find amusing, pray tell?"

Connor shook his head. "Your penmanship. Lovely, 'tis."

Her gaze narrowed in assessment, and he could see the wheels turning as she tried to determine if he was sincerely complimenting her penmanship or if he was mocking her. Apparently politeness won out, and she turned back to the letter.

"Thank you." She dipped the quill once again and continued writing, her bottom lip caught between her teeth.

Connor lost interest in the letter and focused on Isabella, on the curve of her neck, the translucent vein jumping at the base of her throat right next to her delicate collarbone. He wanted to press his lips to the spot and feel her pulse. Then move to the perfect shell of her ear, trail along her cheekbone, letting her lashes tease his lips, and finally claim her mouth with his own once again. What harm would there be in that? He sucked in a breath and closed his eyes.

Plenty.

"What do you think?"

His eyes popped open. Her long, slender fingers held the letter so that he could see.

"It's a beautiful letter. No' sure Quinn can actually read it, though, with all those fancy swirls."

"I'm sorry. It didn't occur to me that he'd have trouble reading it." She started to set it aside. "I'll do it again, and I'll make it easier to read."

"No." Connor captured her wrist, holding the beautiful letter in place. "If he can't make out the words, Mrs. MacDonald can. She's a former schoolteacher."

"If you're sure?" Her brow furrowed, her concern over the letter endearing.

"I'm sure, lass. 'Tis a mighty fine letter."

"Mrs. Butler will see that it's sent posthaste." She held out the quill. "Would you like to sign it?"

Taking the quill from her, Connor leaned over the desk, his left hand resting on her chair, his arm brushing her back. Dipping the quill in the inkwell, he scrawled his name at the bottom of the page.

She glanced up, but just as quickly she lowered her gaze, though she didn't move away. He tilted his head, his lips mere inches from hers. She leaned toward him, or maybe he leaned toward her. He wasn't sure, but—

A door slammed, and Connor jerked away, focusing on the letter between them.

His scrawl and her perfect penmanship jumped out at him from the page.

Opposite as night and day, just like their very different lives.

A day later, Mrs. Butler quietly closed the door to William's room, seated herself, and took up her knitting.

"How is he?" Isabella asked, her own fingers busily tatting a doily.

"Sleeping like an angel, poor boy."

Isabella laughed. "I'd never call William an angel, Mrs. Butler."

A soft look crossed the housekeeper's face. "Ah, but, dear child, you didn't know him as a babe. Sweetest child this side of the pond."

Isabella resisted the urge to let loose with a very unlady-like snort. William had been the furthest thing from sweet all those years he and Jonathan had tormented her as children. "You've been with the Wainwrights a long time, then?"

"Goin' on thirty years. Was nanny to William and his sisters." She cast a sly glance at Isabella. "'Bout time he married and raised up another generation of little ones here at Wainwright House and out at Wainwright Hall."

Isabella lowered her gaze, feigning a sudden interest in the tatting in her lap. She wouldn't hurt the woman's feelings for the world, but marrying William was ... really, it was just about as far-fetched as her and Connor reciting vows. More so, even.

Heavens, she couldn't imagine kissing William. The very idea made her squirm. But Connor—

Her face flamed as she thought of the almost kiss from the day before. No, she couldn't see herself marrying William. In some ways, he was as much a brother as Jonathan had been. Even when he'd visited the plantation the last few weeks and on the trip to Natchez, she never felt as if he wanted to court her, but that he was watching out for her like a big brother should.

If anything, she'd become convinced that he had his eye on Leah. She'd planned to broach the subject with him while in Natchez, but his injury had prevented that. She could think of nothing better than for Leah to find happiness again with someone as steady and dependable as William.

"You don't know how much I've enjoyed this little visit, disregarding the trouble dear William got into." Mrs. Butler looked up from her knitting, her wrinkled face crinkling in a smile. "It's quite lonesome here in the summer with Mrs. Wainwright and the girls out in the country."

Thankful that the housekeeper had moved on to a different subject, Isabella asked, "You're not interested in spending the summer at Wainwright Hall?"

"Goodness, no, Miss Bartholomew." Her eyes twinkled. "In spite of confessing to a few lonely days, I enjoy my quiet time here alone. The hustle and bustle of balls and soirees in the fall and winter will come soon enough, mark my words."

Isabella tossed a teasing glance at the kindly housekeeper. "I can't impose upon you to call me by my given name, Mrs. Butler?"

"Oh no. It would be unseemly, miss." Mrs. Butler gave Isabella's hand a gentle pat. "But it wouldn't be improper for me to address you as Miss Isabella—with your permission, of course."

"Permission granted." Isabella inclined her head, smiling at the improper propriety the two of them managed to maintain.

Mrs. Butler knitted and rocked, her humming soothing as she worked. Isabella dropped a stitch, sighed, then started picking out the mistake. "Mrs. Butler, if you've been with the Wainwrights all these years, you must have known my mother."

"Ah, your mother. Such a sweet young thing. And very

beautiful." Mrs. Butler studied her, then nodded with satisfaction. "You have the look of her. Your eyes, especially."

"That's what my father says."

"She loved your father—and you and your brother—very much."

"Then why did she leave?"

"I can't answer that, child. But I don't believe she went willingly." Mrs. Butler's needles clicked in the room, the only other sound the ticking of the clock on the mantel. "Your mother left everything. Her clothes. Her jewelry. Everything. No young woman I know would do that."

"I didn't know she'd stayed here."

"Oh yes. She'd been here quite some time waiting for the ship to set sail. She had a terrible row with her father the night before he was to leave. I didn't hear all of it, but he wanted her to file papers for a divorce from your father, and she refused. The next morning, he apologized and begged her to accompany him to the docks to see him off. She relented and went with him. She never returned."

Isabella pressed a hand to her middle, trying to quell the churning inside. Her father had been right. "He forced her to return to Spain?"

"I've always believed so. As I said, her life was with your father, you, and your brother, God rest his soul. A few days after the ship departed, your father stormed into Natchez, furious. But there was nothing he could do, short of finding a ship to take him to Spain. Which wasn't an easy task."

"Because there was a storm brewing?"

"Yes. Many storms were brewing, not just the one off the coast of New Orleans. France had ceded the district to England with the Treaty of Paris in 1763, but some were already speculating on how long England could hold on to power. And they were right to worry. Spain took control in 1779, but—that's neither here nor there. All that happened much later, maybe five or six years after your mother left. When word came that the ship carrying your mother had sunk off the coast of Cuba, your father lost all hope of ever being reunited with her."

Isabella wanted to ask if Mrs. Butler believed the ship had been lost, but was afraid of the answer.

Wasn't it enough that Papa believed an act of God and not her own will had prevented her mother from returning to them?

Connor was fit to be tied.

He'd brushed the horses in Wainwright's stables until their coats glistened. He'd toted water for Mrs. Butler to do her washing. Mews and Toby mucked the stables thrice daily, all of them determined not to be a burden while lodging with the Wainwrights.

They'd struck a deal with Mr. Wicker to supply lumber in the coming months. And now Connor needed to get back to Breeze Hill to keep up his end of the bargain. There was a lot of work to do if he was going to make good on the promises he and Isabella had made to Wicker, as well as produce enough lumber to rebuild Breeze Hill.

The doctor wanted William to wait one more day before he headed back home. Connor knew it was wise to wait. But that didn't keep him from being restless.

He hoisted a bag of shingles and headed toward the carriage house. He'd spotted a few broken squares, so he might as well fix the roof while he waited. The hot sun bore down on him as he crawled over the roof.

He'd been tempted to take one of the horses and head back alone, but every time he got the itch to take off, Isabella's face swam before him. Mr. Bartholomew had put her in his safekeeping, and Connor couldn't leave her behind. What if something happened to her and he wasn't there to protect her?

He wouldn't be able to face himself or her father.

So he stayed.

One more day wouldn't hurt.

Unless he went crazy with waiting.

He ripped a rotten shingle off the roof and pulled a fresh-cut one out of the bag. His shirt clung to him like a second skin as the sun climbed higher in the sky. Laughter pealed across the courtyard. Toby and Jack, the Wainwrights' stable hand, led a pair of horses toward the carriage house.

"Morning, boys." Connor used his sleeve to wipe the sweat from his face. "Where are you off to?"

"Mrs. Butler and Miss Isabella need to go to the market." Toby's voice vibrated with excitement. He didn't get much chance to see the sights of Natchez living out at Breeze Hill.

"You lads stay close to the ladies. No running off, you hear?"

"Yes, sir."

In no time flat, the boys had the carriage waiting by the front door. Connor had a bird's-eye view of the street in front of the house, and he paused in his work to watch Mrs. Butler and Isabella as they walked toward the carriage. Isabella hadn't come prepared to stay for days at a time, but her plain brown dress made her look as beautiful as if she wore a satin ball gown trimmed in lace straight from Paris. She didn't need fancy clothes to turn a man's head. Her smile and flashing dark eyes did the job just fine on their own.

As she ducked into the carriage, Connor grabbed a nail and pounded on the shingle with such force the thin wood snapped clean in two.

A borrowed parasol shaded Isabella's face, and a cooling breeze relieved a bit of the stifling heat as Mr. Wainwright's carriage rolled along at a nice clip.

They passed a new house on Jefferson Street, turned down Wall Street, and saw the foundations of two more houses being laid. Natchez was definitely in the throes of a construction boom.

Excitement welled up when Isabella spotted at least four more homes under construction as they traversed the streets heading toward the shopping district. She couldn't wait to tell her father how ripe Natchez was for building materials. No wonder Mr. Wicker had gladly accepted their price.

She chewed her lip. Had they undersold the competition?

No matter. Her father had given her strict instructions on the lowest price he would take, and Mr. Wicker had offered far more than that. A fair price and a good relationship with the contractors in Natchez were worth more than turning a quick profit.

If they could salvage a portion of the cotton crop and sell a bit of lumber along the way, they might be able to limp along until spring when they could plant again. By then, the repairs to the house would be finished, and all the lumber could be sold for profit. Assuming Connor stayed around after his indenture was up.

His crooked smile tumbled into her thoughts, and she thought back to the last time they'd been alone. Two days ago when she'd written the letter to his brother. He'd signed the letter, mumbled something about taking care of the horses, and left without so much as a by-your-leave.

But for a brief moment, she'd thought he might kiss her again, and she would have been powerless to stop him. She angled the parasol to block Mrs. Butler's gaze and pressed a gloved hand to her bosom to slow the pounding of her heart. Not that she'd wanted to stop him. As soon as he'd leaned forward to sign that letter, the feel of his corded arm against her shoulder sent her heart soaring skyward like an eagle in flight, only to plummet the next second with just as much force as it had climbed.

She'd been more than happy to write the letter, only to feel like a show-off when he commented on her penmanship. His crude letters endeared him to her even more. There was no shame in having had little formal education. Her own father had little to recommend him when he'd settled in Natchez. Clearing land had been his slate, planting crops his quill.

The closer they got to the center of town, the shops, and the marketplace, the busier it became. Horses, wagons, and carriages clogged the road. Men shouted at each other. The crowded thoroughfare gave Isabella pause, but the stable boy handled the horses with ease, relaxed and in his element. The press of the crowd allowed them to move forward at a snail's pace.

Isabella drew in her breath as a contingent of slaves shuffled by, fetters around their ankles, chains rattling as they moved in unison across a wide-open parade ground toward an auction block.

"No wonder there are so many people in town today." Mrs. Butler shook her head, lips pursed. "They're going to have an auction."

Unable to tear her gaze away, Isabella watched as the slaves stopped next to the platform, brawny bucks with muscles bulging, women staring stoically ahead, some with babes in arms. One young woman, her head held high, her ebony skin glistening in the heat of the day, caught Isabella's attention.

Gentlemen farmers pointed at the slaves, walked boldly up to the men, and motioned for them to open their mouths so they could see their teeth. They stripped the shirts off their backs and prodded at their muscles.

The carriage moved past the auction site as more men

crowded around. Isabella jerked around at the sound of tearing cloth. The young woman she'd seen stood proud, her breasts exposed. Shocked, Isabella gasped and averted her gaze, shame flooding her cheeks.

She'd seen the auction once in her life, but she'd been too young to grasp the meaning of it all. Now, after learning of her family's history, she understood her father's anger, his helplessness at such a sight.

Had her great-grandmother been subject to the same degradation as the girl she'd just seen? And why wouldn't she have been? An Irish slave wouldn't have been treated any differently than an African slave, would she?

Only a few short years ago, her great-grandmother would have been the one standing on that auction block, being exposed to the greedy eyes of men who claimed to be Christians. Men who would call another out in a duel if his wife or daughter were treated so abominably.

No wonder her father abhorred slavery.

His own grandmother had walked the same path as that poor young woman.

Chapter 21

CONNOR POUNDED the last nail in place, tossed the bag of shingles to the ground, and swung from the low-slung roof.

Mews rounded the corner, jerked his hat off, and rubbed his face with his sleeve. "All done?"

"Yes. It'll hold through the winter." Connor scooped a dipperful of water and took a gulp, the tepid moisture cooling his parched throat.

"Where's Toby?"

"Jack took Mrs. Butler and Isabella to the market, and Toby rode along with them."

Mews frowned. "I don't know if it's a good idea for them ladies to be down close to the wharf today. There's an auction, and I heard there's a horse race too."

Connor grabbed a rough towel off a peg, scrubbed it down his face, and dried his arms. "That shouldn't be a problem, should it?"

"The auction draws a big crowd of plantation owners and miscreants, too. And the race could be anywhere. They rope off several streets for some of those races and have a regular fracas. Bystanders have gotten trampled. A few have even been killed." Hands planted on narrow hips, Mews scowled. "I don't like it one bit. Not Miss Isabella and Mrs. Butler being down there, and not the boys either."

"We'd better go find them, then." Connor tossed the towel toward the peg and headed for the stables. "Better safe than sorry."

They saddled up and headed toward the wharf, Connor letting Mews lead the way. As soon as he saw the crowded streets, worry knotted his stomach. Mews was right to be concerned. Today was not the day to frequent the market. They turned and rode down a street parallel to the course laid out for the race. A group of riffraff surged across the cobblestones in front of him, and Connor sawed back on the reins to keep from running the boys down.

"Is there someplace we can leave the horses?" he shouted to Mews. "It would be better to continue on foot."

"There's a stable not far from here."

"Stable the horses, then. I'll start looking." Connor dismounted and tossed the reins to Mews.

"Head that way." Mews pointed toward the thickest part of the crowd. "You can't miss the market. It's across the way there."

Connor dove into the close-packed crowd, pushing and shoving his way through. He made it to the rope that sectioned off a wide street. People hurried across, intent on getting to their destinations before the horses came tearing through.

"How many riders in the race?" Connor asked a man standing next to him.

"Upwards of twenty is what I've heard." The man's eyes glowed. "My money's on Braxton's thoroughbred. Ain't no horse can beat that two-year-old."

"Braxton?" Connor frowned. Braxton had made his presence known at Breeze Hill more than once over the last few weeks. "He's riding?"

"Of course not." The man gave Connor a strange look. "He's too big. He's got a little Negro boy no bigger'n a washing of soap. Kid clings to the back of that horse like he was born there."

Connor ducked under the rope and headed down the street at a fast lope. He'd have plenty of time to get out of the way, and until the riders showed up, following the course would be the fastest way to find Isabella and Mrs. Butler.

Isabella and Mrs. Butler breezed into the dim interior of Mrs. Simson's dress shop. The proprietor smiled a welcome.

"Mrs. Butler, how good to see you." Then she turned to Isabella, hands clasped, beaming. "And if it isn't Isabella Bartholomew. My dear, you are lovelier than ever."

"Thank you, Mrs. Simson." Isabella curtsied, happy that

the woman remembered her. She hadn't been to the dress-maker's shop over half-a-dozen times her entire life, but the dear woman made a point of keeping up with every lady in the territory, especially if said lady might be a customer someday. "How's business?"

"Slow. It is the summer season, you know. As soon as the plantation wives and daughters return to town, I'll have more business than I can throw a thimble at. Is there something I can do for you?" Her tone sounded hopeful.

"Nothing for me." She nodded toward Mrs. Butler. "I'm staying at Wainwright House for a few days, and Mrs. Butler and I decided to come to the market today."

Mrs. Butler stepped forward. "I would like a nice piece of damask, Mrs. Simson, if you have any on hand."

"Any particular color?"

"A pale rose would be ideal."

"Yes, I do believe I have something that might be to your liking. Please, have a seat." Mrs. Simson motioned toward some chairs and a small table. "May I offer you some refreshment? Some tea or lemonade? We just received a shipment of fresh lemons at the market. Such a wonderful treat, isn't it?"

Isabella fanned herself. "Lemonade sounds wonderful."

"It is dreadfully hot, isn't it?" Mrs. Simson poured two glasses of lemonade and then moved to the shelves lining her small shop. As she rummaged about for the requested material, she continued the conversation over her shoulder. "How's your father, Miss Bartholomew?"

"Much better, madam. Thank you for asking."

"Poor fellow." The woman made a tsking sound with her tongue. "Such a tragedy. Ah, here it is."

Mrs. Butler and Mrs. Simson moved to the open doorway to get a better look at the cloth.

The housekeeper nodded in approval. "This should do nicely. I'll take six yards."

"Wonderful." The shopkeeper placed the bolt of cloth on a cutting table and started unrolling it.

A redheaded stick of a man with a long, scraggly beard leaned in the open door. He jerked his hat off the moment he saw Mrs. Butler and Isabella.

"You ladies might want to stay inside for a while." An excited grin split his face.

"Whatever for, Jeremiah?" Mrs. Simson plopped both hands on her hips. "Have you spotted another skunk under your shop?"

"No, madam. But there's a horse race over on Canal Street."

"Canal Street?" Isabella froze, lemonade held midair.

"Yes, miss. But don't worry. Y'all aren't in any danger. It just might be better to stay here until the race is over and the crowd thins out." And with that, he scurried away in the direction of the race.

"I do declare. Men and their horse races." Mrs. Simson peered out the open door. Men and boys rushed past in a tizzy to get as close to the action as possible. "I shouldn't be surprised, what with the auction today. Men can't pass up the opportunity to have their fun."

Isabella grabbed her bonnet.

"Miss Isabella, where are you going?"

"Toby and Jack are waiting for us on Canal Street. They may be in danger."

The race was on.

Connor didn't hear the horses coming or see anything, but he could feel it in the crowd lining the streets. A ripple of expectation rolled over the men and boys as they craned their necks, peering northward.

Where was Isabella? He hadn't seen the carriage or the women anywhere. Had they changed their minds and headed back to Wainwright House?

The ground rumbled beneath his feet and the crowd cheered. Up ahead, the street veered to the right, climbing a steep hill. He glanced behind him and saw the first wave of horses turn onto the street, jockeys whipping the lathered animals mercilessly. Two horses were in the lead, neck and neck.

One rider plowed his mount into the horse next to him, and the second rider almost lost his seat. They paid little heed to the crowd that pressed in from all sides.

Connor flattened himself against the nearest building as the horses rushed past, breathing hard, pushed to run faster by their riders. A trail of dust rose up to choke him. With the leaders out of the way, Connor knew the rest of the pack wouldn't be far behind.

He sprinted the last fifty feet to the end of the street, hoping to see something of the carriage. If it wasn't here, he prayed they'd left town and headed back to Wainwright's before this deluge of men and horses.

A shout rose from behind him, and he glanced back to see a pack of riders spread shoulder to shoulder across the roadway, the riders kicking, screaming, and slashing at each other for position. He turned to duck into the nearest alley, intent on squeezing himself into the press of men shouting for their favorite horse to win.

Then he saw the carriage on the opposite side of the street a hundred yards away. One of the horses had its foot caught in the traces. Toby fought to hold the frightened animals, while Jack struggled to untangle the lines. Toby threw a wild-eyed look at the oncoming wave of riders. Connor took a step in their direction, then breathed a sigh of relief as Jack got the traces untwisted and the two boys urged the horses toward a nearby alley.

"Toby!"

Pure terror shot through Connor when he heard Isabella scream. He caught a glimpse of her brown skirt billowing out of control as she exited an alley and launched herself across the street toward the boys.

Heart in his throat, Connor shot out of the crowd, his one thought to get to Isabella before the horses did.

The horses swept toward them. Connor snaked an arm around her waist and kept running, launching himself toward the nearest stoop and rolling out of the way as the horses pounded past. He tucked Isabella under him, praying they wouldn't be trampled.

The ground shook with the force of forty hooves slicing into the earth, powered by ten thousand pounds of horse-flesh. Dust churned, men shouted, horses snorted as their riders pushed them hard.

The last of the horses swept past, the crowd following in their wake, rushing toward the finish line to claim victory or weep in defeat. Quickly the crowd thinned, and a few stragglers scurried past, some looking curiously at Connor and Isabella before hurrying on their way.

Isabella stirred, pushed against Connor's chest. "Let me go. Where's Toby? And Jack?"

"They're fine. Jack got the traces untangled and they got out of the way just in time."

She went limp. "Are you sure?"

"I'm sure." Connor helped her to her feet, holding her by the shoulders. "Are ya all right, lass?"

"Yes."

Her hair hung down her back in dark waves. Tears and dirt streaked her face. Fury, mixed with a desire to sweep her into his arms and kiss her senseless, swept over him.

He opted for fury.

"Ya could have been killed," he bit out through clenched teeth. "In all o' holy heaven, what possessed ya t' run out in front o' those horses like that, lass?"

"Didn't you see that Toby and Jack were in danger?" Her eyes flashed.

"O' course I saw. And I would have been able to help them if I hadn't had to rescue you instead."

"What makes you think I needed rescuing?" She glared at him.

"A pack o' horses was breathing down your neck. Or did ya no' see that?" Connor pulled her close and tucked his face next to hers, intent on talking some sense into her. Gritting his teeth, he gave her a little shake. "Don't ever do that again, lass. Ya took ten years off me life."

He sucked in a shuddering breath, reliving the horror of what might have been only moments ago. He reached out a trembling hand, his thumb wiping the dirt away. "When I saw those horses bearing down on you, I thought—"

The tips of her fingers against his lips stopped him, trapping his words beneath their softness. The angry fire in her flashing eyes was gone, only to be replaced by another fire, just as volatile, but much, much more dangerous. Her eyelashes fluttered, lowered, and she slid both arms around his neck and pulled him toward her.

And Connor was powerless to stop her.

It occurred to him as he wrapped his arms around her waist and drew her more fully against him that he didn't want to stop her.

Not now. Not ever.

Nolan stood in the shadows of a building across the street, watching Isabella and the Irishman. When he'd seen her dash in front of the wall of horses, a sudden, irrational fear for her life grabbed him by the throat.

Which was surprising.

He didn't love Isabella. He only wanted her for what she could give him.

Breeze Hill. Along with access to the trace without having to answer to anyone or anything.

He studied them, Isabella's arms entwined about the Irishman's neck, her body pressed against the rough clapboard building, the two of them so wrapped up in each other, the outside world ceased to exist. The Irishman tucked a lock of Isabella's hair behind her ear, his fingers lingering.

Nolan's own fingers curled around the pistol tucked into his waistband, an anger he didn't know he possessed sweeping through him like a forest fire in the dry heat of August. Isabella Bartholomew belonged to *him*. Yes, she was simply the means to an end, but she could be more.

He wouldn't rule out the possibility that he'd finally found a woman who might stand by his side as he rose in power in Natchez. If the Spanish managed to hold on to the territory indefinitely, having a wife with ties to Spain would work in his favor.

Yes, Isabella Bartholomew would serve him well.

His gaze shifted from Isabella toward the man who dared put his hands on the woman Nolan had claimed for his own. A *servant*, no less.

Connor O'Shea would die for touching Isabella Bartholomew.

Isabella held Connor close, all the while thinking she had to stop this madness.

Connor cared nothing for her. What time he hadn't been glaring at her the last two weeks, he'd been ignoring her. A tingle of excitement shot through her, and her lips curved into a smile beneath his. But when he wasn't frowning at her or ignoring her, he was kissing the very daylights out of her, and that made up for all the scowling. Her fingers tangled themselves in his hair, and she forgot all about stopping, about madness, about anything but the sweet warmth of his lips on hers.

Voices reached them as the crowd retraced their steps. Rambunctious men recounting the race, some laughing over their spoils, some cursing whatever fate had led them to bet on losing odds.

Connor pulled away, the tender look in his eyes fading, replaced by something almost like fear. Or sorrow. She couldn't tell which, but whatever it was, it drove the warmth away.

He took her hand and led her down the alley, then another, distancing them from the crowd of men.

"Connor?" Her voice trembled.

"Not here. Not now." He released her and stepped away, just as he'd done on the trip home the first time they'd met, as he'd done after the first time he kissed her. As he always did.

As if he regretted kissing her, holding her, letting himself get close to her.

She felt the impact as his gaze raked her from head to toe; then he lowered his eyes. "Make yourself presentable, mistress."

Isabella gasped, turned away, and swiped at the grime that coated her dress. But it was no use. The only saving grace was that the garment was a plain dark-brown material that covered a multitude of sins and a lot of dirt and dust. Her hair was a different matter altogether. She'd lost most of her pins in the melee. Finally she twisted her hair up as best she could and secured the dark mass under her bonnet, thankful the wide, stiff brim would hide her features from passersby.

When she'd repaired as much of the damage as possible, she turned back to Connor. Without looking at her, he motioned for her to precede him down the alley. "After you, mistress."

Tears pricked her eyes, and she lifted her skirts and turned away, blindly walking toward Mrs. Simson's shop two streets over. She wanted to confront Connor, ask him why he kept her at arm's length with one hand but pulled her close and held her tenderly with the other.

But she dared not ask.

She wasn't sure she really wanted to know the answer.

Chapter 22

Tired of being cooped up inside, William insisted on leaving his sickbed. Isabella accompanied him to the porch so they could catch the afternoon breeze off the river.

Mrs. Butler arranged a mound of pillows behind him. "Master William, don't you think you should wait a few more days before going back to the plantation? The road is so rough, and the carriage—"

"Now, Nanny, don't fret yourself." William reached for her hand and kissed the back of it. "Everything will be fine. Father and Connor took the carriage to the smithy's not an hour past to make sure it's in tip-top shape."

Mrs. Butler pressed her lips together, sniffed, and plumped one of the pillows.

"Besides, Isabella will be in the carriage with me." William winked at her. "She'll make sure I'm all right."

"Oh, I don't need to ride in the carriage."

"Of course you will. I wouldn't dream of riding in all that comfort while you bounce along on a farm wagon."

"Since you put it that way—" Isabella smiled, then inclined her head—"I accept."

"Well, if that's the case, I'd better start packing your things." Mrs. Butler beamed at them both. "And cooking. You'll need nourishment for the journey. Heaven knows what your father will feed you on the way home."

She turned to go, but William called her back.

"Nanny, the girls would never forgive me if I didn't bring home a batch of your freshly baked tea cakes."

"Of course you should take some, Master William, and some lemon squares as well. It'll be a treat for Mistress Wainwright and your sisters."

When Mrs. Butler left, Isabella shook her head. "She spoils you rotten."

"Always has." He chuckled, reached up, plucked one of the pillows from behind him, and tossed it on a nearby rocker. "Always will. Don't know what we'd do without Nanny. She's more like a member of the family than a servant."

"And she's ready for grandchildren."

William's gaze cut to hers. "Really?"

"Really. She mentioned it the other day. Specifically said that you should get married and have children."

"She did, did she?" William rubbed his chin, looking askance at her. "She didn't have anyone in mind?"

"Not that I know of." Isabella tried to keep the smile that squirmed on her lips from showing. Could she get him to admit his feelings for Leah? "Lemonade?"

"No thank you." He stared at the river, a frown on his face.

Isabella poured herself a glass of the tart liquid and took a sip. "I'm confident there's any number of eligible young ladies who'd jump at the chance to become your bride."

"But not you?"

Isabella sputtered, almost spewing lemonade all over her dress. Surely William didn't have feelings for her. No, he loved Leah. She was positive. She arched a brow at him. "Dear William, please don't misunderstand me, but I just can't see us as husband and wife. You're too much like a brother for me to imagine anything else."

He chuckled, an amused smile twisting his lips. "I'm sorry, Isabella, I think I'd better start over. When you came out of mourning, Mother started making noises about my courting you." He shrugged. "I wasn't averse to the idea. We've always been friends, and I suppose it is time for me to settle down and start a family. But—"

"You have feelings for someone else."

"You—you know?"

She smiled. "Of course I do. And I couldn't be more delighted."

William's gaze narrowed, a challenging gleam in his eyes.

"How do I know that you know, or are you just fishing for information?"

"Oh, I know." Isabella nodded, laughing. "I'll set your mind at ease. I've seen the way you look at Leah."

A flush heated his face, and he sputtered out a cough. Isabella took pity on him, poured a glass of lemonade, and handed it to him.

He took a long drink. "And you're not upset about it?"

"Upset? Why would I be upset? It's not like we have romantic feelings for each other." She could never imagine letting William take the same liberties as Connor had yesterday after the race. His lips on hers, kissing her, pulling her closer. Her arms entwined about his neck, pulling *him* closer. She felt her own face heating up, grabbed her fan, and fluttered it to cool her cheeks. Thankfully, William didn't seem to notice but propped his chin on his palm, his attention on a carriage that rattled past.

"I feel like I'm betraying Jonathan somehow."

"William, Jonathan is gone, and he'd want Leah to be happy." Isabella leaned forward and placed her hand over his. "And nothing would please him more than for her to find that happiness with you."

He turned his hand up and squeezed her fingers. "Thank you. I'm glad we had this talk. It eases my mind to know that I have your blessing in this."

"Good." She grinned at him. "Now, when are you going to have a talk with Papa about Leah?"

Before daybreak, the Wainwright party was traveling northward along the trace. A light shower in the early hours before dawn settled the dust and offered a cool morning to start the journey.

But the pleasing traveling conditions didn't ease the knot of tension felt by every man in the party. Because of the delay over William's injury, several of the party had left Natchez two days ago, cutting their numbers in half.

Connor held the reins with ease but kept the flintlock close by. The space next to him on the wagon was noticeably vacant. Isabella rode in the carriage with William, along with two other ladies—a woman and her daughter—Mr. Wainwright had invited to share the ride.

Connor spotted the black top of the conveyance at the head of the column. As could be expected, all the ladies were much more comfortable in the well-sprung carriage than rattling along on a wagon seat, but still Connor missed Isabella's presence beside him.

Even though they were hardly on speaking terms.

They hadn't been alone since he'd escorted her to the dressmaker's after the race and found Toby and Jack alive and well.

Why he'd given in and tasted her lips again was beyond him. Did he have a death wish? Did he want Bartholomew to banish him from the plantation without references? Or worse, have him hanged? Had he learned nothing from his tryst with Charlotte? Nothing at all?

Isabella was better off with Wainwright now, just as she'd be in the future. His gaze jerked away from the carriage.

Master William and Isabella?

He scowled. He'd seen nothing but friendship between the two of them. The younger Wainwright had been a friend of her brother's, so it was understandable that he'd think of her as a pesky little sister. But Jonathan was gone, and Isabella was a beautiful woman and in line to inherit Breeze Hill.

Marriages had been based on far less.

And William Wainwright was a good man. A decent man. A man of Isabella's station set to inherit his father's vast plantation. The two of them would make the perfect match.

Then why did he want to punch the man right now? A man who'd stood by his side in a brawl that had almost gotten both of them killed. A man who was still weak as water and in no condition to travel, let alone defend himself in a fight.

Disgusted with himself, Connor flicked the reins to close the gap between his wagon and the one up ahead. He'd do well to concentrate on his duties this day instead of moping over his master's daughter.

By midmorning, as anticipated, the merciless sun beat down upon his head. The horses and mules plodded along, sleepy-eyed, ears drooping. Other than their sluggish forward motion, one would think the animals were almost asleep. But with each passing mile, as they drove farther along the dark wilderness road, the tension among the travelers mounted.

Even Connor, with his limited knowledge of the trace and the dangers it presented, pushed thoughts of Isabella to the back of his mind and kept his attention firmly on the shadowed foliage and steep banks on each side of the trail.

Muted conversations drifted on the breeze as Mr. Wainwright rode along the trail speaking with each driver in turn. As soon as he came abreast of Connor, he turned his mount to match the plodding pace of the draft horses.

"Don't let your guard down, man. If the devils attack, they can pick us off one by one without any effort at all."

"I understand, sir."

"The bandits usually leave us alone because our party is large enough to thwart attack, but with our numbers cut in half . . ." He trailed off, his gaze sweeping the high bluffs surrounding them, watching for an ambush. "Another reason they rarely bother us is because our pockets aren't as deep as travelers going all the way to Tennessee and Kentucky."

"Not as deep?" Connor glanced at the wagons snaking along the rugged trail.

Wainwright waved a hand at their traveling companions. "Most of these men went to Natchez to trade for supplies, not to sell goods for cash money. The Kaintucks float large flatboats of cotton, corn, pelts, and tobacco down the river to Natchez and New Orleans. Once they liquidate their assets, most times they abandon the flatboats and hike back up the trace toward home, their pockets filled with coin. Many a man has lost his life along this highway. There are some terrible men plying this stretch of road, men without an ounce of decency about them. Some even say the Harpe brothers have been in the area, but I suspect that's just hearsay."

"I've heard o' the Harpe brothers."

"Who hasn't? The very name of Big Micajah Harpe strikes fear in the heart of any traveler." Wainwright held his horse in check, his attention half on the conversation and half on the wilderness around them. "If they strike, keep your head. Under the wagon is risky at best, but it's better than remaining topside."

"Will they charge or try to pin us down?"

"You never know. It depends on how crazy they are. And how desperate." He peered at Connor from underneath the brim of his hat. "Men of this ilk have no regard for human life, not even their own most of the time. They show no mercy. If you get one of them in your sights, shoot to kill. You won't get a second chance."

Connor nodded. He'd been in similar circumstances a few times and didn't have to be told twice.

Pierre Le Bonne flattened himself on the high banks overlooking the sunken trace.

Soundlessly, his men faded into the underbrush, and within minutes, the deep forest became deathly quiet. They'd avoided Wainwright's party for the last year, preying on smaller, more easily defeated groups of travelers. But Braxton had given the go-ahead to attack today, with instructions to kill O'Shea.

Pierre wasn't surprised. Braxton had gotten a bee in his bonnet over the Irishman. Over the girl, if Pierre didn't miss his guess. And the plan suited Pierre just fine. The cocky Irishman had gotten under his skin from the very first time he'd seen him at Harper's Inn.

On a whim, he'd taken matters into his own hands when he'd spotted O'Shea and his companion entering Brice's Tavern. But unfortunately the fight hadn't gone as he'd hoped. It had been so simple, really. A crowded tavern, most of the patrons too sotted to know or care what started the melee or even who started it. A stabbing and the Irishman bleeding out on the floor. Instead, the son of one of the most influential planters in the area had taken the knife blade, and the Irishman had gotten off free as a bird.

Braxton would be livid if he knew of Pierre's involvement in the incident—and his failure.

But Braxton wouldn't find out. The miscreant who'd botched the whole affair was floating in the Mississippi River and wouldn't be telling any tales about what he'd seen or heard.

Failure grated on Pierre, and he scowled at the empty roadbed, anxious to finish what he'd started. Eliminating O'Shea had become a matter of honor, and he wouldn't fail a second time.

Whispers drew his attention.

"Silence!" he hissed.

Instead of the silence he demanded, a rustling of brush followed his order. Even before he looked, he knew that the imbecile wasn't one of his own. His men knew that when he gave an order, it was to be obeyed instantly and without question. And complete silence was the one thing he demanded. No, Turnbull had brought the fool along.

Eyes narrowed to slits, his anger barely held in check, Pierre watched the dolt settle down, getting into position as if he were building a nest and planned to lay eggs. He clenched his jaw, resisting the urge to slit the bumbling idiot's throat right there on the spot. If that one lived through today's skirmish, he wouldn't survive what Pierre did to him afterward.

His gaze slid left, and he could barely make out Turnbull's brown waistcoat in the shadows fifty feet away. The man's presence grated on his nerves like steel on flint. Braxton had foisted the uncouth slave trader on him, insisting that Turnbull and his men learn the nuances of the trace. He'd used the excuse that too many of Pierre's own men were recognizable in and around Natchez, and that one association would lead to another, then to Pierre and back to Braxton himself.

Bah! Pierre could recruit enough men to form an army if needed, and those who were no longer needed were dispatched in the same manner as the one who'd let O'Shea best him. There was always some riffraff willing to slit someone's throat for a bit of coin. And when one couldn't be found, he'd do it himself.

He glared at Turnbull, thoughts churning. Something else was afoot, and he'd do well to keep his eyes and ears open. He didn't trust Braxton, and he trusted Turnbull even less.

A faint jangle pushed thoughts of Braxton's duplicity from his mind, and Pierre froze, his attention fully focused on the job ahead. A cold, quiet calm descended, and he embraced it, holding back the excitement that wanted to rush through his veins, the flush of adrenaline that always hit him before a successful raid. There was an exquisite pleasure in the planning, in the waiting, in being patient.

Minutes ticked by as he waited for the first sight of Wainwright's party. The clink and clank of harnesses grew louder, the snort of a horse blowing hard as it pulled up an incline. Then a flicker of movement through the trees. His heart kept time with the creaking of the wheels as the first wagon rolled into sight. Like ants, lined up one after the other, the wagons kept coming.

He felt a wave of excitement roll over his compatriots.

Patience, messieurs. *Patience.*

Even as he willed his men into complete silence, complete immobility, complete invisibility, it was all he could do to remain still. Like a jockey with a horse at the starting line, he had to hold himself back to keep from charging into the middle of the group of travelers, slashing and shooting his way through to kill the man who'd insulted him.

But he'd learned that success depended on patience and perfect timing, and he'd become a master of both.

The train snaked by. Wainwright rode astride next to his fancy black carriage. From his vantage point, Pierre could see the silhouettes of several women inside. Pierre let the carriage roll on past, ignoring the riches of the fittings and the women inside.

Braxton had instructed him to leave the women alone. Pity. But Pierre knew to abide by the man's order. He'd make it worth their while to leave the women alone if the Irishman died in today's skirmish.

Chapter 23

THE MAN UP AHEAD flinched, reached back, and slapped at a horsefly on his shoulder.

Connor twitched his shoulders in sympathy. Those monsters stung, and they didn't respect man over beast. They'd draw blood from either if the opportunity arose.

Other than the jingle of harnesses, the occasional snort of a horse, and the swish-swish of tails beating off horseflies, all was quiet. The soft dirt muffled the clop of horses' hooves and well-oiled wheels rolled along nearly silent as they made slow progress toward home. Slower than usual in deference to Wainwright's injuries.

Connor hunkered down, elbows resting on his knees, his gaze rimming the edges of the loamy banks that rose high on both sides of the trail.

A small cascade of loose soil tumbled down the bank, and he jerked to attention.

He caught a glint of sunlight off metal and twisted sideways seconds before the sound of a high-pitched whine swooshed by his ear. A musket ball splintered the footrest between his boots. Even as he hauled back on the reins, the man in front of him slapped his shoulder again, but this time blood spurted through his fingers. He toppled from the wagon, hitting the ground with a thud.

Heeding Wainwright's advice, Connor jumped to the ground and rolled to safety as shots rang out all around him. He could see several wagons up ahead moving forward, hear the shouts of the drivers urging their teams out of the tight bottleneck they were trapped in. Any chance of escape was blocked by the unmanned conveyance in front of him.

Where is the carriage? Isabella?

He craned his neck, trying to see through the dust, dirt, and horses rearing in fright. There was no sign of Wainwright's carriage.

Mews and Toby were somewhere up ahead, and he prayed they could get to the women and keep them safe. He rolled to the left, stuck his pistol through a crack in the undercarriage. He squeezed off a shot, the pistol jerking violently. Before the smoke cleared, he tucked the weapon into his waistband and crab-crawled forward. A shot punched into the road to his left, spewing dirt in his face. The horses reared, pushing, pulling back, and snorting in fear.

Connor dove under the unmanned vehicle, crawling

through the flying dust. A quick glance at the driver who'd been shot revealed there was nothing more to be done for the poor soul, so Connor hauled himself up to the driver's seat, grabbed the reins, and slapped them against the horses' withers. "Hi-yah!"

The animals surged forward up the incline, Connor ducking down to avoid any shots fired at him. Bullets slammed into the wood.

Whap! Whap! Whap!

Long seconds later, he cleared the sunken roadbed into an open area. The horses needed little urging to break into a run, traveling a mile or more until he caught up with the rest of the party. Wainwright had stopped the group in a small clearing, where they were busy circling the wagons for protection.

Connor sawed on the reins to stop the wagon before it plowed into those nearest him. He spotted Wainwright shouting orders, giving instructions on forming a barrier with the wagons, putting the injured in the center, and protecting their perimeter.

Standing on the seat, he looked over the chaotic scene. Panic slammed into him with the force of a percussion ball shot at close range.

Mr. Wainwright's fancy black carriage was nowhere to be seen.

He jumped from the wagon, fell to his knees, then scrambled up. Heart pounding, he dodged around the barricaded wagons, the injured, the remaining drivers, looking for Isabella, Mews, and Toby.

"Connor." Toby ran toward him, his face leached of color, his freckles stark against his pale cheeks.

Connor grabbed the boy in a close embrace, grateful to see him uninjured. Just as quickly he set him on his feet, clasping him by the shoulders. "Where's your *da*? Is he all right?"

"There." Toby pointed toward Mews, propped against a wagon wheel. "Shot in the leg, but—but it's ju—just a flesh wound."

Connor jogged toward Mews and knelt at his side, ripping the man's breeches above the knee to see for himself. As he worked to stanch the flow of blood, he gritted out, "Where's Isabella?"

"They took the carriage. That way." Mews pointed down the winding road, then pushed Connor away. "Find her, Connor. Get her back. Toby can take care of this."

Torn between making sure that Mews would be all right and rushing off to find Isabella, Connor hovered over Mews, his hands covered in the man's blood.

"Go, man. There's not much time."

Connor gripped Mews's shoulder, then glanced at Toby. "Stay with him. Keep the pistols primed and ready."

"Yes, sir." Toby's bottom lip trembled.

"I'll be back soon as I can."

"Isabella, are you all right?" William's pain-filled gaze met hers as the carriage careened wildly around each curve, slamming them from one side to the other without mercy.

"I'm fine."

She held tight to the traveling strap with one hand, while trying to support William with the other. He held on with one hand, the other clasping his middle as the carriage tossed them to and fro. The more they jolted over the rough road, the more ashen he became. Across from her, Mrs. Wheeler's wide, terrified eyes met hers, her daughter LouAnn clinging to her, weeping hysterically.

What had happened to the rest of their party? To Toby, Mews, Connor, and Mr. Wainwright? She prayed they were all right, but there was nothing she could do for any of them at the moment.

The pace of the carriage changed, the jouncing becoming less prominent, as the man who'd shot their driver applied the brakes. "Whoa. Whoa, there!"

William straightened and awkwardly drew a pistol from his waistband with his left hand. He leaned forward, addressing Mrs. Wheeler. "Madam, when we stop, I'll try to take out the driver. You and your daughter stay back as far as you can. I'll only have one shot."

The woman nodded, holding her daughter close, trying to shush the girl.

Isabella gripped William's arm. "William, it's too dangerous. You could be killed."

"This man—this barbarian—won't hesitate to kill me—all of us—regardless." His eyes bored into hers. "Killing him first is our only hope."

Tears pricked her eyes, and Isabella searched his face, a

sick feeling in the pit of her stomach. Knowing he was right, she nodded as the carriage came to a complete stop. The only sound was LouAnn's weeping accompanied by her mother's whispered admonitions to hush. A sudden dull thump on the roof of the carriage caused the girl to yelp in terror.

"All right, ladies and gent. Come out of there, and don't try nothing foolish, or I'll blow your heads off."

The door swung open, and William's single shot blasted through the opening. Acrid smoke filled the inside of the small space as William fumbled to reload.

An answering gunshot exploded through the door, ripping a hole in the padded seat inches from the girl. LouAnn and Mrs. Wheeler screamed. Isabella blinked against the smoke rolling in the enclosed space, her ears ringing from the close proximity of both blasts.

"I said get out here now!" the outlaw screamed. "The next bullet will go through somebody's heart. Don't know whose and don't care. But somebody's gonna die soon if you don't do as I say."

There was nothing for it but to obey. Isabella lifted her skirts and exited the carriage. The outlaw grabbed her and held the gun to her head, moving to where William could see him.

"All right, mister, if you don't want me to blow her pretty little head off, you'll throw your weapons out and come out with your hands up."

Silence followed his ultimatum, but then William tossed his pistol out the door and it landed in the dirt with a thud. William followed.

"All of you, out."

Mrs. Wheeler and her daughter stepped to the roadway, clinging to each other, the mother shielding her daughter as best she could.

"You." Their captor jerked his bearded chin in William's direction. "Unhitch the horses."

Isabella wanted to protest. William wasn't up to the task, but he caught her eye and shook his head, so she kept silent. It wouldn't do any good to argue anyway. And as long as the man had a need for William, he'd keep him alive. William moved to the horses and started unbuckling the traces.

"Now, which one of you pretty little fillies am I gonna take with me?" Nuzzling Isabella's neck, the man tightened his arm like a vise around her waist, his stench almost suffocating her. Her stomach roiled in protest, and she thought she'd lose its contents right there on the spot. What would he do if she deposited her breakfast on his scuffed and dirty boots? Would he blow her head off like he'd promised?

Maybe that would be better than the alternative.

Lord, help us. She closed her eyes and concentrated on praying for help, desperately blocking out the sound of the highwayman's heavy breathing in her ear, the stench of his rancid body pressed against her back, the feel of his hard arm clutching her against him so tight she could barely breathe. Suddenly he jerked around, and clutched against his side, Isabella flopped like a trussed goose.

He pointed his gun at William. "Hurry up if you know what's good for you."

William eyed the man over the back of one of the horses. "You won't get away with this."

"Wal, looks like I already have." The highwayman laughed, an evil sound that didn't leave any doubt that he intended to kill them all.

Dear God, help us.

Isabella's gaze latched on to LouAnn. No longer crying, the girl stood within her mother's embrace, rigid, eyes glazed, staring at nothing. She had to do something to get the girl to safety. No matter what, none of them could allow this monster to take LouAnn. Unless he had more than one brace of pistols, he had only one bullet left before he'd have to reload.

She caught Mrs. Wheeler's attention and flicked a glance toward the woods, tipping her chin up a notch. Mrs. Wheeler's eyes widened, but she nodded.

William finished unhooking the horses and led them out of the traces. Isabella leaned back, trying to see the highwayman's face. "I'll go with you if you'll leave the others unharmed."

"Isabella, no—"

"Well, well, well." The man snagged her closer, a lurid grin cracking his face, showing a row of putrid, rotting teeth. "Don't look like I'll have to make a decision after all."

William stepped forward, hands held out. "If you hurt any one of these women, every decent man in these parts will be after you."

"They are already." He shrugged. "Don't matter none."

He shoved Isabella toward one of the horses, pistol cocked

and aimed at William's head. "Help her mount, and if you try anything, I'll shoot you where you stand."

Isabella knew he meant every word. She put a hand on William's arm, silently beseeching him. "Trust me," she mouthed.

He searched her expression, then relented and gave her a boost up. She hadn't ridden bareback since she was a child, but she didn't plan to be on the horse long.

She grabbed the horse's mane, dug her heels into the mare's flanks, and aimed straight at their captor, screaming with all her might.

A scream and a shot reverberated through the forest, and Connor gouged his heels into his mount's flanks.

The horse flew around one bend, then another, as he urged the animal forward, faster and faster. He rounded a bend and saw the abandoned carriage in the road. He sawed on the reins, sliding off the horse's back. He pulled his pistol, not seeing anyone.

"Isabella!"

Mr. Wainwright and another man rode up behind him.

"Frances? LouAnn? Where are you?" The man ran toward the empty carriage.

A rustling in the woods drew his attention. The two women stumbled down an embankment toward them. "George, we're here."

"Frances, are you all right?" The man gathered his

wife in his arms. The girl threw herself against her father, sobbing.

Mr. Wainwright stepped near. "Where are Miss Bartholomew and my son?"

"Father." William's faint voice reached them from the other side of the carriage.

Connor rushed toward William, the senior Wainwright close behind. William's face was covered in blood.

"William?" Mr. Wainwright sank to his knees, a tremor in his voice.

"It's not as bad as it looks." William winced. "The bullet just creased me."

"Where's Isabella?"

Cold dread snaked through Connor when William's pain-filled eyes met his.

"He took her. I tried to stop him, but—" William attempted to sit up, but Wainwright pushed him back down. "I must have blacked out—"

"Lie still. We've got to get this bleeding stopped."

"I've got to . . . go after her. I'm sorry. I tried to stop . . ." William's eyes began to glaze over.

"I'll find her."

"Go." Wainwright jerked his head, his attention on his son. "Kill that blackguard, and bring Isabella back."

Connor swung himself up on the closest mare and spurred the mount forward.

How will I ever find her?

Chapter 24

BILE ROSE in Isabella's throat.

The heartless outlaw had shot William in cold blood.

She'd taken matters into her own hands, but charging the highwayman had gone horribly wrong. He'd sidestepped, grabbed her, and jerked her off the horse, then shot William where he stood.

Everything after that was a blur. She'd been so horrified, she hadn't even resisted when he'd roughly tossed her onto the back of one of the horses, mounted another, grabbed her reins, and took off.

Oh, God. Oh, God. Oh, God.

Oh, Jonathan, is this how you felt when outlaws ambushed

you on this very road? When they shot you and left you for dead? Did you regain consciousness, knowing you were dying but unable to go for help?

Oh, God. Oh, God. Oh, God.

The prayerful litany kept time with her pounding heart, beating out a terrified rhythm.

Terrified but numb.

The man leading her away from William, Connor, Mews, and Mr. Wainwright had more in mind for her than a quick death at the end of his pistol. If a quick death had been his intention for her, he would have shot her after he shot William.

Oh, William.

She wanted to believe that he might still be alive, but the image of him falling, lying still in the ditch, blood covering his face, mocked her hope. The only blessing in this nightmare was when Mrs. Wheeler had plunged into the thick undergrowth with LouAnn as Isabella charged toward the outlaw. Isabella sent a prayer heavenward for the women's safety and clung to the horse as they careened around another sharp curve in the road. She slid sideways and tumbled off the back of the horse, grunting when her body slammed against the ground. Her mount took off, hooves pounding the dirt as it vanished around the next bend. She scrambled to her feet, grabbed at her skirts, and made a dash for the woods.

She'd taken less than a dozen running steps when her captor grabbed her by the hair and jerked her off her feet, leaving her dangling in midair against the side of his horse.

Sharp pain tore at her scalp, and tears spurted from her eyes. Gasping for breath, she clawed at the horse's mane, the saddle, trying to get a grip on something, trying to ease the excruciating pain of the vile highwayman's fingers twisted in her hair.

"I oughta slit your throat." He shook her, and she flopped like a rag doll, feet inches off the ground.

"Please." The word, barely more than a whimper, escaped her lips.

"That won't be the last time you'll beg for mercy, you little chit." He laughed, a crude, guttural sound that turned her stomach. Then he yanked her upward, tossed her over the horse's withers in front of him, the impact knocking the breath out of her. She scrabbled for a handhold, anything to keep from sliding face-first into the dirt.

Her clawing fingers encountered something cold and hard strapped to his leg.

A knife.

She slid it out of the scabbard, gripped it with both hands, and drove it with all her might into his thigh.

He roared, jerking on the reins of the horse at the same time. The animal reared, and Isabella took the opportunity to jackknife upward, the back of her head slamming into her captor's chin. The upward movement propelled them over backward, the horse screaming in fright, the highwayman spouting a string of curse words and threats.

They spilled onto the road, and she rolled away.

A roar of fury exploded from her assailant's throat, and

desperation drove Isabella. She hiked her skirts and plunged into the dark, vast wilderness.

Faster, faster, faster.

Connor's heart kept time with the horse's hooves pounding against the roadbed. He prayed Isabella's captor didn't leave the road. He prayed he found Isabella before—

No, he wouldn't let his thoughts go there. He would find her.

He rounded a bend and spotted a lathered horse, head down, munching the vegetation along the side of the road. He sawed on the reins, pulling his mount to a stop, then slid to the ground and crouched by the side of the road, watching.

The horse continued to pull clumps of grass, meandering along the road. Connor stayed in the shadows and circled around, looking for Isabella or her captor. When he'd made a full circle and found nothing, he paused. It was obvious Isabella and the highwayman were long gone, but why would they leave the horse?

Had Isabella somehow gotten away? And what of the other horse?

As Connor approached the draft animal, she shied away.

"Whoa." He reached out a hand to soothe the mare, and his palm came away covered in blood.

Isabella's?

Please, God, no.

Connor rubbed the sticky red substance between his fingers, his gaze taking in the surrounding area. A steep bank bordered one side of the trail, so it stood to reason that if Isabella managed to get away, she wouldn't attempt to climb the bank.

Connor wasn't much of a tracker, but he was a woodsman, and he could spot a broken limb, scuffed ground cover, or scattered leaves better than most. Yet if the man who'd taken Isabella had any skills at all in the woods, he'd find her before Connor did.

Methodically he searched for signs. The only way he'd find Isabella was to locate her trail and keep a clear head. Running off half-cocked wouldn't do her any good.

As he searched, a cool breeze ruffled the treetops, and clouds rolled in from the west. Frowning, he glanced at the sky. Rain might keep Isabella safe from her pursuer, but it would also make it almost impossible for Connor to track her.

Finally he found evidence where she'd left the roadway. He plunged into the wilderness, praying he wasn't too late.

Nolan waited an hour; then, along with half a dozen recently purchased slaves and a dozen men from Braxton Hall, he rode along the trace to join Wainwright's caravan.

He'd met with Governor Gayoso while in Natchez. Nolan was in his element making small talk with the Spanish governor. Miss Watts had been in attendance, and she'd been fascinated with his knowledge of the arts, the theater, and London's latest scandal.

If he didn't miss his guess, Miss Watts would soon be the next First Lady of the Spanish Natchez District, and being one of her favored guests would put him in good stead with the governor.

He'd even dropped hints of his impending marriage, much to Miss Watts's delight. By the time the weather cooled and Natchez became a hotbed of parties and soirees, he'd have Isabella Bartholomew on his arm, a bride sure to impress the Spanish governor and his American lady.

Today's skirmish was just one step toward his goal.

The closer he rode toward where Le Bonne had attacked the Wainwright party, the more anxious he became. Surely Le Bonne had been successful and the Irishman was dead.

He smiled, visualizing his arrival at the chaotic scene.

He'd order his men and the slaves to help with the wounded, bury the dead, while he consoled Isabella.

Nolan pondered his newfound infatuation with the woman. It wasn't his nature to care overmuch about anyone. He supposed he could blame his mother for that. She hadn't been much of a mother by anyone's standards. She'd been an actress in London, pursuing a career onstage with her eye on making a match above her station.

As alike as two peas in a pod, his father also had an eye on the same, but the two had ended up with each other and with him. The following years had been good, with the two of them fleecing many a lord and lady with their charm and good looks.

But they'd gotten greedy and careless, and his mother's looks had begun to fade. After an unfortunate incident where they'd been caught red-handed in some scheme, they'd been shipped off to the New World with Nolan in tow, each blaming the other for their misfortune. His father had died aboard ship along with many others, including Mrs. Nolan Braxton II, a woman of aristocratic bearing, en route to join her husband at their new plantation home in the Natchez District.

A testament to her acting abilities, Nolan's mother had moved into the woman's stateroom, taken over her identity, and created a whole new life for herself and her son. One that included a plantation where Nolan Braxton II had also passed away and none of the servants had ever met the mistress of the house.

He and his mother had just walked in and taken over Braxton Hall and no one had been the wiser. That had been over fifteen years ago.

She might not have been much of a mother, but she'd proven her worth as a dramatic actress when she'd pulled off the coup of a lifetime.

A coup that had set Nolan up for life. Except that the life of a gentleman farmer's wife didn't hold enough excitement or coin for his mother. When she'd seen the wealth that flowed along the Natchez Trace, she'd put her acting talents into place and started a whole new life of crime.

Nolan's lip curled. His mother's greed would have ruined him if not for her untimely death. While the neighboring plantation owners had come to pay their respects upon her death seven years ago, Nolan had been relieved that she was gone.

It was only a matter of time before her unorthodox

methods would have exposed them for the frauds they were. If Nolan had learned anything from his parents' mistakes, it was to keep his role as gentleman farmer completely separate from his role as highwayman.

But now all that was about to change.

With the ownership of both Braxton Hall and Breeze Hill, a wife of Spanish descent, and a political appointment from the Spanish governor, his dreams of a respectable life would be realized. He could completely cut ties with the rough underworld and embrace the aristocracy that was his due.

Nolan and his men rounded a bend and came face-to-face with the aftermath of the attack on Wainwright's party. A warning shot rang out, coming too close for comfort, and Nolan jerked his mount to the side, a fierce glare aimed at the man who'd fired the shot.

"Halt! Who goes there?"

"Nolan Braxton, owner of Braxton Hall." Nolan schooled his features into one of shocked concern, choosing to overlook the near-fatal accident. "Is this the Wainwright party? Have you been attacked?"

"Lower your weapons, men." Wainwright strode forward, hand outstretched. "Braxton, am I glad to see you!"

The man who'd fired the shot looked sheepish. "Sorry, sir. I thought the outlaws had circled around and were attacking from the rear."

"Is everyone all right?" Nolan dismounted, clasped Wainwright by the arm, and shook his outstretched hand. "Isabella? Tell me she's unharmed."

Wainwright's gaze met his. "I'm sorry, but she's gone."

"Gone?" Nolan froze, not sure he'd heard correctly. "What do you mean by *gone*?"

"One of the blackguards shot William and took her." Wainwright motioned to a black carriage nearby where Isabella's overseer and his whelp hovered over the younger Wainwright. "We're heading for Breeze—"

"Took her?" Nolan's grip tightened on Wainwright's arm. "By God, man, what do you mean, he took her?"

"Kidnapped her and took off with her." Wainwright's jaw hardened. "Connor O'Shea, her indentured servant, has gone after her."

Nolan's blood chilled.

Not only had Pierre and Turnbull failed to kill the Irishman, they'd allowed some foul imbecile to make off with Isabella.

The fools!

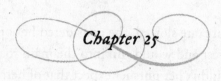

Chapter 25

ISABELLA RAN, briars and brambles tearing at her skirts.

Finally she could run no more. She stopped beneath a large pine, gasping for air. As she caught her breath, the forest sounds loomed loud. The creak of a twig, the thump of a pinecone falling set her heart to racing all over again.

A crashing noise to her right had her scrambling away, looking for a place to hide. A scream lodged in her throat when she spotted movement, and she backed away. The bushes shook; a deer leapt from the wild tangle of brush and bounded off, tail alert. A massive tree loomed in front of her, and she crouched at its base, heart pounding.

After the deer's flight, all was quiet. No birds chirped, no leaves rustled. Not even a breeze stirred the oppressive air beneath the thick canopy. Sweat dampened her dress, and the fabric clung to her, sticky and hot. Her stomach roiled. She was lost in this wilderness with a killer after her.

Think. She had to think. She had to be still if she was to survive.

As her heart rate slowed, she considered her options. She could head west and would run into the main road. But did she dare? Wouldn't her pursuer expect that of her? Or was he out there right now, watching her, waiting to pounce like a barn cat toying with a mouse?

She shuddered.

What had happened to Connor, Mews, Toby, and the others? Were they all dead?

Please, God, no. Please, Lord, keep them safe. She suppressed a sob. *And William. Lord, please have mercy on William. Let him live. Let him—*

Guilt filled her as desperate prayers shot through her frantic thoughts. She'd shied away from truly seeking God's help, blaming Him for Jonathan's death and the misfortune that had befallen her family. How foolish. God never promised her that she wouldn't have trials and tribulations. He'd never promised a life of ease, not to her or anybody else who trusted in Him.

But He had promised life eternal, and she could cling to that. She *must* cling to that because the odds of her making it out of this alive were unlikely.

The chirping of birds penetrated her consciousness, and a tiny rustling in the leaves revealed that the animals were stirring again. Her headlong flight and that of the deer had silenced them for a brief span of time, but no longer.

She'd never had to know how to move in the wilderness, but she'd heard the men talk. If she was to stay alive, she'd have to move as slowly and quietly as possible.

Please, Lord, give me strength. Give me courage.

With the Lord's help, she would survive.

Clouds rolled in, dimming the sun but doing little to ease the humidity on the ground. With the trees and the clouds obscuring the sun, she had no way of knowing which way was north. But she had to move. Taking a chance, she crouched and eased deeper into the wilderness, hoping to find a creek soon. She'd go upstream, away from the trace. A niggling in the back of her mind warned that upstream could lead deeper into the untamed wilderness, away from civilization and help. But to go back the way she'd come would lead her into the highwayman's snare.

Cold dread snaked down her spine. She'd take her chances in the wilderness.

As she stumbled through the forest, the sky grew darker, the trees swaying as the storm clouds moved closer.

What seemed like an eternity later, she stopped, slumped against a tree, and attempted to get her bearings. Her skirts clung to her legs, cloying and suffocating. She hiked her skirts and ripped off one of her petticoats. Eyeing the ripped and torn garment, she tossed it to the ground, flipped up her skirts again, and stripped off another one.

The relief would be short-lived, but maybe she'd be able to move easier without the weight of so many garments swishing around her limbs. At home, she didn't wear so many layers, but custom demanded that she look presentable in Natchez and while traveling.

She bit back a hysterical laugh, glancing at the heap of muslin on the ground. Who cared if she had on three petticoats out here?

A twig snapped from somewhere off to her left.

She froze in place, her heart thudding so hard her chest ached.

Had he found her?

The forest fell silent, or maybe she just no longer heard the melodious sounds of the birds singing over the blood pumping through her veins.

She caught a whiff of something foreign on the breeze—woodsmoke, leather, male—and did the only thing she knew to do.

She ran.

In a blur, a form blocked her path. In the fraction of a second before she plowed into the man's broad chest, his battered cotton shirt with laces dangling flashed across her vision. She collided with her captor, a scream of terror clawing its way from the back of her throat to her lips.

Bands of steel wrapped around her and she was swept against the hard length of a man's body, his arms circling her waist and lifting her off the ground.

"Shh, it's all right. I've got you. I'm here."

The scream on her lips died to a whimper.

Connor had come for her. He'd found her.

Thank You, Jesus.

Connor relaxed his hold, and she tilted her face to his. One long welt graced his cheek, and streaks of grime and sweat covered his face, but his eyes glittered, the color of the forest surrounding them.

He was the most beautiful sight she'd ever seen.

She threw her arms around his neck and held on, gut-wrenching sobs pouring out of her like water from a busted barrel. He hugged her close. As long as Connor held her, she'd be safe. She didn't think she'd ever let him go.

"That man . . . he's . . . he's out there," she whispered.

"I know, lass."

He loosened his hold, and she slid down his length, her feet touching the ground. One hand cupped her chin, turned her face up to his. His jaw—nay, his entire body—clenched tighter than a coiled rattler.

"Are ya hurt?" His gaze took in the scattered petticoats, and his face blanched white. "My God, did he . . . ?"

The heat of shame rushed to her cheeks when she realized what he was asking.

"No," she whispered, barely able to expel the word. "No, I am not hurt."

Time stood still as his gaze searched hers. Finally, as if accepting the truth of her statement, he nodded.

"You're shaking." His hands roved up and down her arms. "It's the shock."

"He . . . he shot William." She remembered the sound of the bullet slamming into William, her scream. The blood.

Nausea rolled through her. "His head . . . blood. So much blood. He died trying to save me."

Hands on her shoulders, Connor forced her to look at him. "William's alive."

"Alive?" Her heart leapt with hope, and she clutched Connor's shirt.

"Yes. Wainwright is taking him to Breeze Hill. We'll meet them there."

"And Mrs. Wheeler and LouAnn? Mews? Toby?"

"All safe and sound. At least they were when I left." He pulled out a flask and tipped it against her lips. Isabella gulped the water before he withheld the flask.

"Enough for now. Come on, let's go." Connor grabbed the discarded petticoats, twisted them together, and tied them with a piece of string. His gaze swept the sky, darker than before. "Pray for rain to cover our tracks. Hopefully our man isn't much of a tracker."

He took her by the hand and led her deeper into the forest.

Isabella stumbled to keep up with him, her skirt snagging on branches and thorns, shredding it to bits. But she no longer cared.

Connor had found her, and he would get them out of this mess.

Connor followed the sound of running water.

A major tributary would run into a larger body of water and would cross the main road at some point. They'd be heading away from Breeze Hill, but if they could make it to Mount Locust or even back to Natchez, they'd have a better chance than roaming around in the woods. Once they made it back to the trace, they might even find the horses.

Still, did he dare risk running into Isabella's assailant?

What other choice did they have? There was nothing but wilderness, swamps, and no-man's-land to the east and a storm brewing in the west.

They drew closer to the waterway, the sound growing louder. They walked out from the trees onto a high bank, looking down on the stream. The water flowed fast through a narrow channel cut into the soft, loamy dirt.

"We'll go downstream a ways, try to find a place to cross."

"Home should be that way." Isabella pointed in a north-easterly direction.

Connor paused. Her internal compass was a bit off, enough that she'd be traipsing into an uninhabited wilderness if she'd been alone. His chest tightened at the thought of her heading northeast never to be heard from again. "You don't know what direction the tributary goes if you head that way. If we cross, then follow it downstream, we'll find familiar territory."

"But what about the men who ambushed us?" Her eyes were wide, luminous and terrified.

"We'll just have to take our chances." Connor moved to her side, cupped her face in his hands. "Do you trust me?"

"I do."

Connor dipped his head, giving in to the desire for a taste

of her one more time. Her lips were soft, warm, and pliable. He snaked an arm around her waist and pulled her closer, reveling in the feel of her slender frame pressed against his.

Slowly he lifted his head, like a man awakening from a deep sleep on a hot, muggy afternoon. Her lashes swept up, and her eyes, softened with the wonder of his kiss, met his. Her lips, moist from the pressure of his, parted.

He sucked in a breath as the truth hit him with the force of a felled tree slamming against the forest floor.

He loved her.

And it was the love of a man grown, not the infatuation he'd felt for Charlotte Young so many years ago.

His thumb moved over her cheekbone, and a tempting smile turned up the corners of her mouth. He'd fought this attraction to Isabella since the day he'd met her, but she'd woven a spell around his heart that he could no longer deny. What he would do about it was another matter altogether, and one best left to ponder after he got her back to her father.

One last sweep of his thumb across her cheek, and he dropped his hand, stepping away.

"We'd better go." His gaze swept the sky. "We need to find shelter before it starts raining."

Isabella felt cherished and protected.

Regardless of the fact that she and Connor were trekking through the hot, muggy wilderness, lost.

No, not lost.

Connor had found her out here in the middle of nowhere. He could get them home. Back to safety. She really did trust him. With her entire being.

Her heart swelled with gratitude. She paused, her gaze lingering on his broad shoulders as he slashed through the vines barring their way, creating a path through the woods where none existed. Really, there was no need to pretend. The feelings she had for Connor weren't just gratitude. She loved him.

Now she understood why her father and mother had bucked custom to marry, why Jonathan had chosen Leah, whose aunt had been a washerwoman in Natchez, why Mr. Horne and his wife endured the ridicule of others.

All because of the love they had for each other.

Surely she and Connor could overcome any obstacles to their love, couldn't they?

Even the first few drops of rain that plopped down through the trees didn't dampen her mood. Lost in her daydreams, Isabella bumped into Connor when he stopped on a high bluff overlooking the water. He glanced at her. "Are you all right?"

She nodded and gave him a tentative smile. No need in letting him know that while he'd been fighting his way through the thick undergrowth, she'd been happily following in his wake planning their future. "I'm fine."

A quizzical look crossed his face; then he turned back to survey the swift current.

"We can't cross here. We'll keep going—" Connor broke off as a covey of birds took flight. He grabbed Isabella's wrist and crouched down, pulling her with him.

She dropped to her knees, heart pounding. "What—?"

He put a finger to his lips.

They waited in the shadows, listening. Other than the drizzle of rain against the leaves and the roll of thunder in the distance, everything was quiet.

"Stay." Connor inched forward.

Isabella reached out, touched his arm. His eyes met hers, and she poured her feelings into that one glance. He squeezed her hand and gave her a lopsided smile meant to reassure her.

He moved away, keeping low to the ground. Isabella eased into the undergrowth, watching his progress, her gaze darting from bush to bush, from tree to tree, worry causing her to see bandits where there were none. Every shadowy shape turned into a frightening specter intent on murdering Connor and then coming after her. All too soon, he disappeared into the foliage, and she barely resisted the urge to call him back.

Lord, keep him safe.

The rain fell harder, and still she waited, crouched in the shadows. She had to be strong. Panicking now would get them nowhere. Her heart slammed against her rib cage when she spotted something moving to her left. Another deer? Or a man? Remaining motionless, she squinted.

There!

A man. Definitely a man. Moving stealthily toward Connor, the rain masking any sound of his movements.

She caught the glint of a pistol.

"Connor!"

Chapter 26

Connor launched himself sideways as Isabella's scream coincided with a boom of thunder and the sound of a misfired weapon.

Fast on the heels of the first attempt, a second shot peeled bark off the tree behind him. Taking a chance that the man would have to reload, Connor palmed his knife and plowed through the undergrowth toward his assailant.

He broke from cover, the rain falling steadily. Less than ten feet away, he spotted the highwayman, knife in hand, lumbering toward Isabella with a slight hitch in his gait. She swung a half-rotten tree branch, the effort puny in the face of the knife he wielded. With a primal growl, Connor threw his own knife. The blade glanced off the man's shoulder, and he turned, coming at Connor.

Connor jumped back, reaching for the extra knife in his boot.

For the first time, he got a good look at the man who had taken Isabella. Greasy buckskins covered his body, and long, stringy hair hung past his shoulders. A multitude of scars crisscrossed the haggard map of his face. He grinned, looking half-wild, the rain running in rivulets down his face, into his beard, and sluicing off his buckskins.

Connor gripped the knife in his hand, weighing his odds. From the looks of the outlaw, he knew how to fight, or he'd be dead already.

"I'll do you in, and after that I'll take care of your woman." The bandit made slashing motions with his knife, then lunged forward, striking at Connor, missing by inches. "How do you like that?"

Connor ignored the verbal jabs, saving his energy and his wits for the fight ahead. He made a quick jab and jumped back as the man took another swipe at him. White-hot pain lanced his forearm as the blade sliced a three-inch gash.

He slashed downward, clipping his opponent's knife with the tip of his. The knife went flying over the side of the bluff. With a roar of rage, the outlaw grabbed a piece of deadwood and swung at Connor. Connor jumped back, crouched, and circled, watching for a chance to end this once and for all.

Out of the corner of his eye, he saw Isabella rush forward, her club raised. Before he could yell at her to stay away, she swung. The highwayman pivoted, swinging his own weapon at her, the blow connecting with her shoulder. Her feet slipped on the wet leaves. One moment she was teetering on the bank, arms windmilling; the next, she lost her footing and plunged over the cliff, her scream tearing at Connor's insides.

He heard the splash as she hit the water.

The bandit turned, a wicked grin on his face.

Connor drew back and threw his knife. Not taking the time to see if his aim was true, he took a running leap and launched himself over the edge of the bluff. He hit the water, drew in his legs, and went down, down, until his feet hit the bottom. He kicked off, giving himself momentum to shoot back up. He broke the surface, and the water swept him downstream. He spotted Isabella several feet away, fighting the current. Then she went under, the weight of her skirts pulling her down.

Connor sucked in a deep breath and dove downward but couldn't find her. When he surfaced, he spotted her once again.

"Isabella!"

She tried to turn toward him, but then the force of the current pulled her under again. Connor knew this was his last chance. He dove forward, down, aiming for where he'd last seen her.

His grasping fingers caught hold of a flutter of cloth, and he tugged, tangling his fingers in the material, pulling, grappling, hoping, praying, all in one second of desperation. Then he got a firm hold on her, pushed off from the bottom of the creek bed, and broke the surface. Isabella lay limp in his arms, no longer fighting.

The rushing current carried them past sheer banks that would be impossible to scale. Connor rode the current, half-swimming with one arm, keeping Isabella afloat with the other. Rain fell in sheets and lightning flashed overhead. He'd almost given up hope when he spotted a sandbar. With the last of his strength, he kicked toward it. His feet hit bottom, and he renewed his efforts, dragging both himself and Isabella clear of the current.

The two of them fell across a half-submerged log, and he lay there gasping for breath. Isabella lay limp as a rag doll. He crawled to her and lifted her in his arms, pounding on her back, her stomach, trying to expel the water she'd swallowed or inhaled.

Suddenly she threw up, liquid gushing out of her mouth and nose.

He held her as she purged herself of the foul swill, thankful she was alive.

"Isabella?"

Her lashes, dark and spiked, feathered against her cheeks, and her full lips were parted as her head lolled against his arm, but she didn't respond. He smoothed back her hair, his hands trembling as he watched for signs of life. Her chest rose and fell with the rhythm of her breathing.

She moaned, then coughed again. Connor held her close, his gaze sweeping the tributary, the high banks barely visible through the rain. Had his aim been true? Was the highwayman dead? If he'd survived the knife, Connor prayed the idea of crossing the fast-flowing stream would deter him. But he couldn't take the chance. He gathered Isabella close and staggered away from the water's edge.

He left her in the shadows, took a brush top, and swept away the evidence of their passing. Even as he did so, the rain pounded the sandbar smooth as if they'd never been there.

He hurried to Isabella's side, picked her up, and plunged into the underbrush.

Isabella opened her eyes to darkness, save a small campfire. Woodsmoke hung in the air, along with the clean, soft scent of rain.

She lay on a bed of pine needles covered with furs, a quilt spread over her. Some kind of canopy stretched overhead, creating a makeshift lean-to. Even now, she could hear an occasional plop as water dripped against the top of the canvas. She heard voices, turned her head, and saw a clearing dotted with small campfires, protected against the rain with more lean-tos, tents, and wagons.

"You're awake." Connor crouched at her side, the space under the canopy hardly big enough to accommodate his sizable frame.

"How . . . ?" She swallowed, her throat burning. "Where are we?"

"On the main road." He fed the fire with a few more large sticks. "How do you feel, lass?"

"Like I've had the ague. How did we get here? I don't remember anything after falling in the water." Everything came back in full force. She closed her eyes and shuddered. "That man . . ."

"You're safe. He can't hurt you here."

Her hand rested on her stomach, her thin chemise the only thing between her fingers and her skin. Her gaze jerked to Connor's even as her face flamed. "Where are my clothes?"

"Easy, lass." He hooked a thumb over his shoulder. "There's a couple o' women in this caravan, and they helped you out of your wet clothes. They've got stew simmering over the fire if you're hungry."

Her stomach rumbled as the scent of cooking meat and vegetables registered. She hadn't eaten since . . . she couldn't remember when. Sometime before they'd left Natchez. Was it only this morning? It seemed like a lifetime.

"Yes, please."

Connor moved toward the open side of the lean-to.

"Wait." She bit her lip and inched away from the edge of the canvas, jittery with the thoughts of the men who'd attacked their party. "Do you think he's still after us?"

Connor shook his head. "If he's still alive, he wouldn't try to hurt you among so many."

She wanted to believe him. But every time she closed her eyes, all she could see was that man shooting William, grabbing her by the hair, and tossing her on the back of one of the draft horses, then the nightmare minutes, hours that followed until Connor found her.

"Don't leave me."

"I'll only be a minute. Just over there." Connor waited, his expression filled with concern.

"All right." Getting a grip on her fear, she pulled the quilt closer. "Where are my clothes? I'd like to get dressed now."

He motioned to a pine bough behind her, protected by the canopy over her head. Her dress, ripped and tattered, draped over the limb. "It's mostly dry. Do you need assistance? I can fetch someone."

"No. I can manage."

"I'll round up some o' that stew, then."

He flipped a piece of canvas down over the front of her shelter, giving her a measure of privacy. Still, she could see glimmers of the campfires spread out before her, hear the faint sounds of conversation as the other travelers settled in for the night. She fumbled with her clothes, dressing as quickly as she could while lying semi-prone under the lean-to.

It wasn't an easy task, but she managed it, feeling like a weak kitten by the time she was done. She leaned back against the furs, eyes closed, trying to catch her breath.

"Are ya decent, lass?"

Her eyes popped open. Heart pounding, she pulled the quilt up to her chin. She must have dozed off again. "Yes."

Connor raised the canvas, a bowl of stew in one hand. Her mouth watered. Struggling to a sitting position, she leaned against the large pine tree that formed the back of the shelter. "I can't believe I'm so weak."

"Ya almost drowned, lass. That can take a lot out o' a

body. You'll feel better after you've eaten and had a good night's rest."

Isabella took a bite of the stew, and Connor moved away, putting distance between them in the small space. She quickly consumed the small bowl of stew and set it to the side. Leaning her head back against the pine, she watched Connor. He hunkered near the fire, poking it with a stick. The flickering flames cast his profile into stark relief.

His brown hair fell across his brow, wild and unfettered. Her fingers itched to smooth the strands back, to . . .

To do what? To declare her love? To wring promises of the same from him? Yes, that's what she wanted. She loved him with all of her being. And she knew that he loved her, too. He'd risked his life for her. He'd thrown caution to the wind and followed her captor into the wilderness to get her back. He'd carried her to safety.

And deep in the forest when they'd been battling for their lives, he'd held her in his arms and kissed her. And the memory of the desperation in his kiss haunted her.

But he hadn't said he loved her. Then again, neither had she. The time hadn't been right for words, only actions, reactions, feelings, and honesty of the heart, not of the head.

He turned, caught her staring, then motioned to the empty bowl. "Would you like some more?"

"No thank you. One bowl is enough."

Connor stood, stalked toward the lean-to, stooped, and held out his hand for the bowl. She searched his face, but he didn't meet her eyes. Disappointed, she handed the bowl over, and he moved away. "It's stopped raining. I'm going to gather a bit o' wood for later in the night."

Isabella resisted the urge to call him back. He vanished into the night, and she scooted to the rear of the lean-to, pressing against the pine tree, staring at the campfires ringing the clearing. Was Connor right? What would stop the highwaymen from attacking this party as they'd attacked the Wainwright party?

Movement across the way caught her attention as the shadowy form of a man stood and walked away from his campfire. Her heart lodged in her throat when he crossed the clearing and disappeared into the woods not far from her lean-to.

The intermittent plop of rainwater against the canopy became more frequent as it started raining again. Isabella burrowed deeper into the furs, waiting and watching. Where was Connor? What was taking him so long?

A clatter beside the lean-to had her scrambling toward the light cast by the fire. She barreled straight into Connor as he ducked under the canopy.

"Whoa." He grabbed her shoulders, his brow furrowed with concern. "What's wrong?"

Her face heated when she spotted the firewood he'd dropped on the ground. "You startled me."

"Sorry about that." He let her go, and she swayed on her feet. He urged her back under the shelter out of the rain. "You'd better sit. You're too weak to stand."

She bit her lip and glanced up at him. "Will you be here all night, standing guard like you did at the inn?"

A tiny smile tilted up one corner of his mouth, and he chuckled. "All night, mistress."

As he helped her to the bed of furs, she sighed. His face, shadowed by a daylong stubble, hovered over hers, his concern making her stomach do more backflips. "Why do you call me mistress?"

He studied her; then he let her go and moved away, even though there wasn't much room in the small shelter. If she wanted, she could reach out and touch him.

And she wanted. But she didn't dare.

"Connor?"

She heard a long-suffering sigh in the semidarkness. "Because you are the mistress o' the house."

"But you call me Isabella, too."

"It's a slip o' the tongue, that's all."

"I give you leave to use my given name," she whispered.

His eyes glittered in the firelight, flitting to her lips before catching and holding her gaze. "And you see where such familiarity has gotten us so far."

"Where?"

Instead of answering her with words, he growled low in his throat, then swooped down, his lips claiming hers. Heart pounding at the ferociousness of his kiss, Isabella wrapped her arms around his neck and pulled him closer, reveling in the taste of his lips on hers. A low moan escaped his mouth, and a thrill of pleasure shot through her. He longed for her and her only. And she for him.

Like a meteor shower on a hot summer night, the

realization burst across the landscape of her mind that she wanted to spend the rest of her life with this man, not with any other. Somehow they'd find a way to be together.

Another groan tore from his throat, and he broke away, his chest heaving as he stared down at her. Isabella cupped his face, loving the feel of his jaw, warm against her fingers. He closed his eyes and leaned into her touch. His lips brushed the palm of her hand, and shivers of delight arched through her. "Connor, I love—"

"No." His eyes flew open, glittering with something other than the passionate kiss they'd just shared. "Don't be sayin' that."

"Why not?" She reached to caress his face, and he jerked away. She persisted. "It's—it's true."

"You know nothing of love." He scowled, untangled her arms from around his neck, and backed away.

A coldness settled over her, having nothing to do with the dampness brought on by the rain. "And what do you know of love, Connor O'Shea? You've already determined that these feelings I have for you are nothing. What of your feelings for me? Tell me they're nothing."

"I won't deny that I have feelings for ya, mistress. But nothing good can come from it."

Hot tears pricked her eyes even as sorrow pierced her heart. "Why? Why do you say that?"

"I'm a servant, lass." He leaned down, his face inches from hers. "That's all I am."

"No, Connor, don't say that." She rose up on her knees,

one hand against the rough cotton of his shirt. "You're not just a servant. America is different from Ireland. You can be anyone you want, become anything you want."

"That may be true, but right now I'm a servant, and you're the daughter of the master of the house. You'll marry someone like Braxton or Wainwright and produce heirs to carry on the legacy of both plantations. Tell me I'm not right."

Isabella's mouth opened and closed like that of a fish tossed up on the shore, gasping for breath. How could he know her thoughts so clearly? How could he know she'd once mapped out her life to do exactly as he'd said?

That was, until she'd lost her heart to an indentured servant determined to stay in his place.

"You're wrong." Isabella lifted her chin, glaring at him. "I can marry anyone I choose."

It was all Connor could do not to throw caution to the wind and gather her in his arms again. But it would do no good. She didn't know what she was talking about. Neither of them had much choice in whom they would marry. How could he make her see that?

"Believe that if you wish, lass, but when the time comes, you'll do whatever it takes to save your family's land."

"You don't know me, and you don't know my father."

"I know how the landed gentry—the upper crust—operate."

"Ha!" She threw her arms out to encompass the crude shelter. "As if my father and I are part of the upper crust.

Has it occurred to you that we're barely making ends meet at Breeze Hill?"

"It's not about how much you own, but your position in society, lass. And your position and mine are too far apart. Just trust me on this."

"I know you're being honorable, Connor, but—"

He snorted. "There's more to it than being honorable."

He'd spent the last eight years being honorable, making a vow to God and to himself that he'd avoid women above his station. As a bonded journeyman to Master Benson, he'd been forbidden to court, to take a wife. And when Benson had given him liberty to do so, he'd had little time, money, or desire for the company of women. Being shipped half a world away from family over the whims of a woman like Charlotte made a man think twice before becoming embroiled in affairs of the heart.

But that was before he'd met Isabella.

"Tell me, then. Tell me why you keep pushing me away."

Connor clenched his jaw, picked up a stick, and poked at the fire. Maybe if she knew the truth, she'd leave him be.

"Her name was Charlotte. Like you, she was the master's daughter. She was young and beautiful and could have any man she wanted. And she wanted me, nothing more than a stable lad. I was young and foolish and thought I had the world at my feet. But it all came crashing down the day her father made arrangements for her t' wed an English baron's son. It was an advantageous marriage, he said. And Charlotte agreed. She laughed in my face when I asked her t' run away with me, t' be me bride. The next thing I knew, I was bound for the colonies, courtesy o' Charlotte's father, who didn't want anything or anyone t' besmirch his daughter's good name." Connor laughed, the clipped sound completely devoid of amusement. "It was better than the hangman's noose that he first suggested."

Connor glanced up, caught Isabella's stunned expression. He inclined his head stiffly, holding on to his heart with just as much rigidity.

"So forgive me, mistress, if I'm no' wantin' t' be caught in the same sticky trap again."

Chapter 27

TIRED, IRRITABLE, and just plain angry at the world, Connor jounced along in the back of a farm wagon on the way to Breeze Hill.

The caravan plodded along slowly, the pace chafing on his nerves. And he could tell by the way Isabella fidgeted with the shawl loaned to her by one of the other women that she was anxious to get to Breeze Hill as well.

And who wouldn't be?

Her father, Leah, and the Wainwrights would be worried sick. He frowned. He hoped Mews and William had fared well from their injuries.

Eyes at half-mast, the jostling of the wagon and the heat of the day nearly lulling him to sleep, Connor watched Isabella. She'd said she loved him. He scowled. She didn't know the first thing about love.

He was a nobody from Ireland, and her father had carved a living out of the wilderness in the Natchez District. He'd want his only child to marry another plantation heir and build on what he'd made for himself.

Somehow Connor had to convince her that he was no good for her, and the best way to do that was to get her safely married off. And William Wainwright seemed the logical choice. Somebody that Connor could stomach without wanting to rip his head off for looking at Isabella. She could do a lot worse than William as a husband. William would be heir to his father's plantation, and the Wainwrights seemed like honest, hardworking men.

If Connor could steer her affections toward William, the pain that would come his way when she realized she was only infatuated with him would be easier to bear.

It was midafternoon by the time they reached the cutoff that led to Breeze Hill.

Isabella passed word to the leader of the caravan that they could find food, water, and safe lodgings for the night. The travelers were grateful, and Isabella was indebted to them for their protection and provision throughout the day and the night before. She shuddered at what might have happened to Connor and herself if he hadn't stumbled on their camp.

She champed at the bit to borrow a horse and ride on ahead. But her impatience had to be endured for a bit longer as there wasn't an extra horse to be had.

Connor sat in the opposite corner of the wagon on top of a bag of ground meal. They hadn't spoken much throughout the day, but it was hard to carry on a conversation as their driver, a grizzled old man, had kept up a monologue most of the day. He slapped the reins against the backs of the horses. "It won't be long now, missy. I hope your friends are all right, what with them highwaymen attacking them. A shame, a downright shame, what this world is coming to."

"Thank you." She grimaced. "The trip to Natchez was my idea."

Connor glanced at her. "You and your father did what you thought was right."

"But I keep thinking that there's a better way than traveling to Natchez every fortnight and risking someone's life."

The driver spat a stream of tobacco juice over the side of the wagon. "If the law-abiding citizens scurry to their homes and plantations every time there's a little set-to, these outlaws will take over this country. The only way to take it back is to go about our business. Ain't none of us will survive if we let 'em run roughshod over us."

Connor nodded. "He's right."

"I know." She faced forward again, the long, winding road that led home stretching out before her, her thoughts on the cold, lonely grave in the family plot. "But it doesn't make it any easier when you bury friends and family."

Just a few more minutes, and they reached the plantation. Wagons and horses milled about the yard, blocking Isabella's view of the porch.

When the wagon stopped rolling, Connor jumped out, reached up, and helped her down. As soon as her feet hit the earth, Isabella lifted her tattered skirts and hurried toward the house. Tears gathered in her eyes as she spotted her father, Mews, Toby, and Mr. Wainwright standing near the porch.

"Papa."

A grimace that only those who knew him well would recognize as a joyous smile lit up his face. He hurried toward her, his gait halting.

His hug was fierce and stronger than it had been in weeks. He pulled away and cupped her face in his gnarled hands, tears shimmering in his eyes. "We were gathering a search party. I was afraid I'd lost you—"

"I'm safe." She gripped his hands. "How's William?"

"The lad's hurt pretty bad, but he's still holding on. Time will tell."

His attention shifted, moved past her to where Connor waited. Her father stepped forward, grasped him by the arms. "I owe you a debt of gratitude that nothing will ever repay, Connor. Thank you for saving my daughter's life."

Connor nodded.

Her father turned to the leader of the caravan. "We don't have much, but what we have is yours. You're welcome to stay as long as you desire."

"One night will be sufficient, sir. All we require is water for our animals and a place to bed down for the night."

"You shall have it. Toby, show them where to go."

Isabella's father wrapped his arm around her and led her toward the porch, where Leah waited with Martha and Susan. As Leah gathered Isabella in her arms, she saw Nolan standing in the shadows, jaw tense.

She followed his line of sight to where Connor walked along the path toward the sawmill.

Connor barely had time to change into a clean shirt and breeches before Mr. Bartholomew sent for him. He stood, feet braced apart, blood boiling.

Restraining himself, he focused on a knothole in the paneled wall of Mr. Bartholomew's sitting room. Otherwise, he'd launch himself across the room and wipe the smirk off Nolan Braxton's face.

Mr. Bartholomew stood tall, his scarred face splotchy with rage. "Have a care, Braxton. This is my daughter you're speaking of."

Braxton bowed stiffly. "I mean no disrespect, Mr. Bartholomew, and I wouldn't say or do anything in the world to malign Isabella's character. I have the utmost respect for her. But—" his gaze slid to Connor—"others might not be so kind when it becomes common knowledge that your indentured servant foisted his attentions upon her."

"While I appreciate your concern over my daughter's

reputation, sir, I'm afraid you've overstepped your place and completely misunderstood the situation. My daughter was accosted and kidnapped by highwaymen, and it was most fortunate that Mr. O'Shea, my *trusted* servant, was able to rescue her from the clutches of the deviant who made off with her."

"Be that as it may, sir, I feel compelled to speak my mind, if I may."

"You may."

Braxton eyed Connor. "In private."

Mr. Bartholomew sighed. "As you wish. Connor, please wait outside."

"Yes, sir."

Connor strode toward the door, making every effort to walk as befitting a servant. He barely restrained himself from slamming the door. The veranda and courtyard were empty, but the grove of trees beyond the well was peppered with the caravan that had seen them safely back to Breeze Hill.

He resisted the urge to pace and stood stoically outside the door, his gaze fixed straight ahead toward the wasteland that had been the west wing of Breeze Hill.

He was well aware that his life hung in Mr. Bartholomew's hands. All he'd wanted was steady work and to be reunited with his brothers. Was that too much to ask? His heart squeezed tight. Braxton had accused him of taking advantage of Isabella. And while he hadn't done anything to warrant such an accusation, he had kissed her. Not once, but several times. Not even a gentleman, a freeman, could get away with that if a woman chose to take offense.

One word from Isabella, and Braxton would have his way.

But would she turn on him? He couldn't believe it of her. She wasn't Charlotte.

After a length of silence, Mr. Bartholomew barked, "Connor, get in here."

Connor entered the room, finding Isabella's father alone, Braxton nowhere to be seen.

"Braxton's gone. I sent him on his way."

Connor stood at attention, as befitted his place as Mr. Bartholomew's servant. The two of them had spent many nights poring over the drawings for the new wing of the house, selecting the best lumber for the floors, the walls, and the beams. They'd chatted amicably as only two men who had an understanding and appreciation for crafting a pleasing structure might. But in a single moment, with Isabella's reputation at stake, there had been a subtle shift in their relationship.

Mr. Bartholomew shuffled across the room and dropped into his favorite chair, scowling. "He offered a solution to this *delicate situation*, as he put it."

"Mistress Bartholomew's reputation is without question, sir, and any man who says otherwise is a liar, including Braxton." Connor knew he'd gone too far, but he wouldn't back down. Braxton had planted seeds of doubt about Isabella in her father's mind, and no gentleman would do that.

"Watch yourself, Connor." Bartholomew's clawlike hands gripped the arms of his chair. "Even though I agree with you, such talk about a plantation owner could land you in serious trouble. Regardless, that doesn't negate the fact that Braxton is right about one thing. The scandal will ruin Isabella's chances of an advantageous marriage in these parts. None of the suitors who've been calling will have anything to do with her now."

"Begging your pardon, sir, but if those men are willing to throw away Isabella's reputation so easily, they never really cared for her anyway."

"I see that you feel strongly about this. Tell me something, Connor." Mr. Bartholomew stared at him, his fingers drumming the arm of his chair. "With Isabella's reputation at stake, what would you do if I gave you your freedom and insisted you marry my daughter?"

Connor jerked his head up, his gaze landing on Mr. Bartholomew. He shook his head, unable to fathom the idea of Isabella's father being serious. Had the man gone mad? "What about Wainwright? Surely he doesn't think ill of Miss Bartholomew."

Mr. Bartholomew snorted. "For a smart man, O'Shea, you're not very observant. Young Wainwright's half in love with my daughter-in-law. It's simply a matter of time before he asks permission to court her."

"Master William and Miss Leah?" Yes, he'd definitely missed that. William would make Leah a fine husband, but it put a kink in Connor's plans.

Mr. Bartholomew placed both hands on the armrests of his chair and, grunting with the effort, pushed himself to his feet. He straightened to a commanding height and faced Connor.

"Connor O'Shea, I release you from the terms of your indenture."

Connor stood speechless, staring at Mr. Bartholomew. To be put in stocks or whipped, or even have his indenture extended by a year or two all because of Braxton's misguided accusations—yes, that was to be expected. But this? "You would send me away without references? What about my brothers?"

"I didn't say anything about sending you away." Mr. Bartholomew scowled. "Have you not heard a word I said, man? I'm freeing you and asking you to marry my daughter."

Connor gaped at the man.

"Well, are you going to answer me, or do I need to do as Braxton suggested and have you put in stocks?"

"Marry Connor?" Isabella's heart stuttered in her chest. "Papa, you can't be serious."

"You were alone in the wilderness. Your reputation is ruined."

"Nothing happened." Heat suffused Isabella's face as she remembered the passionate kiss they'd shared when Connor had found her and later when she'd thrown herself at him and confessed her love.

Right before he'd rebuffed her and told her she knew nothing of love.

Did she? Did she truly love him? Or was she just thankful that he'd managed to save her from a fate worse than death?

Yes, she loved him, but she didn't want him to be forced to marry her.

And nothing had changed from the time he'd told her that he didn't want to be trapped again. Unless—

"I won't marry a man just because you coerced him into it. Please." She shook her head.

Her father's face flushed. "I've never asked anything of you, Isabella. I've always given you free rein to do as you please, but this is one time you must listen. After this, none of the plantation owners would dare propose marriage to you."

"Connor rescued me from a highwayman. He didn't abduct me and haul me off to the woods to ravish me."

"There's no need to be crude, Daughter."

"Well, if he hadn't done what he did, you'd be dealing with more than the thought of my reputation being ruined. You'd be dealing with my death at the hands of a ruthless killer who wouldn't have cared one whit for my reputation, let alone my life."

"I don't like this any more than you do, but what can I do?" Her father reached out a trembling hand. "Connor's a good man and will make a fine husband."

Isabella looked away, hiding the sudden tears that burned against her eyelids. "Yes, Papa, he's a good man, but I can't marry him."

"Isabella, look at me."

She complied, blinking back the tears.

"Answer me honestly, and I'll not pressure you again. Is your heart set on another?"

"No."

"So you do love him? Or at least care for him deeply?" When Isabella didn't respond, he prodded. "Isabella?"

"Yes." She nodded, miserably aware that her love for Connor was one-sided at best. After what had happened to him in Ireland, he couldn't bring himself to trust her, let alone love her. "But I can't marry him."

"I don't understand you at all." Her father slumped back in his chair. "You admit that you care for him, but you won't marry him. What will you have me do? As Braxton suggested?"

Isabella jerked her head up. "What? What did Nolan want you to do?"

Her father scowled. "He suggested I have Connor horsewhipped or confined to Gayoso's garrison."

Isabella cringed. "Please, Papa. You can't do that."

"Do you want me to send him away? I told him I would release him from the terms of his indenture."

Isabella's heart broke. If her father sent Connor away, she'd never see him again. But how could she marry him knowing he'd been forced into the arrangement by her father?

It was one thing to indenture him to Breeze Hill for a brief span of time, but to forcibly bind him to her through marriage when he wanted his freedom would be like sentencing him to a lifetime of servitude. He'd hate her for it. And she'd end up hating herself.

She hung her head. "If—if he wants to go, send him away."

"Very well, then. I'll send for him first thing in the morning and tell him that he's free to go."

Chapter 28

THE DARK CLOUDS matched his foul mood when Connor stormed out of Mr. Bartholomew's quarters early the next morning.

Isabella had refused to marry him, and she hadn't even had the gumption to tell him to his face.

As soon as she was safely back home and the whispers had started, she'd backtracked her declarations of love. Even in the face of a scandal, she wouldn't stoop to marrying a servant. Just as he'd predicted. He glanced up at the second-floor gallery and saw her standing motionless, watching him. Resisting the urge to go shake some sense into her, he turned his back on her and stalked toward the grape arbor.

He'd been right to tell her that she didn't know anything of love. He'd tried to do the honorable thing by marrying her to save her reputation, but just like Charlotte, she'd thrown his proposal back in his face.

Even with her father's blessing.

A light mist showered the grapevines with moisture, and he paced, replaying the conversation with Mr. Bartholomew. It had been short and to the point. Mr. Bartholomew had called him in and told him she'd refused. He'd given Connor the option of staying and completing his indenture or of leaving with the promise of glowing references.

Neither option sat well. But he couldn't stay.

At least this time the choice was his. This time there was no family to ruin, only Connor himself.

The harder the rain fell, the more he paced, and the madder he got. He slammed the palm of his hand against a corner post and a spray of raindrops showered down on his head. Growling, he scrubbed his sleeve over his face, wiping the moisture away.

He glanced toward the upper veranda. He deserved some answers, and Isabella Bartholomew was going to give them to him.

Isabella froze at the sight of Connor charging toward her.

He marched through the courtyard straight toward the steps that led to the gallery beneath hers. She stood rooted to the spot, knowing that running was fruitless.

Her heart pounded, keeping time with his boots as he mounted the stairs, the impact of his footfalls shaking the second floor where she stood. She turned toward the stairs. Better to face him head-on instead of acting like a scared ninny.

But when his head popped over the stairwell and his stormy moss-green eyes clashed with hers, she stepped back. She'd never seen him so incensed.

It was all she could do to hold her ground as he cleared the stairwell and advanced on her. He stopped a few feet away, his jaw jutted out in fury. His shirt lay plastered to his skin, the hair on his uncovered head tousled with wind and rain.

"What is the meaning o' this?" Anger turned his eyes to a tempestuous shade as dark as the roiling clouds in the sky.

"I don't know what—"

"Don't give me that rot, lass. You've played me ever since I got here. First, you bought my papers t' fix this house; then I had t' put that task aside and gad about Natchez on a whim."

"Going to Natchez was not a whim. We did what we had to." Isabella clenched her fists within the folds of her skirts. "You knew that when you agreed to go."

"As if I agreed. I was ordered t' go, and you insisted on going as well."

"I can't undo what's been done, Connor." He was determined to put her in a bad light over the trip to Natchez. As if she didn't feel bad about it already. "I had no way of knowing we'd be attacked by highwaymen."

"But you knew the state of affairs here at Breeze Hill when

you bought my papers." He took a step closer, his demeanor daring her to deny the charge. "Didn't you?"

She looked away.

"The truth, Isabella."

Thunder clapped, and she jumped. "I knew. But—"

"But you signed those papers anyway. All the while asking if I could abide by the terms, when you knew you'd have a difficult time o' it yourself."

The heavens opened up and poured out buckets of water. Connor advanced, his ire rolling across her in waves. Isabella glanced around, wishing for someone to come to her rescue. Martha. Susan. Or even little Lizzy. But everyone had taken shelter during the thunderstorm.

"I'll abide by the terms of our agreement." She lifted her chin, determined to show him that she wasn't afraid. She stepped back as he moved closer. Well, maybe she was. A little.

"Ah, ya will, will you? And how, pray tell, will you do that, lass? I've wasted three months here." He held up three fingers and shook them in her face. "Time I could've been working somewhere else to earn passage for my brothers."

Tears sprang to Isabella's eyes and she just stood there, unable to answer his question, unable to undo the damage she'd done. She'd messed things up so badly, Connor hated her and there was nothing she could do about it.

"I'm sorry. I never meant—" She stopped. An apology wouldn't fix things. So she stood, her back against the railing, her heart breaking.

Suddenly the fury leached out of him, to be replaced by

a coldness that shook her to the core. He closed the remaining distance between them. She pressed her back against the spindles, willing her shaking limbs to hold her upright.

"Why? Why did you bid on my papers?" His eyes narrowed, searched hers with an intensity that ripped her heart out. "Was it because you truly needed someone to repair the damage done to Breeze Hill, or did you like what you saw on that auction block?"

He caught her hand before it connected with his cheek.

"How dare you," she sputtered, unsuccessfully tugging against his hold.

"Oh, I dare, Isabella. Or should I revert to Mistress Bartholomew?" He pulled her toward him, the fury once again in full force. "What happened to your declarations of love? Surely you haven't forgotten so quickly."

"No, I haven't forgotten, and neither have I forgotten your reaction. I'll not marry a man who only asked for my hand to save his own skin." Isabella lifted her chin, glaring at him. "I'll sign your papers. You'll be free to go."

"There's no need, mistress." He let her go as if the thought of touching her turned his stomach. "Your father's already given me my freedom."

She willed her pain to stay hidden behind a cold, emotionless mask. "It's what you want, isn't it?"

The storm raging in his eyes dimmed, and he searched her gaze. For a moment she thought this whole nightmare would end, and he'd declare his love. But he didn't. He stepped back, paused, then bowed low.

"Yes, lass, it's what I want."

Then he turned and walked away.

Pretending all was well gave Isabella a headache of magnificent proportions. But she sat on the veranda overlooking the courtyard, hemming a gown for the baby, half-listening as Leah chattered about this and that.

She smoothed the delicate white lawn pooled in her lap. The impending birth of Jonathan's child was the one light in an otherwise-dark world. Connor was leaving on the morrow, and her loss was almost more than she could bear.

Leah sighed, shifted her position.

"Are you feeling all right?" Isabella tossed a concerned look toward her sister-in-law.

"Just having trouble getting comfortable." Leah reached for another pillow and positioned it behind her. "My back's been giving me fits the last few days. Martha says it's a sign that the baby is ready to be born."

She smoothed her hand down her rounded stomach, a tiny smile gracing her face. "I've decided on a name."

"You have?"

"Yes. If it's a boy, I'm naming him after his papa—Jonathan William Bartholomew II." Leah bit her lip, sudden tears shimmering in her blue eyes. She blinked them away. "He won't ever know his father, but he can carry on his father's name."

"You seem pretty confident that the babe is a boy."

"I am." Leah nodded. "A boy who looks just like Jonathan is what I've been praying for."

Isabella reached out and took Leah's hand. "Me, too."

Lord, give Leah the desires of her heart. She's suffered such a great loss.

The baby garment in her hands blurred as unshed tears pooled in her own eyes. Without question, Leah's loss was greater than her own. Jonathan was gone to his grave, never to return, never to see the birth of his child. At least Connor was still alive even if he would be gone by morning. Maybe in time she'd forget him. And maybe in time people would forget her indiscretion.

Her lips twisted at the ironic turn of events. If nothing else, the scandal had given her more time, as suitors would hesitate to call on her in the foreseeable future. Even neighbors would be likely to press on to Mount Locust to avoid being tainted with her disgrace. For that she could be grateful.

The two of them fell into a comfortable silence as they worked. Frowning, Isabella concentrated on the tiny stitches as she put the finishing touches on the gown's neckline, angling the material to catch the best light.

Finally, last stitch in place, she held it up for Leah's inspection. But her sister-in-law's attention wasn't on her sewing. Isabella followed her gaze to the far end of the courtyard, where William sauntered toward the grape arbor.

Leah shifted her focus, saw Isabella watching her, and her alabaster skin flushed scarlet. Isabella pretended to be engrossed in examining her stitches. "Isn't it wonderful how well William is getting along?"

"Yes, wonderful." Leah sounded as if she were choking on a persimmon.

Isabella couldn't help but tease her. "I suspect he'll be well enough to travel within the week."

"So soon?" Leah's gaze flitted back toward the grape arbor. "Surely the journey on those rough roads isn't good for him. Not to mention those barbarians plying the trace." She shuddered, her wide blue eyes beseeching Isabella. "Isabella, you must convince him of the need to stay."

Isabella gave Leah a pointed look and a teasing smile. "I'll do my best. But you, my dear, have much more sway with our Mr. Wainwright than I ever will."

A fresh wave of embarrassment flooded Leah's face, and she lowered her gaze to her lap. "Surely you jest."

"It's no jest. He's in love with you but has bided his time until you're ready for his suit." She placed a hand on Leah's arm, forcing her to meet her gaze. "Do you think you could love him? He'll make a fine husband and father to the babe."

"It's too soon, but to my shame, I do have feelings for William." Leah clasped Isabella's hand, distress stamped on her delicate features. "Just saying those words out loud makes me feel as if I've betrayed Jonathan's memory. Please forgive me."

"There's nothing to forgive." Isabella shook her head, then glanced over her shoulder. "Now wipe your tears and tidy your hair. He's headed this way."

"Oh no," Leah gasped. "He mustn't see me like this."

Leah, big with child, tossed her sewing into the basket and clambered out of the rocker before Isabella could assist her. She waddled through the nearest door faster than Isabella would have believed possible had she not seen it with her own eyes.

The door clicked shut moments before William mounted the steps. "I thought I saw Leah—"

"She retired to her rooms." Isabella gave him a sunny smile. "You just missed her."

Disappointment shadowed his features, and he plopped down in the rocker still warm from Leah's presence. "She's avoiding me."

"Yes." Isabella smiled again, nodding. "This is true."

William scowled at her. "I don't see what's so funny about it."

"She's avoiding you because she doesn't feel pretty around you right now."

He stared at her so long that Isabella thought she'd have to beat him over the head with the truth. Suddenly his eyes widened; then his face turned beet red. "So I have a chance, then?"

Isabella laughed, then reached for her sewing. "I'd say you have more than a chance, my friend."

Martha stepped into Leah's sitting room and motioned for Isabella.

She laid her embroidery to the side and tiptoed out, careful not to wake Leah. The poor dear had just dozed off after a restless night.

"Yes, Martha?"

"You have a visitor."

So much for her hope that she would be left in peace for a change.

"Who is it?"

"Mr. Braxton."

"Show him to the parlor."

"Yes, ma'am."

Isabella tidied her hair and straightened her dress, then descended the stairs. Nolan stood the minute she entered the room.

"Nolan. So good of you to come."

He strode to her, took both her hands in his, and kissed her cheek. Isabella pulled back, alarmed. He'd never been so forward. "Sir, you presume too much."

"My apologies." He had the grace to look contrite. "I'm just so overwhelmed with gratitude that you have returned home unharmed."

"Thank you." Isabella stepped back. "Would you like some refreshment?"

"No thank you. I can only stay a short while." He eyed her, his scrutiny making her nervous.

She fidgeted. "Is something wrong? You're not quite yourself today."

He blinked, then shook his head. "I'm sorry. I was just thinking."

"About what, pray tell?" She'd never seen Nolan quite this way. Usually he was talkative, regaling her and Leah with his latest exploits in Natchez or his many trips to New Orleans, but this quiet, reserved side of him was new to her.

He stepped closer. "May I be frank, Isabella?"

"Of . . ." Isabella cleared her throat. "Of course."

"Your unfortunate . . . uh . . . incident with the highwaymen is common knowledge, and . . ." He paused and took a turn about the room before glancing at her again. "And it's also common knowledge that your indentured servant, Mr. O'Shea, rescued you from the miscreants."

"Yes, that's correct. And if I'm not mistaken, you suggested that my father have Mr. O'Shea incarcerated for the offense of—" she lifted a brow—"*rescuing* me?"

"Ah, he told you." He spread his hands, looking sheepish. "I was beside myself with worry over your welfare and may have overstepped my place. Forgive me?"

Isabella inclined her head. "You're forgiven."

"I take it that your father didn't heed my advice after all?"

"No. Mr. O'Shea will be leaving Breeze Hill posthaste."

Oh, Connor, if you just loved me enough to fight for me.

"I see. Well, it's for the best, don't you think? I know you'd never do anything to tarnish your reputation, my dear, but the sooner he's gone, the sooner people will forget . . ." He shrugged, letting his words trail off.

Isabella's face flamed. Was Nolan here to berate her for her foolishness in going to Natchez in the first place? Did he, along with all the other gossips of the Natchez District, assume that she and Connor had engaged in a lovers' tryst while trying to escape from a ruthless killer?

At the sound of wagons outside, she moved to the window and peered out. Yet another group of travelers was setting up camp at the foot of the hill to avoid the risk of camping along the main thoroughfare.

Like lightning flashing across the sky, she realized why Nolan was here and why he was stumbling through his rehearsed speech. He'd come to withdraw his proposal of marriage. She'd refused him so many times because she didn't love him; instead she'd been holding out for someone she really cared about. She'd used the excuse that her father needed her, that Leah and the babe needed her, but all the time, she'd wanted to marry for love.

But the man she did love could barely stand the sight of her. She almost laughed out loud. Her father and Nolan were right. Her reputation was in tatters, and no decent man within miles would offer for her hand now.

A bittersweet thought took root in the dark corners of her heart. She wouldn't marry at all. There was no longer the need to. The babe would be her father's heir. A male child to carry on the Bartholomew name would set her free. Free to grieve love lost. Free to grieve over Connor.

Lord, give Leah a son, I beg of You.

"Isabella?"

Her gaze snapped to Nolan. "I'm sorry. I was lost in thought. Again. You were saying?"

"My offer of marriage still stands. I won't pretend that I'm offering you a love match, but I think you and I respect each other. Mutual respect can go a long way toward making a successful marriage." Nolan moved to stand beside her, facing the window, his hands clasped behind his back. He turned to her and smiled. "As well as a desire to protect and provide for family and to see your father's legacy restored to its former glory."

Isabella bit her lip. How did he know her so well? Everything he said was what she'd thought she wanted. All of it was important, but couldn't she do the same thing and have love, too?

Chapter 29

NOLAN STOOD beside Isabella, his patience growing thin.

Acting the solicitous suitor was just one more role he had to play to get her right where he wanted her. But it seemed as if she wouldn't be swayed.

No, he'd come too far to change course now. The next few weeks would see the rise of foot traffic along the trace, plantation owners and their families returning to Natchez for the cool winter months, pockets lined with coin ripe for the taking. His men needed better access to the trace, and he needed money to gain access to the Spanish governor's ear.

And he needed Isabella's cooperation.

Would he have been better served to take Pierre's

suggestion that he focus on Leah instead of Isabella? The odds of Leah's child surviving to adulthood were unlikely. So many children died; even the governor had lost his own wife and child soon after arriving in Natchez.

But what of Isabella? With her mixed European and Spanish heritage, she'd seemed the logical choice to stand by his side and influence the governor. Still, there was more than one way to convince her to do his bidding.

He motioned to the motley group of travelers camped on Breeze Hill's lawn. "Isabella, all this talk of highwaymen and desperate travelers is worrisome. Breeze Hill is so close to the trace, and word has gotten out that your father won't turn anyone away. Anything could happen to you, to Leah or the babe. Braxton Hall is much safer for all of you. Marry me. Let me take you all away from Breeze Hill and the danger that the trade route presents."

She shook her head. "Papa would never leave Breeze Hill."

"Perhaps in time he might reconsider."

"Perhaps."

Nolan took her hand in his. "Isabella—"

"Nolan, please, don't press me. Not today. Leah's not feeling well, and I fear for her and the child."

He lifted her hand to his lips, curtailing his irritation behind a solicitous smile. "Of course. You're distressed, and I'm making things worse. Forgive me."

She gave him a distracted smile. "Thank you."

The door flung open, and Martha rushed into the parlor. "Miss Isabella, come quick. I think it's time."

Connor separated his tools from those belonging to Breeze Hill.

An unamused snort escaped him as his gaze swept over the pegs and shelving along the workshop walls. It hadn't taken long for him to make the cabin his home, start using Bartholomew's hammers, lathes, and saws as his own.

He'd immersed himself in life at Breeze Hill as if he expected to stay forever, just as he'd grown too close to Isabella, allowing himself to fall in love with her.

Fool that he was.

Had he learned nothing from the trouble back in Ireland? Was he destined to let a pretty face turn his head?

He knew better. Or did he?

It had been nine years since he'd let Charlotte lead him astray. When he'd come to his senses somewhere in the bowels of a ship bound for America, he realized he'd never loved her. He'd been infatuated with her. With the beautiful, articulate Englishwoman who'd cast her laughing smile on him, flirting and enticing him to do her bidding. And he'd done it all willingly.

But in the end, when she'd threatened to expose him, to lie about their time together, he'd realized the type of woman she was. She'd already turned to the man her father had chosen for her by that time—someone of her station and set to inherit a title.

Just as Isabella would marry a plantation owner.

Which was as it should be.

But knowing how highbrow society worked didn't make the truth any easier to swallow, not when Isabella should be his.

He tossed a broken saw blade to the side.

"That could be fixed."

Connor glanced up to find William leaning against a corner post, looking pale as if the short walk from the house out to the sawmill had almost been more than he could handle.

"There's probably enough left to make a good one-man saw. Too short for the pit, though."

Connor reached for a chair, plunked it down beside him. "Begging your pardon, sir, but you look like you're about to pass out. Maybe you should sit."

One hand hugging his bandage-wrapped waist, Wainwright lowered himself to the chair, stretched out one leg, and rested his head against the cabin wall. "Please, don't *sir* me. After all we've been through, I'm more your equal than your better."

"Old habits are hard to break." Connor shrugged. "And some might not see things the same as you do."

"'Tis true enough." Wainwright shifted, then winced.

Connor jerked his head toward the big house, the gabled peak of Isabella's second-story rooms barely visible above the tree line. "Does Martha know you've escaped?"

Isabella would probably be worried as well, but he couldn't bring himself to think about her, let alone bring her into the conversation intentionally.

"Martha has better things to do right now than to worry

about me." William skewered him with a look. "The babe should make an appearance any time."

"All is well?"

"Yes." William looked toward the house, concern written in the lines of his face. "For the time being. I couldn't stand waiting around any longer, watching the women run back and forth, shaking their heads every time I asked about Leah or the babe. And besides, I wanted to talk to you." He straightened, groaning with the effort. "I didn't realize I was still so weak."

"Your actions saved the lives of three women. Being housebound for a few days is a small price to pay."

"While I can't take credit for saving anyone, I'll suffer gladly knowing they're all safe." Wainwright's gaze met his. "You should take credit where credit is due. If it hadn't been for you, Isabella wouldn't be here. Bartholomew owes you a debt of gratitude."

"And you, Master William? Do you owe me a debt of gratitude as well?"

"Of course. We're all glad to have Isabella back safe and sound." A frown pulled Wainwright's brows together in a deep V. "Are you implying more?"

Connor moved to the edge of the porch, staring across the treetops toward the house. The trip to Natchez, the attack, and rescuing Isabella had unraveled the carefully woven fabric of his and her lives. "I'm leaving. Mr. Bartholomew released me from our agreement. I'm free t' go."

Go where? He doubted he could find work in Natchez. Better to head north and let everyone believe that he'd left without marrying Isabella, instead of that she'd refused to accept him.

"Why'd he release you? Surely he doesn't believe that rot about you and Isabella?"

Connor flinched. Even William was clueless to the truth. "It doesn't matter what he believes if others believe it."

"You're going to leave Bartholomew to face this alone, then?"

"Pardon?" Connor jerked his head up.

Wainwright leaned forward, then clutched his side. "Blast this injury." He fixed Connor with a glare. "I'm afraid someone really is after the Bartholomew estate. Jonathan's death, Bartholomew's injuries, the fire—all of it is a calculated ploy to destroy this family. Someone needs to marry Isabella to protect her from this threat."

"Then marry her and that will solve your problem," Connor growled.

William assessed Connor. "You're in love with her, aren't you?"

"Are you daft, man? Would I be handing her to you if I were?"

"I didn't get the impression you were handing her to me as much as trying to make sure she was properly cared for when you're gone." William leaned back in the chair. "But it doesn't matter. My heart belongs to another, and when the time is right, I'll court her proper."

So Mr. Bartholomew had been right. "You're speaking of Miss Leah. Do you think Mr. Bartholomew will accept your suit, knowing that someone is after Breeze Hill?"

William grinned. "He's already agreed. When we were in Natchez, I had Bloomfield draw up papers stating that in the event of my marriage to Leah Bartholomew, I relinquish all claims to Breeze Hill, leaving it to her child should he be a boy. If it's a girl, then Isabella inherits the property."

"Why haven't you pressed your suit before now?"

"Leah is still in love with Jonathan. And what of you? You didn't declare your intentions to Isabella?"

Connor clenched his jaw. "I have no intentions."

"Rubbish. I may be half-dead from a stabbing and a gun-shot, but I'm not blind."

"She won't have me."

"I can't believe that. She—"

"I agreed to marry her to save her reputation—with her father's blessing, I might add. She refused."

William stared at him, then burst out laughing. He winced, clutching his side. "Oh, don't make me laugh. It hurts too much."

Connor scowled. "I fail to see what's so funny."

"No wonder she refused. I doubt she wanted to marry a man who was forced into it."

"I wasn't being forced."

"Sounded like it to me." William shrugged. "Did you tell her that you wanted to marry her because you couldn't live without her or that you were doing it because it was the honorable thing to do?"

The accusation hit too close to home. She was the one who'd refused. Not him.

His jaw tightened. "She made her choice."

"Even if her choice means marrying Nolan Braxton? He paid a call earlier today." Wainwright eyed him. "What if he's the very threat the Bartholomews are trying to avoid? Or even Samuel Hartford. Although I doubt Hartford could summon enough energy to be devious."

Connor shook his head. "Neither of them have any reason to get rid of the Bartholomews. Braxton has his own plantation and Hartford is in line to inherit Hartford Hall."

"That may be true, but both properties adjoin Breeze Hill. Any plantation owner worth his salt is always looking to expand his holdings."

"Even you?"

"Think what you will." William's jaw clenched. "My intentions are noble, and I will honor Jonathan's memory. His son—should Leah have a boy—will inherit Breeze Hill, and that will be the end of it."

"Which means that your piece of paper leaving Breeze Hill to the male heir puts the child in even more danger than before."

William froze, his gaze narrowed as he pondered Connor's words.

"Connor! Mr. William!"

They glanced up as Lizzy raced down the dirt road toward the mill, her pigtails flying. William stood. "What news, girl?"

Lizzy glanced from one to the other, a grin splitting her face from ear to ear.

"It's here."

"And Miss Leah?"

"Fair to middling, according to Miss Martha."

"And the child? Is it a boy or a girl?"

"Boy."

Connor sucked in a breath. If Bartholomew and Wainwright were correct, the Bartholomew family's troubles were far from over.

Isabella held the babe close, unable to tear her gaze away.

Her nephew was perfect.

Ten tiny toes, ten fingers that wrapped around hers and held on tight, a head full of dark hair, the spitting image of his papa.

"Welcome to the world, Jonathan William Bartholomew," she whispered, her heart full to overflowing.

Susan appeared at her side, a soft smile gracing her face. She cupped little Jon's head with her palm. "God's precious gift."

Tears burned Isabella's eyes. "Yes. Jonathan would be so proud."

"No tears, Miss Isabella. Today is a day of rejoicing."

"You're right." Isabella sniffed. "I'll try not to be too maudlin."

They both glanced up at the sound of a soft knock at the door. Susan patted her shoulder and hurried to open the door. William stood there. His attention shifted, landed on the baby, a look of wonder in his eyes. "May I?"

"Please, come in." Isabella nodded, turned the baby so that he could see.

He gazed at the peaceful sleeping face of little Jon, then reached out and touched his cheek. His face clouded, and he expelled a long, slow breath.

Isabella frowned. "What's that for?"

A tiny smile kicked up one corner of his mouth. With a glance at Susan, he gave a small shake of his head. "Nothing."

"Would you like to know his name?"

"Jonathan, I'm sure."

"Yes. Jonathan William Bartholomew II."

"William?" A pleased look crossed his face.

"It was Jonathan's middle name."

"Ah, yes. I had forgotten."

"Fitting, though, don't you think?" Isabella grinned at him.

A flush stole over William's face, but he didn't acknowledge her teasing. Little Jon woke and stretched, a frown pulling at his tiny bow mouth. He let out a squall and turned his face toward Isabella. She snuggled him against the hollow of her throat, but still he fretted, rooting at her neck.

"Susan." Isabella stood and handed the babe off to the nurse. "Why don't you take little Jon to Leah? I think he needs his mother."

"Yes, ma'am."

After they'd gone, she returned to the settee. "Papa told me you asked for permission to court Leah."

William sat, his hands dangling between his knees. "Do I still have your blessing?"

"Of course. You and Leah are perfectly suited to one another."

"Let's hope Leah feels the same way."

"I think you'll be surprised. Yes, she misses Jonathan, and she's been afraid for the babe. Now that he's here, I think she'll be more open to your suit. But it might take some time."

"Time is the one thing we don't have." William cleared his throat. "Did your father tell you that I forfeited all claim to Breeze Hill if Jonathan's child was a boy?"

"Yes." Isabella blinked back tears. "William, you couldn't have given my family a better gift than that. Thank you."

"Well . . ." William shifted, looking uncomfortable. "I'm worried that my actions may cause more harm than good."

"What do you mean? If Papa is right and someone is after Breeze Hill, then—"

"But that's just it. What if my actions put the child in even more danger?"

Isabella's heart leapt to her throat. "No. Nobody would be that cruel, that—" her voice broke—"heartless, to hurt a child."

William took her hands. "We have to consider it. If someone killed Jonathan, tried to burn the house down, and even tried to kill you on the Natchez Trace, then they might not stop at trying to harm Leah and the babe. I thought I'd figured out a solution by removing Leah from harm's way and leaving the land to the baby, but Connor—"

"Connor? What's he got to do with this?"

"Nothing." William searched her gaze, then shrugged. "Everything. I know that he offered for you."

"He offered because Papa gave him his freedom in exchange for marrying me. I won't be bartered like a side of beef."

"You'll not change your mind, then? He'll be gone by morning if the weather clears."

She'd spent the day hoping and praying he'd come to her, make things right, declare his love, but she hadn't seen him. And she wouldn't go to him.

"No, I won't beg him to stay." She lifted her chin. "He made his choice, and his choice was to leave."

William chuckled. "Funny, that's the same thing he said about you."

Chapter 30

CONNOR CLOSED THE DOOR on the sawmill one last time, shouldered his pack, and walked down the lane toward the house. He stopped on the front lawn and stared up at Isabella's rooms.

The wind whipped the tops of the cedars, and thunder rumbled in the distance.

Fitting.

A rainstorm had blown in the day he was sold to Breeze Hill and another on the day he was leaving. Gray clouds hovered over the house, giving it a dark, dreary look in the early morning light.

But even now the front of the house had an elegant

appearance that belied the burned and razed wing in the back. Eventually Bartholomew would find someone to rebuild, and it would be as good as new.

He turned away, hoping to make it to Mount Locust before the next wave of rain hit. Hopefully, there would be a caravan he could join, going north or south. It didn't matter which. Any direction was fine, as long as it took him away from Breeze Hill.

The front door slammed open and William called out to him. He hurried down the steps, his face contorted with worry. "Isabella's gone. She left a note with Martha saying she was going to Braxton's. I'm afraid she's in danger."

Connor's heart twisted with the need to see her, to rush to her rescue once again, but he slammed a lid on the yearning. What Isabella did or didn't do was no longer his concern, and the sooner he put distance between the two of them, the better off he'd be. Someday he might convince his heart to distance itself as well.

"I'm sure she'll be fine. She'll take shelter at Braxton's until the weather clears." His words came out stiff and cold, blown away by the blustery wind whipping the cedars.

William scowled at him. "I'm not talking about the weather, but from Braxton himself. Captain Minor stopped by last night, and he was asking questions about Nolan Braxton. Word has come from England questioning his ownership of Braxton Hall. Seems there's no record of the elder Braxton having a son. From all accounts, he had no heirs. None at all."

"This isn't the first time that an inheritance has come into question. Won't be the last."

"I'm not the least bit concerned about whether Braxton is the legal heir to Braxton Hall. The governor can sort that out. But until then, Isabella needs to stay away from him, because if he's not a Braxton, who is he? Leah's beside herself with worry, and Mr. Bartholomew threatened to go after her himself." William walked away, toward the stables. "I promised I'd find her."

Connor followed. "You're not in any condition to be traveling."

"I'm going, regardless. I don't trust Braxton. Never have."

Connor caught up to him, motioning toward the heavy, dark clouds. "Look at those clouds. You'll catch your death if you go out in a rainstorm."

William's attention whipped southward, his jaw firming. "We might be in store for more than just a bit of rain this time. Look how those trees are twisting in the wind. If I don't miss my guess, this squall is coming off the ocean. It has the taste, the smell of a hurricane."

"A hurricane? This far inland?"

"Yes, sometimes. All the more reason I need to find Isabella and bring her home. I'll take Toby or Jim with me if it makes you feel better."

The stables were empty, and William insisted on saddling his own horse instead of taking the time to find one of the boys. His face grew pasty white as he struggled to lift the saddle into place, but he gritted his teeth and hoisted it onto the back of his mount. After watching him struggle to saddle his horse, Connor unlatched a stall and led out another mare.

In the shape he was in, Wainwright would be passed out on the road between here and Braxton Hall, and no one would be the wiser. Connor might be wiping the dust of Breeze Hill from the soles of his boots, but in good conscience, he couldn't abandon a man he'd come to call friend.

He ignored the bittersweet realization that he'd have an excuse to see Isabella one last time. He hefted a saddle and threw it across the horse's back. "Master William, but you're a stubborn one, for sure."

Alone in Nolan's parlor, Isabella twisted her fingers in her lap.

Was she doing the right thing?

She didn't know, but she'd sat in the rocker in Leah's sitting room in the darkest hours of the night, wrestling over little Jon's future. There was one man who was powerful enough and close enough to Breeze Hill to offer protection for her nephew. And that man was Nolan Braxton.

And in spite of the scandal attached to her name, Nolan still wanted to marry her. She'd accept his proposal with the stipulation that Jon would inherit Breeze Hill. Nolan and William could both be trusted to keep their agreements secret until Jon was old enough to take over the plantation himself.

She jumped when a loud clap of thunder rattled the windows. What was keeping Nolan?

His housekeeper—wide, frightened eyes darting to the

huge oaks bending and twisting in the wind—had said that he was indisposed. Isabella asked to wait out the storm, and the woman had shown her to the parlor, then quickly disappeared, muttering about devil winds and the cellar.

As the wind picked up, Isabella stood, moved to the windows, and pulled the heavy drapes back. The sky toward New Orleans had turned a sickly blue-gray in the hour she'd waited, and the trees whipped back and forth in a frenzy. The storm was worsening at a frightening rate.

She bit her lip. Should she attempt to go home or wait out the storm? Sighing, she turned away, but movement on the road caught her attention. Ah, maybe Nolan had arrived after all. A fresh wave of uncertainty that had nothing to do with the weather flitted through her stomach. Could she pledge herself to a man she didn't love, even as her heart ached for Connor?

Yes, she could. Just as Connor had predicted, she'd do what it took to protect Jonathan's child.

Three horses came racing through the yard toward the stables. Two men dismounted and urged their horses inside before she could tell if Nolan was one of them. But just before the barn door closed, the wind snatched the third man's hat away. As he bent down to retrieve it, she recognized the man who'd kidnapped her.

With a gasp, she let go of the curtain as if she'd been burned, then backed away from the window.

What was *he* doing here? Had he simply sought shelter in Nolan's barn? And what of the men with him? Were they highwaymen as well? But Nolan's plantation was the least likely place that lawless men would take shelter in a storm. Breeze Hill was much closer to the trace, and there were no other main thoroughfares near Braxton Hall.

Heart pounding, Isabella hurried to the settee and picked up her riding cloak. She had to go home, regardless of the hurricane-like winds buffeting the house.

She turned toward the door and came face-to-face with Nolan Braxton.

The wind howled around Connor, whipping sheets of rain against his face, and it was all he could do to keep up with Wainwright.

For a man who'd just survived a stabbing and being shot in the head, he was showing strength of determination as he urged his mount toward Braxton Hall. Connor raced after him, praying he wouldn't have to scrape Wainwright off the roadway.

A thunderous crash ripped through the wind and rain, and a massive oak twisted from its moorings and slammed toward the earth not twenty feet ahead of his horse. The animal whinnied and reared in fright. Connor fought to stay seated but found himself flat on his back on the ground, his mount racing toward home.

By the time he got to his feet, swaying against the gale-force winds, Wainwright was gone. There was nothing for it but to keep going. It couldn't be far to Braxton Hall.

He vaulted over the tree and continued onward. Finally, through the trees, he spotted a stately three-story plantation home surrounded by oaks. Where was Wainwright? There! He'd dismounted and was leading his horse toward the stables set off to the side of the house. Connor leaned into the wind, aiming for the open door. He'd catch up with Wainwright, and then they'd find Isabella and go home.

If she was still here.

It had been hours since she'd left home, and with each passing minute, he'd grown more worried. He was supposed to be gone by now, putting miles between him and Breeze Hill, putting thoughts of Isabella out of his heart and out of his head. But here he was, running to her rescue even as she ran to the arms of another man.

He scowled as he struggled across the open space between the trees and the barn. The similarities from eight years prior couldn't be ignored, except for the fact that Isabella's father hadn't come after him with a flintlock and a hangman's noose.

But once again, the ones who suffered the most from his stupidity ended up being his brothers. As soon as they got Isabella home, he'd leave, even if he had to hunker down somewhere until the storm passed.

Movement at the side of the barn caught his attention, and Connor pulled up short as he recognized the broad-shouldered slave Turnbull had forced to dance to his pistol.

"Massa. Massa," the slave whispered, motioning him to the side, away from the barn door. "Come."

What was going on? Had William sent the slave to him?

But why not enter through the barn door? The slave beckoned again, and he followed him out of the roar of the wind.

"Where's Wainwright?"

"Massa Turnbull, da Frenchman, an' another man, they have da other massa in the barn." The slave hurried toward the back of the structure, waving him forward. "Come. See."

"Wait. Why are you doing this?"

"You were there the night the scarred man used the whip on Massa Turnbull. I will help you in return. We must hurry before they kill him."

For a fraction of a second, Connor considered finding Wainwright on his own. But the man's panicked state convinced Connor to trust him.

"Lead the way."

Moving quietly for such a big man, he eased open a door at the rear of the barn and crouched down, pressing a finger to his lips, signaling silence. Connor flattened himself against a wagon wheel. Over the roar of the wind, he heard bits of conversation from the front of the barn.

"I say we just kill him—"

The wind snatched the words away, but the voice was unmistakably Turnbull's. No doubt he was talking about William, but whom was he talking to? The slave had mentioned a Frenchman.

Connor motioned to a carriage parked in front of the wagon. "Closer."

"No, suh." The slave plucked at his arm. "Massa Turnbull kills you, too."

But Connor shrugged him off and padded forward, keeping in the shadows. He had to get closer if he was going to be any good to William. He stumbled over a pile of discarded harnesses, thankful for the wind that slammed against the barn walls, masking the clatter as he fell against the carriage. He hunkered down and peered through the undercarriage. What he saw shot fear through him.

Turnbull had a pistol pointed at William's head, a hungry look in his eyes that spelled death. The Frenchman from the inn stood in front of him.

William's face was battered and bloody, and he slumped against a post. The Frenchman slammed the handle of a pitchfork into his side where he'd been stabbed and William doubled over and fell to his knees, clutching his stomach. Connor pulled his pistol and felt for the knife at his waist. The pistol would do little good in the close quarters, since he had only one shot.

The Frenchman spread his hands. "For the last time, *monsieur*, why did you brave this ferocious storm to ride all the way to Braxton Hall?"

William glared at him but said nothing.

Frenchie twirled the pitchfork, the tines sparking against the light of a single lantern. "Silence isn't going to help you."

"Would ya look at this." The third man led Isabella's horse out of the shadows. "It's one of them fancy sidesaddles."

Connor's blood turned hot and angry when he got a look at the man's face, scarred and pocked from numerous fights. It was the highwayman who'd kidnapped Isabella. His gaze jerked from the highwayman to the Frenchman, then to Turnbull, the pieces falling into place like a clock striking twelve. They were all in cahoots. His stomach clenched with a new worry. Was Braxton party to whatever nefarious deeds the three had been up to? And Isabella was in the house with him.

He fought the urge to rush to her rescue. William needed him more than Isabella at the moment.

God, please keep her safe until I can find her.

Frenchie moved to inspect the horse and saddle. He chuckled. "*Mon dieu*, Braxton has pulled it off. The Bartholomew dove has flown here to roost. Most interesting. Maybe we should all retire to the house and join the party."

Turnbull waved his pistol at William. "I don't care one whit about the woman, but this young whelp knows too much."

"Very well." Frenchie shrugged and stepped back. "He's all yours. I, for one, plan to make the acquaintance of a certain young *mademoiselle*."

As soon as the Frenchman let himself out of the barn, Turnbull pulled back the hammer.

Connor stood, took aim, and pulled the trigger.

Click. His pistol misfired.

Turnbull and the highwayman whipped around, facing him. William slumped to the floor, barely conscious. The men spread out, minimizing the odds of Connor taking both of them out.

Tossing the useless pistol to the side, Connor palmed his knife, waiting.

"Well, if it isn't the Irishman."

The highwayman reached for his own blade. "He's mine, Turnbull."

"No worries, mate. I'll just wound him; then you can have your fun." Turnbull raised his pistol and pointed it at Connor. "Would you care to wager your life that my pistol misfires as—?"

With a grunt, Turnbull broke off midsentence, his eyes going round. His weapon tipped downward, and in disbelief, he looked at his chest, where the tines of a pitchfork protruded. The big slave stood behind him, pitchfork in hand. As Turnbull pitched forward, the highwayman roared and charged.

Connor flicked his wrist and threw his knife.

Chapter 31

NOLAN CARRIED a silver tray into the parlor. Isabella still sat in the same spot where he'd left her only minutes before. He placed the tray on a table and reached for the pot of tea.

"I'm sorry I can't offer you anything more substantial. But my housekeeper is deathly afraid of storms. At the first sign of inclement weather, she scurried to the cellar. At least she left a pot of tea on the stove." He reached for a spoon. "Cream and sugar?"

"Yes, please."

The house groaned under the force of the wind, and Isabella's gaze jerked toward the windows. Calmly, Nolan handed her a cup of tea, not surprised to see that her hands were shaking. Women as a whole were really quite delicate creatures. "Don't worry, dear. I'm sure this storm will blow over in no time, and I'll see you safely home before nightfall."

"I'm afraid it's going to get a lot worse before it gets better."

"Perhaps." Nolan wasn't the least worried by the storm. He smiled. "We can retire to the cellar with the slaves if you like, although that's not exactly my idea of a relaxing evening."

"If it becomes necessary." Isabella took a sip of tea, then placed the delicate cup on the table, seeming to gather her nerves about her like a well-worn cloak. Her dark eyes met his. "Nolan, I'll get right to the point. I came here to accept your proposal. On one condition."

"Well, this is unexpected but delightful." He reached for her hand and pressed a light kiss to her knuckles. She really was quite beautiful. He'd made an excellent choice. He could taste victory even now. "Anything you ask, my dear."

"I ask that you help me ensure my nephew, Jonathan William Bartholomew II, inherits Breeze Hill."

"So Leah had her child?"

"Yes. A boy."

"I would think the child's birth would be an occasion for rejoicing, not concern."

"My father is convinced that Jonathan's death and the misfortune that has befallen our family is no accident." A worried frown creased her brow. "If he's right, then little Jon could be in great danger."

"Surely you jest?" Years of playing the part of a sympathetic plantation owner served him well.

"It's no jest. I want to protect my nephew at all costs. Our agreement would allow you to oversee Breeze Hill until he comes of age, when he could take over himself."

"You don't need my agreement to accomplish that, Isabella. The child is legally the heir, regardless."

"If he lives."

"You're—" Nolan paused, allowing a look of absolute horror to creep over his face. "Surely you're not suggesting that someone would kill the child for the land. And what of your sister-in-law's future husband? What if she remarries? What might her new husband have to say about such an agreement?"

"Her future intended—should she accept his suit—has already drawn up papers relinquishing ownership of Breeze Hill to little Jon."

"Admirable." He lifted a brow. "May I ask who the lucky man is?"

"William Wainwright."

"Ah."

"I have no illusions that we're marrying for love. This is a business arrangement, pure and simple. But it means a lot to my father—and to me—that Jon inherit Breeze Hill."

"Of course it does, and rightly so." Nolan eyed her over the tips of his steepled fingers. "Isabella, I hate to bring up such a macabre suggestion, but the odds of the child living to adulthood are slim even without this . . . this far-fetched and barbaric idea that someone would intentionally try to end his life."

"True. But I couldn't live with myself if anything should happen to him." Her lips trembled, and she blinked back tears. "I can't believe I'm sitting here so calmly talking about a newborn's death. It's just that I didn't sleep at all last night. If his life is in danger, then I've got to do whatever I can to protect him."

"Of course you do."

Her proposal could actually play into his plan nicely. With access to the long stretch of the trace that ran the length of Breeze Hill, his men would be able to come and go as they pleased. As he gained favor with the governor, he'd slowly distance himself from Pierre and Turnbull's activities along the trace—extorting a stipend for his silence, of course. His need for Breeze Hill would be long gone by the time the child reached adulthood.

"Isabella, I think it's admirable that you want to leave Breeze Hill to your nephew. I'll certainly do everything I can to protect you and the child and to build the property to its former glory."

"Thank you." She bit her lip, her gaze straying to the windows.

"Was there something else?"

"No—actually, yes. Are you aware that some men took refuge in your barn today?"

"Pardon?"

"While waiting, I couldn't help but keep an eye on the storm. I saw several men ride up and take shelter in your stable."

"Well, I can hardly refuse shelter to anyone in this weather."

"I agree, but I recognized one of the men."

"Really?" Nolan took a sip of tea.

"I thought it was one of the highwaymen . . ." Her voice trembled. "The man who kidnapped me."

Nolan choked on his tea. "Surely you're mistaken."

"I wouldn't be mistaken about something like that."

Nolan stood, moved to the window, and peered out. Had Pierre and his henchmen ignored him and come to the plantation after all? He'd taken great pains to keep their association separate. All his hard work could come undone with one careless act.

He spotted Pierre hurrying toward the house. He dropped the drapes, turned, and strode across the room. "I think I'll find a couple of men and check the stable. Will you be all right?"

Isabella blinked. "Yes, yes, of course."

Both Turnbull and the highwayman who'd kidnapped Isabella lay dead, their blood seeping into the hard-packed dirt floor while the storm raged outside.

Connor dropped to one knee beside Wainwright. "William, are you all right?"

"I think I'll live." Wincing, he pulled himself to a sitting position against the wall, still holding his side. "I'm beginning to think that you're an unlucky man to be around, Connor O'Shea."

Connor grinned. "The feeling's mutual, Master William."

William chuckled, then groaned. "Don't make me laugh."

Silence filled the barn, save the howling wind that clawed at the building, the horses snorting and pawing at the ground in the stalls. William glanced at the bodies, then at the slave. He hadn't moved but stood over Turnbull's body, pitchfork in hand. William addressed him. "What is your name?"

"Abraham, suh."

"Who owns your papers, Abraham?"

"Massa Braxton most recently, suh." The slave's chin jutted in stoic defiance; his gaze flicked to Turnbull's body, then to Connor and William. "He deserved to die. He was evil. Not just to you, but to my people as well."

"Abraham, I'm about to tell you something, and I want you to listen to me very carefully." Even slumped against the wall, his face covered in blood, William somehow managed to convey the proud bearing of someone who expected to be obeyed. "I killed Turnbull. You were never here. Is that clear?"

Abraham seemed to be on the verge of refusing.

"It's for your own good. They will kill you even though you were protecting O'Shea and me. Let me repay you in this manner. Please."

After a long moment, Abraham lowered his gaze. "Yes, suh."

William closed his eyes, and Connor gripped his shoulder. "William?"

"I'm fine." His words were slurred. "Help me up. We've got to find Isabella."

"William, please, stay here and let me—"

Connor caught William as he swayed on his feet, slumping against him, unconscious. He lowered William to the ground, motioning to Abraham. "Stay with him. No, hide the bodies, then get out of sight." Connor nodded at William. "And take him with you. The Frenchman might return at any time."

"Yes, suh. There is a cellar. He would not know of it."

Connor nodded. "Good."

He headed toward the barn door. *Now to find Isabella.*

Suddenly he stopped, turned, and addressed Abraham. "Does Nolan Braxton know of Turnbull's connection with the highwaymen?"

Abraham nodded. "He knows. He is the highwaymen's massa."

Nolan strode into his office to find Pierre snipping the end off a cigar.

"What are you doing here?"

Pierre waved the cigar. "*Pardon, monsieur.* I knocked, but no one answered."

Nolan gritted his teeth. Pierre knew he didn't mean here, in his home, but anywhere on his land. The Frenchman loved to intentionally pretend to be obtuse, but word games got on Nolan's nerves—unless he himself instigated them. "I told you to never come here. Speak your peace and get out."

Pierre grinned. "*Au contraire*, my friend. Do you not want to know what we found in the barn?"

"It seems you are going to tell me regardless."

"Young Master Wainwright came to collect Mademoiselle Bartholomew, but there is no need to worry about him."

"And why not, pray tell?"

"Turnbull is taking care of him as we speak." Pierre examined his nails.

Nolan didn't have to ask what Pierre meant. He pinched the bridge of his nose. Another plantation owner's son dead, and in his own barn. "Why?"

Pierre shrugged. "He knew too much, and he saw too much."

"He wouldn't have seen anything had you and Turnbull stayed away as instructed."

Nolan eyed Pierre, thoughts churning. Too bad Wainwright had followed Isabella. But this too could work to his advantage. If Pierre ended up dead this night, he would be blamed for killing Wainwright, and Nolan could wrap it all up in a nice, neat package.

"Listen, Pierre, everything is riding on my marriage to Isabella Bartholomew. Not only will we gain access to the trade route through Breeze Hill, but we'll have the governor's ear as well."

"How so?" Pierre arched a brow of disbelief.

"Isabella's mother was Spanish, from the same region as the governor." Nolan spread his hands. "If you remember correctly, you foisted your attentions on Miss Bartholomew at Harper's Inn. Perhaps you can rectify the situation at a later date, but tonight is not the time for introductions. She's already distressed enough as it is."

"Very well, *monsieur*." Pierre stood. "I will wait out the storm in the barn. But don't think you can play me for the fool."

Nolan smiled and shook his head. "I wouldn't dream of it."

Chapter 32

ISABELLA PACED the length of the parlor, nerves on end.

She should be relieved that Nolan had agreed to her request to maintain Breeze Hill until Jon came of age. If the babe was safe and his future secure, that was all that mattered, wasn't it?

But instead of relief, a knot of dread tightened in her stomach. She'd just pledged herself to a man she didn't love for the sake of her nephew, while the man she did love walked out of her life forever.

She steeled herself against longing for Connor. She'd learn to respect Nolan, even if she never loved him. It would be enough.

A crack and a loud crash shook the house and had her

racing to the window. A mighty oak lay uprooted, its branches reaching like claws toward the three-story structure. The wind picked up in intensity, the remaining trees writhing as if in pain.

What was taking Nolan so long? She'd insist that they retire to the cellar as soon as he returned. The hurricane-force winds could spawn a tornado at any time. No sense in risking their lives for propriety's sake. They were to be wed, after all.

As she watched, the porch shuddered, then flipped upward, slamming against the side of the house. Isabella rushed out of the parlor, the sound of splintering wood and shattering glass following in her wake.

"Nolan?" she called out. "Nolan, where are you?"

Even though it was midday, darkness shadowed the hallway, save for scant light through a window at the far end. A flash of lightning illuminated stairs to the second and third floors. In the brief flicker, she spotted a man at the end of the hallway.

"Connor?"

She moved in his direction, stopping just shy of touching him. "What are you doing here?"

A deep-throated chuckle rumbled through his chest. "I could ask you the same thing."

"I thought you were gone."

"Ah, lass, I would have been. But that fool Wainwright was determined to get himself killed by coming after you, so I was obliged to come along to keep him safe."

Isabella bit her lip. "So you only came to keep an eye on William?"

Lightning flashed, illuminating his furrowed brow,

eyebrows dipped over eyes filled with pain. But Isabella didn't need to see his face to know what he looked like. His features were branded on her heart.

"No, I came for you, Isabella. Will you forgive me for being an *eejit*?" He reached out a hand, smoothed her hair back, then stepped forward and wrapped an arm around her waist. "I should've believed you when you declared your love. Instead, I let my past blind me to the truth.

"I love you, Isabella," he whispered. "From the beginning, I've loved you."

A sob broke free, only to be swallowed up when Connor's lips closed over hers, claiming her breath, her heart, and her love.

Tears trickled down her cheeks, and Connor pulled back. His thumbs swiped at the tears. "Ah, lass, what's this?"

"It's too late, Connor."

"Too late for what?" He kissed her tears away.

"For us." She shuddered. The touch of his lips on her face almost made her forget her promise to Nolan, the storm battering the house, everything but Connor and the way he made her feel. "I told Nolan I'd marry him."

Connor shook his head. "You can't. He's—"

The front door slammed open, and Connor whirled.

Nolan Braxton stood in the open doorway.

He advanced, ignoring Connor, his gaze on Isabella. "Isabella, are you all right?"

"I'm fine, but—" Isabella moved from behind him, but Connor blocked her, keeping her safely out of harm's way. "Nolan, we need to seek shelter immediately. The storm—"

"Of course." He motioned to the stairs. "We'll seek shelter in the cellar below."

In one fluid motion, Connor pulled his pistol, cocked it, and pointed it at Braxton. The weapon was useless, his powder wet, but Braxton didn't know that. If he could just buy enough time for Isabella to get away. "No. We'll settle this once and for all. Now."

"Connor, what are you doing?" Isabella gasped even as Braxton halted his advance toward them. "Please. Put the gun away. Nolan isn't any danger to me."

"Did he tell you who's in the barn?" Connor narrowed his gaze, watching Braxton for any sudden movements. "The highwayman who kidnapped you, the Frenchman from Harper's Inn, and Turnbull, the slave trader."

"They were just taking shelter from the storm. Nolan sent them away."

"They almost killed William."

Isabella gasped. "William's hurt? Again? Where is he?"

"He's safe." At least Connor hoped he was. The Frenchman was still unaccounted for, and who knew how many other highwaymen were afoot this night. "Turnbull's dead, Braxton, and so is the man who kidnapped Isabella. Mr. Bartholomew was right. An influential plantation owner was behind Jonathan's death and the attacks on Isabella's family. That plantation owner was you."

"Isabella, don't listen to him. He's gone mad."

"I have, have I? Who are you, Braxton? Or should I call you that? The elder Braxton didn't have a son. He didn't have *any* heirs."

Braxton's composure slipped, and his eyes widened.

"What, no answer for the lady? Even now the authorities in Natchez are combing ships' manifests to figure out how you managed to assume the identity of an heir who didn't even exist fifteen years ago. It's over, Braxton. Give yourself up now, and the governor might grant leniency."

The look on Braxton's face told Connor that he knew the futility of that argument.

"Nolan, is this true? Did you kill Jonathan?" Isabella's voice cracked.

"Unfortunately, yes. I had my future mapped out, and Breeze Hill stood in the way of my success." Nolan's gaze shifted, met hers. A tight smile graced his features. "With you by my side and the governor's blessing, we could have risen to heights of glory and riches that the common man only dreams of."

Lightning flashed behind Nolan, blinding Connor. He blinked, and when he opened his eyes, Nolan had his pistol drawn. The man aimed and fired. White-hot pain slashed through Connor's right arm, and he dropped the pistol.

"Connor!" Isabella screamed.

He grabbed a heavy candlestick off a nearby table and flung it toward Nolan, then shoved Isabella toward the stairs. "Run!"

He turned back toward Nolan even as the man pulled a second pistol, cocked it, and leveled it at him. Connor froze as a roar unlike anything he'd ever heard swept toward the house. The vortex reached through the open door, sucking at everything inside, seeking to turn the house inside out. Horror spread across Nolan's face, and he reached toward Connor.

In the next instant, the monster wind grabbed Nolan and sucked him through the open doorway.

Connor dived for the stairwell.

"Connor!"

The deafening roar swallowed up Isabella's scream, but she felt Connor behind her, half-pushing, half-carrying her down the stairs to the pitch-black servants' kitchen. They fell in a heap at the bottom of the stairs. Connor grabbed her around the waist and pulled her beneath the staircase, wrapping his arms around her, his body cocooning hers.

Memories of the day they'd sought shelter from the hogs assailed her, but that had been nothing compared to the wind that ripped the house apart over their heads. They huddled together, the screech of splintering wood, glass shattering into a million pieces, furnishings flung hither and yon, all overshadowed by the ferocious howl bearing down upon them.

The staircase shook, shuddering against the force of the wind. Isabella clutched Connor's shirt, holding him close, the warmth of his body pressed against hers in the small space beneath the stairs. This time they were going to die. She knew it in her heart. Knew that she'd brought death on herself by coming to Nolan's in the first place. And God forgive her, she'd brought it on Connor and William as well. *Dear William.* She prayed he'd made it to safety.

Oh, God, spare us, but if you must take Connor, take me, too. I can't bear to see him cold and lifeless, his life snuffed out even as he tried to save mine. Please, God.

Her prayers mingled with her tears and thoughts of the foolish decisions she'd made. Decisions that had cost so many their lives.

Just as suddenly as the tornado struck, it passed, and with one last groan, the battered staircase shuddered and became still. Isabella opened her eyes to light and sky and rain splattering against the kitchen floor, the wind blowing gusts of moisture under the staircase and dampening the hem of her skirt. She sucked in a breath as she realized the entire outer wall on this side of the house was gone, save the staircase under which they huddled.

Connor shifted, turned her in his arms so that he could see her face. He smoothed her hair back, his gaze raking over her. Heart pounding, fingers shaking, Isabella caressed his face, every nerve ending conscious of the stubble on his jaw, the way his brow furrowed, his lips, every precious breath he took.

"We're alive," she whispered. "And we're together."

"We are." He gathered her close. "And I'll never let ya go, lass. Never ever again."

"Promise?"

"I promise. Isabella, I thought I could leave you to some rich plantation owner, but I can't." He cupped her face, his gaze holding hers a willing captive. "I'm asking ya again, lass, will ya be my bride?"

Isabella lifted a brow, then reached up to smooth back a wayward lock of his dark-brown hair. "Now, Connor O'Shea, why would I say yes to such a grave proposal?"

"Because—" His steady gaze wavered, and the remnant of a younger man who'd been burned in love flickered across his face. Then his jaw hardened and frown lines creased his brow. "Because I love ya, that's why, and by all that's right and holy, I won't see ya married off to another. We'll be poor, what with Breeze Hill goin' to little Jon, but—" He broke off, then placed her hand over his heart, beating hard and fast beneath her palm. "I'm offering all I have. I'm offering my heart."

Isabella slid her hand up from his chest and around his neck. And as she pulled him to her, she whispered, "Yes, Connor O'Shea, I accept. I'll marry you."

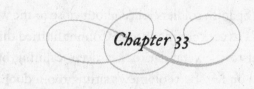

Chapter 33

Dawn was breaking over the horizon when the sound of pounding on the cabin door jerked Connor awake.

"Connor? You awake?" Toby yelled. "Mr. Bartholomew is asking for you."

The events of the day before came flooding back. Rushing to Isabella's rescue. The fight in the barn. The tornado that ripped Braxton Hall apart and sucked Nolan Braxton out the door. Then Isabella agreeing to be his bride. The whole thing had been a nightmare and a dream all rolled into one.

As inhumane as it sounded, Connor hadn't stuck around to assist with the cleanup or to search for Braxton. When William and the slaves emerged from the cellars unscathed, and William insisted that he could ride, Connor, William, and Isabella had hurried back to Breeze Hill, the trip fraught with worry. Darkness had fallen by the time they arrived to find that the tornado had spared Breeze Hill any damage.

Quickly he dressed and followed Toby to the main house. A garrison of Spanish soldiers lolled about close to the well, at ease. *Soldiers?* His concern mounting, Connor hurried through the courtyard to the veranda, took a deep, calming breath, then knocked on Mr. Bartholomew's sitting room door.

"Come in," Mr. Bartholomew's gravelly voice croaked out.

The master of the house glanced up from his customary chair. Captain Minor stood next to the fireplace, and William and Mr. Wainwright shared the horsehair settee. Mr. Bartholomew waved him over to the group. "Ah, Connor. Please join us. The captain has news of Braxton."

"Nolan Braxton is dead. We found him late last night in the rubble of Braxton Hall. But there was something very strange about the corpse. As was to be expected, the body was pretty battered from the tornado, but that wasn't what killed him. His throat was slit, the deed clearly done after the storm. I can only surmise that his own men took it upon themselves to kill him." Minor spread his hands, looking sickened by the discovery. "Who knows why with men who have little regard for human life?"

Mr. Wainwright shook his head. "What cruel fate to survive a raging tornado, only to be killed by one of his own."

"What of the Frenchman?" William asked.

"Not a trace. I expect that's one body that might never be found." Captain Minor slapped his hands together and said, "But that's not exactly why I'm here. Mr. O'Shea, my presence concerns you and your brothers."

Connor jerked to attention. "My brothers, sir?"

"First things first." Minor opened a satchel and riffled through a stack of papers. "Bartholomew, it's my understanding that Mr. O'Shea is indentured to Breeze Hill. Is that correct?"

"Yes. And no."

"No?" Captain Minor paused in the process of pulling papers out of his satchel.

"Recent—" Mr. Bartholomew tossed Connor a glance and cleared his throat, a twinkle in his eyes—"um . . . developments necessitated that I release Connor from the terms of our agreement. He's a free man and soon to be my son-in-law."

"Excellent." Minor nodded and sorted his papers. "That takes care of the first step in this process."

Connor scowled. What process? One glance at Mr. Bartholomew's face revealed that Isabella's father was wondering the same thing.

"Captain, I know you have a flair for the dramatic, but this is getting tiresome." Mr. Bartholomew drummed his fingers against the arm of his chair. "Speak your mind, sir. I have yet to break my fast this morn."

"Very well, then." Minor seemed to be enjoying himself. He looked through his papers and held up one with a flourish. "Ah, here it is."

He turned to Connor. "Mr. O'Shea, your actions on the day the highwaymen attacked Miss Watts's escort did not go unnoticed by the governor. It came to the governor's attention that, per the terms of your agreement with Breeze Hill, Mr. Bartholomew had made inquiries about your brothers back in Ireland. Hence, the governor, at Miss Watts's urging, has made arrangements for passage for your brothers to the Natchez District, posthaste."

Connor stood rooted to the spot, stunned. His gaze swept from William's battered face, to Mr. Bartholomew, back to the captain. "My brothers? All of them? At once?"

Minor chuckled. "All of them. When Governor Gayoso wishes a thing done, it's done as soon as is humanly possible."

"I—I don't know what to say. Thank you."

"Don't thank me. Thank the governor—and Miss Watts. And there's more." He pulled a sheet of paper bearing the governor's seal from the stack of papers. "As you all are aware, the man known as Nolan Braxton was an impostor and had no legal claim to the tract of land listed as Braxton Hall. By order of the governor of the Natchez District, for services rendered, I, Captain Stephen Minor, on August 15, in the year of our Lord 1791, do grant said property to Connor O'Shea."

Minor handed him the deed to more land than he could have ever hoped to own as a poor Irish lad. Rendered speechless, Connor could only stand there, staring at the official-looking piece of paper stamped with the governor's seal.

"What say you, O'Shea?"

William stood, his bruised and battered face already turning blue, one eye swollen shut. "I say that is a most noteworthy wedding present." A lopsided grin pulled at his puffy lips, and he held out a hand toward Connor. "Congratulations, my good man."

Isabella gave little Jon one last kiss, then placed him in his crib. Careful not to disturb Leah, she tiptoed out of the nursery and quietly let herself out of Leah's rooms.

Male laughter came from her father's sitting room, and she frowned. Who would be visiting at the crack of dawn? Hardly anyone was stirring at such an hour. She turned and froze as she spotted the garrison of soldiers near the well.

What in the world? Soldiers at this time of day?

Her father's sitting room door opened and Connor emerged. He spotted her, and a wide grin split his face. He quickly closed the distance between them, grabbed her hand, and tugged her into the entryway that led to the front porch.

As soon as the door closed behind them, he swept her against him, and crushed her lips with his. Shocked at his brazen and sudden display of affection, Isabella could only return his kiss until she was breathless.

All too soon, she pulled away, breathless and giggling, but oh, so happy. "Connor O'Shea, what in the world has come over you?"

He threw back his head and laughed, practically shouted with glee.

Isabella clapped a hand over his mouth. "Hush," she whispered. "Someone will hear you."

His lips curved into a smile beneath her hand, and he kissed her palm, the featherlight touch setting off a fluttery feeling inside. "Let them. I don't care."

He dropped onto the third step of the stairs and tugged her down to the steps, scooting her flush against his chest, his arms wrapped around her from behind. Isabella leaned into his embrace and sighed, loving the feel of his broad chest at her back, his arms around her, holding her close.

"Captain Minor came to call, and I—I still can't believe it." Awe filled his voice.

Isabella threaded her fingers through his and smiled. "Tell me everything."

And he did. When he was done, Isabella sat, stunned, fighting tears of joy. Connor's initial excitement had waned, and he held her close, hunched over, his cheek pressed against hers.

"To think that everything I've worked for during the last eight years is all coming t' pass at once. My brothers here by spring. And my own land," he whispered, his voice breaking. "A wife. Isabella, what did I do to deserve all this? To deserve you?"

Isabella turned in his arms. Her heart broke at the tears pooling in his eyes. She reached up and gently kissed one eyelid, then the other, his tears salty on her lips. "You were simply being you. Showing your love for your brothers, your determination to care for them as the elder of the house. But you couldn't be content to save only your brothers; you had to save me—more than once, I might add—you saved Miss Watts, you saved William—"

"More than once." His lips twitched in amusement.

"Yes, definitely more than once." Isabella smothered an indecorous snicker. She lifted her hand, cupped his jaw, and smiled. "You can't help fixing things, fixing people, saving and protecting them. It's who you are, my love."

"I'll spend the rest of my life protecting you, saving you, if you'll let me." Connor's gaze raked over her face, his brow furrowed in intense concentration. He leaned forward until his lips just barely touched hers.

"I love you more than life, Mistress Bartholomew. Promise you'll be me bride, forever and always?" he whispered, his Irish brogue thick with emotion.

"Yes," Isabella breathed as his lips claimed hers. "Forever and always. I promise."

TURN THE PAGE FOR A PREVIEW OF ANOTHER NOVEL BY PAM HILLMAN.

★ CLAIMING ★
MARIAH

PAM HILLMAN

"(Hillman is) gifted with a true talent for vivid imagery, heart-tugging romance, and a feel for the Old West that will jingle your spurs."

Julie Lessman,
author of the Daughters of Boston series

★ AVAILABLE IN STORES AND ONLINE ★

CHAPTER ONE

Wisdom, Wyoming Territory
Late spring, 1882

Dust swirled as the two riders approached the house.

They stopped a few feet shy of the steps, and Mariah Malone eyed the men from the shadowy recesses of the porch. Both were sun-bronzed and looked weary but tough, as if they made their living punching cows and riding fences.

One man hung back; the other rode closer and touched his thumb and forefinger to the brim of his hat. "Afternoon, ma'am."

"Afternoon." Wavy brown hair brushed the frayed collar of his work shirt. A film of dust covered his faded jeans, and the stubble on his jaw hinted at a long, hard trip. "May I help you?"

"I'm here to see Seth Malone." His voice sounded husky, as if he needed a drink of water to clear the trail dust from his throat.

At the mention of her father, a pang of sorrow mixed with longing swept over her. "I'm sorry; he passed away in January. I'm his daughter. Mariah Malone."

The cowboy swung down from his horse and sauntered toward the porch. He rested one worn boot on the bottom step before tilting his hat back, revealing fathomless dark-blue eyes.

"I'm Slade Donovan. And that's my brother, Buck." He jerked his head in the direction of the other man. His intense gaze bored into hers. "Jack Donovan was our father."

Oh no, Jack Donovan's sons.

A shaft of apprehension shot through her, and Mariah grasped the railing for support. Unable to look Mr. Donovan in the eye, she focused on his shadowed jaw. A muscle jumped in his cheek, keeping time with her thudding heart.

When her father died, she hadn't given another thought to the letter she'd sent Jack Donovan. She'd been too worried about her grandmother, her sister, and the ranch to think about the consequences of the past.

"Where is . . . your father?" Mariah asked.

"He died from broken dreams and whiskey."

"I'm sorry for your loss," she murmured, knowing her own father's sins had contributed to Jack Donovan's troubles, maybe even to his death. How much sorrow had her father's greed caused? How much heartache? And how much did his son know of their fathers' shared past?

The accusation on Slade Donovan's face told her, and the heat of fresh shame flooded her cheeks.

"My pa wanted what was rightfully his," he ground out. "I promised him I would find the man who took that gold and make him pay."

Tension filled the air, and she found it difficult to breathe.

"Take it easy, Slade." His brother's soft voice wafted between them.

Mariah caught a glimpse of Cookie hovering at the edge of the bunkhouse. "Miss Mariah, you need any help?"

Her attention swung between Cookie and the Donovan brothers, the taste of fear mounting in the back of her throat. An old man past his prime, Cookie would be no match for them. "No," she said, swallowing her apprehension. "No thank you, Cookie. Mr. Donovan is here to talk business."

She turned back to the man before her. Hard eyes searched her face, and she looked away, praying for guidance. "Mr. Donovan, I think we need to continue this discussion in my father's office."

She moistened her lips, her gaze drawn to the clenched tightness of his jaw. After a tense moment, he nodded.

0   0   0

Malone was dead?

Leaving Buck to care for the horses, Slade followed the daughter into the house. She'd swept her golden-brown hair to the top of her head and twisted it into a serene coil. A few curls escaped the loose bun and flirted with the stand-up lace of her white shirtwaist. She sure looked dressed up out here in the middle of nowhere.

Then he remembered the empty streets and the handful of wagons still gathered around the church when they'd passed through Wisdom at noon. He snorted under his breath. Under other circumstances, a woman like Mariah Malone wouldn't even deem him worthy to wipe her dainty boots on, let alone agree to talk to him in private. He couldn't count the times the girls from the "right" side of town had snubbed their noses at him, their starched pinafores in sharp contrast to his torn, patched clothes. At least his younger brother and sisters hadn't been treated like outcasts. He'd made sure of that.

He trailed the Malone woman down the hall, catching a glimpse of a sitting room with worn but polished furniture on his right, a tidy kitchen on his left. A water stain from a leaky roof marred the faded wallpaper at the end of the wide hallway. While neat and clean, the house and outbuildings looked run-down. He scowled. Surely Seth Malone could have kept the place in better repair with his ill-gotten gain.

Miss Malone led the way into a small office that smelled of leather, ink, and turpentine. She turned, and he caught a glimpse of eyes the color of deep-brown leather polished to a shine. The state of affairs around the house slid into the dark recesses of his mind as he regarded the slender young woman before him.

"Mr. Donovan," she began, "I take it you received my letter."

He nodded but kept silent. Uneasiness wormed its way

into his gut. Did Miss Malone have brothers or other family to turn to? Who was in charge of the ranch?

"I'm sorry for what my father did. I wish it had never happened." She toyed with a granite paperweight, the distress on her face tugging at his conscience.

He wished it had never happened too. Would his father have given up if Seth Malone hadn't taken off with all the gold? Would they have had a better life—a ranch of their own maybe, instead of a dilapidated shack on the edge of Galveston—if his father hadn't needed to fight the demons from the bullet lodged in his head?

He wanted to ask all the questions that had plagued him over the years, questions his father had shouted during his drunken rages. Instead, he asked another question, one he'd asked himself many times over the last several months. "Why did you send that letter?"

Pain turned her eyes to ebony. "My father wanted to ask forgiveness for what he had done, but by that time he was unable to write the letter himself. I didn't know Mr. Donovan had a family or that he'd died." She shrugged, the pity on her face unmistakable.

Slade clenched his jaw. He didn't want her pity. He'd had enough of that to last a lifetime.

She strolled to the window, arms hugging her waist. She looked too slight to have ever done a day's work. She'd probably been pampered all her life, while his own mother and sisters struggled for survival.

"I hoped Mr. Donovan might write while my father was

still alive, and they could resolve their differences." Her soft voice wafted on the still air. "I prayed he might forgive Papa. And that Papa could forgive himself."

"Forgiveness is too little, too late," Slade gritted out, satisfaction welling within him when her back stiffened and her shoulders squared.

She turned, regarding him with caution. "I'm willing to make restitution for what my father did."

"Restitution?"

"A few hundred head of cattle should be sufficient."

"A few hundred?" Surely she didn't think a handful of cattle would make up for what her father had done.

"What more do you want? I've already apologized. What good will it do to keep the bitterness alive?"

"It's not bitterness I want, Miss Malone. It's the land."

"The land?" Her eyes widened.

He nodded, a stiff, curt jerk of his head. "All of it."

"Only a portion of the land should go to your family, if any. Half of that gold belonged to my father." Two spots of angry color bloomed in her cheeks, and her eyes sparked like sun off brown bottle glass. "And besides, he worked the land all these years and made this ranch into something."

Slade frowned. What did she mean, half of the gold belonged to her father? Disgust filled him. Either the woman was a good actress, or Malone had lied to his family even on his deathbed.

"All of it."

She blinked, and for a moment, he thought she might give in. Then she lifted her chin. "And if I refuse?"

"One trip to the sheriff with your letter and the wanted poster from twenty-five years ago would convince any law-abiding judge that this ranch belongs to me and my family." He paused. "As well as the deed to the gold mine in California that has my father's name on it—not your father's."

"What deed?" She glared at him, suspicion glinting in her eyes. "And what wanted poster?"

Did she really not know the truth? Slade pulled out the papers and handed them to her, watching as she read the proof that gave him the right to the land they stood on.

All color left her face as she read, and Slade braced himself in case she fainted clean away. If he'd had any doubt that she didn't know the full story, her reaction to the wanted poster proved otherwise.

"It says . . ." Her voice wavered. "It says Papa shot your father. Left him for dead. I don't believe it. It . . . it's a mistake." She sank into the nearest chair, the starch wilted out of her. The condemning poster fluttered to the floor.

A sudden desire to give in swept over him. He could accept her offer of a few hundred head, walk out the door, and ride away, leaving her on the land that legally, morally, belonged to him. To his mother.

No! He wanted Seth Malone to pay for turning his father into a drunk and making his mother old before her time. But Seth Malone was dead, and this woman wouldn't cheat him of his revenge.

No matter how innocent she looked, no matter how

her eyes filled with tears as she begged for forgiveness, he wouldn't give it to her. Forgiveness wouldn't put food on the table or clothes on his mother's and sisters' backs.

"No mistake." He hunkered down so he could see her face. "You have a right to defend your father's memory, I reckon. But I'll stick by what I said. The deed is legal. And that letter will stand up in court as well. You've got a decision to make, ma'am. Either you sign this ranch over to me, or I'll go to the sheriff."

Silence hung heavy between them until a faint noise drew Slade's attention to the doorway.

An old woman stood there, a walking stick clasped in her right hand. Her piercing dark gaze swung from Mariah to him. He stood to his full height.

"Grandma." Mariah launched herself from the chair and hurried to the woman's side.

The frail-looking woman's penetrating stare never left Slade's face.

He held out his hand for the deed. Silence reigned as Mariah handed it over.

"I'll give you an hour to decide." He gave them a curt nod and strode from the room.

A Note from the Author

A BOOK ISN'T BORN out of one person's imagination, but from an entire cast of characters: artists, editors, agents, family, and friends. And during edits, an author of historical fiction realizes that not just those who actually have their hands on the project have a say, because the historians who have made it their lives' work to document history have a chance to shine.

I've had the pleasure of working with the same editor on this project as my first two books released through Tyndale. Erin Smith cracks the whip gently, but she knows me well. Once an anachronism is discovered, I cannot rest until I've exhausted every effort to fix it. I'm not saying I'm always successful, and any errors are mine and mine alone, but I'm glad to have Erin on my team.

Writing about the Natchez District in the 1790s was especially challenging, but also rife with potential as it was a melting pot of French, British, Spanish, African, and Native American.

Breeze Hill Plantation, the Bartholomews, Braxtons,

Wainwrights, and Hartfords, as well as their respective plantations, are fictional, as are Connor O'Shea and the majority of the secondary characters.

Actual historical figures who play a part in the story are Manuel Luis Gayoso de Lemos Amorín y Magallanes. Gayoso was the governor of the District of Natchez, also known as West Florida, in 1791. His second wife, whom he married in 1792, was indeed Elizabeth Watts. Unfortunately, she died three months after their wedding.

Another historical figure was Stephen Minor. Born in Pennsylvania, Captain Minor served in the Spanish Army before being appointed as the secretary to Governor Gayoso de Lemos. He later went on to become a successful planter and banker, as well as one of Natchez's richest residents in the early 1800s.

I hope you enjoyed this first book in the Natchez Trace series. I can't wait to share Quinn and Ciara's story with you.

Pam Hillman

About the Author

CHRISTIAN BOOKSELLERS ASSOCIATION bestselling author Pam Hillman writes inspirational historical romance. Her novels have won or been finalists in the Inspirational Reader's Choice, the EPIC eBook Awards, and the International Digital Awards.

Pam was born and raised on a dairy farm in Mississippi and spent her teenage years perched on the seat of a tractor raking hay. In those days, her daddy couldn't afford two cab tractors with air-conditioning and a radio, so Pam drove an old model B Allis Chalmers. Even when her daddy asked her if she wanted to bale hay, she told him she didn't mind raking. Raking hay doesn't take much thought, so Pam spent her time working on her tan and making up stories in her head. Now that's the kind of life every girl should dream of.

Visit her website at www.pamhillman.com.

Discussion Questions

1. Connor and Isabella both feel a strong sense of duty to care for their families, even to the point of reversing the parent-child roles. In what ways is their commitment commendable? Where might they go too far in accepting this responsibility? How do you find balance with boundaries in your life?

2. After losing both her mother and her brother, Isabella stops just short of placing blame squarely on God's shoulders. How would you answer her question that, in allowing their deaths, God had essentially taken them from her? Is that the same as blaming Him?

3. The Bartholomews have a rather progressive stance on slavery for their time. What convinces Matthew that "Every man has the right to prove himself regardless of race or creed or his bloodline"? Where do you still see inequalities in today's society? What can you do to help overcome prejudice?

4. After the Hornes arrive and place an extra burden on the Bartholomew family, Isabella wonders how she'll find the resources to compensate them. Describe a time in your life when you or someone you know was asked to make sacrifices for the sake of others. What actions did you take? How did things turn out?

5. Isabella is greatly affected by Mr. Horne's sermon focused not on Job, but on Job's wife. Mr. Horne says, "What man or woman among us hasn't questioned God in our hour of sorrow?" Is it okay to question God as long as we "sin not"? Was Isabella on the verge of taking her questions and her blame too far?

6. In chapter 12, Isabella believes her prayers didn't save her mother or brother or the plantation. How does Connor respond to her in that moment? What would most comfort you if you were facing a similar situation?

7. After Connor shares a little about his family with Isabella, she reminds him, "It's never too late to make amends." Have you been in a situation where you felt it was too late to make amends? Were you able to repair the relationship?

8. In John 16:33, Jesus tells His followers: "Here on earth you will have many trials and sorrows. But take heart, because I have overcome the world." What does this reminder mean to Isabella? What does it mean to you?

9. In today's society, parents want their children to have a better life than they themselves did. For the middle class, this usually means a college education and a good job. In the 1700s, it wasn't unusual for parents to indenture their children. While this might seem cruel to us, if this was the only way to improve their child's lot in life, do you think it was the right decision for the parents to make? Why or why not?

10. Given the melting pot of classes and cultures that made up Natchez in this time period, it was inevitable that there would be marriages across different classes. Isabella unsuccessfully tries to ignore her attraction to Connor because of her parents' ill-fated marriage. Should anyone ever make life choices based on family history? Is Isabella's conviction to marry within her social class instead of for love an issue that couples face today?

11. Nolan Braxton thinks he can rise above the thievery and trickery that had characterized his entire life. He hopes to marry Isabella and become a respected member of society. Do you think he would be able to turn over a new leaf? What would it have taken for Nolan to redeem himself in the eyes of the law?

12. Luke 15:11-32 tells the story of the Prodigal Son. What parallels or similarities can you draw between the biblical account and this story?

"[Hillman is] gifted with a true talent for vivid imagery, heart-tugging romance, and a feel for the Old West that will jangle your spurs."

JULIE LESSMAN, *author of the Daughters of Boston series*

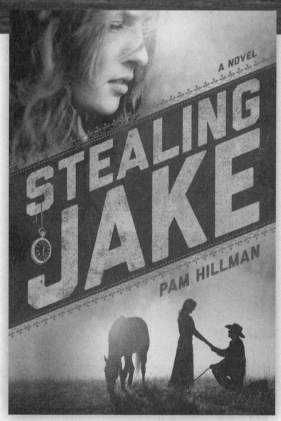

TYNDALE HOUSE PUBLISHERS
IS CRAZY4FICTION!

Fiction that entertains and inspires

Get to know us! Become a member of the Crazy4Fiction
community. Whether you read our blog, like us on
Facebook, follow us on Twitter, or receive our e-newsletter,
you're sure to get the latest news on the best in Christian
fiction. You might even win something along the way!

JOIN IN THE FUN TODAY.

 www.crazy4fiction.com

 Crazy4Fiction

 @Crazy4Fiction